THE STORYTELLER SERIES | BOOK ONE

THE STORYTELLER'S WAR

GEOFFREY CHAUCER
RELUCTANT SPY

J.C. CORRY

Black Rose Writing | Texas

ISBN: 978-1-68513-597-3
Library of Congress Control Number: 2025930952
PUBLISHED BY BLACK ROSE WRITING
www.blackrosewriting.com

Printed in the United States of America
Suggested Retail Price (SRP) $23.95

The Storyteller's War is printed in Minion Pro

*As a planet-friendly publisher, Black Rose Writing does its best to eliminate unnecessary waste to reduce paper usage and energy costs, while never compromising the reading experience. As a result, the final word count vs. page count may not meet common expectations.

PRAISE FOR
THE STORYTELLER'S WAR

ACKNOWLEDGEMENTS

Many writers inspired me to try my hand at historical fiction. Robert Louis Stevenson's *Treasure Island* captivated me as a boy, more so after seeing my son's similar reaction to the story. Jack Whyte's *Dream of Eagles* series hooked me. As did Patrick O'Brian's Aubrey and Maturin, Bernard Cornwell's Richard Sharpe and Ken Follett's *Pillars of the Earth.* Closer to home, I was inspired by Chris Humphreys' *Jack Absolute.* More recently, Lauren Groff and Maggie O'Farrell have shown the magic than can be woven by masters of their craft.

Of course, Geoffrey Chaucer's writing and life had a huge part to play in all this. I can thank my first year university English professor (whose name sadly escapes me) for bringing not only Chaucer's writing but also his life, to life, and sending me along this journey.

I must first thank my family for being there for me every step of the way. Thanks also to Kate for the support in the early days, when writing a novel was just a dream.

Laurie, thank you for co-piloting the many research trips and helping me live that dream, and for being such a supportive reader and editor.

Historical fiction is bolstered by the research done before and during the writing. So many biographies and historians provided the foundation for this novel, but two stand above the rest—Marion Turner's *Chaucer: A European Life,* where I found the genesis of the story idea, and *To Win and Lose a Medieval Battle,* by L.J. Andrew Villalon and Donald Kagay, the most comprehensive analysis of the Battle of Najera and the historical and political context and events leading up to it. I am deeply indebted to these (and many other) researchers who provided the solid ground upon which this story is built, and I take full responsibility for sacrificing veracity for verisimilitude at the altar of storytelling.

Some say writing is a lonely vocation. I say it is a world of possibilities inhabited by like-minded souls, and I have been so very fortunate to have met other writers, editors, agents and publishers who have enriched, informed and educated me in so many ways.

The first was Merle Nygate, an extraordinary editor and writer who agreed to work with a neophyte writer and who generously provided to me invaluable direction and support when I was first trying to write my way into Chaucer's story and world.

The Surrey International Writers' Conference is where I began to build my tribe, and I am grateful to all the volunteers, writers and editors who help make SiWC happen each year. And where I could meet a wonderful editor like Genevieve Gagne-Hawes, whose supportive feedback and encouragement meant so much.

Trees Writing Group grew from SiWC, and I can't thank AK White, Laura Fauth and Michelle Baudais enough for their support over these past few years; it has meant the world.

Through SiWC, I also found the Creative Academy and the historical (or, as some of us call it, hysterical) writers meet-up, which has also been so important—thanks to Jenny Lang, Donna Conrad, Sharon Michalove, Jacquie Paul, Adrienne Stevenson, Brian Wyvill, and the many others who have provided so much encouragement and support.

And of course I am grateful to writer-historian Kerry Cathers, PhD (Medieval History), for her helpful pointers on medieval warfare, and to writer-historian Sharon Michalove, PhD (History of Education) for her period-specific corrections and POV suggestions (you were right!). A very special thank you to Griff Hosker, Donna Conrad and Chris Humphreys for their encouragement and feedback.

Many thanks are also due to Corinne Aarsen for her multitude of edits, and a very special thanks to Jenny Quinlan for asking the hard questions and helping focus this as Chaucer's story.

And finally, I am so very grateful to Reagan Rothe and the entire team at Black Rose Writing for taking a flier on this old dog, and for literally helping turn my dream into a reality.

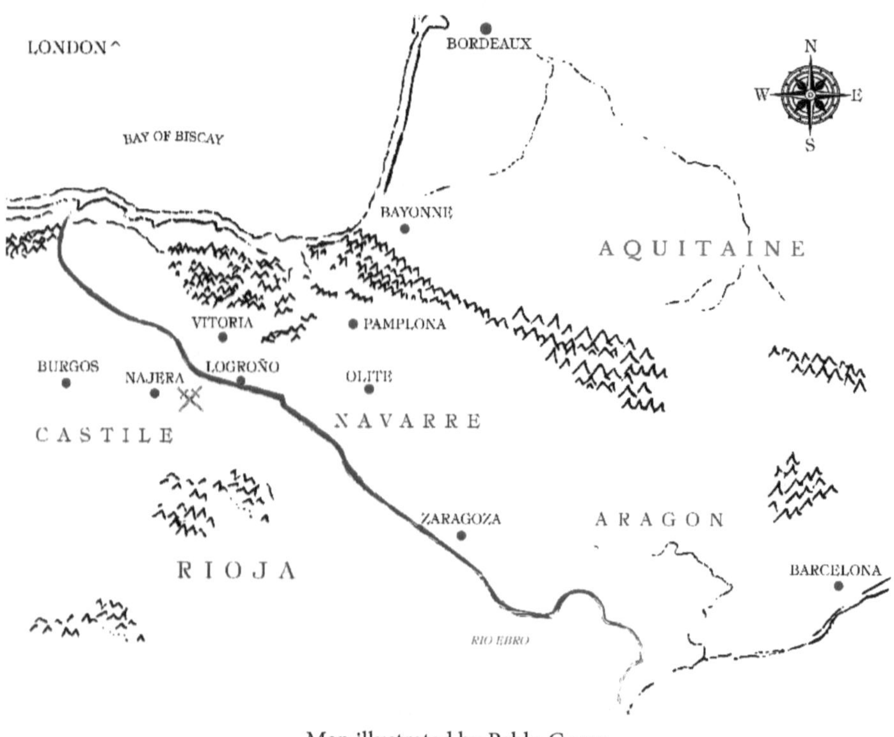

Map illustrated by Pablo Corry

Northern Iberian peninsula, 1365

THE STORYTELLER'S WAR

To Pablo and Diego

Non altus, non humilis, sed progressus

"Women desire to have sovereignty
As well over their husband as their love,
And to have mastery of him above."
– Geoffrey Chaucer, *Wife of Bath's Tale*

"For how might sweetness ever be known to him who has never tasted
bitterness? Nor can any man be truly glad, I believe,
Who has never been in sorrow or some distress."
– Geoffrey Chaucer, *The Knight's Tale*

PART 1
LOST

CHAPTER 1
LONDON, DECEMBER, 1365
CHAUCER AND PIPPA

Three Cranes Wharf Tavern, The Vintry
Geoffrey Chaucer waved the wine goblet in his right hand about as he told his story. With each emphatic word and gesture, he painted drops of burgundy across the tavern's oak floorboards. His three friends around the table leaned forward as he approached the story's end.

"…he escaped from Olite after the battle, and finally returned to Bordeaux with the much needed wine, and said these fateful words to his wife waiting there…," he said, and paused.

The moment I most savour, when they yearn for the end above all.

"Go on then, what did he say?" asked the older of the three men.

Ah yes.

"He said to her, 'Expect no less from a pie seller.'"

Silence, then all three burst into laughter.

"Snapes! Another round for Chaucer," one friend said.

"Another round for all of us," another shouted.

"Where'd you hear such a story?" the third asked.

"One hears things at court…," Chaucer replied, taking the empty seat.

"So is we at war with…?" the third man began, before a deep, clear voice from across the room cut him off.

"Geoffrey Chaucer is it?"

All four heads turned to a tallish man leaning against the corner of the bar.

"What ill-bred heanling interrupts?" shouted Chaucer as he stood up, swayed, then jabbed his goblet toward the interloper, spilling more wine.

"Sir Christopher Croker, formerly of the Vintry Guild, now servant to our lord King Edward. I heard your tale clear across the tavern, and I would a word with you," Croker replied, stepping forward.

Chaucer sized up Croker, who did indeed appear more Vintry than palace, his boots worn, his clothes well-made but not too grand.

"Vintry, eh? Don't know of a Croker."

"I know the name Chaucer," Croker replied, his tone dismissive. He stood before Chaucer as if goading him.

"Begone!" Chaucer replied.

A few heads turned as Croker took one step toward Chaucer and, standing a foot from him, said in a quiet voice, "You're a tattling tale-teller, and should quell your tongue and hear me out."

"And you, sir, bleat and bray and blore like a wounded farm animal and should quell such threats. Hear *me* out, and begone!" Chaucer replied, and then looked to his friends, clearly pleased with his nimble rejoinder. He took a long pull from his goblet.

Croker smacked Chaucer's head with his fist, sending Chaucer's goblet flying across the room and Chaucer backwards, tripping on a chair and falling to the floor. Croker stood over him and commanded, "Gentlemen, they'll be no more of Chaucer's tale telling this eve."

Croker pulled Chaucer up by his worn cloak and dragged him to the tavern entrance, held him against the door and whispered in his ear, "You will leave now and turn west to your home and sleep off your wine. You will attend to the king in the morn. He will speak to you of a task of great importance. Do you understand me, you drunken babbler?"

Chaucer was about to reply when Croker opened the door to a blast of winter air and shoved Chaucer out. "Home! Now!"

Chaucer stumbled out onto the cobbled street and shivered at the cold. He was alone save for the beadles crying, "Curfew!".

What in the God-forsaken name of Lady Fortune just happened? And who did this damnable Croker think he was, hitting me so and ordering me about? I have a mind to go back and give him my own hand.

Chaucer rubbed the side of his head where Croker's fist had found purchase. Perchance not. He turned toward his home and paused.

I'll need to explain my face to Pippa, for it is as surely bruised as my pride.

He instead turned east and walked the few blocks along Thames Street to the warehouse of Chaucer & Company.

•   •   •

Thames Street, The Vintry

"You're out past curfew," Pippa said from behind the kitchen table, Chaucer's mother Agnes and father John standing beside her. "Have you been brawling?" she asked.

Nothing gets past her.

"I was accosted by Edward's latest page, nay storied henchman. Name of Croker," Chaucer said loud enough for the neighbours to hear, then he took off his sodden cloak and hung it on a wooden peg by the door.

"I know not the man. He had good reason?" Pippa replied.

"That overweening brute did not much like the tale I was telling."

"And what did you say to offend him so?"

"I know not."

"Not all enjoy your stories, Geoffrey."

He said nothing.

"No matter. Come sit and warm yourself by the fire."

Chaucer did, and Pippa joined him. He studied the face of Pippa Rouet, the woman he loved.

Does she truly know me?

She sat angled to him in a similar hard-backed oak chair on the other side of the crackling fire. He knew he was but a stout 23-year-old merchant's son with unkempt tawny hair. She was two years younger, shapelier, with darker hair—and the daughter of a knight. He oft wondered why she had chosen him, and not some handsome, wealthy squire.

Behind them, John stood counting coins at the large oak table that took up much of the kitchen, muttering numbers to himself. Agnes chopped vegetables on a wooden block next to him, backlit by the only window in the room.

"You were drinking," Pippa said.

She knows me too well.

"After I was accosted at the Three Cranes, I found William at the warehouse where he told stories of Navarre, Rioja and Castile," he replied.

"And by told you mean 'poured' wine-soaked stories from those same kingdoms."

He smirked a reply.

"So, you heard rumour at court that this journey to Navarre still proceeds?"

Perchance, my time to prosper, and our time to wed, has finally arrived.

"Yes rumour says our good King Edward will ask me to travel there anon," he replied, then turned and read in his mother's raised eyebrows, *You see, our son gains stature.*

"Why there? Why now?" asked Pippa.

"Fill me a goblet if you be so kind."

Pippa hesitated, then poured wine into a goblet and handed it to him.

He tilted his back and drank deeply.

"And?" she asked.

"England's wine in Bordeaux is threatened by mercenaries and brigands."

"And why would King Edward send you, a mere page, on such an important journey to find wine?" she asked.

He drank again.

Does she jibe?

"A fair question, for you are not yet a valet, let alone esquire or knight," piped up John from behind.

Chaucer turned his head to gape at his father, then turned back to Pippa.

They fail to grasp what is plain for all to see.

"I know wine, and surely will be tasked to find a reliable supply of the famous blended wine made in the monasteries of Rioja. In lands controlled by King Pedro of Castile, but accessed only through the mountain passes of Navarre. As to why me, you well know that I earned the trust of Prince Lionel during my service in Eire, and of Prince John in Picardy, and have since earned King Edward's trust at court," he snapped.

Pippa tilted her head and raised her eyebrows, as if asking, '*You really think that to be true?*'

"And I will be treated one station above my rank on such a journey, as valet and courier, not mere page," he added. Chaucer had been page at court for seven years, a position that allowed him time to write, drink, and compete in the storytelling competitions, or 'puys', that he so enjoyed. And time also to woo Pippa.

Poorly on this day, for Pippa snorted. "You hear one rumour, and I another, for I hear Edward may be less keen than you think."

"What rumour? From whom?" Chaucer asked, and drank again.

"That says you know wine far too well, and tell too many outlandish tales for a page. But now this page must indeed turn and tend the fire. But take care, or both page and story will be singed and branded so," she said.

I do so enjoy her wordplay, yet would have less play at my expense.

"Yes, put another log on the fire, Geoffrey," Agnes said as she cupped the chopped vegetables, stepped toward the blaze and dropped them into a pot of boiling water that hung over the flames.

Chaucer placed his goblet on the small table beside him, leaned forward, lifted a log from the woodpile next to the hearth and thrust it atop the others, shooting sparks at his hand.

He shook his fingers, then shook his head.

"My journey will require a few tales told well," Chaucer said, puffing up. "And if my tales be so ill-formed, then you speak ill of our king's judgement."

Agnes smiled as she returned to her chopping board. "Oh Geoffrey, you are ever so easy to tease," Agnes said.

I gain no favour in this home.

"'Tis jealous words I hear, for I have some talent for teasing out such talented tales."

"Surely the reason is simpler," John said, placing the bag of coin aside. "Edward would choose one who speaks French, Latin, and some Castilian, learned on the wharf or at court. As former deputy wine butler to the king, my name is respected at court. And as founding member of the Vintner's Company, I am a trusted wine merchant, more so since the Company received its royal charter from King Edward but one year ago. The name Chaucer is one to be trusted and treated with respect in both the palace and the city. And our hard won charter is never to be put at risk by drink or rumour. Do you hear me?"

John's tone had hardened, and Chaucer's mouth flinched at his father's words, as if he'd been lightly slapped.

"What route would you take?"

Why such a pressing need to remind me of his name? I shall progress and make my own name.

"Geoffrey? What route do you take?" John asked again.

"To Bordeaux, and then across the Pyrenees to Pamplona, and then south, I expect."

"Winter is no time to cross those mountains. Seek to delay a month."

"Haste follows the import of my task. It may take a month or more for me to sail to Bordeaux, arrange a guide and horses, and reach the pass at Roncesvalles. By then, it will tilt more spring than winter, and safer for such a crossing," Chaucer replied.

John said nothing, so Chaucer carried on. "Once through the pass, I will travel the Camino de Santiago through Navarre and Rioja to Castile."

"Via Logrono?"

"Methinks so. You know of the route?"

"I travelled it once to find the Rioja wine I used to import before the pestilence struck," John replied, staring ahead, as if remembering.

"I did not know you had been to Navarre."

John ignored his question. "If you must journey in winter, bring a heavy cloak and sheepskin," he added. "From Pamplona, first travel south to Olite and seek a pass from King Carlos to travel freely through his kingdom. Then west to Logrono. But expect to pay dearly for such a pass. And be warned: you may find yourself a friend arriving, and an enemy departing, for Carlos is a snake."

Chaucer nodded at his father.

"When will you return, Geoffrey? You two have much to discuss," Agnes asked as she stopped chopping, put down her knife, and eyed her son.

All three heads swivelled toward her.

"You know well what I mean. When will you two finally wed?"

"When will Pippa have me, no sooner, for I have asked and been found wanting."

Pippa blushed, a rare sight, then turned toward Agnes and said, "I will marry your son when favour at court returns to him a higher station and more regular coin."

"Yet people talk. It would set things right to set up your own home, do right by your daughter," said Agnes.

"Let them talk, parley, jangle, and giggle. Nay, let them cackle and cluck, grutch and grunt, say la-la-la all the day long. I care not, for I have nothing to set right except this oversized man-boy before me," Pippa said sharply.

Agnes glanced toward Pippa, shook her head, opened her mouth and then shut it.

"We plan to move into our tenanted space at St. Botolph-without-Aldgate that Agnes inherited from her father after his recent passing," John said, breaking the tension.

"Pippa, I know you must attend to the queen when she is at the palace, and Geoffrey the king alike, but we would that you have this house after we move," Agnes said. "As a home for you two and Elizabeth, a home for a family."

Pippa and Chaucer shared a glance, mouths half open, eyes wide open.

"That is…so very kind of you," Pippa replied, looking first to her future mother-in-law, then back to Chaucer, who smiled his agreement. Neither had expected as much.

"Once you are wed, of course," she added.

Chaucer, eyes still on Pippa, had no ready answer this time.

"Right then, that's settled," John said and got up, mumbling something about needing to speak with William at the warehouse, and pulled on his cloak. Agnes said she needed to pop next door for more carrots for her soup and followed him out the door.

Chaucer and Pippa sat facing each other and smiled, for they both knew the excuses for leaving were made up so they could be alone.

"Perchance upon my return from Castile?" Chaucer asked.

"Perchance, if you do go, but only if you survive the wintery mountain passes, the war brewing there, and of course the dark-skinned, black-eyed beauties who have slain more men than the Moors of Granada. And progress there and return home with higher rank. Then we shall see," she said.

"Black-eyed beauties? I hear they eat over-spiced food and argue incessantly. Not so unlike the women I know here." Then added, "Yes, we shall see upon my return."

"And let me remind you of the words I have said before. As a wife, I will be free to do as I want and will not be shackled by any man, like so many women that I know."

"Freedom brings responsibility…" he started, but she cut him off.

"Easy for a man to say. It's a different world wearing a wimple."

"I know not how I or any man would ever shackle you," he replied.

"But I know you, Geoffrey Chaucer. I know your kiss lands upon your goblet more often than my lips, and your quill is grasped more often than my queynte, the soft vellum of your sacred books stroked more often than my own skin…so yes, why indeed would I or any woman seek to be bound to a man with so many leather-bound mistresses whose call you always answer first? Why indeed?" she shot back.

Yes, in that she knows me well enough and knows what I love.

"And in that, most men would be the same, save the quill and vellum," he said.

"That leaves few men with a clever tongue worth having."

"And yet quill and vellum are but a stage for the clever tongue you say you enjoy…you will admit our tos and fros are most enjoyable, if too rare."

She paused before making her reply. "Yes, your clever tongue is enjoyable…and our tos and fros rarer. But with you gone…who am I to share such enjoyment with?" she replied.

"While that joy is lost, another is found, for when I'm gone, you are free, unshackled."

"In that, I cannot argue. And I enjoy your returns, and in making up for time away," she said, eyelids fluttering, a blush spreading across her cheeks.

"I should go and come more often."

"Come and go daily," she quipped.

"You would exhaust ten of me."

Pippa stifled a laugh. "In time, you shall learn much about women and their desires."

"I know enough of women's desire," he replied in a tone suddenly much cooler. The truth of who had fathered their daughter Elizabeth was a question that lingered. Pippa had spoken once of Prince John of

Gaunt in his cups, making an advance upon her at the palace. It was near the time they themselves had first lain together, some three and a half years before. Gaunt had already fathered one bastard by Marie St. Hillaire, another lady-in-waiting at the palace who worked with Pippa, so after this news he tried not to imagine the same of Pippa. But he was hesitant to ask her more, for he well remembered the pain in her eyes when she had told him, and of her saying only that she had dealt with the matter and it was behind her. So he had left the question unanswered, and yet still he wondered.

She angled her head, a questioning expression upon her face.

"And what do you mean by that?" she asked.

"Please ensure you visit Elizabeth while I am away. A three-year-old needs her mother."

Pippa flinched, as if slapped.

"Of course I will visit my daughter. Why say such words? It is her soon to be absent father who should consider such service," she shot back.

Whomever that father may be. Service indeed.

"I say so because St. Helen's Bishopsgate has lessened the time allotted to visitors as they repair the entrance to the nunnery," he replied, his eyes searching Pippa's face.

"I see," she sighed.

And I see we recede from each other toward opposing shores.

A pause lay between them.

"Let us return to your task. Should Edward ask you to go, and should you succeed in your task, are you assured a higher position at court?"

"Nothing is assured in this life but death, taxes and writing that is yet undone."

Chaucer rose and padded to the small table tucked in a corner of the room where he wrote. He lit a candle set on the table.

"Finish here and we can finish there," she said, looking skyward to the bedroom.

But he had already settled himself in the chair and was checking the quill.

"Tarry not, or you shall miss your reward."

He was silent and did not lift his head. She sighed. Both knew he would write until the black of night.

•   •   •

"Come to bed?" Pippa asked some time later as she popped her head into the kitchen. Chaucer still sat at the small table, three half melted candles before him.

"I will," he replied absently. "We need the income from this translation of Ovid."

"You may miss your chance to come and go," she said, trying to restart their banter. She approached him and noted a second translation on the table and picked up the first pages and read aloud. "By Jean Froissart. I didn't know that snake translated such works."

"It's three years old, and not a fine translation, but good enough for the simpletons at court," he said as he took the page out of her hands, voice now edged. "He stopped translating after he won his first puy and become court poet," his envy palpable.

He flung down Froissart and picked up his own translation and began writing.

"Ah yes, the puy…where only the finest poets compete in telling stories——or is it lies? You still dream of becoming puy champion and court poet." It was not a question.

He gave no reply and kept working.

She opened then closed her mouth, left, but soon returned, replacing the three melted candles. "I did not want to interrupt you, but two messages arrived when you were at the tavern. The first said that I am to attend Queen Philippa at the palace, for she and King Edward return two days hence. The other methinks is a summons to court, the task Croker spoke of," she said, holding out a sealed, folded note.

He got up, snatched the note from her hands and sat back down and wrote.

She muttered something, waited for him to read the summons, shook her head and left.

In time, Chaucer put down his quill and examined the wax seal. It was stamped with an effigy of King Edward standing upon the prow of a boat. Chaucer snapped the seal and noted a narrow strip of vellum adhered to the top. As he broke the strip, he tried to unfold the letter, but first had to pull the narrow strip through a small hole made at a corner of each fold. Clever, for anyone who broke the wax seal thinking they might rejoin it later by heating it would face a locked letter, unable to continue unless they broke the thin strip of vellum. He had never seen such a device before. Chaucer saw that the note was carefully folded four times, and that "Master Chaucer" was written on the inner fold. The honorific "Master" was only given to a valet, or esquire. And he was only a page at present. A lowly position, surely about to change. A shot of excitement ran through him as he read the brief message. Pippa was right: he was to attend to his king at the palace on the morrow.

My time has come, finally. But first I must write.

He worked until the three new candles began to flicker, the wax again flowing across the table. He set his quill down and blew on the vellum, done with the translation of a poem from French to English. He would share it with the duchess, the beautiful Blanche of Lancaster, the wife of Prince John of Gaunt, for he knew she enjoyed his poems in English. The rest of the French court be damned.

His neck and back ached, but he was not yet done, for now he would write his own words; an ode to Blanche begun some weeks ago. He had been smitten by her on his first day at court five years ago. She was comely, intelligent, and said that she enjoyed hearing his poetic phrases and had read some of his recent short poems. The poem he had started spoke of an unrequited longing, and he dreamed that his scratches upon vellum might become a book one day that she might read aloud at a puy, defeating the French fop Froissart, and becoming court poet. One day. But this day was not that day, and this day was not done.

He lit another candle and took a swig from his near-empty goblet—just enough to give a warm glow to his mind. He found he wrote better with some wine in him. Let his mind free itself and fly. But not too much, or he'd think his words better than they were. He picked up a small knife and his quill and cut a fresh angle off the quill, picked up a clean piece of vellum, dipped the quill in the ink, blotted the first drops of ink on another piece of vellum and began to scratch words about Blanche, whom he desired but could not have, for she was a duchess, far above his station. And he loved Pippa. Yet desire would not rest, and so his words about desire and duty would not let him be, like the now incessant cawing of a large black crow outside the small kitchen window, where dawn slowly pulled back the cover of night.

•　　　•　　　•

Palace of Westminster

"Arise Chaucer, before your knee breaks from shaking so," King Edward said. His rich burgundy robes could not hide his bent stance and paunch, his shaven but deeply lined face showing every one of the forty years spent atop the throne that he now stood in front of as he glared at Chaucer.

Chaucer slowly rose and stood before his king. Croker stood behind Edward, expressionless.

"You arrive late, again," Edward said.

"My lord. I was too enamoured of my sleep." While his words were ill formed, the truth was best, for he had learned that Edward could too easily sniff out a lie.

His wine-soaked breath only deepened Edward's scowl.

"Too enamoured of your drink, you mean."

Chaucer's brow furrowed.

"I was to send you to Bordeaux and then Navarre on the king's business."

"Thank you, my lord."

Finally, the truth of it.

"I have reconsidered," Edward added.

Chaucer's face fell. "May I ask why, my lord?"

"No, you may not!" Edward snapped. Then added, "But I shall tell you, for you may yet learn something on this day. Last night at the Three Cranes Tavern, one of my loyal and sober knights could not help but hear of your boasting of a journey to Navarre on the king's business. You are incapable of discretion, lack circumspection, and I would circumcise such swelling."

"But my lord, it was merely a story told of a journey to Navarre…," Chaucer began.

"Do not interrupt your king, you damnable cur!" Edward shouted back.

Chaucer closed his mouth.

Edward leaned toward Chaucer, his voice quieter, for Chaucer alone to hear.

"Croker heard you speak of Bordeaux and Pamplona, Olite and Logrono. Turning rumours at court into tales. Any fool would know such a journey there with war brewing would be in service as courier or spy—or both. Which makes you a babbling tattler who cannot keep his tongue from wagging so."

Then louder again.

"I will send Sir Alan Richards in your stead, for he is more sober both with words and drink. Go back to the Vintry, go back to your trade in wine, whence you belong," King Edward said, his voice as stern as his face.

Chaucer did not move; the shock of his king's words struck his ear like a poleaxe.

"Go!" Edward cried.

Chaucer stumbled backwards. With slumped shoulders, he awkwardly stepped away from Edward while still facing him. To turn his back on the king was to turn his back on his career. Too late. Near the entrance to the Great Hall, he tripped over a courtier who sniggered at the sad figure who turned and shambled down the corridor, for such a deep cut from the king at court was a wound needing time, and surely the hand of Lady Fortune, to try and heal. It was a wound most would not recover from.

Croker stepped toward King Edward after Chaucer's ignominious exit and whispered, "My lord king, it is true that Chaucer too much enjoys his wine, and has a loose tongue, but he possesses two qualities that would profit this journey."

Several supplicants hovered nearby, straining to hear.

"My good Sir Christopher, such qualities escape both the eyes and ears of this crown. He has shown his true nature, one unfit to serve."

"My lord, his truest nature, as storyteller, would still serve well. He knows the local Castilian tongue gained in the Vintry, and can craft a courtly verse. You speak of Sir Alan to replace him, but that man has no art with words. Nor can he speak the local lingua. And Sir Alan knows not wine. Chaucer's task, under the guise of seeking a supply of Rioja, is to travel to Castile and find Sir Hugh Calveley, your former knight and now mercenary who leads 400 other mercenaries and who fights for the bastard Enrique. When Chaucer finds Calveley, he must convince him to switch his allegiance to your cousin Pedro and so help him keep his crown. Sir Hugh would welcome Chaucer, but would likely turn away from Sir Alan. Richards is high born, whereas Chaucer, like Calveley, is a man born of the city. They are two of a kind, my lord, and would I think profit from each other," Sir Christopher said.

Edward stared right through Croker to some point, or time, in the distance, then faced Croker.

"Yes, fine, agreed. Calveley must be turned, there is no getting away from that. Pedro and I share the same bloodline, and he is the rightful claimant to the Castilian throne. It would not do to have that bastard Enrique rule Castile and stain our royal lineage."

"Agreed, my lord king. And King Charles of France backs Enrique, so if Enrique defeats Pedro, Charles will control him and all of Castile, and so threaten the southern border of Aquitaine that your son Edward rules over," Croker replied.

Edward turned to Croker. "Yes, Charles is a much greater threat than his father King John ever was, and I would not see Charles regain any more power than he already has. This journey is of outmost importance, and as for who might succeed in turning Calveley, I value your opinion as a knight who knows such trade," Edward said.

"If anyone can gain the ear of Sir Hugh, it is a man like Chaucer. But can he turn Calveley back toward the warm embrace of Pedro? That I cannot say, my lord."

"We must decide anon, for Pedro's man Córdoba arrives on the morn to hear my plan."

"We could send another to watch over Chaucer. One who could complete the task if Chaucer fails," Croker replied.

"*When* he fails, for he would be a reluctant and strange spy, and will surely drink wine and babble secrets in some tavern in Burgos. Agreed, he may need to be replaced if his indiscrete tongue threatens our cause. Your advice pleases me not, yet holds merit. But who would suit, let alone accept, the odious task of being that fool's keeper?"

Croker bowed. "My lord, I would be honoured to serve so."

"Ah yes, of course. Go. Follow and protect Chaucer. And ensure his success, for failure would not be kind to you or Chaucer, or our plans there."

Croker bowed once more, then backed away and once he was out of the Great Hall he strode quickly down the corridor that led to the entrance and caught up to the hunched figure of Chaucer and pulled him aside.

•   •   •

The Vintry

"I will be no sacrificial lamb for Edward under that tyrant Croker," Chaucer cried.

"Yes, you will Geoffrey. For us. For Elizabeth," Pippa replied as she put a log on the kitchen fire.

Chaucer paused for but a moment, cloak half off.

"Edward would have me some kind of spy, and Croker, my keeper."

"Good sense that," Pippa replied.

"I have my pride…" he began.

"You bristle with pride like a hedgehog, wounding any who offer help," she snapped.

At that, he turned away, shrugged his cloak back on and left, slamming the door behind him.

I will seek solace elsewhere, for I receive none here.

•   •   •

Palace of Westminster

Chaucer stifled a yawn as he stepped toward Edward and knelt on one knee for the second time in two days. After his embarrassing public scolding the day before, followed by Croker's heavy-handed offer and Pippa's jesting, he had again gone to the Three Cranes Tavern to salve his wounds. He had slept poorly from the excessive wine imbibed. He was awoken to a thunderous knocking at the door. Bleary-eyed, head pounding, he had stomped down the stairs and opened the door, ready for murder. A squat young page handed him a missive. He was to return to court that afternoon.

The king surely seeks to mete out more punishment.

The afternoon light streamed through the tall narrow windows set on the south side of the great room, the silvery grey Thames sliding past not one hundred yards away. Chaucer was ignored by the dozens of courtiers and ladies who chattered and drank, save one, a well-dressed, sun-kissed man Chaucer didn't recognize standing to the right of King Edward, who sat atop a gilded chair set upon a raised platform. The damnable Croker stood below to Edward's left, clutching a rolled parchment in his tawny, leathery fingers. Chaucer glared at him with his best version of a frown.

"Welcome Chaucer. I see you are hardly less unkempt than at our last encounter," King Edward said in a tone only slightly less harsh than the day before.

Chaucer swivelled his head to face Edward. "My lord," he said, knee still bent.

Edward waved his right hand toward the stranger. "This is Señor Don Martín López de Córdoba of Burgos, Master of the Orders of Alacantra and Calatrava and King Pedro's Senior Steward, from the Kingdom of Castile. Señor Córdoba departs on the morn to return to my dear cousin and the rightful king of Castile, Pedro," Edward said.

Córdoba tipped his head slightly.

"Geoffrey Chaucer, page to our lord king," he said, knee shaking.

Edward scowled slightly, as if Chaucer's words rang false. "Up dammit."

"I am honoured to make your acquaintance, Master Chaucer. I am also page, and courier, to King Pedro the Just of Castile," Córdoba said.

Chaucer stood and faced Córdoba, who was equal in title, but unequal in every other way. Chaucer knew himself as stout and wore a plain cloak and wine-stained leather boots. Córdoba was surely ten years older, bearded, tall, and lean. He appraised Chaucer with striking green eyes, wearing a purple silk jupon, supple dark brown leather boots and a golden dagger encrusted with jewels that hung at his belt. He dressed as a nobleman, while Chaucer dressed as the son of a merchant that he was.

"Pedro the Just? He has been called other names as well."

"Such as Pedro the Cruel? He is called both, but not to his face," Córdoba said.

Refreshingly direct.

"My father trades wine, and has brought many bota bags of your fine Rioja to London." Stating he was a merchant's son was a calculated risk; most at court covered over such ignoble roots.

Córdoba returned an easy smile.

"My family were also merchants, and I have served Pedro as waiter and pastry chef."

Straightforward, honest. Rare at court, and he must hold Pedro's trust as his courier.

"You wonder why a mere pastry chef stands before you? I saved the life of Don Pedro's son Juan a few years ago."

Another similarity. Chaucer's father had saved Prince John of Gaunt, the king's second eldest son, from drowning. Similar stories. Similar backgrounds.

"What brings you to the Palace of Westminster?" asked Chaucer.

"I do the bidding of my king who would bind our kingdoms closer together. And you? Will you follow in your father's footsteps and travel to Navarre and Castile for our famed Rioja wine?"

"I did not say my father had travelled to Navarre, only that he traded in that wine."

What does the man know about my family and my journey?

"Only the finest wine comes from Navarre and Rioja, so forgive me, English is not my first, nor even my second language," he replied smoothly.

Chaucer nodded.

"Will you travel to Navarre?" Córdoba pressed.

"Only if my king wills it," Chaucer said, looking to Edward.

Edward's face gave no hint of his thoughts.

"If you do ever journey there, write to me, for I have family there who will show you the hospitality of my beautiful land."

Chaucer gave a brief bow. "You are too kind."

"My lord, I would beg your attention to the matter we were discussing yesterday," said Croker.

Edward turned to him.

"Sir Christopher, please share the proclamation with Senor Córdoba."

Croker unrolled the parchment and read aloud, "All English mercenaries shall put down their weapons and fight no further against our cousin Pedro, the rightful claimant to the crown of Castile. Sir

Hugh Calveley will at once give up his allegiance to the Bastard, Enrique Trastamara, and return to our lord king's good grace," and went on, finishing with, "…as proclaimed by our most gracious King Edward the Third, on this fifth day of December in the year of our lord, thirteen sixty-five."

"I trust that will suffice, Córdoba. It will be shared from here to Castile, so all mercenaries shall hear of it," Edward said.

"My lord king will be pleased," Córdoba replied, then bowed.

Edward nodded, slowly stood up and stepped down past him. Croker followed behind.

Chaucer and Córdoba listened to the echo of Edward's fading boots as he left the hall.

"If you do travel to my land, be careful, for fealty and fidelity are the first to suffer in times of war," said Córdoba.

"Pedro is at war?" asked Chaucer.

"Pedro is always at war," Córdoba said.

Chaucer tilted his head in understanding. At seventeen, he had joined the unsuccessful siege of Reims and was captured. Memories of the cold, mud and blood had faded, but he still remembered the men who had sold their fealty for their life.

Fealty and fidelity indeed. Which war to be had now? An ongoing battle here with Pippa, to gain neither gold nor elevation. Or a new field of battle there, and so use my wits to survive and perchance advance? If I succeed, the rightful king and newly crowned king will sit atop his throne in Burgos, and the rightful valet and newly ringed husband will sit atop his humble throne in London.

CHAPTER 2
BURGOS CATHEDRAL, DECEMBER, 1365
PEDRO THE CRUEL

"My lord king, the cloister is yours to use for as long as you need," the priest said, bowing. "I have asked the brothers to move their mid-morning prayers of Terce to the rectory."

"I am grateful, Juan. It is difficult to find a place absent prying eyes. Your discretion shall be rewarded," King Pedro replied with a slight lisp.

"My lord," said the priest as he bowed again and backed away.

Pedro stood by a stone well in the middle of the cloister, a square of quiet and green enclosed by the cathedral, and he turned to the man behind him. "Don Pero, you have been my trusted servant for what, ten years now? What say you of this…man?" he asked.

Ayala noted that Pedro's lisp was now heavier, which usually meant trouble. He would need to be careful.

"My lord, I have served you for eleven years and say this man, Javier de Alfonso, is of noble blood, and as he is betrothed to your daughter, deserves to be heard," Ayala replied.

Pedro faced Javier, who stood across the well. Two guards stood on either side of Javier, reflected sun glinting off the swords hanging at their waists. Although dressed in the clothes of a wealthy noble, Javier's countenance was more that of a scared child before an angry father.

Ayala noted the difference in the two men. Pedro was over six feet tall, slender but muscular, and his size, very light blond hair, pale skin and blue eyes were a striking contrast to the dark-skinned, diminutive young man quivering before him.

"Tell me…what name do they call me on the street?" Pedro asked.

Javier hesitated, looking to Ayala for his answer. Ayala offered no help.

"I know not what the people of the street call you…King Pedro the Cruel?" the overdressed and perfumed Javier finally said, his brow moist from sweat.

"Ah, you think I am cruel. Cruel to those who do not deserve my cruelty? Or too harsh in my choice of punishment? Which do you mean?" asked Pedro.

One bead of sweat had formed and now hung at the tip of Javier's aquiline nose, like his fate.

"Not what I…I…think…what others…" was all Javier could stutter.

"Stop that damnable stuttering. It is abhorrent to my ears. Say what you mean, dammit!" Pedro shouted.

Ayala's face twitched at Pedro's words as the poet in him failed to ignore the irony of a lisping king mocking a stuttering young noble. Pedro's lisp was now even heavier.

"I think such a name is spoken out of respect, my lord," he finally squeaked.

"And yet spoken by an obsequious mole who seeks to marry into my noble lineage and whose name I keep forgetting…what is it? Jacquerie? Janus?"

"Javier," he whispered.

Ayala knew that Pedro, King of Castile and Leon, relished the epithet spoken by the people, for 'Pedro the Cruel' spoke to their fear of him, and fear led to respect and obedience. But he knew Pedro also relished his other name—'Pedro the Just'—spoken by the courtly sycophants around him since he became king at the age of sixteen. "Am I cruel or just?" he would ask to see whom he could trust. Most said 'just'. Those who responded with both 'just' and 'cruel', he knew to be honest. Those who said 'cruel' often ended up in the dungeon of his castle here in Burgos. And so he was true to his name.

The most deserving of his cruelty might be Enrique, Pedro's half-brother. Enrique the Bastard. Who had no rightful claim to Pedro's crown. And so too the mercenaries Bertrand Du Guesclin and Sir Hugh Calveley helping him to wrest the crown from Pedro. Calveley was an English sell-sword, and leading him Du Guesclin, called the 'Eagle of Brittany' and 'Black Dog of Brocéliande'. No more than a dog leading a pack of braying hounds is how Pedro described him.

Pedro stepped around the well and leaned forward, flicking the droplet of sweat from Javier's nose with the index finger of his right hand.

"Janus, it is time for you to seek a blessing," Pedro whispered.

Javier's face brightened.

"My lord, you are most just," Javier said, relieved. "And my name is Javier."

Pedro burst out laughing. He then turned to Ayala.

"I will baptize this two-faced Janus in the waters of my blessing."

Pedro nodded to the guards, and they grabbed Javier by his arms, lifted him upside down, and then lowered him by his ankles into the well.

"No, my lord, no!" shouted Javier.

"The water lies far below, my lord," said Ayala.

Pedro replied with the slightest nod.

"Guards, please let Janus kiss the holy water and find a blessing there," Pedro replied.

The guards glanced at each other, shrugged, and let go of Javier's ankles.

Pedro smiled at the echoes of his screams and the faint sound of a splash. Then silence.

The corners of Ayala's mouth curled almost imperceptibly downward.

"That heanling was no match for my daughter," Pedro said.

Ayala said nothing.

"Padre?" called a high voice.

Pedro turned to his raven-haired, statuesque daughter standing at the edge of the cloister, some twenty feet away.

"Padre, I heard screaming just now, and it sounded like Javier." She stared at the men by her father. "Where is Javier?" she asked.

"I'm sorry, my dear Beatrice. I thought you were with your sisters," he said.

She awaited his answer.

"Javier disrespected my name, and he will not be marrying you."

She began to tear up. "Javier? We shall not marry?"

"No, my child. He was not suitable. You deserve a better man for a husband, like a prince, and I have an idea of who that may be," Pedro replied.

"But where is Javier? I would say goodbye."

"I have sent him to find a blessing, my child."

"I see, padre," she said, her resigned tone belying her words, and speaking of previous such disappointments.

She turned to leave then hesitated and turned back. "Padre?" she asked.

"Yes?"

"Are the rumours true? Does the army of Uncle Enrique approach? Will he attack us?"

"He is not your uncle. He is the bastard child of my father. And seeks my crown."

"Will you defeat him?" she asked.

"If not today, then tomorrow, for I have signed a peace treaty with King Carlos of Navarre to ensure Enrique cannot attack us from the north. He must come through Aragon, and my forces will defeat him there. Have no fear, my dear," he said.

"I will try not to, padre," she replied, and she turned and disappeared into the shadows.

"Do not worry," Pedro said after her, and left the cloister.

Ayala watched him go. His spies had told him that du Guesclin and Calveley had already arrived in Barcelona, with King Pere of Aragon providing them gold and more soldiers. Pere, another claimant to Pedro's throne, had battled Pedro for years.

Ayala knew Pedro might lose the coming battle, but this was a war that had lasted decades, not weeks. For Pedro to win the war, he would need to look north to Bordeaux and Prince Edward and his vast army, who could surely help put an end to Enrique.

Regardless, more blood would be spilled for the crown, of that he was sure.

CHAPTER 3
BARCELONA, DECEMBER, 1365
DU GUESCLIN AND CALVELEY

Bertrand du Guesclin sat atop his huge destrier. His grey eyes took in the golden city far below, the weak December sun shimmering on the Mediterranean Sea. Above the sound of the riders and infantry jostling behind him, he could hear the faint ringing of bells newly added to the unfinished cathedral by the water, Santa Maria del Mar. They rang to celebrate the birth of Christ and the first of twelve days of Christmas. His horse whinnied and stamped his hoof as if in response. Du Guesclin patted its neck. After his journey across France to gather his mercenary army, both were impatient to begin the battle that lay ahead.

Du Guesclin had named his destrier Ironhoof because the massive blonk was surefooted and had never failed him, and like its owner, was tough. Trained for battle, the huge beast was draped in as much fine steel barding as du Guesclin. Many years earlier, when fighting the English, he'd seen archers shoot the horses from under the French nobility at Crecy, and again at Poitiers. He would never allow that to happen to Ironhoof. The barding weighed over a hundred pounds, but his horse was huge, two hands taller than any other, and was accustomed to the extra weight. He had been told that they appeared as two animals—human and horse—that had become one, fearsome to behold. Ironhoof had carried du Guesclin for over five years through countless battles, responding to every twitch of his knees, as close as any two animals might be.

Du Guesclin loved his horse but felt no love for the soldiers who marched past him, only respect, for they were very good at killing. But they were mercenaries, here to win battles and reap the spoils of war, loyal only to du Guesclin's abilities as skilled tactician and laying siege to wealthy towns to force capitulation with gold paid to be spared. King Pere of Aragon and the Pope had paid a lot of gold for du Guesclin to hire mercenaries and lead them to Barcelona, conveniently ridding France of the same. Most of the soldiers' faces were pale northerners from Normandy and England, Hainault and Flanders.

Du Guesclin watched them crest the hill and begin their march down the valley toward Barcelona. A gentle golden hue lit the ancient, fabled city as if hinting at the riches below. He patted his horse. "We shall have a brief rest this evening," he said. The horse's ears twitched at his voice. "And then we shall go to war," he added.

His horse gave a soft whinny at the word "war".

A huge dark-skinned Moor marched past clad in bronze armour.

"Saludan, how fare the men?" du Guesclin asked.

Saludan glanced briefly at du Guesclin but did not break stride. "They fare well, my lord, for Barcelona is the end of one journey and the beginning of another," he replied.

"My lord, I have news," said a mounted squire that approached and halted his horse before du Guesclin.

"Yes?" du Guesclin snapped.

"The banner you asked after has been seen at the Palace."

"Are you sure? What device was upon it?" du Guesclin asked.

"Three calves on a silver field, a red sash between the top two and bottom calf."

"Sir Hugh Calveley. I know his device well, having soiled it with blood more than once. I would send Sir Hugh a brief missive. Remember my words, then write them down and deliver the message." After hearing the message, the squire nodded and backed his horse away.

•   •   •

Calveley stood in the shadow of the Palau Reial Mayor, the palace of King Pere the Ceremonious of Aragon. Calveley looked up at the dying sun to the west, and to the east, the glinting armour of troops cresting the mountain range that encircled the city. Du Guesclin and his army of mercenaries had finally arrived. The war was soon to begin. He would fight with an old enemy against an ally of his king. Much had changed since he had left England.

Two guards walked past him; they were also looking toward the glint of metal on the mountain top.

"It's du Guesclin and his mercenaries," said the taller one. Clearly the guards hadn't seen Calveley, who overheard one say, "I hear du Guesclin was poor, came from nothing, and fought his way to his position through skill."

They stared up at the distant line of men and horses.

The first one continued. "They say he was a squire who attended a famous jousting tournament in Le Mans. He followed each tilt closely and felt he could do just as well, yet had not the means to compete. So, he begged to borrow his cousin's armour. Visor closed, no one knew who jousted, and he unseated fifteen chevaliers in a row before being unhorsed on the sixteenth tilt, earning the respect of his parents, who until then had looked poorly upon him."

Calveley made a noise, and they turned, surprised to see him.

"And he looks down upon us all now from above," is all Calveley said through his long teeth that projected from his mouth like insubordinate children, then he climbed the steps of the palace entrance.

A valet handed a note to Calveley as he reached the top step.

He read the note as the valet shifted his weight from one foot to the other. Calveley looked up and noted the valet glancing at the sword at Calveley's waist. The lot of a messenger was always tenuous, for an unpleasant message might cause any number of reactions, and why the valet surely stayed a full sword's length away.

An odd smile spread across Calveley's face. Not one of mirth or joy, but of malice.

The valet took a half step backward.

"Do not worry—my sword seeks another."

"Do you have a reply, my lord?" the valet asked.

Calveley pondered his reply. "Say 'King Pere has asked to meet two old friends upon our arrival, and that it has been too long since our last…entreatment.' You have it?"

The valet nodded, mumbled, "My lord," and let out the air he'd been holding as he turned on his heel and left.

•   •   •

Bertrand du Guesclin climbed the steps to the palace, where Pere had ruled the Kingdom of Aragon for twenty-five years, nearly as long astride the throne as Edward of Windsor in England. Over that time Pere had solidified his grip on the kingdom. His palace, the embodiment of such control and wealth, was huge, sprawling and majestic.

Du Guesclin followed the valet along a corridor, his broad shoulders, short, thick legs and long arms giving him an ape-like appearance. Saludan followed two steps behind. The valet stopped by a large set of bronze doors and knocked. The doors opened from the inside and du Guesclin stepped into a vast airy room, light streaming through large vertical windows of coloured glass. A man sat atop a throne on a dais at the far end of the room, surely the king. Several courtiers and knights stood before him and turned as du Guesclin entered.

"Du Guesclin. I am King Pere. Welcome to Barcelona and my palace. Please, come forward," Pere said, his mellifluous voice easily carrying across the hall, sounding younger than the 46 years Guesclin knew him to be.

As du Guesclin approached, he could see that Pere was dressed plainly, gold thread running throughout his simple white cotton tunic. Atop that, he wore a plain but fine wool cloak. A jewelled ring on his right hand—now extended toward him—was the only sign of his station. Unlike many sovereigns du Guesclin had met, Pere clearly felt no need to impress his guests.

Du Guesclin climbed the five steps to the top of the dais, bent and kissed Pere's ring. Then standing, he replied, "My lord, I am grateful for your hospitality."

"I hear Gascony in your voice," Pere said.

"Yes, my birthplace," du Guesclin said, not offering more, for information was valuable in time of war.

"Please, sit," Pere said, pointing to two chairs set before his throne.

"I would stand, my lord, for I have sat for many days atop my horse."

Pere nodded his permission, then cast his eyes about the space.

"This is a beautiful hall, my lord," du Guesclin noted.

"I had it built by the master architect, Guillem Carbonell. He built his arches over the vaults constructed three hundred years earlier, that were in turn built over arches created by the Visigoths some seven hundred years ago, that were raised upon what the Romans had built. So, you see, this room, like this kingdom, was built upon the great works of those who have come before. I trust you are here to build upon what has gone before, not destroy it, du Guesclin?"

The question caught du Guesclin off guard, and he hesitated, so Pere continued.

"I know the pope has paid you a bountiful quantity of gold for your crusade to eradicate the Moors, or at least that is what he said to those who had ears to hear. But we both know the true reason for your journey," Pere continued.

"Ah…yes, of course, my lord, to the point of the matter," du Guesclin stated. The gold he had received was from both the pope and King Charles, and served three purposes. The first was to rid France of mercenaries like himself who, without a war, had been pillaging the country to survive. The second, the public reason, was to rid once and for all the Moors of Granada, the last remaining since they had attacked Iberia over six hundred years before. But the third task was indeed the true task, to defeat Pedro and put Enrique on the throne. "I am here to serve in your efforts to capture or kill King Pedro, for he has dishonoured all by his treatment of the rightful Queen of Castile."

"Indeed, he has. We agree you will provide to me a one-quarter portion of your proceeds from any cities taken as you pursue Pedro," said Pere.

"Yes my lord," du Guesclin said, "I understand Calveley will join our endeavour?"

"He is expected shortly. Success is more likely with such an alliance. Should you succeed, you shall receive the gold, land and titles as outlined in the letter I sent," he said. "As well, I shall grant you the hand in marriage of my daughter, Leonor."

Du Guesclin tilted his head. Marriage would bind him to Pere and limit any potential damage he might bring to Aragon after defeating Pedro. And the reason why Pere would make such an offer.

"My lord, I am honoured by such generosity," du Guesclin said, matching Pere's overly respectful language. "I had expected gold and land, but not a princess."

"Does that not please you?"

"It does, my lord."

"Good, then you will meet Leonor tomorrow, after you and your men are rested and bathed," he said. Du Guesclin and his men were indeed dirty, dusty and overripe.

"Yes, I would feed my soldiers and horses after I've seen Calveley." And put a sword deep into his chest as soon as Pedro had been defeated. But business first.

At the sound of a door opening, approaching footsteps and a sword withdrawing from a scabbard, du Guesclin's hands went to his own scabbard, but his sword was not there. He had relinquished it at the door.

Calveley handed his sword to a guard as he entered the vast room.

"Calveley," du Guesclin grunted.

"I saw your soldiers arriving and sought to welcome you," Calveley replied as he approached and stood next to du Guesclin.

"The last time you welcomed me your men took several arrows for their troubles."

"And yours as well."

"You know each other well," Pere said from his throne.

"Too well," du Guesclin growled.

"We have much to discuss… please approach and sit here before me in these chairs," Pere said.

Both du Guesclin and Calveley remained standing.

Pere ignored the slight and continued. "I will get to the heart of our meeting. You each received my letter with an offer."

Du Guesclin turned to face Calveley, ignoring Pere. He said nothing to Calveley and just stared at him, his hatred for the man clear upon his face.

Pere continued. "Calveley, du Guesclin has agreed. Calveley, do you also accept the…?"

Before Pere finished and Calveley could answer, du Guesclin interrupted.

"We assume Calveley does, and I must feed and water my horses and troops," said du Guesclin as he gave the slightest bow to Pere, then turned and left the way he came in. Turning his back on a king, this king, as he left was yet another slight.

"Yes, of course," Pere said, his brow expressing annoyance at such disrespect.

"I too must tend to my men and horses," said Calveley, turning to follow after du Guesclin, whose footsteps echoed from the outside corridor.

"Sir Hugh? The terms are agreeable?" Pere asked after him.

Sir Hugh Calveley paused and turned to face Pere. "Serving under that bastard is not agreeable, no. But I will consider your terms and provide my response once we reach Zaragoza."

"I cannot wait any longer than that for my answer, as we shall attack Pedro's cities just west and north of Zaragoza," Pere replied.

"You will have your reply then." Calveley bowed, turned and strode away, his boots snapping on the marble floor, matching his curt response.

CHAPTER 4
BORDEAUX, JANUARY, 1366
CHAUCER ARRIVES

The voyage from Southampton did not go well. After sailing half a day south, a winter storm blew in suddenly from the northeast, driving Chaucer's cog farther west than planned, the captain struggling to make headway toward the coast of Bordeaux. Ten stormy days later, they reached La Rochelle. They restocked water and supplies for the final two-day sail to the Gironde. After that, it took them another day to sail upriver to Bordeaux, the Port of the Moon.

The delay gave Chaucer time to ponder his life, and Pippa. He had to make something of this journey, or she would surely choose a more suitable suitor, some highborn knight befitting her noble status. Why she had chosen him, a lowly merchant's son, he could not fathom. But they had an easy banter, and she understood his wit, and could hold her own, nay best him in their verbal battles most oft.

And of course, there was their daughter Elizabeth, born out of wedlock nearly three years earlier at the Chaucer house and recently placed at the convent at St Helens Bishopsgate. It was Pippa's choice to continue serving the queen at court. She hated the thought of not staying at home and mothering her child, but needed to earn coin, for Chaucer earned not enough for them both. She also loved such service, for she had the ear of Queen Philippa. The cost of providing food and board for Elizabeth had been paid for by an anonymous donor. Chaucer had tried and failed to find the donor's name. Pippa might know, but it was a subject neither was ready to speak of.

But tongues wagged, for rumour was a valued currency at court. More than once a conversation had been halted mid-sentence upon their entry, but not before the words "cuckold", "daughter", and "noble" were spoken.

So they tried to ignore such mutterings.

Chaucer desperately missed seeing Elizabeth, but supported Pippa's choice. And now he had to succeed in his task so he could earn a better position at court and better support Pippa, and one day bring Elizabeth home. And perchance have another child together. Properly, as man and wife.

Upon his return, he would ask for Pippa's hand in marriage again. And end such rumours.

And yet, no matter how much he wanted to make things right with Pippa, his thoughts wandered to Blanche, the Duchess of Lancaster. He had fallen for Blanche years before. She had sparked in him some strange desire he seemed unable to quell. She was the source of many of his dreams—both waking and asleep—and also of several poems he had written. Including a new one he struggled with now.

He sighed. A woman he loved, a girl he missed, a duchess he desired. Three who filled his heart one day, and broke it the next. Yet on good days, such feelings were, he knew, also a deep well he could drink from to quench the thirst of his poetic muse.

He dipped his quill into the ceramic inkwell placed into the depression in the oak table before him. The carpenter who had built the table knew his business, for the cavity stopped the inkwell from sliding about as the ship dipped and swayed.

He scratched the letters onto the vellum until the first lines of a poem arrived before him. He blew upon the last letter to set the ink and picked up the vellum and read aloud:

> 'This love has so placed me that he will never fulfill my
> desire; for neither pity, mercy, nor grace can I find.

Yet even for fear of death, can I not root out love from my sorrowful heart.

The more I love, the more my lady pains me; through which I see, without remedy, that I may in no way escape death.'

Chaucer sighed again and put down the vellum. He noted that his quill did not roll as it had done earlier in the morning. In fact, he only felt a gentle roll and sway. And just then a deckhand's shout of "Bordeaux" broke through the incessant noises that passed for silence on the ship, the cacophony of squeaks and flaps, howls of wind and pattering of rain drilling into his head for the past weeks.

After putting away his writing tools into his two leather travel bags, he made his way to the bulkhead and climbed to the deck as the veil of rain lifted with the sun's arrival, setting alight the bustling city of Bordeaux that lay before him. His father had said there were some thirty thousand souls—as many as London—and he could see a great cathedral nearly as large as St. Paul's that loomed over the port, close to two other massive stone edifices.

His father and the men he had worked with on the wharf had told him much about the city. He knew that Bordeaux, the capital of Aquitaine, had been under English rule since Eleanor, formerly queen of France, married King Henry the Second two centuries earlier after divorcing King Louis the Seventh, becoming both queen of England and the first duchess of Aquitaine. Together they made Bordeaux into the force it was now, with the wine from the surrounding countryside one of the primary sources of income filling King Edward's treasury, and paying for much of the city that lay before him.

Seagulls laughed at Chaucer as he shuffled down the rain-soaked plank on wobbly legs. He breathed a sigh of relief as he finally stepped onto the cobbled stones of the wharf and felt the solidity of land. Not for him the vagaries and unending sway of the ocean. His da loved to sail, but Geoffrey preferred to walk. He chose a porter from the many waiting to carry his bags and smiled at the warm afternoon sun that kissed his face and familiar sounds that filled his ears. There were some similarities to London, for a high stone wall also marked the city's perimeter, and a beehive of workers unloaded wool from the cogs at the docks and loaded barrels of wine for the return voyage. The Port of the Moon, named for River Garonne's crescent shape, resembled the Thames. What was different were the hills to the north, and the three massive stone structures to the west that loomed over the city. He had asked the grizzled porter to take him to Prince Edward, and the man had begun walking northwest toward one of them.

"The cathedral?" Chaucer asked, in French, of a stone edifice furthest in the distance.

"The Cathédrale St-André," the man said, nodding. "Kings and queens of Aquitaine, married and buried."

"And that?" Chaucer asked, as he gestured at the palatial building next to it.

"The archbishop's palace. Called Archibescat. When Prince Edward arrived ten years ago, he took possession of the palace and told the archbishop and clergy within to vacate. After initially huffing and puffing about the injustice of such a request, they vacated when they saw the hundreds of well-armed knights accompanying the Prince."

Chaucer began to huff and puff himself as they reached a broad, tree-lined avenue with an imposing structure at the end.

"English princes like their buildings large," said the porter. "Make up for other things small?" he asked, smiling.

"Perchance. What is this? A palace or a castle?" Chaucer asked of a third hunk of stone.

"Both. The Palaise de l'Ombrière, home to Edward's ancestors since Eleanor of Aquitaine and the second King Henry resided there. Edward break tradition and made it seat of military and judicial administration."

"Why the name 'l'Ombrière?" asked Chaucer.

"Means 'shade' in your English tongue, for the shade of the large trees on the avenue before you," he said.

Chaucer nodded.

"Finished some fifty years ago," the porter said. "See huge square donjon there. Has vaulted staircase leading to the Great Hall with beautiful round stained-glass window. Two-story tower added by second Edward there," he said, pointing. "Now home to the prince, his seneschal, Sir John Chandos, and the arsenal. A place no outside force has ever set foot in," he said as they approached the massive building.

Chaucer noted more well-dressed merchants and courtiers milling about the palace entrance. Chaucer also noted a black iron fence that wrapped around the palace. Human heads, some revealing white skulls beneath, and some with eyes picked clean but still with flesh and hair, had been set on pikes behind the fence. They were arranged every twenty yards or so around the fence. The message was clear.

"What happens to rebellious lords that no like Edward," the porter said as they both stood and stared.

Chaucer tried to ignore the heads and proceeded to climb the massively wide stone steps to the entrance. A huge flag flapped above him bearing Edward's coat of arms of three ostrich feathers waving at those who sought ingress. The motto "Ich Dien" was written below each feather.

I serve indeed.

At the gateway, Chaucer passed two large guards who eyed him warily, for he was not dressed as a wealthy merchant, nor a lord. But he was not stopped and passed through the main entrance to then climb a twenty-foot-high set of narrower, well-worn stone steps. At the top step, Chaucer's porter rapped on a small door set within a much larger oak door, reinforced with strips of iron and hung on hinges as large as his head.

After a lengthy pause, what Chaucer took to be a guard, clad in full armour save a visor, opened the door halfway and asked, "Your business?"

The man was in his late forties. A diagonal scar ran through a stubbled salt and pepper beard, ending in a disfigured eye. The confident gaze of his left eye gave Chaucer pause. This was no ordinary guard.

Chaucer stepped forward. "I am Geoffrey Chaucer, courier to King Edward," he said evenly, trying not to stare at the black hole where the guard's right eye should have been.

"I ask again, what is your business?" the man demand.

"I arrive from London, bearing a letter for Sir John Chandos given to me directly from the hands of our lord and ruler, King Edward the Third," Chaucer said, pulling out the leather pouch holding the letter to emphasize its importance.

This haughty guard best understand that I should not be trifled with.

The door opened, and the man gestured toward the expansive room, as if to say come in.

But when Chaucer took a step forward, the guard laid his steel-covered hand on Chaucer's chest, blocking him.

"Are you a loyal man, a trustworthy man, who will keep all that is told here secret?"

Strange questions for a guard to ask.

"Of course, or the king would not have entrusted me with this letter," Chaucer snapped.

"That is what I had hoped to hear. Good day, Geoffrey Chaucer. I am Sir John Chandos, seneschal of Prince Edward's army in Aquitaine," the man replied.

Chaucer let out his breath, relieved.

"Please forgive my words and actions, for I have seen many like you arrive these past few weeks saying that they were seeking passage to Navarre and Castile to join arms in the war burgeoning there. But some were spies, unearthing information for our enemies. Those spies are now either rotting in our dungeons, or their heads sit atop the pikes outside."

Chaucer's eyes widened, nodding.

"Sir John, you have no need to apologize. It is my honour to meet such a celebrated warrior and noble," said Chaucer, his words sincere and drained of the biting tone he had intended for his reply.

Chandos smiled. "Please excuse my visage. Most men would cover an injured eye or wear a visor. I prefer to leave the hole exposed as a reminder that a soldier is not a pretty carpet knight who dances at court and only ever wields his tongue or cock. I love the ladies, 'tis true, but I love even more to serve my lord and wield my sword."

"You lost your eye in a battle?" Chaucer asked. Chandos was celebrated far and wide, the stories of his many victories well known. The story of the loss of his eye was not.

"No, that would make for a better tale. Three years past I was hunting a stag. A massive beast he was, carrying twelve tines atop his huge head. After felling him with three arrows, I went to pull one arrow from his chest, and he threw his head in one last death throw and caught me in the face with his tine. That's him there," he said, nodding toward the massive stag's head mounted on the wall above the hearth that crackled and smoked from newly added wood.

"I've not worn a visor since," he said, "except in battle, that is. I'm not stupid," he added.

Chaucer knew that Sir John was surely the most famous knight in all of Europe, and the mastermind behind King Edward's victories at Crecy, Poitiers and Auray. He was also one of the founding members of the Order of the Garter, and a close friend of Prince Edward. In Chandos, Chaucer was gazing on the flower of English chivalry, and a man of proven military genius. As seneschal of Aquitaine, he was responsible for maintaining order, which included quashing rebellious lords and rooting out spies.

"Come in, sit. Roland, some wine for our guest," Chandos said, turning to a red-haired giant of a servant.

The grizzled porter set Chaucer's bags on the floor, palmed the proffered coin and departed.

Chaucer took in the expansive room as he followed Roland's limping hulk toward a side table. Coloured light streamed through stained-glass windows running along the top of the southern wall of the room, casting fantastic multihued shapes along the floor and opposite wall. Beautifully wrought scenes of battle were displayed in the detailed wall hangings around the room. The roaring fire in a massive hearth cast heat and light upon two finely carved gilded chairs and an oak table, where two jewel-encrusted silver goblets awaited. A room that spoke of great wealth and refined taste.

"You note Roland's limp. I faced him on the battlefield at Auray last year," Sir John said, motioning Chaucer to be seated. "It's a good story."

Roland's bearded face gave away nothing as he moved away from them to the table and turned the wooden handle on a small barrel. Deep burgundy coloured wine flowed in a narrow stream into a silver flask.

"He was one of the toughest warriors I have ever fought. The soldiers of Charles of Blois, Duke of Brittany, had folded and run. He alone stood his ground, protecting the mercenary Bertrand du Guesclin. You may know of du Guesclin?"

Chaucer nodded.

"Roland already had a spear embedded in his leg as he wielded his axe against me and my second, Sir Hugh Calveley. After a furious fight, we disarmed him, and I accepted du Guesclin's surrender. Then I saw that Roland had fallen into a pool of blood. I thought him dead, but he came around. He had already taken several sword strokes to his chest, back, and arms. The spear was still lodged in his leg. It's a miracle he could still fight. I could have killed him then, but it is rare to find such a warrior and so I offered him life, in service to me, which he gladly accepted. After his wounds healed, he became my loyal servant, and has remained so since."

Roland limped towards them, carrying the silver flask and two silver goblets. His beard looked like he had plunged his face into a vat of salt and then pepper, but it did not hide the proud curl of a smile as he acknowledged Chandos' story, his English good enough to understand the compliment. He set down the flask and goblets and shuffled to the doorway where he took up his stoic stance.

"Yes, I would gladly take your drink," Chaucer said, thirsty for the Bordeaux he had come to relish ever since his father had begun importing the wine some five years earlier.

Chandos filled each goblet.

"You fought du Guesclin, the Eagle of Brittany? He has a fearsome reputation."

"Yes, with the aid of Sir Hugh Calveley, I captured him. He can be beaten," he said, then awkwardly settled onto a large chair, his legs splayed before him. Visorless, he wore armour on his chest, arms and legs, is if ready for battle. Odd.

"You note my armour. I was just training some men at arms in the finer details of hand to hand combat."

"I interrupted…"

"Not at all. Let us toast to your successful passage. The Channel can be treacherous this time of year."

"To Bordeaux," Chaucer said, raising his goblet.

"To Bordeaux!" Chandos replied.

They clanked their goblets together, and Chaucer took a sip.

"You have a letter for me?"

Chaucer nodded, put down his goblet and fished it out from his jerkin and handed it to Chandos.

Chandos broke the wax seal, broke and pulled out the vellum strip, opened the folded note and read the letter.

"Yes, just as I assumed," Chandos said.

Chaucer was desperate to ask, but held his tongue.

"You must wait to hear our king's words, as I must first inform my prince," he said, rising, then added, "A servant will take you to your room, as I'm sure you are tired from your journey. We shall speak on the morrow."

Chandos clicked and clanged his way to the door, leaving Chaucer in silence, save for the crackling of the warm fire.

"More wine, Master Chaucer?" Roland asked in a thick Gascon accent.

"Thank you, Roland. Please join me."

"I cannot while I attend to you," he said. "But I join you in talk," he replied.

"Your English is good," Chaucer said.

"Not so good, no," Roland said.

"Is it true that English is spoken by all the lords in Bordeaux now?"

"Most, yes. The prince say nobles must speak English, sign of loyalty. Some make ugly sound not English. In private, one lord laughed. Edward's valet overhear. That lord's tongue cut out in front of other nobles. Edward say this noble never again have any trouble with English. Most now speak English."

Chaucer took a drink. *A fair punishment for such disrespect.*

"Even though English control Bordeaux for two centuries now, nobles in mountains north of Navarre and Castile still rebel. They would prefer to be ruled by King Carlos to Prince Edward. Some of their heads on spikes outside."

The servant suddenly appeared.

"Master Chaucer. I will escort you to your bedchamber," he said.

Chaucer rose and nodded to the servant then turned back. "Thank you Roland. I will stay only two days, and then must depart for Pamplona."

"Be careful crossing the mountains," Roland replied.

•   •   •

Chaucer's bedchamber was filled with rich tapestries, a comfortable bed and a platter of bread, cheese and wine on a low table by the roaring fire. After supping and undressing, he was sound asleep in moments.

The sound of birds awoke Chaucer. He had slept well for the first time in days. Dawn was far off, and he was famished, so he dressed quickly, ate what crumbs remained on the tray, and followed his nose to the massive kitchen—empty of servants—where he fell upon a slab of hard cheese and crusty bread. He ate standing, washing the food down with some more Bordeaux red. It was extraordinary how good simple food and wine tasted at certain times.

He looked out the stone slit where fingers of light clawed apart the cloud-scudded dark.

"Geoffrey Chaucer, is it?" a woman's voice asked.

He turned and faced a woman standing before him, a woman of pure beauty. "My…l-lady," he managed to stutter, bowing.

"I am Joan, wife of our lord, the prince, and countess, and I am pleased to meet you."

Joan of Kent. My God, what a vision.

"Countess," Chaucer replied, now kneeling, almost spilling his goblet of wine. He knew Joan to be nearing 40 summers in age, and her beauty was undeniable. Her eyes struck him first. Bright blue, with flecks of green that shone from her oval face, where her wide smile and full, red lips were framed by golden hair that was not yet tucked into a wimple, flowing over her partly exposed shoulders. She was informally dressed in a shift covered by a loose cloak that was partially open, revealing more of her shapely form beneath. He lowered his eyes, realizing he was staring.

"Careful Chaucer, you wouldn't want to spill the lifeblood of England," she said.

"I have tasted many wines, for that is my father's trade, and this is indeed one of the finest."

"Your father was also deputy wine butler to our king, yes?"

Chaucer nodded, impressed at her knowledge of his humble family.

"Please stand."

He stood.

"Is it wine that brought you here?"

He hesitated but for a moment. "Our good king sent me to seek out the finest Rioja wines and establish relationships with vintners there."

"You choose an unfortunate time for such trade, with war afoot," she said. "One would hope you do not have to trade Rioja for blood."

"Wine cares not for politics or the fates of kings and queens," he replied.

"And yet you could just as easily serve our good king as spy, gathering information."

Of course, King Edward has informed his son Prince Edward, who has told his wife Joan of my task. But I must be careful here.

"My lady's imagination is as fertile as the lands she rules. I travel as a lowly courier and am of little import to any king or pretender in Navarre or Castile."

She smiled at his carefully worded reply, as if he had passed some test.

"You have a clever talent with words. Be not too clever, for one false move in Navarre and Castile may cost you that fine tongue of yours."

He nodded.

"Prince John's lady Blanche told me you are a poet of some talent."

His Blanche had said that of me?

"I am but a poor master of words," he replied.

"I would have you share with me a composition inspired by your journey upon your return," she said, adding, "So return safely. Now I must attend to my duties, and you to yours."

The kitchen fire light embraced her. His tongue failed him.

She swept out of the kitchen.

She wanted to hear a composition? Inspired by my journey?

He recalled then the story Pippa had told him of how Joan had come to marry Prince Edward. A knight had fought with Prince Edward at Crécy and Poitiers. The prince asked how he could repay him for his loyal service. He said, "Would my lord ask for the hand of the recently widowed Joan Holland, Countess of Kent, on my behalf?" Prince Edward approached the countess, for he knew her well from their time spent together in their youth. He had always loved her, and as she was even more beautiful than he remembered, he asked for her hand in marriage himself. His father, the king, was incredulous at such behaviour and denied him, for she was Edward's second cousin. But Prince Edward would not listen and married her. Joan had already been married once before, to Sir Thomas Holland, and had several children with him, but he had died five years earlier. To be wooed by a knight and wed by a prince; few others could say as such.

They each married for love. Rare for a noble or a peasant in these times.

• • •

Chaucer had made his way to the central market to seek out books, local stories and a guide. Then spied a tavern. Not long after, he was downing his third goblet of Rioja at a small table near the back of the tavern when a man's voice called "Geoffrey Chaucer?"

Chaucer faced the familiar face of a knight who stood before him.

"Sir Christopher Croker," Croker said.

"Ah yes, Croker, I was wondering if you might re-appear," Chaucer replied in a tone far less welcoming than Croker's.

And knock me to the ground again.

"Chaucer once was a name to be respected, thanks to your da," he said.

Was? What did he mean by was?

Croker was middling of height and weight, a well-fed belly pushing against his plain woolen coverlet, good quality boots—one could tell a lot about a man or woman from their footwear—and without gold or jewellery. His dress suggested no untoward ambition, and no suggestion of falsity. Yet the "Was" hung in the air like a foul odour.

"How do you know my father? He has never mentioned your name."

"I told you back in London that I was of the Vintry. Your da and I, vintner's men both," Croker said, now sitting across from Chaucer.

"Yes, so you had said. Which vintner?"

"Stodie, up on Gracechurch Row by the market. Know of 'im?"

"A storied history. Stodie's father was banished from the Vintry district for watering down his wine, the worst sin a vintner could ever make."

"There may be worse sins," Croker replied.

True enough, and any man tied to the Vintner's Guild was bound by its laws, which gave Chaucer some confidence in Croker's word.

"You said Chaucer was a name to be respected, and imply it no longer is."

"I tell you only what I see and hear. At court, the name Chaucer now produces a smirk, and words like chatterer, clatterer, bibber and drunk."

Chaucer was mid sip of his goblet and pulled back his head as if slapped, spilling the Rioja on his chest. He put down the goblet. The words stung, and he sat up straight.

"You do not varnish your words."

"My task is to ensure your success, not flatter you like some painted whore."

"What do you want, Croker?" Chaucer asked.

"The path from Bordeaux to Castile is dangerous. Others less well-disposed to your success may also know of your journey," Croker said.

"So now you would offer me protection for some exorbitant fee, rather than do your duty to your king."

Croker smiled and shook his head no. "Our good king only asked that I keep you alive and to see *you* do your duty."

"Do you seek to accompany me?"

Croker shook his head. "Best if I stay in the shadows. But I'll share a flagon with you."

Chaucer was unsure of the company Croker might provide.

But Croker took Chaucer's silence as assent and shouted, "Barman! A flagon and cheese."

CHAPTER 5
NEAR ZARAGOZA, FEBRUARY 18, 1366
ENRIQUE TRASTAMARA AND HIS BROTHERS

Enrique Trastamara rode at the head of some eight thousand Castilian knights, men-at-arms and exiles. Many had been fighting with Enrique against Pedro for more than a decade and proudly bore the scars of those battles. Beside Enrique rode his brothers Sancho and Tello, who had both survived Pedro's various attempts on their lives over the years; they were Enrique's only surviving family. Enrique was the eldest at thirty-three. Sancho was the youngest, twenty-three, handsome, tall, and even-tempered. Tello was twenty-nine but seemed younger than Sancho in many ways, for he was headstrong, more vain, and lacked the honour of his two brothers. He had briefly aligned himself with Pedro five years earlier after a sibling fight, and had never been able to wash away that stain in the eyes of his brothers.

But Tello, for all his flaws, was alive, while Enrique's other brother Fadrique was dead, murdered by Pedro. Tello's presence was a reminder of what Enrique still had to fight for.

"Sancho, have you heard any news of King Pere's cousin, the Count of Denia, and his army? Will he join us?" Enrique asked.

"He will, and he has also brought together Felipe de Castro, Pedro Boil, Juan Ramirez de Arellano, Juan Martinez de Luna, and the Count of Ribagorz to join, and together they are a force even larger than your own."

"Our own. We command these forces together, my brother," Enrique corrected. "And together we shall defeat Pedro. Isn't that right, Tello?"

Tello shifted in his saddle and smiled, part wry grin, part grimace. "We all know who is truly in command, my brother," he replied.

"I command as the king without a crown, but I command only because you both support me. Never forget that," Enrique said.

Enrique was not an attractive man, of average height, physically unimposing, but he had a feral, animal-like quality inflamed by anger that he could not easily hide. When his father King Alfonso had suddenly died of the Black Death, and his half-brother Pedro was made King of Castile, Pedro immediately cast out Enrique, his brothers and his mother. Enrique never forgot the looks, the curses, the belittlement of those at court who now looked down upon him as a mere bastard of Alfonso. Each slap to his honour added more fuel to his desire for revenge. He had spent the last fifteen years seeking to regain his honour and battling Pedro for a throne he felt was his, joined by King Pere of Aragon, who had been fighting Pedro almost as long. Now, with Calveley and du Guesclin joining the army, the seeds of victory lay before him.

Tello nodded at Enrique in agreement, but his curled lips spoke of something else.

"We are but three miles away from Zaragoza, brother. We should consider making camp and sending out scouts," Sancho said.

"Yes, agreed. And du Guesclin and Calveley? Any news? Are they nearby?" Enrique asked.

"They also approach Zaragoza," Tello replied.

"Good. And what of Pedro? Has he been found?"

"He retreats as we advance; our spies last placed him near Logrono."

"I will capture that foul Jew-loving beast, torture him to within an inch of his life, parade him before our people in a gibbet cage, and have him quartered in the public square of Burgos where he was crowned. His body torn apart, limb from limb, and his head taken off and hung upon a spike so that all may see what Pedro has become," Enrique shouted.

Enrique's vehement outburst quieted both Sancho and Tello. They knew better than to interrupt him, for he would not sleep, would not stop, until he had captured and killed the man who had taken so much from Castile, and from their family.

CHAPTER 6
PAMPLONA, FEBRUARY 21, 1366
CHAUCER MEETS HIS GUIDE

Chaucer let out a sigh of relief and his breath danced before the snow-covered peaks of the Pyrenees that rose above the walls of Pamplona to the north, west and south. He wanted nothing more than a warm fire and a goblet of wine on this frigid February afternoon. He had travelled south from Bordeaux with another wine merchant, and then at Dax, a knight and his valet had joined them on their pilgrimage to Santiago de Compostela. They hired a guide who was poor at his job, and after making it through the pass at Roncesvalles they became lost twice and nearly froze. His father had been right about waiting until spring. But he had survived and finally reached Pamplona.

Chaucer led his horse toward the cathedral overlooking the Rio Arga. At a nearby barn behind a tavern he paid for his horse to be sheltered and fed. He entered the tavern, dropped his leather satchel by the long bar and ordered a long-sought after goblet of wine. A good-sized fire burning in a hearth near the back warmed his cold bones, and he began to feel better. He smiled at the taste of the Rioja. Lighter than the Bordeaux he had recently become used to. The inn filled up with travelers as he waited for Córdoba, who had replied to his letter saying he would meet him here on this day. His thoughts turned to home and to Pippa.

Will she find some noble while I am here on this mad quest? Like Gaunt? And what of Gaunt? What of Pippa? What of them both?

He sighed and turned over in his mind the relationship between Gaunt and Pippa, and if Gaunt could be the father of his daughter. Then, tired of what might be, considered what could be, and his thoughts turned to the poem he had been trying to compose. And he sighed again.

The damnable words escape me. Why pretend that the dull letters that fall from my stony head upon the barren pages might yet be fashioned into cunning words to make others feel what I feel? A madness, to think my base words might yet speak of such feelings?

He shook his head, sighed a third time, ordered food, and shifted his focus to those around him. He understood enough Castilian to hear the talk of Enrique's rapid advance west. After wolfing down sausage, hard, tangy cheese and crusty bread, he thought of leaving, for Córdoba was clearly not coming and Calveley would not be found at the bottom of his goblet. But go where? He tapped his fingers upon the dark, fine-grained red wood, admiring the colour and feel. The wood was darker and smoother than the oak used in most London taverns. More like teak.

"Que?" he tried to ask the barman.

The man tilted his head, trying to understand. Chaucer pointed to the wood.

"Ci. Madera de caoba. Afric," he replied, refilling Chaucer's goblet.

"Is Mahogany, in English," said a voice to his left.

Chaucer turned to face a white-haired man with a tanned, leathery face above a worn black cloak at the end of the bar. He hadn't noticed him arrive. The man could have been forty or sixty, it was hard to tell. But his intelligent brown eyes shone brightly.

"English?" the man asked.

"Yes, how did you know?" replied Chaucer between bites of his chorizo.

"Boots," the man said, pointing at Chaucer's boots. Indeed, the boots of the other patrons were of a different cut, the leather more supple. But Chaucer was more surprised by the man's use of English, normally spoken by nobles and lords. Yet he was clearly no lord by his simple clothes.

"Where did you learn your English?" Chaucer asked, his curiosity stoked.

"Buy wine, I tell," the man replied.

"I am Geoffrey Chaucer."

It took a flagon of wine to get the story and the man's name.

Alfonso had worked in King Pedro's court as a wine butler, learning a smattering of languages from the men who unloaded wine. Like Chaucer.

"Your father—is he a vintner or merchant like mine?" Chaucer asked.

"In some way, yes," was his vague reply. He said he now worked as a guide and translator for the English, French and Gascon nobles and soldiers who crossed the Pyrenees into Navarre to seek gold as mercenaries. Hundreds of them now clogged the streets of Pamplona.

"You go where?" Alfonso asked.

"I cannot say," Chaucer replied, careful of revealing too much.

"Cannot, or will not?" Alfonso asked.

"It is the same," Chaucer replied carefully.

"In time of war, look to those you trust, and trust those that look to you," Alfonso replied.

Chaucer looked to Alfonso.

Perchance he is more than just a guide.

Alfonso looked back, searching Chaucer's eyes. "Man die in mountains…cold, bandits, thieves. You will need help," Alfonso added.

"But how do you know I'll be going through mountains?"

"You are in Pamplona. North is mountains. South is mountains. Mountains every way," Alfonso said, then asked, "You have pass to travel through Navarre from King Carlos?"

"Not yet. I leave for Olite tomorrow to request one," he replied.

"Wise," Alfonso simply said.

"How much do you charge?" Chaucer asked, his interest piqued.

"How much you have?" Countered Alfonso.

He didn't think he could afford the man's services. His five gold nobles had to last his entire journey. Yet he could ill afford to wander the valleys of Navarre looking for Calveley—let alone Córdoba—without knowing his way. His gut told him that Alfonso was trustworthy, and he had begun to learn to listen to his gut.

"Tell me your fee," Chaucer asked again.

Alfonso got up and put out his hand. "Pay me when arrive," he said.

Guides always ask for gold up front. What is he playing at?

"After, not before?" Chaucer asked, ensuring Alfonso understood what he said.

He nodded. "When leave?" he added.

"Cock's crow," Chaucer replied.

"Best sleep good now. No sleep soon," Alfonso said.

Something about Alfonso's eyes stayed Chaucer from asking why. He seemed to know things. That was enough for now.

"Cock's crow," Chaucer repeated.

•   •   •

Cocks had crowed and dawn was burgeoning across the mottled sky when Chaucer stepped out of the dimly lit tavern. Fog drifted in and out of sight. A figure in the shadowed space between the tavern and the barn shifted.

"Alfonso. You startled me," Chaucer said.

"You late," he said.

"It's just dawn. Give me a moment to gather my things and get the horses."

"I bring horses, things," he said. Chaucer noted the two saddled horses behind Alfonso, recognizing his leather sack already strapped behind the saddle of the second one.

"But how...?" he began to ask.

"Must leave," Alfonso replied, his tone suggesting darker things afoot. "Must leave to make Olite before nightfall," Alfonso added, and mounted and he trotted south on the cobblestoned street.

Chaucer awkwardly mounted and followed his strange guide. As his rouncey tapped out a rhythmic clip-clop south along the cobblestoned streets of Pamplona, he pondered his future and what he had got himself into. War was beckoning. Enrique and du Guesclin approached, with Calveley amongst them. How would he find Calveley, not get killed, and then turn him away from Enrique and toward King Edward and Pedro?

I will need Lady Fortune to smile kindly upon my journey.

CHAPTER 7
OLITE PALACE, FEBRUARY 22, 1366
CHAUCER AND KING CARLOS

Thirty miles south of Pamplona.
Chaucer and Alfonso welcomed the light, if not warmth, of the weak sun as the fog burned off and they bounced upon their rounceys along the hilly trail in the valley leading south from Pamplona. When they reached the base of the ruins of an ancient castle at Tiebas, they stopped to rest and eat at a nearby hostel. When the owner learned of their destination, he warned them to be careful, for the route to Olite was winding and dangerous, with many brigands about.

The sky was azure blue and the slanting afternoon sun almost warm as they left the mountains behind and descended into a heavily wooded valley filled with deer and innumerable grouse. They emerged from the forest onto a plain and a city appeared. Rising above the city was the Royal Palace of Olite, a fortified castle with crenelated towers over a hundred feet tall.

As they approached, Chaucer spied a massive wall covered in a film of green and brown, surely the famed hanging gardens of Olite that Alfonso had described to him, the leaves already turning green. Chaucer was struck by how difficult it would be to assault such a fortress. Alfonso had told him that Olite had been attacked ten times in the past thirty years, yet no army had breached its walls, which ensured King Carlos' tight hold on power in Navarre.

As they rode towards the castle gatehouse, Chaucer noted merchants selling their wares in stalls that lined either side of the roadway at the foot of the castle walls, spoken in unknown languages whose origins he could only guess at.

"Alfonso, what language are those two speaking?" Chaucer asked of two dark-skinned men dressed in long robes haggling over a fine blot of aubergine silk.

"Arabic, master. Language of Moors, Muslim belief," Alfonso said.

"Don't call me master, Alfonso. And that language?" Chaucer asked of a well-dressed merchant and his wife.

Alfonso listened for a moment before replying.

"Hebrew. Judaic belief, master," Alfonso said.

"My father told me the Jews were expelled from London by King Edward some fifty years before I was born," Chaucer said. "I have heard the language only once…a merchant from the Palatine. And that? I also heard that in Pamplona," Chaucer asked of two black-haired men wearing embroidered doublets who were laughing and shouting.

"Basque," Alfonso replied.

"Uh, yes. You said the native language of those who live in the mountains. My father spoke of the Basque, how their language was different than any other, and had never been overtaken by Castilian," Chaucer said. "Do they follow a different faith as well?" he asked.

"Some Christians, of a kind. Some pagan. Proud people, never conquered," Alfonso said.

"How is the peace kept in Olite? I would not think that Christian, Moor, Jew and Basque could live side by side," Chaucer said.

They were only fifty yards from the city gate, and the walls and towers loomed above. Chaucer glimpsed the upper bodies and heads of guards on the ramparts.

"In Olite," Alfonso said, "king's word shouted in city squares Thursdays, mosques Fridays, synagogues Saturdays, churches Sundays. City of many faces, many beliefs. Carlos' master crossbowman is Amet Alhudaly, a Muslim."

"A Muslim as master crossbowman to the king? Unusual, no?" Chaucer replied.

Alfonso shrugged.

They arrived at the main gate to the castle, where they were admitted after a knight on a steed covered in fine livery warmly welcomed Alfonso and motioned for them to follow him.

Alfonso appeared to be well known and respected.

They rode through a narrow entrance that opened into a wide street. They then climbed and passed through a second guarded archway that led into a large square courtyard, with gates at two corners opening to other streets. Chaucer was struck by the flurry of activity. Hundreds of workers scurried up and down the castle walls, hammering, sawing, banging. The courtyard and the streets beyond were also a beehive of industry.

"Carlos prepares for war, strengthens city walls and fortifications," Alfonso said, before Chaucer could even ask the question.

Just like Visconti in Milan.

The knight signalled a halt, and they dismounted and handed their reins to servants, who led their horses away to be watered and fed.

"That is the entrance to the Great Hall," Alfonso said, pointing to broad steps leading to a massive iron and wood door set in the castle wall topped by three imposing towers.

They followed the knight inside, where Chaucer eyed carts piled with food and an alcove that looked like a chapel. Two massive oak doors set on huge hinges blocked the Great Hall.

"Please follow this steward," the knight said in precise Castilian, gesturing to a neatly dressed servant. "He will provide a room where you can bathe and change out of your travel attire, as well as a tray of refreshments. Await there. A meeting with our lord, the king, will be arranged."

They turned right down a corridor and then climbed a set of stairs, and Chaucer was soon lost.

•　　　•　　　•

King Carlos stood in the antechamber of his sleeping quarters and looked out the narrow slit in the stone wall over the lower turrets of his castle towards the white tipped mountains to the north. Enormous black clouds threatened more snow.

"I'm always cold in this godforsaken palace. I cannot wait to return to Normandy and decent food, wine and company," he said. "Marie, child, please fetch my cloak."

"Yes papa," said the young, raven-haired girl behind him as she dashed from the room, eager to please her adored papa.

"Ancelo, bring me my writing table. I would write to King Pere of Aragon."

The small, wiry Ancelo bowed to his master and hurried from the room.

Both returned shortly and Carlos, his cloak over his shoulders, settled himself near the window to compose a letter.

"And put more wood on that fire, for I cannot seem to get warm this day," he added to Ancelo. "This damnable mountain air remains winter cold as spring arrives elsewhere."

"Spring is delayed here this year, says my mother," Ancelo offered.

"Your mother is seldom wrong," Carlos said with a sigh.

"The snow will last longer in the passes," Ancelo added.

Carlos smiled. "Yes. And more snow means delay for any army in the north that might be stupid enough to attempt to traverse the pass."

"Some merchants have done just that. We received a request today, my lord king, from a page in King Edward's household with connections to the wine trade. He has just arrived and is seeking a pass," Ancelo said.

"His name?"

"Geoffrey Chaucer, bearing a letter of trade from King Edward."

Carlos looked out the elongated window. Below the other turrets and towers lay the roots and stems of the hanging garden covered in the barest hint of green and, below that, the stark branches of the orchard, showing the first sign of blossom.

"Marie, get me an orange," he asked.

"But papa, it is still winter," she replied, confused.

"Yes," he said. "It may take some time. Do your best," he added.

Her brow still creased, she nodded and slowly left.

Carlos waited until the door closed before turning to regard Ancelo. "Bring the Englishman."

"Yes, my lord," Ancelo said, backing to the door and leaving.

•   •   •

Chaucer had waited in his chambers until an ancient valet collected him. The man gesticulated for Chaucer and Alfonso to follow him. He was more spry than he appeared and stepped through a small doorway, down a corridor, then up a marble staircase. Stained-glass windows showered colour across an upper corridor as they approached and then ascended a second staircase to a walkway.

Once they reached the second floor, they followed their guide through a large reception room empty of people, then through another archway and out onto a covered portico. Looking up, he could make out the extent and enormity of the castle itself, and also the hanging gardens he had spied on approaching the castle.

The gardens framed the portico, covering one entire wall and draping past the stone balustrades down to a lush square two floors below that was filled with trees, plants and winter flowers, protected from frost by awnings attached to the stone walls. Protected also from the wind, many fruit trees, including lemon and orange, had begun to blossom. In February. Such an unexpected sight.

Chaucer noted creatures moving amidst the trees, and then a fearsome growl froze him.

"Worry not, that is the lion that my lord keeps in the gardens. Here, I will show you," said the valet. He led them past the tops of the fruit trees to an uninterrupted view of the gardens where several exotic animals were penned. In one gated corner was a tawny-coloured beast with a long beard of hair hanging about his massive head. He lay upon a rock that jutted above the scene, his long tail flicking. The weak sun had found its way to the rock and the lion lazily turned and lifted his massive head toward the visitors. As Chaucer's mouth gaped open, so did the great maw of the beast as it yawned, revealing huge white fangs and a long tongue.

"That cry of my lord's lion is one of hunger. He watches the other animals below and wants what he wants," the valet said.

Indeed, all manner of beasts wandered below the lion, separated from the creature by a wooden fence that did not look nearly high enough to keep him out. Chaucer saw fat horses striped black and white, and a squat beast twice the size of a bull with a long pointed horn set on its snout. Brightly coloured birds with huge fan-like tails stalked the grounds. A large cat-sized creature with stripes leapt from one branch to another. Two large furry rodents with nuts in their mouths rummaged amongst the leaves. The animal most strange was a long-necked tawny-coloured creature covered in large brown spots that towered over the others as it nibbled on a tall tree's green shoots some fifteen feet above the ground, its head nearly level with the visitors. Chaucer had heard stories of such creatures from his father, and from the sailors who arrived from faraway lands, but he thought them fancible tales and hadn't really believed them, until now.

The valet saw what held Chaucer's gaze, and said, "It is called a giraffe. From Afric, the land of the southern Moors."

"Can the lion not leap over that fence and attack the giraffe? The fence does not look high enough," Chaucer said.

"Indeed, once he is hungry enough, he will do just that and take down a giraffe or a zebra—the horse with stripes—or anything else he chooses," the man replied. "Such is the way of nature."

"Are you not worried he will escape and attack one of you?" Chaucer asked.

The valet shook his head as if conversing with a child.

"Come, our lord awaits," the man said.

Chaucer and Alfonso dragged their eyes away from the strange beasts and continued along the portico, through another archway and into a hallway. He peered into the rooms they passed and noted that each had a hearth, a luxury for any castle. By the time they passed under an intricately carved stone entrance into a hall, Chaucer knew he could not have found his way back to where they'd started in this vast castle. The room looked familiar, and he realized they were back near the entrance as they entered past the huge oak doors set in iron hinges he had seen upon arrival. Inside the Great Hall, a roaring fire burned in a massive fireplace set in an alcove in the middle section of the wall. Most of the room's occupants stood near the hearth, warming themselves. Light streamed in from the many windows that lined the long length of the massive room. Alfonso left to find a garderobe, complaining of aching bowels.

At the far end of the hall was a raised dais with two chairs. A man was seated in the larger chair whom Chaucer assumed by his fine clothing to be King Carlos. Chaucer stepped toward Carlos and paused before the raised dais.

"Geoffrey Chaucer, welcome to the Royal Palace of Olite. You speak French? It would be a blessing to speak the language of my childhood with you, for I must speak Castilian here to be seen as ruler of this kingdom."

Chaucer nodded. He spoke French at court, as most did. His Castilian was poor, learned on the wharf and in the warehouse, but he could understood much of what was said, and he would prefer Carlos not know how much.

"Good. I am King Carlos of Navarre," Carlos said in his heavy Norman accent. Chaucer remembered his father telling him that Carlos' father Philip of Evreux had married Joan, the only child of King Louis the Tenth, and Carlos had been raised there until the age of eighteen in Normandy, when he first travelled to Navarre.

"Geoffrey Chaucer, wine merchant and page to King Edward," Chaucer replied as he knelt on one bended knee.

Chaucer noted the intricate design of the gold thread woven throughout the rich burgundy of Carlos' well-fitted paltok, and the matching burgundy shoes with gold laces.

"Up, Chaucer," Carlos said.

Chaucer stood straight.

"Thank you for your warm welcome, my lord," Chaucer said.

"You arrived from Pamplona?" Carlos asked.

"Yes, and before that, Bordeaux," Chaucer replied.

"I trust you had a safe journey across *my* mountain pass?" Carlos asked,

Carlos's emphasis on the word "my" was unmistakable.

"Yes, it was uneventful, other than my previous guide almost leading us into an abyss."

"The pass can be dangerous. Even seasoned guides make mistakes. The weather can turn in a moment, and a snowstorm can drop a foot of snow in the blink of an eye. A mudslide could take out the path, a rockslide bury its travelers, or a sudden flood carry off horse and rider," Carlos said. "One can defend such a pass with but a few men. Many have tried to breach Navarre's borders over the centuries. None have succeeded," he said.

Chaucer just blinked.

"Tell me, what brings you to my kingdom?" Carlos asked. "Most pass through Pamplona on pilgrimage to Santiago de Compostela."

"A worthy journey for another time," Chaucer replied. "I travel here for three reasons, my lord. The first concerns my good King Edward, who would increase trade in wine and many other goods between our two kingdoms, and so would also seek to ensure the passes between Bordeaux and Navarre remain open all year. Their recent closure was of concern to some English merchants who were unable to move their goods," Chaucer said, choosing his words carefully.

As he was talking, Chaucer's gaze strayed to the helmeted, dark-skinned hulk of a man standing silently to the left of Carlos. In his left hand, he balanced the top of a massive crossbow, the feathers from a sheaf of quarrels poking above his head. In his right hand he grasped a gold tipped spear, half again his height. The man looked born to hunt and kill prey.

The master crossbowman Alfonso had spoken of?

Carlos noted the look of apprehension on Chaucer's face.

"He has that effect on most men, but have no fear. This is my master crossbowman, Amet. Amet is the finest bowman in Europe, and can strike a deer at fifty yards with his spear. And yes, he is of the

Muslim faith. I allow Muslims, Jews and Christians in Navarre, for I believe tolerance leads to less war, and war is expensive," he added.

Chaucer dipped his head slightly toward Amet, who did the same in response.

"Yes, I noted the variety of languages as we travelled through the streets," Chaucer said.

"I like to believe that they inhabit Olite because we are more tolerant of their differences. Less likely to round up one group or another, take away their wealth, and expel them," Carlos said. "Like that ignorant pig, Enrique, who hunts the Jews and would sooner have them all killed," he added.

Chaucer nodded.

"And what is your father's occupation?" asked Carlos.

"My father imports wine from all around Europe, including Gascon, Rhenish, Rochelle, Trent, and the famed blended Blancos Pardillos from Navarre and Rioja, which is why my king has assigned me this task. The closure of the passes limits my father's trade and both his and our king's profits," Chaucer said.

"And yet, if the passes are open and easy for such merchants as yourself to traverse, then an army may just as easily travel close behind," Carlos replied.

"War and trade are not good bedfellows, my lord," Chaucer replied.

"Unless that trade is in war," Carlos shot back.

"Or in stories of war."

"One's trade may be in stories of war, yet any such war may wound such stories."

"Yet every story may give birth to war, just as every war may give birth to more trade in stories," Chaucer said.

"And yet to die in a war for one's story would be to war with one's own story that may be told," he said just as quickly.

"I am at war with *this* story, my lord, for I can no longer tell of its meaning," Chaucer said, throwing his hands up.

Carlos chuckled. "You have a clever head and a sharp tongue, Chaucer. One that could too readily cut another. What is the second thing you would discuss with me?" he asked.

"I would seek a pass to travel freely through Navarre to meet wine suppliers on my lord king's behalf. It would be beneficial to assure them that their wine will reach England and it would keep open that same market for your benefit. On my travels through your lands, I would also seek new suppliers for my father, for to expand trade with England would benefit Navarre, with wool coming to your land and wine to mine."

"And how long do you plan to journey through my kingdom?"

Chaucer hesitated but for a moment. "Until the end of May, my lord, after which I will return to Olite and pay my respects before returning home," Chaucer said.

"Three months seems not long, and yet we may hope your stories told then will do no harm," Carlos said. "And the third reason?"

"I am a poet of small repute, and would collect stories to turn into poems, my lord."

"A storyteller during a time of war? You will find many stories here, but be careful which stories you tell," Carlos said.

"Of course…" Chaucer began, before Carlos cut him off.

"For it would be a shame to see such a storied emissary at war with my kingdom. That, I think, would be a very short and very unsatisfying story," Carlos said, his brow suddenly furrowing, lips tight, then just as quickly his frown replaced by a wide smile.

"You may cross pens or, more likely, goblets with the poet soldier, Ayala. Have you heard of him? No? He is Pedro's lieutenant, but also a talented poet. If so, take care, for he cuts with tongue and sword," Carlos added.

"I am grateful for the warning, my lord," Chaucer replied.

"As to your safe passage, I will grant you the same," Carlos said. "For two months, you said?" Carlos asked.

"Three months, my lord," Chaucer corrected. "Which should suffice to find the wine sellers I seek, and arrange payment and transportation back to London, my lord."

"Yes, yes, granted. Ancelo will provide the missive to you come morning," Carlos said.

Chaucer bowed. "I am again grateful, my lord," he replied.

"Rest. Eat. Enjoy my hospitality," he said.

"There is one more thing I wish to ask, my lord," Chaucer said.

"Yes, what is it?" Carlos asked.

"The strange bestiary you keep in the gardens."

"Ah, yes. What think you of it?" he asked.

"Impressive. Why do you collect such animals?" Chaucer asked.

"I gather such creatures so that the wonders of the world can be shared," he said. "I also keep them to remind myself—and my visitors—that predators feed on those less able to protect themselves. It is the law of nature."

Chaucer blinked, aware of the point Carlos had made.

"Thank you for sharing such a gift with this humble traveller, my lord," Chaucer said.

"Oh, and one more thing. The price of such a pass is one gold noble, which will ensure safe passage along your journey. You may pay Ancelo."

"Of course, my lord." Chaucer tried to retain his composure and not show the shock he felt inside.

A year's salary. A price far above what I had been told, and far above what I had accounted for.

"Good evening," Carlos said, and Chaucer bowed, backed away and left Alfonso behind.

Which leaves me four gold nobles, and I am no closer to finding Calveley.

* * *

Chaucer tried to find his way back, but was soon lost again. The castle was vast. After several wrong turns, he found himself in a narrow mezzanine above a small meeting hall. At the sounds of male voices, he crept on silent feet to peek through the balustrade. Below him, Carlos and an advisor he did not recognize sat before a fire. Their conversation, about the art of war, was dull, until he heard them speak a name he would never forget: Eustache d'Auberchicourt. Six years earlier, the then seventeen-year-old Chaucer had been a young soldier north of Reims, and had witnessed d'Auberchicourt turn the French countryside into a killing field, felling the English like wheat.

Chaucer felt chills up his spine as he listened to Carlos's words.

"Garcia, prepare safe passage for d'Auberchicourt's war machines. We will welcome and celebrate him. Give the order to every walled town within fifty miles to fell trees and fortify their defenses. d'Auberchicourt may well turn on us, and I would be prepared."

"It shall be done, my lord," his advisor replied. "Is that all?"

"Get Chaucer on his way early, before d'Auberchicourt arrives. I would rather he not know of my plans. Find out what he is really up to, and if he proves to be Edward's spy, then do with him what we have done to other spies."

The advisor bowed and left.

Chaucer shook his head.

Do with me what he has done to other spies? Put my head on a spike, like Chandos had done in Bordeaux?

Chaucer suddenly felt the weight of the task put before him. Until now, his journey had been an adventure. Now it had turned into a serious business.

He found his way back to his dimly lit room and closed the door. One of the two sconces had gone out. He looked out the narrow gap in the wall at the nearly full moon that cast a bluish hue upon the jutting turrets of the castle, and the Pyrenees beyond.

Chandos had warned him that Carlos played both sides and was dangerous. Now he had the truth of it. A less than noble life. It would cost Carlos much less than a noble to take his life. A groat or two would surely suffice. He would need to send a message warning Edward about Carlos bringing in the French murderer d'Auberchicourt, and try not to get himself killed. And try to make his gold nobles last.

He needed to put such worries at bay. For he needed to write, scratch words upon the blank vellum he carried with him, and could not write with such worries upon his mind. He pulled out his one remaining quill and carefully lit a fat, stubby candle set upon the small writing table by his bed. He sat down, dipped his quill into the small pot of ink, and began to scratch his words. Words of new things, of creatures as impossible as the love for a highborn woman. Of hope and despair. Of what being apart from the one you love feels like. And of a war about to blossom like the fruit trees below, a deadly fruit soon to ripen and be cast forth.

CHAPTER 8
ZARAGOZA, FEBRUARY 23, 1366
SIR HUGH CALVELEY AND KING PERE OF ARAGON

Dawn was threatening as Sir Hugh Calveley and some eight hundred mercenaries followed a black cloaked rider toward Aljaferia Palace at Zaragoza. Calveley and his men had pushed northwest from Barcelona along with du Guesclin. The aim was to rendezvous in Zaragoza and then strike toward cities controlled by Pedro, only a day's march away. The stranger had arrived at their camp in the black of night, saying he was a trusted knight in Pere's employ, displaying Pere's seal, and offering to lead them safely through the forest and into the castle. After hesitating—would the rider lead them into a trap?—Calveley ordered his men to follow. The rider led the horsed soldiers along a nearly hidden path in the forest that opened into a copse of trees and then into a field a hundred yards south of the imposing palace.

Even in the faint light, Calveley could see what lay before him was unlike any palace he had ever seen. He craned his neck to take in the unfamiliar curves and designs. The Moors built it some three centuries earlier in a mixture of Moorish and Romanesque designs, and looked as if a Crusader castle from Outremer had been lifted and dropped into Aragon. Several round crenelated towers bisected a high stone wall, with Roman-looking arches connecting each tower. A massive square keep set into the northeast corner of the structure dominated the towers. Calveley could make out dozens of soldiers walking atop the towers and under the archways. This was not just a palace; it was a heavily fortified castle that would be very difficult to attack. Many had tried, for the walls were pockmarked by stones flung from trebuchets, bearing testament to the castle's name, Qasr al-Surur—the Palace of the Joy. Joy for defenders, but little joy for those foolish enough to attempt to mount its battlements. Zaragoza had been at the centre of the war between Pere of Aragon and Pedro for many years, but had never been successfully taken by Pedro.

The guards above the shut portcullis at the main gate demanded they identify themselves.

"I lead Sir Hugh Calveley, who is here at the request of his highness, King Pere the Ceremonious," the guide shouted back.

After a pause, a guard cried, "Open the gate!" and the huge iron portcullis slowly rose.

Calveley motioned to a knight by his side, who leaned toward him.

"Take your men and camp outside the palace. I will take my personal guards inside. Be wary of a trap. I will send a rider later to say all is well. If you do not see the rider, attack at dawn. Understood?" Calveley said.

The knight dipped his head and motioned for his soldiers to follow on a cart path that wound its way beside the castle on the far side of the drawbridge.

Calveley kneed his destrier and followed the black-robed guide forward and they clopped across the palace's drawbridge. The guide then led Calveley and his twenty personal guards into a central rectangular plaza that was surrounded on three sides by a covered portico. While a military man through and through, Calveley still appreciated art and beauty, and his mouth hung open at the intricate curved designs carved into the portico's columns, the multitude of colourful flowers and plants, and the intoxicating, unfamiliar smells that enveloped him. The chill of the winter morning hung in the air, yet the smells were of a summer months away. They dismounted and unloaded their horses, and servants led them away to be watered and fed.

King Pere stepped into the courtyard and greeted them. "Sir Calveley. Welcome to Zaragoza and Aljaferia Palace, the home of my family for decades. It will be to share."

"My lord, I am honoured to be welcomed to your home," Calveley said, bowing. "Indeed, it is exceptionally beautiful," he added.

"You and your men must be thirsty and hungry. Follow me for some refreshments," Pere said, leading them through a heavy, intricately carved door of dark wood into a massive room that appeared to be outside, but was under a roof made of glass.

Colour burst from every direction. Huge blooming flowers in a panoply of shades and surprisingly vibrant colours vied for attention, competing with the colourful and intricately designed mosaics made from Moorish tiles. Multi-coloured prisms of light decorated the tiled floor from the stained-glass windows above. A cupula made of deep cobalt blue glass glowed above them. The humid, warm air felt more like July than February.

Calveley craned his head to take in every detail of the room's unusual beauty.

"Come, let us enjoy some sustenance," said the King.

They entered a smaller room; the walls covered by even more intricate mosaics and inlaid wood. Calveley noted that the black-robed rider had disappeared.

But there was du Guesclin, standing to one side of a bench. And beside him stood Saludan.

A roaring fire behind cast yellow light across du Guesclin's face.

Calveley gave du Guesclin the briefest of nods, and received the same in return. A servant set down a flagon of wine, and then filled the goblets set before both men.

One wall of the room was covered with wall hangings. Exotic flowers burst from vases, and their scent, along with some unnamed spices, created a tantalizing smell to relax any visitor, impossible now due to the enmity between the two men who stood before Pere.

Du Guesclin remained standing.

"You meet again," Pere said, looking from one sworn enemy to the other.

Du Guesclin said nothing.

"Let us drink to our future together as allies in our mutual struggle to unseat Pedro the Cruel," Pere said.

They raised their goblets. Pere clunk his goblet first against Calveley's, then du Guesclin's. The two men did not do the same.

"Please sit," Pere said, and they did.

Two servants, each bearing a small chest, stopped and placed these on a table before each man. Pere opened both lids. Each chest was filled with gold coins; du Guesclin's chest held more.

"I would finish the discussion begun in Barcelona and agree on the terms," Pere said.

"Where is Enrique? We are gathered here to fight for him, yet he chooses to not attend?" Calveley asked.

"He has been delayed, and asked that we continue," Pere said.

Calveley and du Guesclin nodded in unison. Pere continued.

"In return for the gold, land and titles described in the letters you hold, Enrique and I ask for your assurances that you will both remain loyal to our cause for the duration of this war or until Pedro has been captured or preferably killed, when you are released from this bond and may return to whatever war and serve whatever king you wish."

"My lord, I accept your terms save the last, for though I sell my sword, I am beholden and give my fealty to King Edward of England, and no one else," Calveley said.

To fight for gold was one thing, but featly to a foreign king was too much to ask.

"Come now, Sir Hugh," said Pere, nodding toward the chests. "You have travelled far into my realm for a purpose—to use your skills to earn this gold that your king does not offer to you. Give your fealty to me now, and you can give it to your king after our successful venture," Pere said.

"My lord, I repeat, I will fight for gold, but I am King Edward's man," Calveley said.

"And your loyalty to your king is admirable. I do not ask you to abandon such loyalty. I only ask you to use your God-given skills in my battle with Pedro, a battle that has nothing to do with your king. In return, you shall be well rewarded," he said.

When Calveley said nothing, Pere continued.

"Sir Hugh, let me revise the terms to entice you to swear but a temporary oath to me. I will grant you an annual stipend of two thousand florins from lands in the Kingdom of Valencia confiscated from Pedro, and I shall offer to name you Baron of Aragon. The spoils of this war shall be divided two quarters for du Guesclin, one quarter for you, and one quarter for my kingdom. As proof of my word, this chest of gold will be yours upon agreeing to these terms. But you must swear homage to me and Enrique until your contract has concluded. In return, I acknowledge that you retain your fealty to good King Edward."

It rankled Calveley that du Guesclin would gain twice the gold he would, but Calveley knew that his quarter share would make him a rich man. He looked at Pere, searching for an emotion that might belie any discordant thoughts. Finding none, he rose from his chair and knelt, taking Pere's hand in his. He kissed his signet ring, and then said, "I cannot deny the sense of your words, my lord, and so will accede to your terms," and rose.

Du Guesclin also rose, and the two soldiers now stood side by side, neither deigning to look at the other, gold and power bonding them in the present, but mutual enmity bonding them to their past and likely also their future.

"Good, then dine with me tonight and celebrate our common bond," Pere said.

"I thank you for your kind offer, my lord, but I would return to my men and ensure they are prepared to move at first light to advance upon Tarragona and Magallon, two cities that Pedro controls. There is much yet to be done," du Guesclin said. He glowered at Calveley as he spoke the words, his eyes unmoving.

And Calveley stared back and said, "As I must also, my lord. We shall celebrate once victory has been achieved."

"So be it. When we next meet again, it will be to share food and wine and toast a new king atop the throne of Castile. God bless you both," Pere said. His voice expressed no surprise, nor even disappointment, in their answer.

Pere watched the two enemies depart, the sound of their armour a reminder of how close the war before them lay.

A few moments after their echoing steps receded, Enrique Trastamara stepped out from behind a hidden door and approached Pere.

"Well done, Pere," Enrique said with a triumphant snarl.

"You are satisfied, Enrique?" asked Pere.

"The two plainly hate each other, but wealth is like heat in casting a powerful weapon, for it tempers the metal of a man. I will only be satisfied once I see Pedro on his knees before me, begging for his life, his army destroyed, his treasury in my hands. Then I will take great satisfaction in torturing him, cutting off his balls and stuffing them into his mouth. And then plunging my sword through his neck and watching his lifeblood drain across the cold stone floor of the dungeon. Then, when I know his loins will not produce any more of his line, and when his blood has stopped flowing, when I will finally be crowned the King of Castile, then yes, Pere, then I will be satisfied," Enrique said, his eyes blazing at Pere.

Pere asked, "How should we ensure Du Guesclin and Calveley play nicely?"

"Play nicely? I care not how they play. I care only that they succeed in bringing Pedro to his knees. You should not worry about the tactics, my friend, only the outcome," Enrique replied.

"But what if their enmity leads to discord and a falling out?"

"Then they will not receive their gold, or land," Enrique answered.

"I worry that their enmity may ignite in an untimely manner, before a battle or a siege," Pere added, pressing his point.

"We cannot control the fates of such men. We must trust that their desire for gold and land outweighs their distaste for each other. As long as they defeat Pedro, I care not what else happens between them. Now I must give orders to Tello and Sancho and prepare."

CHAPTER 9
LOGRONO, FEBRUARY 26, 1366
DOÑA CONSTANZA AND AYALA

Chaucer wandered the cobbled streets of Logrono as the afternoon light tipped the steeple of the city's cathedral. He and Alfonso had crossed over the Rio Ebro at the bridge and entered the city that afternoon and then found a tavern to stay for the night. After a simple meal, Chaucer left Alfonso at the tavern, intent on exploring the city before darkness fell. Alfonso had warned him to return before sunset and curfew, or be at risk from the night patrol.

Chaucer passed a cart that held two prone, injured soldiers wearing Pedro's livery.

"Fight war?" he asked in his limited Castilian.

One of the two tilted his head to understand Chaucer's mangled words. Chaucer pointed to them and made a sour expression.

"Escaped west of Zaragoza yesterday," the man replied.

Enrique has already advanced to Zaragoza?

Enrique's advance was much faster than Chaucer expected. When he left Bordeaux, the bubbling war had not yet boiled over. Rumours of du Guesclin's arrival from France had reached him as he passed through Roncesvalles. Calveley's location was still unknown to him, but Chaucer assumed he would be near the fighting. The speed of the advance was disturbing, for Enrique was now but a two-day ride away.

Am I already too late to find and reach Calveley? Or will he find me here first?

Logrono was also two days southwest of Pamplona, where any army from the north or east would surely pass through on its way to Burgos, the capital of Castile. The ancient city lay at the easternmost reach of Castile at the border with Navarre, and control of Logrono was critical for control of the valley leading to Najera, then Burgos. Logrono would surely be Enrique's next target, with Calveley by his side. Chaucer knew from Alfonso that the people of Logrono had long been loyal to Pedro. Many were Jews, whom Pedro protected. Enrique would not.

Chaucer continued up the central calle, and he passed several nervous faces. Around a corner he found the market, but merchants there were packing up. One short, wiry merchant saw him and cried "rare and beautiful books" in Castilian. Chaucer hugged his sheepskin coat closer against the frosty air and approached the merchant where a truly beautiful book lay before him.

"You seek beautiful books?" the merchant asked as Chaucer approached. "Five reals," the merchant said, "for this, and I have two more, better." Odd to see such a valuable book at a merchant stall, but Chaucer could not take his eyes away from the book. He carefully picked it up. It was a beautifully bound copy of Petrus Alfonsi's *Disciplina Clericalis*, the first example of a frame-tale, a device made popular by the Florentine author Boccaccio Chaucer had heard of from Froissart.

The merchant said a wealthy noble owned the book, and had two more books he wanted to sell. He said the second book was *Libro de Calila e Digna,* describing it as an anonymous collection of stories that had been commissioned by Alfonso the Tenth a century earlier, based on a collection of Arabic moral beast-fables that was, in turn, based on a lost collection of Persian stories that were based on a third-century Hindu story collection. A palimpsest of stories that would be fascinating to read.

The third book he said was a masterpiece of Castilian poetry, *The Book of Good Love* by the Archpriest of Hita, Juan Ruiz, a semi-biographical account of his romantic adventures. Chaucer had heard the book was prized for its beauty and poetry, and for its colloquial Castilian and Arabic, classical sources like Ovid, and its French fabliaux and ancient fables.

The book before Chaucer was illustrated with richly detailed, multi-coloured illuminations and gorgeous gold-leaf letters, and covered in a thick leather binding, the title also embossed in gold leaf. The others would probably be similar. None of the few books Chaucer owned were any near as beautiful nor as valuable.

Chaucer shivered and fingered the coins in the soft leather purse that lay under his coat. He was unsure how to value the offer. He only had four of King Edward's newly minted gold nobles left in his purse, four years of pay as a page. Based on the cost of a goblet of wine and the livery barn, five reals were worth about one and a half nobles and he might be able to haggle him down to one.

He enjoyed many things in life—dallying with Pippa, partaking in wine and competing in puys—but buying and reading books was one of his greatest loves. Some men were weak before a beautiful woman (and Chaucer was not immune to a woman's charms), but a rare, beautiful book held a particular grip on Chaucer's heart. Buying one was a stupid thing to consider, and yet…

"I take you to seller and show you others. Follow me."

Chaucer nodded, and the merchant packed his items into a sack and put the book into a separate leather bag and Chaucer followed him along the Calle Laurel. He turned right through a door into a courtyard, and then into another door and upstairs through a door to a large room well-lit with candles. A single chair was set in front of a hearth where a fulsome fire gave off welcome heat. On a table next to the fire lay two beautiful books with gold lettering on their spines. His eyes were drawn to an iron poker laying with the sharp end in the fire.

Why is that poker in the fire?

Chaucer stepped through the doorway toward the books and was met by a tall man with a scarred right cheek wearing a black cloak. He looked more like a soldier than a wealthy book collector or noble.

"Welcome. I am Seigneur Jean de Harcourt. And you are?" he asked in a strong Norman accent.

"Geoffrey Chaucer, wine merchant from London." Chaucer kept looking away from de Harcourt to the beautiful books arrayed on the table.

"A merchant with a passion for books, I see."

Something about this man made him think of Carlos, and what Carlos had said about spying, but then Chaucer approached the books and ran his fingers over the spine of the first and forgot about his worries.

"Such a passion is no fault in a man, yet any man's passion can lead them astray, for their heart forgets what lessons their head has taught," said de Harcourt.

What? What does he mean?

Chaucer turned at the words, for they implied a threat, and then his world went black.

He awoke sitting in the chair facing the fire, his head throbbing. His ankles and wrists were bound with strips of leather, and the now glowing red end of the iron poker was held by de Harcourt an inch from his right eye. The merchant, or whatever he was, guarded the door.

Bound, trapped and at the warm end of a poker. The man's accent. That was it. Norman, like Carlos. Surely hired by him. How in Hades will I escape this?

"You are a spy for King Edward the Third, sent to learn Lord Enrique's secrets and the strength of his army, yes?" de Harcourt asked.

"I have been sent by King Edward to expand his son's wine trade, for the trade of Bordeaux suffers because of brigands and mercenaries like yourself." Chaucer glowered at de Harcourt as he said 'brigands'. The glowing poker stared back at him, an inch from his face.

"I am sure you have seen many things on your journey here. They will soon become the last sights you will ever see, for I will take out both your eyes if you do not tell me the truth…"

"What more can I tell you?" Chaucer said.

Harcourt pushed the poker toward his eye.

"If you have nothing more to say, then I will begin with your left eye."

Just then, the door crashed open, and a man carried through and swung his sword at the merchant, who held up the leather bag to protect himself.

It is Croker! Thank God.

Croker sliced the bag and the book inside fell out. He then faced the soldier and lunged straight at him, but the soldier parried Croker's thrust with the poker, sending sparks flying. Croker quickly dispatched the poker with a flick of his wrist and the soldier whipped out one of his swords and went on the attack.

The merchant hesitated by the door as if deciding to help or flee. After several clashes, the soldier pulled out his second sword, and Croker had to be quick to defend himself from the two-handed assault. As the two moved about the room thrusting and parrying, Croker caught Chaucer's eye and gave him the slightest nod and then began a furious attack, forcing the soldier backwards to the fire past Chaucer, who thrust out his bound legs like a branch, causing the man to stumble just enough to open his side, and he was quickly dispatched with a long thrust by Croker. The merchant ran from the room.

"Your entrance was well timed, Croker," Chaucer said as Croker sliced through his leather bindings, freeing his hands. He rubbed his sore wrists. "But how did you find me?"

"I found Alfonso, who said he had followed you to the market, and you had left with a merchant, and I just caught sight of you from the market but lost the trail. I saw light from the street and guessed the right room," he said.

Chaucer let out a breath of air—of both exhaustion and relief.

I could be blind, or worse, if not for Croker.

"Then I am doubly lucky on this day, and thank you," he replied, his voice shaking.

Chaucer slowly stood, swayed and sat down again.

"Take your time. Facing death can leave even the most courageous knight week in the knees."

Chaucer nodded, let out several more breaths and then once he had calmed down he got up, dressed, slipped the two books on the table into his leather satchel and added the third book the merchant had left on the floor in his haste to get away. He followed Croker out of the entrance to the building and Croker paused.

"I must return whence I came," Croker said.

"I am in your debt," Chaucer replied.

"A debt I will claim one day. Until then, try to stay alive," he said, and they parted ways.

●   ●   ●

Chaucer wondered who would have sent de Harcourt. Probably Carlos, given the accent and what he had overheard. But Carlos could have easily interrogated him in Olite. Why wait for him to leave for Logrono? Enrique made more sense, for de Harcourt had mentioned his name. But Enrique would only know of him if he and Carlos were allied and had recently been in contact. Which was entirely possible. His task had suddenly become much more knotty.

He turned a corner and did not recognize the street. His treasured books were slung over his shoulder in the leather satchel, and he needed to get them, and himself, to a safe place.

He wondered then about Pippa, and if she was safe in London, or Westminster, or Kettlethorpe Castle or wherever the queen was, for the king and queen travelled regularly. He knew Pippa was the woman for him, and Pippa had expressed her love to him. He knew in his heart that she loved him. They were meant to be together.

But she had made it clear that she would only marry him when he advanced to a higher position at court earning regular gold, and gave up his folly writing poetry and entering puys, the storytelling contests he loved. Only then would she consider his hand. Yet he was no closer to success or advancement, for Calveley was still a ghost, and now he was marked as a spy, and had come a sword's length away from never seeing Pippa again.

He had been daydreaming again and hadn't realized time's passing as he approached two men lighting sconces on the street. Dusk had fallen. The cry of curfew that followed rang out across the city, fully waking him from his reverie. The dull pink sky in the west was being swallowed by darkness. He needed to get back to the tavern, or he'd likely be caught by a patrol and thrown in a dungeon for his troubles.

He sighed with relief at seeing the street sign "Calle de Laurel", where he had found the market. He spotted the tower of the cathedral to his east. Looking to fix his position, he noted the warm glow from candlelight behind the glass windows in the homes he passed. He was surprised at how many residences in Logrono had windows of fine glass. Alfonso had told him that the Moors, who used to control most of the Iberian Peninsula, had introduced such windows five centuries earlier. The Moors now inhabited only the south, in Granada, but their architecture, algebra, literature, and glass remained.

His eye caught the figure of a woman closing a curtain, her face softly lit from the lantern inside. He himself must have been standing under a lit sconce to be seen, for she smiled back at him. His heart dropped, for even at thirty paces he could see that her smile was luminous, her tanned, oval face beautiful. A blend of the Moor, Jew, Basque and Christian faces of this land.

"You! How dare you peer into windows!" cried a voice behind him in Castilian.

Chaucer turned to face two rough looking characters, both wielding short swords and their suspicious faces harshly lit by the sconces they held. The night patrol.

"Well then? What have you to say? It's after curfew," the larger of the two said.

Chaucer understood enough of the Castilian and attempted to reply as best he could. "English. Lost, seek tavern," he said in his halting Castilian, hoping to be understood.

Understood well enough. "English? Which tavern?" one asked.

Chaucer paused, for he couldn't remember the name.

"It matters not," the larger man said. "It's irons for you."

"But..." Chaucer tried to protest as the shorter fellow grabbed his arm.

"What's in the satchel?' the larger man asked.

"That's mine," Chaucer protested and the smaller man smacked him across the head.

"You're coming with us," the larger man said, trying to twist Chaucer's arm behind him.

"Let that man go," cried a woman's voice.

It was the woman behind the window, now covered in a heavy woolen cloak and holding a candle, standing before her open front door. Her feet were set apart and her open cloak revealed a shift beneath.

"Now why would we listen to you?" asked the larger thug.

"Because I am Doña Constanza Enríquez de Castilla, cousin to Enrique Trastamara, and lady-in-waiting to the Queen of Aragon," she said evenly.

Fear of Enrique's name was all over the thug's face, even in the sputtering light of the weak torch he held. He moved backwards.

"Then this English scum is your problem," the man said, and the smaller man let go of Chaucer's arm and they both turned and clattered away down the cobbled street.

•　　　•　　　•

"It's not much, but you may rest on this pallet until the curfew has passed, then I would ask that you return to wherever you were going," Doña Constanza said to Chaucer.

They stood inside the dimly lit anteroom of Doña's house. A door he assumed led into further rooms behind her, the door to the street behind him and between them a bed of straw covered by what looked like linen, and beside it a small table. She'd placed her lit candle on the stool by the pallet. A window to the street was covered by dark material.

His eyes met hers, which were of deepest black. As was her hair that framed her face and hung in ringlets down her back. Her skin was smooth bronze, her delicate fingers graceful as she removed her cloak. She was almost as tall as he was, and her curves beneath the simple shift were undeniable. She gestured for him to remove his cloak and then hung it on a hook on the door. Looking over her shoulder at him, she caught his eyes lingering on her body.

She showed no concern and held his gaze, no doubt inured by the gazes of countless men.

"I am grateful, Doña," Chaucer said in his halting Castilian as he put down his satchel of books and sat on the palette and tried and failed to look away from the beauty who stood before him. "My name is Geoffrey Chaucer."

"Doña is for ladies," she said. She lit a taper and as she stretched to light the candle in the first of two wall sconces, Chaucer couldn't help but stare again at the curves of her hips and breasts. "While my father had noble blood, he was a bastard, bless his soul, and so, as the daughter of a bastard, I will never become a lady, especially at the Aragon court where I served my queen. But those louts wouldn't know that, so I use the term when needed."

"And you are cousin to Enrique?"

"More of a distant cousin, but cousin serves its purpose," she said vaguely as she finished lighting the second sconce and sat down on the stool, facing him.

Cinnamon and something sweet wafted his way, almost overwhelming his senses.

"So, tell me your story, Geoffrey Chaucer," she said.

He told her of his journey to find Rioja wine for his father and King Edward, making no mention of his search for Calveley.

All the while, he fell deeper into the inky black pool of her eyes.

"So, you travel all this way from London to search for Rioja wine in the middle of a war," she said in the same, even tone she had used earlier with the thug.

He nodded.

"And you expect me to believe that?" she asked.

He said nothing.

"I would say there is more to your story, except we both know some things must not be said. And do you have a woman you think of in London?" she asked.

Chaucer hesitated. "There is a woman, yes. I have known her for years, named Pippa, whom I love, and who is the mother of our daughter."

"How long have you been married?"

"We are not yet married," he replied.

"I see. A woman you love who you won't marry, despite her having borne your child?"

"No! You have it wrong. It is she who refuses to wed me until I advance my station in service to my king and earn more gold."

"And perchance this journey will help advance your cause?"

He gave the barest nod.

That is it exactly.

"Ah. A story about a battle of hearts?" she continued.

"A story about a war, yes," he replied.

"A story set amidst war, yes, but of a war of hearts where the cutting is done more often by tongues and eyes than swords, perchance," she said, a slight smile curling.

He nodded.

"And this Pippa. This woman that you say that you love. What is it do you think that she most desires?"

As she had leaned forward to speak, her shift opened to reveal the shape of fulsome breasts.

"She would have me advance here, so I may advance there," he said, trying not to stare at her body.

Doña looked at him with a small smile, as if speaking to a child.

"And you think that will be enough to claim her heart? You may appreciate a woman's beauty, but you are young and have more to learn of a woman's desire."

"I know enough of a woman's desire."

"I doubt that very much, for a woman must live within a world of men. Her true desires must be well hidden or she will be named witch or whore. Think on that when you think on your Pippa."

Chaucer said nothing, for he had indeed not thought of that before.

She stood as if to go, but he did not want her to leave.

"Doña? Will you return to our bed?" asked a male voice.

Chaucer hadn't noticed the inner door open. A man now stood in the doorway, looming behind Doña. He was tall and dark-skinned, with an impressive black moustache, dressed in only the thinnest of breeches. His muscled thighs and near naked midsection made it clear to Chaucer why Doña might want to return to her bed.

"A moment, my love," she said affectionately. "Greet Geoffrey Chaucer, wine merchant and page to King Edward, he says, but I think there is more beneath his crude surface. Chaucer, let me introduce you to the poet Don Pedro López de Ayala, also second lieutenant and special advisor to King Pedro the Just," she added, practically spitting the king's moniker.

Ayala dropped his head toward Chaucer but said nothing.

Ayala, the soldier poet, whom Carlos spoke of.

"I have written a few verses myself," Chaucer said, getting up to shake Ayala's hand.

"Well met, Chaucer. What do you write about?" he asked, barely glancing at him, his impatient eyes still upon Doña.

"I write of love," he replied, then looking to Doña, added, "and war, and the war raging in our hearts, for what else is there to write of?" Chaucer replied.

At that, Ayala looked at Chaucer more closely. He nodded in agreement.

"You are in the employ of King Pedro? You may know of a Córdoba, whom I met in Westminster," Chaucer asked.

Ayala's face clouded as he leaned a shoulder against the door frame. "Yes. He is Pedro's chef, whom Lady Fortune favours, for now."

"Córdoba called him Pedro the Just when we met in Westminster, as you and Doña did, yet I have heard the name Pedro the Cruel spoken as well," Chaucer said.

"Then you would be wise to call him simply King Pedro, should you ever meet him."

"How did you come to be in his employ?" Chaucer asked.

"Our families have known one another for centuries," Ayala said.

"And does Pedro not have a queen? I have heard no mention of one."

Again Ayala's face darkened. "He killed his first and second wives, Maria de Padilla and Blanche of Bourbon, and left his third wife, Juana de Castro, after two nights. He does not, it seems, look favourably upon the women that he marries," Ayala said.

"He prefers men?" Chaucer asked.

"No, I have not heard of such. He takes several mistresses, but does not trust women. This may have to do with his mother, but that is a story for another time and it is getting late. What is in that satchel?"

"Books purchased at the market," Chaucer replied, not wanting to go into the details of their hard-won purchase.

"A booklover must be careful, for such treasures can attract the wrong kind of attention."

Something about Ayala's comment gave him pause.

Does he know of the attack?

"You are welcome to stay here, but Doña, I would you return to our bed, for we have unfinished business," he said, returning his hungry gaze to her.

She rose and moved toward Ayala. Chaucer's heart sank, for he wanted to converse with this beautiful, keen woman a while longer.

She turned back. "You must leave at dawn, for to have you here would raise more questions than answers for both of us. Understand?"

He nodded.

"Goodnight then, Geoffrey Chaucer. Perchance our paths will cross again."

"But how can I repay you for your kindness, Doña?"

"We shall see in time," she said, before closing the inner door behind her.

The candles were getting low, and he was about to blow them out when he noticed a slim, leather-bound book on the table by his pallet. He picked it up and read aloud the title on the spine, '*Libro Rimado de Palacio…Rhymes of the Court,*' and the author's name, Pedro López de Ayala. He opened the book and began to read. Ayala had talent. The poetry made him think of the poem that he had been trying to write.

My bane.

He had been struggling with a poem about a knight who goes to war to escape his unrequited love for a noblewoman. He struggled because his unrequited love was for Blanche, the Duchess of Lancaster, and he had felt this way about her for five years since he had first laid eyes upon her after joining the court. He had hoped that his journey to Navarre would take his mind off her, but it had only made him pine for her more. Such desires had begun during his days as a 15-year-old page at the court of Elizabeth of Ulster, first wife of Prince Lionel, Gaunt's elder brother by two years. Elizabeth, poor dead Elizabeth, had dressed him in tight-fitting hose and a codpiece and then paraded him about, along with the other pages, for her own pleasure. And his own pleasure. He had been less porcine then, and his well-developed manhood was prominently displayed by the codpiece he had to wear. He enjoyed being gazed at by the duchess and the other noblewomen at court. The desirous looks he received inflamed his own desire. Thoughts that Pippa also inspired in him. Now inflamed once again by Doña.

Impure thoughts, unrequited love and a woman's desires. My love life leaves me discomfited and undone, when it should leave me in rapture and ecstasy. Such is the way…

He awoke to a rooster's hail. Ayala's book lay open on his chest, lit by a sliver of grey peeping through a crack in the window covering. He had slept fitfully, the sound of Doña's voice somehow merged with Ayala's stern face looming over him; he was unsure if it had been a dream or no.

He reluctantly returned the book to the table—he had only read a few pages. He would seek a copy, for even with his poor grasp of Castilian he could tell that Ayala was a fine poet.

He left and relieved himself in an alley, where the sound of his piss mixed with a few grunts, crowing roosters and the squeaking of a cartwheel of a merchant heading to market. Stepping lightly along the ancient, cobbled street, he tried to find his way back toward his lodgings, his thoughts turning to Doña as he wondered why she had chosen to help him. As he strode along the street, he noted with pleasure the vibrant colours of the painted flowerpots, doors, and windowsills, decorated in intense ochres and yellows and reds and blues, such colours as he had only ever seen in the stained-glass windows of the churches and cathedrals of London and Westminster. The colours lifted his spirits as he navigated the streets of Logrono in the angled morning light. He paused upon encountering a man begging, holding out a small tin cup. Chaucer dropped a coin in the cup and the small man lifted his face and smiled up at him. Chaucer recoiled at the sight of two scars that ran from his forehead down to his chin, across dark, empty sockets where the man's eyes had once looked out. Chaucer's gaze dropped to the scrap of dirty white cloth hung around the beggar's neck. On it was written, "Enrique took my eyes."

CHAPTER 10
CASTILE, FEBRUARY 23-26, 1366
FEAR AND LOATHING

Ayala stood outside the largest tent on the hill where Pedro and his forces had paused their flight to rest and eat. Ayala had ridden twenty miles southeast from Logrono to Pedro's camp in Tudela, halfway to Zaragoza, arriving before dawn. Ayala could tell that things were not going well. News had arrived that Calveley and du Guesclin had left Aljaferia Palace and Calveley had led his eight hundred English and Gascon mercenaries southwest to the nearby city of Tarragona. After a brief battle, his superior force easily took the city. Du Guesclin and his army of twelve hundred mercenaries had approached the city of Magallon, some forty miles northwest of Zaragoza, and set about laying siege. The war had begun in earnest and Pedro's army was reeling. Pedro was irritable.

Ayala knew at such times it was better to stay near Pedro, but not too near. He gazed across the camp and wondered how long this war would last after such rapid losses. His eye caught movement, and he spied a mounted rider—a knight by the look of him—arriving from the southeast. As he got closer, Ayala saw the knight's mount was sweat-drenched and foaming at the mouth. Ayala's heart sank. The knight had ridden hard, which probably meant the news was not good. The knight slid off the horse, said something to a guard, who pointed toward Ayala and the tent, and hurried toward him. He looked familiar.

Ayala ducked his head into the tent. A torch in a sconce hung from a tent pole lit the entrance. Pedro stood at a table, peering at a map lit by another sconce. "My lord, a rider from the direction of Magallon has arrived," Ayala said.

"Show him in," Pedro replied, his furrowed brow, his eyes furtive.

Ayala stepped back outside to greet the knight.

"Raise your visor," Ayala ordered.

He did.

"Welcome Don Jimenez."

"Ayala, it has been too long," Jimenez replied in a friendly tone.

"Whatever news you bring—be thoughtful in your words."

Jimenez nodded, and Ayala led him inside Pedro's tent.

Pedro faced the knight. "Well, what news?" he asked.

"My lord, Magallon has fallen," said the knight.

"Magallon? That is impossible! I left eleven hundred soldiers there to defend the city. Who led the attack?" Pedro asked.

"A Gascon knight of some renown, according to the men who escaped, by the name …," Jimenez replied.

"Do not say his name!" Pedro snapped.

"My lord, are you unwell?" Ayala asked.

Pedro had leaned back against the post holding up the tent flap, and then slumped, suddenly devoid of all vigour.

"The eagle of the prophesy…," Pedro said in a monotone voice.

Ayala attempted to help Pedro, but he pushed him away.

"Prophesy, my lord?" Jiminez repeated.

Just then, a figure clad all in black with his head covered by a cowl emerged from the darkness in the back of the tent and stood over the slumped Pedro. The figure was more shadow than man.

Jimenez jumped backwards as if before a ghost.

"The prophesy foretold that the Castilian throne would befall a disaster brought on by an eagle crossing the Pyrenees from the north of France," the dark-robed figure said. Ayala had never seen the man before and felt an unease.

Pedro began to moan and mutter, listening to the words of the cowled man.

"This leader. What creature did he bear upon his shield?" the shadow asked.

"Two eagles. The man is known as the Eagle of Brittany, my lord," Jimenez replied.

Anger, then fear, crossed Pedro's face as his whimpering increased in volume.

The voluminous cowl hid the face of the dark clad man. His voice was deep, sonorous, calming. "Come. You must be tired and thirsty," he said, addressing Jimenez. "I have fine Rioja to share in thanks for your duty. Please, follow me," he said.

Ayala watched Jimenez stare briefly at the figure of his whimpering king before him, and looked to Ayala for guidance, but he had no words to offer, so Jiminez followed the man into the shadowed depths at the back of the tent.

Ayala cringed inwardly at the rasping sound of a blade unsheathed, followed by a muffled cry, another sound of a weight being dragged, and then the shadow re-emerged before Pedro, holding his bloody blade.

Ayala had known Jimenez well, knew he had given many years of good service, and now this honourable man had been killed for merely doing his duty. Such a waste. At the hands of some faceless murderer. Done only to silence a witness to a frightened king. There was no honour here, and this was no way to fight a war. He himself was now the only witness.

"My lord, the prophesy is but an old wives' tale. Pay no heed. You are a great leader, and we will defeat the Bastard," said the shadow.

Pedro looked up. "And the knight who delivered this news?"

"He will never share what he heard and saw, my lord," he replied.

"Yes," Pedro said.

"I merely do my duty," the shadow replied.

As he turned to leave, the man's face was briefly lit—and Ayala saw a pale face with one eye blue, and one black. The man smiled at him, as if responding to a joke, and his face was the face of evil, for he had taken great joy in murdering his friend. The face sent a shiver down Ayala's back.

And then he was gone.

That could have been me, for Pedro will be protected first, above all.

•   •   •

Calveley heard that du Guesclin had taken Borja, twenty miles south of Tudela, and also that King Pere was so pleased on hearing the news that he named du Guesclin the Count of Borja as a reward.

Calveley had marched north from Tarragona to Tudela and run into du Guesclin's rear guard, who reported that Pedro's army, encamped near Tudela, had left two days earlier and was probably near Logrono. He found du Guesclin a short while later.

"Calveley. You finally arrived," du Guesclin said atop Ironhoof; a full hand taller than Calveley on his piebald destrier.

Calveley wrinkled his nose at the rank smell emanating from du Guesclin. "My God, you stink! With all of your newfound wealth, surely you can manage a steam?"

"What took you so long?" du Guesclin demanded, ignoring his comment.

"I took my men west for two miles so that Pedro's spies would think I was attacking Soria, and then at night turned north," Calveley said.

Du Guesclin grunted.

"We shall rest here for what remains of the day," du Guesclin said. "On the morrow, you are to follow the Ebro north and west and take Alfaro. I will take my men northwest and attack Calahorra. Enrique's force will serve as our rear guard in case Pedro has any designs on a flanking move. Then we will move together northwest toward Logrono. Enrique will follow with his force."

"Understood?" du Guesclin asked.

Calveley asked, "What is that God-forsaken, devil-spawn odour?"

Du Guesclin smiled. "You lasted longer than most. A knight threw up his breakfast right after riding next to me," he replied. He pulled an object out of the leather satchel tied to his saddle. Holding the severed head by the hair, du Guesclin turned what remained of the face toward Calveley.

"He is the fifth of six men who have crossed me and who I have vowed to kill. I found this one cowering in the keep of his castle. Took a couple of days to ram the gate after we lit it on fire. Oak takes a while to burn, you know. Then I put an axe through his face; he's not such a pretty lord anymore," du Guesclin said, looking upon the head with admiration.

Calveley tried to hide how he felt as he regarded the grotesque object. The face was cut in half, the flesh rotting, and maggots crawled out of its brain. The smell was even more horrific than the sight. Calveley had seen many, many men cut, bludgeoned, burnt, flayed and disembowelled, but witnessing du Guesclin's unperturbed delight in his rotting trophy was disgusting. He felt queasy.

"Fine, I'll bite. Who is number six?" he asked with pretended nonchalance.

Du Guesclin smiled wider. "I am looking at his living corpse now," he said quietly, so the other knights could not hear.

Calveley froze. His right hand quivered, for he wanted nothing more than to pull out his sword and run du Guesclin through, but he knew he would be dead before his sword was free of its scabbard. Instead, he fought to gain control of himself, and said in as pleasant a voice as he could muster, "And I the same. We shall give each other satisfaction one day, but until then, we have a task to complete, a task that will bring many riches, land, and titles."

Du Guesclin nodded, then wheeled his horse away toward his own soldiers. He would need to tread carefully with du Guesclin.

The next morning Calveley crossed into Rioja. Following the course of the Ebro northwest, he led his men through the southern tip of Navarre, and reached the walled fortress of Alfaro, where Enrique and his men were waiting. The city was defended by Pedro's knight, Orozco, a clever tactician who well understood the power of a strong defensive position and high stone walls. When the town refused to surrender, Calveley suggested that Enrique bypass it and he agreed and they continued northwest and laid siege to Calahorra. They took the city without firing a single arrow.

They approached Logrono. Enrique wanted to attack but chose to bypass it on the advice of his brothers and both Calveley and du Guesclin, as the effort of attacking it was too great and would have slowed his advance toward Pedro, who was last seen near Najera heading west toward Burgos. Here the armies diverged. Enrique and du Guesclin carried on west. Calveley rode northwest with his men toward Najera, and had neared the town of Huercanos, a few miles north of Najera, by March 6.

CHAPTER 11
NEAR HUERCANOS, MARCH 7, 1366
LOST AND FOUND

Geoffrey Chaucer opened his left eye to a blood-red dawn, tried and failed to lift his head off the cold, flat and empty bota, and shivered. His stomach burbled. He needed to piss.

I am lost.

He and Alfonso had left Logrono unseen. They had been travelling for over a week and were low on food and water. Two days earlier, they heard Pedro was at Burgos, Enrique was near Najera and Calveley had headed northwest. So, they had crossed the Ebro the day before and climbed west along a rocky goat path, then dismounted and camped at the lip of a gorge somewhere north of Najera, Navarre's ancient capital. Yet somewhere was nowhere, Calveley was still a ghost, and Pedro was losing the war. There was little time left to succeed in his task.

Chaucer opened his right eye, lifted his aching head and sat up. Alfonso was already standing. When he saw that Chaucer was awake, he gestured toward the valley below. Chaucer followed his gaze to the remains of a village by a bridge. On the opposite side of the river gorge overlooking the village lay the ruins of a castle keep. And no sign of any soldiers in the keep.

"Here not good, bota almost empty. We need water. We go down," said Alfonso.

"Yes, that is plain," Chaucer replied.

"What 'plain?'" asked Alfonso, tilting his head.

Chaucer did not reply and stood and pulled himself free of his breeches, releasing a forceful yellow stream toward the broiling river far below. Alfonso had said Enrique's scouts might be nearby, or even in the castle keep, and if so, would soon be up with the sun.

Lifting small packs onto their backs, they descended the dusty path toward the river. They left their horses tied to bushes, hidden from the eyes and ears of scouts. They would be quieter and less likely to be seen without them.

As he descended, Chaucer pondered his future. Turn Calveley away from Enrique and toward Pedro and the war might still be won, with advancement at court and the hand of the woman he loved.

But will Pippa Rouet marry a mere merchant's son, esquire or no?

It mattered not, for success was as distant as the sun that refused to rise with each step taken toward the God-forsaken shadow of a village below.

They were soon making their way past scraggly trees, rocky outcroppings and tumbledown buildings. Chaucer licked his parched lips.

The morning light revealed the shape of a narrow stone bridge beyond the abandoned village, and then the same goat's path winding up to the opposite lip of the gorge past the ruined keep. The water in the angry river lay out of reach amidst boulders some fifty feet below the bridge. Chaucer swivelled his head back and forth between each side of the gorge. Still no sign of a human, let alone an army.

They eased their packs off their backs and sought refuge by a ruined building so as not to be seen by anyone above looking down. Chaucer shifted back and forth, uncomfortable at staying still, his thirst shouting for him to move.

"Village empty," said Alfonso.

"Again, you state what is plain. Why do you feel such a fervent desire to state what is so plain for anyone with eyes to see?" Chaucer snapped.

"This word plain, please tell?" Alfonso asked evenly.

Chaucer stared at Alfonso, shook his head and sighed.

"Where are we?" Chaucer instead asked.

Alfonso paused for a moment. "Plain, yes?" he said, tilting his head.

"No, it is not," Chaucer replied.

"Lost," Alfonso said, pointing at Chaucer.

Chaucer's head swivelled. Alfonso clearly understood more than he let on.

"You're not a very good guide," Chaucer said.

"Guide?" he asked, again tilting his head.

"You guide us to Calveley. That was your only task," Chaucer snapped. His head ached and his mouth was parched. He needed some water. Or wine. "We are lost."

"I am no lost," Alfonso replied, pointing to himself.

Alfonso stared at the flat bota slung over Chaucer's shoulder, shook his grey-tufted head dismissively and lifted his own half-full bota, pulled out the cork and squeezed.

"Empty bota bad luck. Also bad for bota," he said.

Alfonso sent a stream of red liquid into his mouth.

Chaucer would have given a gold noble for some wine, but Alfonso was not sharing.

"Water here," Alfonso said, pointing down to the river gorge.

"Again you state what is plain, but the water is fifty feet down, and we've no way of reaching it. We are lost and will die of thirst." Chaucer said, his mouth gritty.

"No. You lost, will die of thirst. I survive," he said, stepping forward. Alfonso sighed heavily, then gestured for Chaucer to follow.

"This Rio Yalde," he said, pointing down as they walked. "Huercanos near, three miles to Najera. This only bridge for army to attack Najera," Alfonso added.

In thirty paces, Alfonso stopped beside a well. It was in disrepair, missing planks from its small roof, but the broken and useless handle was still attached to the spindle with rope wound around it, a bucket sitting on the stone lip. Using his dagger, Alfonso fashioned a functioning handle and unwound the rope, then dropped the bucket.

After many turns, and an eye on the fraying rope, they heard a distant splashing sound, then repeated the process in reverse to raise the bucket. They took turns turning the spindle and were both sweating profusely by the time they were rewarded with a leaking bucket half full of cold, fresh water.

Alfonso was about to take a drink but instead offered the bucket to Chaucer, who drank deeply, let out a long "Ahhh", and offered the bucket back to Alfonso, who hesitated, looking at Chaucer.

"You're not thirsty? It will all leak out," Chaucer said.

Alfonso eyed Chaucer for a few more moments, then finally took the bucket and drank.

"It would take but a few men to hold such a bridge," Chaucer said, wiping his mouth with his dusty forearm.

"Is plain, yes?" Alfonso said, without a hint of a smile.

"Plain, yes Alfonso," Chaucer said, finally chuckling, for Alfonso clearly understood its meaning. He had thought Alfonso but a simpleton, but what his father said was true: *A beautiful book cover may yet contain empty words, and a rough-hewn cover a work of great quality.*

"But if the bridge holds such import, why are there no soldiers here?" Chaucer mused.

"All dead; people stay away," Alfonso said slowly, his face clouding over like the billowing black clouds that had suddenly appeared above the western lip of the gorge.

Chaucer formed a question about murder, but Alfonso cut him off. "Rain comes," he said.

"Rain? Don't be a dorbel. It's a sunny day," Chaucer said, peering up.

Shortly after, their botas filled—filling a bota with water instead of wine was not condoned, but surviving was—they'd returned to the ruin where they'd left their packs and huddled under the remaining portion of its dilapidated roof. Clouds scudded across the sky and in no time they were inundated by a downpour. Alfonso had been right. At first, the noise of the onslaught of rain and thunder drowned out the river below and all else. But then they heard the familiar noises of a whinnying horse, jangling harnesses and the clanging of iron against wood. And men's voices, shouting orders.

Soldiers. From the castle ruin, and sleeping no more.

"Enrique Trastamara's men," said Alfonso, peering around the edge of the wall. "They will think we are spies and kill us," he added quietly.

"Then we must disappear," said Chaucer, "But there is nowhere to hide," Chaucer added.

"Our horses too far. Only one place can hide. The well. Come." Alfonso said.

"I do not enjoy enclosed spaces."

"Enjoy coffin more?"

Chaucer shook his head.

"Come," Alfonso shouted.

A cannon crack of thunder followed immediately by a shaft of lightning stalled them. The storm was now directly overhead.

"Wait!" Chaucer said, grabbing Alfonso by his leather jerkin. The well was ten yards away, but the soldiers were already entering the village. It was too late.

"Wait for a lightning strike, then run for it once you hear the thunder," Chaucer said. He hoped the lightning might cause anyone looking to turn away.

It didn't take long. Another white rent of the black sky, another boom of thunder.

They made the well as if shot from a longbow, soaked to the skin, their packs on their backs. Alfonso climbed onto the stone lip of the well as Chaucer pulled the dagger out and let the bucket down a few feet. He stabbed the dagger back into the wooden dowel to block it from turning and nodded to Alfonso. The dagger was still there, and might signal their presence, but it was a risk they had to take.

Chaucer eyed the frayed rope.

"Hold?" Alfonso asked, his question barely audible amidst the thunder as he climbed over the well lip and took hold of the fraying rope.

The rain was now so heavy they couldn't see the soldiers, which meant they probably couldn't be seen, but they could hear them getting closer.

"It must," Chaucer said, and climbed on top of Alfonso.

They hung, Alfonso with his legs wrapped around the rope, sitting on the bucket, and Chaucer sitting on Alfonso's lap facing him, head lowered to only a foot below the lip of the well.

Seconds later, the neighing horses and curses of their riders echoed above them.

"We should water the horses before riding," a soldier shouted in Castilian, the jangling of harness suggesting he was dismounting.

Chaucer knew enough Castilian to understand; his stomach sank. With Alfonso's face.

"No, we must not stop until we find Pedro's scouts," said another.

Chaucer lifted his head.

"It will take but little time to fill a bucket of water," the first voice said.

Chaucer could hear his footsteps approaching the well. At any moment, the soldier would peer into the well and see them hanging there.

"No! Most wells here are poisoned to ensure Pedro's men can't use them," replied another.

Chaucer looked down at Alfonso, who looked up at him. The villagers had been murdered by poison. And they had both just drunk deeply from the well.

Chaucer now understood why Alfonso offered the bucket to him first. He wanted to say something vile to Alfonso but held his tongue, for as suddenly as the storm began, it abated.

Then they heard shouting. The jangling of a harness; a new horse and rider arrived.

Chaucer heard, "Pedro's forces have been seen two miles west, heading south."

"We must not dally here," said another.

"But we were to meet Calveley one mile east of this bridge," said the first.

Chaucer lifted his head at Calveley's name, but all he saw was the dilapidated roof.

"He will need to catch up to us then, for we cannot wait," said another.

"Mount up!" shouted a voice of authority. "We ride!"

Chaucer listened as the sounds of the mounted troupe began moving once again. That's when he noticed the strands of the rope fraying before his eyes.

The jangle of horse and rider continued. The army passed by, slowly. The rope frayed.

Chaucer had lifted empty oak wine barrels as a youth and while he was more porcine than stout now, he knew he was still strong. He waited a few more moments and pulled himself up the rope and put one hand on the lip of the wall and another on the dagger handle that held the rope.

He saw the last soldier ride past, but the rider was looking forward toward the bridge.

The fraying rope gave way.

Chaucer flung his other arm out and Alfonso caught his hand as the bucket bounced off the inside walls of the stone well.

The two hung off Chaucer's one arm and four fingers gripping the edge of the wet lip, unsure if the last rider had heard the racket. The rain was still falling, albeit less heavily.

Chaucer could just see the head of the soldier turn in his saddle at the sound of the bucket clanging down the well, but he must have decided the sound was nothing but an echo of the thunder of hooves and turned back and carried on over the narrow bridge. Chaucer began to lose his grip. He dropped his head.

"Climb up my arm," he whispered, "and be quick about it."

Alfonso gripped the lip with one hand as Chaucer lost his own grip and grabbed Alfonso's leg, and together they heaved themselves up over the edge and lay panting in the mud, their backs to the wet rock of the well.

The two men lay slumped beside the well.

"Thank you. You saved life," Alfonso said.

"We would both be captured and probably thrown down this well if not for your quick thinking. I'd say we saved each other's life," Chaucer replied. "At least we haven't been poisoned," Chaucer added. Alfonso's 'courtesy,' was not so easily forgotten.

"Poison may take time," he replied.

"Ah. Time then to sort out how we will find Calveley without horses," Chaucer said.

"They said meet one mile east. I take you short way," Alfonso replied, rising and retrieving his dagger from the well.

"Let me guess. By a goat track," Chaucer said.

First, they climbed the path they had descended to retrieve their horses—but they were gone. How was unclear, but it mattered not now—they would have to proceed on foot.

•   •   •

The morning climb northwest was gruelling. The early March sun unseasonably warm, the path steep. The brief downpour was over, and the sun soon baked dry the ground. They had crossed a trickle of a stream earlier and filled their botas. The heat and effort of the climb drained their muscles and their botas. Alfonso suffered more, for he refused to drink the last of his diluted wine, for an empty bota was a bad omen.

How far I am from finding Calveley, and from finally marrying Pippa. Both connected, both so distant.

"Climb make you tired? Or life?" Alfonso turned and asked, responding to the Englishman's heavy sigh.

Chaucer stopped and looked at Alfonso and grunted a yes to both.

I am tired of my own thoughts circling round and round like a crow chasing an eagle.

"You storyteller?" Alfonso asked, as they both resumed walking. "Tell stories. Pass time."

Not the worst idea.

"I will tell you a story of my king and his son," Chaucer said, moving to walk beside Alfonso as the path widened.

"Good story, yes?" Alfonso asked.

"Yes." Chaucer told the story of King Edward's first victory at the Battle of Crecy, beginning with some of the history leading up to the battle, then the climax of the battle itself.

"Watching the battle from a hilltop, King Edward saw his sixteen-year-old son, also named Edward, struggling to hold the line. A lord watching with the king asked, '*Your son, the prince, struggles. Should we send reinforcements to aid him?*' The king replied, '*No, let him earn his own spurs this day. I will not send help,*' and he did not, and Prince Edward overcame the French and was victorious. A victory for both father and son."

Alfonso nodded, "I know story but not like this," he replied. "You good storyteller. You compete in puy?"

Chaucer rolled his eyes. "Yes. I have competed in puys."

He had competed in several puys, and had yet to win any gold. Yet he kept composing verse and paying to enter puys. Pippa frequently told him to stop wasting his time, for both poetry and entering puys were impractical efforts, bringing in no gold. Yet.

And there lies the rub.

Composing was what gave life to his soul. For Pippa to marry him, he would need to find success at court—her definition of success—and also give up that which gave him joy and succour. Perchance she asked too much of him.

"Your turn," Chaucer said.

Alfonso told a story about the civil war that had been raging in Navarre, Castile and Aragon for over a decade. Chaucer had heard bits of the tale from the dockhands and merchants he had dealt with at his father's wine business in the Vintry. But what Alfonso was sharing was new to Chaucer.

"King Alfonso of Castile had one son, Pedro, with his wife Maria, of Portugal. But the king and his lover, Eleanor de Guzmán, had four sons," Alfonso said. "Twins Enrique and Fadrique Alfonso. Then Tello and Sancho."

Chaucer nodded to show he understood.

"My mother name me same name," Alfonso said.

Chaucer looked at him more closely.

Is he related?

"The king made Enrique Count of Trastámara. Eleanor gave many titles to sons. Make many nobles angry. Most angry is wife, his queen Maria. Her son Pedro is the Cruel…and Just." Alfonso said the second eponym as if spitting.

"When King Alfonso die and Pedro new king, Eleanor flee, take sons away."

Alfonso paused to lick his chapped lips, and Chaucer considered offering some of the water in his bota, but then remembered how Alfonso had not offered to share his wine.

"Pedro find Eleanor and kill her. Enrique escape to France, serve King John of France, King Charles's father, and plan revenge."

"After seven year, Enrique come back, join King Pere in war against Pedro. Enrique defeated. Prisoner in Nájera. Then liberated and exiled to France once more."

"Pere then attack Castile. Enrique help Pere to fight Pedro. Same war still, many years now. This time Enrique will win."

"Why do you think he will win this time after so many failures?" Chaucer asked.

"Du Guesclin and Calveley, and two thousand mercenaries."

Calveley. Yes. But I must turn him so they do not win.

"So what happened next?" Chaucer asked.

"This happen next," replied Alfonso, pointing to Chaucer and himself, then spreading his hands outward to the desolate scene before them. He licked his lips and stopped talking.

They collapsed later above a narrow pass, too hot, tired and thirsty to continue, their lips too parched to continue telling stories, agreeing to wait out the heat of the day, but desperate for water or wine. There were no trees or bushes, just rocks. It was a desolate place where nothing lived.

"Alfonso, we will die of thirst if we stay here," Chaucer croaked. His thirst was becoming unbearable.

"We die of many things," Alfonso said.

"I would prefer to die of *too* much drink. I would give my first born for a goblet of wine right now," Chaucer said. With no shade, he lay on a rock, looking up at the deep blue cloudless sky, trying to lick his lips.

"We all die, no escape from death," Alfonso croaked. He too lay with his head on rock, and closed his eyes.

Their eyes opened together to the sound of horse hooves and harnesses.

They sat up, heads swivelling as one to the valley below. There, at least fifty riders approached on the wide track they had veered off a few moments before, led by a number of scouts. They had been seen and this time there was nowhere to hide. Sure enough, the scout ahead of the main body of riders signalled and several more riders trotted forward to join him, and they carried up the path straight toward them.

Alfonso pointed to the standard held by one of the riders. It was Enrique's men. "Not good," Alfonso said.

"Yes, that much is plain Alfonso," Chaucer muttered.

The riders climbed toward them, steel flashing in the sun.

One rider trotted ahead of the others and, nearing the boulders, dismounted.

He was not young, surely in his late 40s, but huge, over six and a half feet tall, and as wide as two men. He effortlessly pulled out a long, curved sword from his scabbard and strode toward them. His visor was closed, as if expecting trouble.

Chaucer stepped out from behind the boulder, holding his own short sword in front of him with two hands, his arms shaking, and shouted, "Halt!"

His leather satchel with his treasured books was slung over his shoulder.

Alfonso stepped out behind him, his sword still in its scabbard.

The armoured man did not pause and continued forward at an angle. He flicked his wrist and swatted away Chaucer's sword, leaving his own sword tip an inch from Chaucer's heart.

Still Alfonso did not move.

"I have a letter from King Edward. Let me show you," Chaucer said, and moved to pull out the sealed leather pouch from inside his doublet that contained the letter.

Again, the man flicked his sword and batted Chaucer's hand away, this time drawing blood at his wrist.

Alfonso moved faster than Chaucer thought possible, pulling out from somewhere in his clothing a concealed dagger and flinging it effortlessly at the behemoth, striking him in his shoulder between the joints in his armour. The hulk barely registered any pain and, with his left hand, pulled the dagger out, flung it to the ground, and approached Alfonso, who stood wide-eyed and very still. Chaucer noted some blood on the tip of the dagger.

The remaining riders arrived and began to dismount, and the hulk did not turn at their approach.

One of the dismounted riders approached the enormous man.

"Du Guesclin asks that you return to camp, for he has new orders."

The behemoth faced the soldier, shook his head, and made a dismissive sound.

"Tell him I return when this business done," he replied in broken Castilian.

He turned back to Chaucer and Alfonso, his sword drawn.

"The squat young one is English, and the older one is local, I would wager," he said, this time in English.

"I am Sir Hugh Calveley, from Bunbury, Cheshire," the behemoth added, also in English.

Chaucer's eyes widened in surprise—and a smile spread over his face.

"My lord, at last. I have travelled far to find you and I am very pleased to meet you," Chaucer replied, his relief at finally finding Calveley clear in his voice.

Thanks be to God; I thought this day would never arrive!

Calveley let out a "Hmmm" sound, as if appraising Chaucer.

Chaucer in turn kept his eyes on the massive knight, for his size belied his swift movements. He had learned of Calveley from speaking to soldiers and valets before departing London. They had told stories of a knight that was cool in the heat of battle, yet quick in his movements. He had an enormous appetite and drank as much as ten men. He was known to be kind and chivalrous, honoured among men, and he had great strength that matched his stature. Yet he was a religious man, and whenever he seized booty, he had it sprinkled with holy water, to absolve him of his sins in taking it. A complex, imposing man nearing fifty stood before him, wielding a massive sword with the ease and strength of a young, virile knight.

Calveley lifted his visor to take in his captives with his piercing blue eyes. He had an unusually angled face with high cheekbones, and tufts of red hair poked out from his helmet.

"And do you have a name?" Calveley asked through extraordinarily long front teeth.

"Geoffrey Chaucer, page and courier to King Edward, and wine merchant from the Vintry district of London, here to seek Rioja wine in trade, and to bear you a letter from King Edward," Chaucer said, picking up the leather pouch he had dropped.

Despite Chaucer's claim to have a missive from his king, Calveley looked unimpressed.

Chaucer noted the knight's dented armour that may have once shone but was now a dull snow grey, no doubt from recent use. The only signs of wealth were a gold cross worked into the brim of his conical steel helm, a gold-pommeled dagger shoved into his belt, and small gems encrusted on the hilt and pommel of his long sword, which he held in his gauntlet as if a play toy. This knight was all about war, not wealth. The tip of a third sword strapped between his shoulders poked up from behind his helm. He wiped away droplets of sweat from his face.

Calveley finally turned to address Alfonso. "And you?"

"Sancho Alfonso," he said evenly.

Chaucer jerked his head toward Alfonso. He'd thought his first name was Alfonso.

"King Alfonso had a bastard son named Sancho Alfonso," Calveley said.

Alfonso said nothing.

Chaucer looked more closely at Alfonso—that would be an interesting possibility. But he just as quickly discounted it, for Alfonso was surely too old, and gave no notion of nobility.

"He's my guide," Chaucer said.

"And to where are you guiding him?" Calveley asked Alfonso.

Alfonzo shrugged. Calveley turned to Chaucer for an answer, and Chaucer gave his well-practiced answer.

"To find vineyards where the famed Rioja grows. And then, after I have concluded my business interests, return to Bordeaux," Chaucer said.

"You are nowhere near any vineyards," observed Calveley, his tone suggesting he didn't believe a word Chaucer had said.

"I also seek you, my lord," once again offering the leather pouch.

"You have found me."

"I think it is you who found us. Might we have some privacy?" Chaucer asked, his eyes flitting to the soldiers behind Calveley. "And perchance a dram of water or wine?" he added.

Calveley ignored the question and asked, "And what is in that leather satchel that you cling to like a king to his gold?"

"Indeed, it is my own treasure, three books I purchased in Logrono."

Calveley took the satchel from Chaucer, peered into it then slung it over his own shoulder, and said, "A wine merchant and a bibliophile. A curious combination…"

"But those are…" Chaucer blurted.

"Now my surety to ensure good behaviour until I can verify who you say you are," he said. "To be returned if your story holds water," he added.

At the word 'water', Chaucer tried to wet his lips. Parched.

Calveley turned and attached the satchel to his saddle and climbed back on his horse. He said something quietly to the lead rider who motioned for Chaucer and Alfonso to follow, and then proceeded back down the rough path toward the main goat track.

After stumbling down the now dust-filled goat track to the main body of men, Chaucer and Alfonso were offered two horses. As they rode, they gratefully drank a full bota of diluted wine before eating stale bread, hard cheese and dried meat that Alfonso called chorizo sausage, similar to what Chaucer had eaten in Logrono. They were escorted for some time before making camp on top of a small plateau within a copse of trees by a spring. The setting sun lit a line of red cliffs to the southeast.

"Najera," Alfonso said when he saw Chaucer looking that way.

After dismounting, Chaucer saw no sign of Calveley and he wondered how he might regain his books, for they would be hard to replace and constituted the bulk of his assets in Navarre. He had only four gold nobles left of the five Prince Edward had given to him. But he had found Calveley. Now the hard work of trying to turn him began.

He and Alfonso sat by a newly made fire, their thin cloaks failing to keep away the chill of the March dusk. Chaucer shivered and looked north to where the Pyrenees, and his way home, loomed, the snow-clad peaks gilded burnt yellow by the last rays of light.

But how to turn Calveley?

By the time the fires had shrunk to embers, darkness enveloped the camp.

Chaucer was almost asleep where he lay on the ground when one soldier prodded his boot with a sword.

"Chaucer. Up. You too, Alfonso. Sir Hugh wants to see you."

Now fully awake, Chaucer and Alfonso dusted themselves off and followed the soldier into Calveley's tent. Three scones lit the inside. Armed guards surrounded him.

"Guards out," said Calveley.

They made a noisy departure with their armour and weaponry.

Standing behind Calveley, four men remained, fully weaponed. Chaucer thought he recognized one of them, but he could not recall the name.

"These are my loyal companions. Anything you have to say to me, they can hear," Calveley said, gesturing at each man as he introduced them. "Sir Lewis Clifford, my right hand. Sir Robert Knowles, Sir William Beauchamp, and Sir Richard Sturry. Good sirs, before you stands Geoffrey Chaucer, wine merchant, page and courier to King Edward. With him stands his guide Alfonso."

All four nodded to Chaucer, and ignored Alfonso.

Chaucer noted their calm demeanour, their clear respect for Calveley, and their well-worn, oft repaired and dented armour—all were dressed for battle. These were warriors. A powerful group of men who showed no sign of disrespect when Calveley spoke of King Edward.

"You have a message for me from the king?"

Chaucer removed the leather pouch with the letter from the inside pocket of his doublet. He held it out to Calveley. "Yes, my lord. I am to deliver this message to you, and to you alone."

Calveley undid the cords of leather wrapped around the pouch, pulled back the leather flap, and extracted a folded piece of parchment.

He broke the seal and read the document, then looked up and addressed his companions.

"Gentlemen, it is indeed a message from our good King Edward," his tone grave.

The men exchanged similar solemn looks.

"He beseeches us to lay down our arms and no longer fight for Enrique. We are to take up our arms for the king's cousin Pedro, his loyal ally, and by doing so, return to the warm embrace of our king. Our disobedience in ignoring previous requests will be forgiven."

The knights looked at one another, then at Chaucer.

Sir Richard suddenly let out a guffaw, and the others, including Calveley, joined in.

"Sires…hold fast. You scorn both me and your good king with your strange mirth," said Chaucer, indignant. But Chaucer's protest only set off another round of cackles.

Calveley finally paused long enough to sputter, "This business…has nought to do…with you, good Chaucer. Our mirth is solely for…ahaha…King Edward, for he sends his demand," he lifted the letter and tossed it to the floor, "without gold…to men who serve only for gold…these past eighteen months."

"To scoff at our king is to hasten treason," Chaucer replied.

The men laughed even harder.

Calveley finally gathered himself enough to string words his together without laughing. "Chaucer, come now. We have been loyal to Edward in the day, when he most needed our swords. But the Treaty of Bretigny ended the war over five years ago. Edward sailed home, leaving us holding our balls in Picardy with our men, horses, armour and swords to maintain, and no war or way to earn our keep. The Free Companies beckoned with gold, and so we said yes and joined them. That led us south to serve Enrique and Pere and his gold. For Edward to ask us to give up this gold, for nought in return, would cause even the pope to smile."

Chaucer saw the truth of it, for Edward's plea relied solely on fealty.

"When we have broken Pedro's army, and he has been captured, then yes, we will consider returning to our good king's service, assuming he has gold to pay. Edward will no doubt want our swords if he needs. Until then, eat, sleep and get what rest you may, for on the morrow we attack Pedro," Calveley said.

Calveley's words echoed, and Chaucer felt at that moment like his future was but a dream, made of nothing that was real. And then remembered Olite, and what Carlos had said. Perchance he could prove useful to Calveley.

"One more thing, my lord. In Olite, I overheard King Carlos saying he had invited Eustache d'Auberchicourt and his war machines to Navarre. He did not want that known by me."

Calveley looked at Chaucer, assessing what he had said. "Now that is useful information. Carlos would only hire D'Auberchicourt if he was planning a siege. Or selling his services to another who was planning the same. Like Enrique. Thank you."

A soldier appeared at the entrance to the tent, interrupting.

"Yes?" Calveley asked.

"Du Guesclin is ready for you, my lord," he said.

Calveley's lips tightened at the mention of du Guesclin's name.

"Chaucer, I must leave you now and attend to matters of war. You have my answer to give our good king and his son the prince. But I suggest you delay your departure until we have won tomorrow's battle, or you will risk capture."

"I understand, my lord. Thank you for seeing us." Chaucer and Alfonso left the tent.

"Not good," Alfonso said to Chaucer as they returned to their now extinguished fire.

"No, not good. I have no idea how I will turn him," he said, more to himself.

"Turn him? Yes. You are, how you say…?" Alfonso asked.

"Carked," Chaucer replied.

"What this mean?" Alfonso asked.

"Weighed down by worries," Chaucer said, saying no more, as he was tired of explaining.

I have failed to turn Calveley, and Enrique is about to defeat Pedro.

"Pass me the bota. I want to get drunk," he said.

"English strange," Alfonso said.

"Is what makes English so interesting," Chaucer replied.

"No, just strange," Alfonso replied.

"Here is to my strange language in your strange country," Chaucer replied, taking a long squirt from the bota. Alfonso joined him.

•   •   •

"My spies tell me that d'Auberchicourt and his war machines are in Navarre," Calveley said.

Du Guesclin stared at Calveley. "I have heard no such thing."

"Carlos may be preparing to switch allegiances," Calveley said.

"We shall see in time. Pedro is our only concern now."

"And Pedro's army is retreating. We must attack," said Calveley, his tone cool.

"I lead this army, and I make the decisions, not you. We will regroup and attack Briviesca first," du Guesclin said.

Calveley scowled, no longer trying to hide his feelings. "You miss an opportunity. We must strike fast and run them down or they may escape," Calveley said.

"No. We will prepare to attack Briviesca. Once we take that town, we attack Burgos," du Guesclin replied, just as vehemently. "Burgos is the capital of Castile and Pedro's seat of power. Taking the city would be the end of Pedro. But it will take some thought, for the city is encircled by walls and backed by a powerful force."

Calveley stared at the smaller man with anger and disgust.

"I think your plan is flawed," Calveley said.

"I care naught what you think," du Guesclin replied.

"And I think less of what you care," Calveley replied in his clipped tone.

"I respect your abilities on the battlefield, but ever since I defeated you at the Castle of Montmuran, you have held a grudge against me," du Guesclin replied.

"Defeated me? That's a good tale you tell. You lost twenty men," Calveley said.

"After my archers killed forty of yours before you even reached the castle! And you failed to take the castle," du Guesclin snapped. "To call such a defeat victory is to call night day, and hate love," he said. "Or is it love that you hate?"

The corner of Calveley's mouth twitched.

"You loved Jeanne de Laval once, did you not?" du Guesclin asked.

"You ravaged her," Calveley replied in an accusing whisper.

"Ravage would be the wrong word to use, given her screams of delight during my…sally," he replied.

Calveley's hand on his sword hilt twitched. "It is not love that I hate. It is you that I hate, du Guesclin. It is only gold that allows me to bend a knee to you," he said in an even tone. His right hand was now clenching and unclenching above his sword pommel.

Du Guesclin smiled.

"Despite your defeat and capture at the Battle of Auray at the hands of Sir John Chandos."

This time it was du Guesclin whose jaw clenched. He paused for a beat and then replied, "Carlos ordered the attack against my advice, and valued me so highly that he paid my ransom of one hundred thousand francs without a moment's hesitation."

They stared at one another, hatred and respect uncomfortable bedmates.

Du Guesclin finally broke the tense silence. "One truth is clear, Calveley. Carlos, or Enrique, or Pedro, or whomever wields power in this God-forsaken land does not know how to lead an army. But I do, and I will end this ten-year-old war. And you will follow my orders and we will be paid enough gold and given enough titles and land and never have to fight with nor see each other again."

Calveley said nothing, unwilling to admit to the truth he spoke.

"We move on Briviesca in the morning. Within the week, Pedro will be gone from Castile, preferably dead," du Guesclin said, more to himself than Calveley.

Calveley turned to leave.

"One more thing. Who were those two men you captured earlier today?"

Calveley hesitated for a moment, surprised that du Guesclin even knew of Chaucer and Alfonso's capture. "Another English wine trader seeking to buy Rioja wine, and his local guide," Calveley said. The truth was close enough to the mark, if not quite in the centre. That his employment was tied to King Edward and dependent on turning Calveley was a detail du Guesclin need not know.

"Be sure he is not also one of Pedro's spies, for they are everywhere among us these days," du Guesclin said, then turned away.

Chaucer may indeed be a spy for King Edward, but for Pedro? Of that he doubted, but if so, Chaucer would pay dearly. Only time would tell.

PART 2
DEFEAT

CHAPTER 12
NORTHWEST OF LOGRONO, MARCH 8 1366
LOST AGAIN

"What do you know of du Guesclin?" Chaucer asked Alfonso.

Alfonso didn't reply for a few moments, gathering his blanket around him to ward off the evening's chill…or Chaucer's question.

They had ridden the horses provided by Calveley for the morning, trying to keep up to Calveley's swarm of soldiers chasing Pedro's army fleeing west. Du Guesclin had allowed Calveley free rein to pursue Pedro's rear guard, but only toward Briviesca. Calveley's main force, that included du Guesclin, and now also Chaucer, Alfonso and their guards, were half a day's ride behind. What would likely be the final battle would occur soon, within a day or two.

They had camped on a ridge and filled their bellies with food and wine taken from the villages they had passed, but they were now chilled, with the smell of snow hanging in the air. Their fire was kept small and low as there was little firewood, and it gave off little heat, so both huddled close by it. The sound from the hundreds of soldiers was surprisingly muted as dark settled over the camp. Pinpricks of light were sprinkled in a rough line to the southwest, where they become a larger glow that must surely be Burgos. A smaller group of lights lay nearer to the east. Briviesca, their first destination. The impending battle no doubt sobering each soldier at the prospect of death come the dawn.

"You said you are a bastard. Did you ever meet your father?" Chaucer asked.

Alfonso lifted his head. "Now dead," he replied.

"What was his name?"

Alfonso looked at Chaucer, weighing his reply.

"Alfonso. Like me."

"What was his surname?"

Alfonso hesitated, then said, "Trastamara."

Chaucer lifted his head.

"Yes. Best known as King Alfonso," Alfonso said, his voice lower.

Chaucer's head shot up further.

"You didn't tell me you were the son of a king, or *that* king," Chaucer said.

"You no ask," replied Alfonso.

"It's not something one would expect to ask a guide," Chaucer replied, and regretted the words as soon as he said them.

Alfonso stared at him across the small fire. "*Lowly* guide, you mean?" he replied.

"As if I had said I was related to King Edward," Chaucer said to deflect his blunder.

The curl of Alfonso's mouth said enough.

"Which makes you brother to Enrique, soon to be crowned a king?" Chaucer asked.

Alfonso nodded. "Half-brother, yes. But Enrique no Edward. Edward rule England forty years, yes? Victor of Sluys, Crecy and Poitiers, yes?" Afonso said.

"Yes," Chaucer replied.

"Edward known across Europe, father to greatest warrior of all, his son Prince Edward, yes?"

"Yes."

"Alfonso father many bastards. Enrique was first. I second, from different mother. I am problem for Enrique. Is plain, yes?" Alfonso said.

"Yes, plain," Chaucer said, shivering. The fire had collapsed to glowing embers.

"So, I say little. Lady Fortune maybe smile on Enrique, maybe smile on Pedro. So I watch and wait. Plain, yes?" Alfonso said, now needling Chaucer.

Chaucer nodded, wrapped his cloak about him tighter, and he lay on the cold ground. "Yes Alfonso, plain enough to see," he said.

Silence filled the space between them as Chaucer pondered what Alfonso had just told him. His knowledge of the land, his connections in every town, it all made more sense now. But one thing remained.

"I nearly forgot. You helped me find Calveley and your fee is now due. What do I owe you?" Chaucer asked.

Alfonso shifted his body and looked squarely at Chaucer. "Help avenge the death of my mother by killing Enrique."

Kill Enrique? I am no killer.

"I cannot."

"Then help *me* kill him."

What? And have me arrested as your accomplice? What madness is this? What has Alfonso got me into? My simple task now approaches madness.

•　　　•　　　•

"To arms!" shouted a voice, waking Chaucer.

Alfonso was already up. "Scout say Calveley find Pedro's rear guard and attack."

They were soon mounted and heading west. Only the faint glow in the east suggested dawn's approach. After a short period of riding, Chaucer could make out a mass of knights ahead, no doubt those of Calveley or du Guesclin, and just visible ahead of them, a larger swarm that must be Pedro's men, running west. Mounted, armoured knights against infantry would be a short story.

And it was, for Calveley's knights soon rode over a gentle ridge and caught some of Pedro's men resting—or hiding—in a meadow.

There weren't many, suggesting Pedro was in a full retreat and willing to give up the ground.

Pedro's men ran for their lives across the meadow toward a copse of trees, and within a short time several of Calveley's knights had caught them just before they had reached the trees, leaving Chaucer and Alfonso guarded by two of the knights.

Suddenly, shouts were followed by hooves and the jangle of sword and armour. Chaucer turned to see a group of ten armed riders—by their banner, Pedro's men—flying out of another copse of trees behind, galloping straight at them.

The two knights guarding Chaucer and Alfonso understood the odds of success were against them. They dropped their reins, sheathed their swords, and put their hands in the air.

They were quickly surrounded.

"Off horse!" shouted the leader in broken Castilian, an ugly-looking fellow with a scar running across his left cheek.

The four dismounted and huddled together.

"Drop weapons," he shouted again.

They did. Chaucer and Alfonso dropped the daggers they had pulled out.

"Now we see if Enrique's men squeal when stuck like pigs," he said, kneeing his horse closer, his sword raised.

Just then, another shout rang out.

A group of eight knights—Chaucer recognized Sir Clifford Lewis in the lead—rode hard toward them, swords raised. A few moments later, they were upon the group. Chaucer also recognized Sir Christopher Croker and Sir Robert Knowles.

The scarred leader wheeled his horse to face Sir Clifford, but he was too late, as Sir Clifford sliced his sword arm down, cutting through the leader's hardened leather jerkin and opening him from neck to bowels as he galloped past. Blood spurted across Lewis as the now lifeless body of the leader slid sideways off his horse.

The two knights who had been with Chaucer and Alfonso immediately picked up their swords and joined the fray. Pedro's riders were quickly dispatched save for two who galloped away. Alfonso and Chaucer gathered the reins of the horses of the eight dead men.

Lewis, Knowles and Croker turned as Chaucer approached.

"My lord Sir Clifford, I thank you, for you have saved our lives. We were surely about to meet our maker," Chaucer said.

"Croker spied Pedro's men erupting from the trees and alerted me. You owe your life to him," Sir Clifford replied.

Fear, anger and relief flowed through and overwhelmed him, and his voice wavered as he tried to form words in reply.

"Croker…I thank you again… for your aid," Chaucer replied, his emotions dampening his usual verbosity.

Croker ignored the compliment. "Take what you can from the dead and mount up, for we need to catch up to Enrique, Calveley, and his men before any more of Pedro's stragglers catch up to us."

I would be dead save for Croker. I need to stay close to him now, or may not see Pippa or Elizabeth again.

·　　·　　·

The next day Calveley and du Guesclin surrounded Briviesca, a strongly defended town fortified with double walls.

Calveley attacked the Jewish quarter. Du Guesclin, battle axe in hand, led his French soldiers to attack the walls. One of du Guesclin's knights, Alain de la Houssoie, climbed with twenty soldiers to the top of the battlements, but they were beaten back. Houssoie was thrown from the walls into the moat.

Calveley had more success and breached the southern wall.

Du Guesclin, seeing his men floundering, said to his exhausted soldiers, "The English have already advanced into the city. If we do not prevail, they will win all the rich booty that lies within." They believed him and began a renewed attack on the walls.

Finally, a Breton soldier mounted the walls with one of du Guesclin's pennons, followed by his comrades, who, with the aid of ropes and grappling hooks, crawled up the walls like apes. The governor, seeing further opposition was hopeless, surrendered.

Calveley and his men slaughtered the inhabitants, seizing rich booty. A mere three weeks after beginning the invasion, they were now only twenty miles from Burgos. Enrique, du Guesclin and Calveley rode side by side as they rode west.

"What happened to that English wine trader and his guide you mentioned?" asked Enrique. "I did not meet them."

"Pedro's men nearly killed them, but they were saved by Sir Clifford. Why do you ask?" asked Calveley.

"I was musing that they might indeed be Pedro's spies. I would see the trader interrogated if he was still in custody," Enrique replied. "Bring him to me."

"I would not want to worry you with such trivial matters. I will undertake that task and report to you after, my lord," Calveley said.

Enrique looked at Calveley for a moment, then simply said, "Fine."

CHAPTER 13
QUINTANAPALLA, NORTHEAST OF BURGOS
RETURN TO CALVELEY, MARCH 15, 1366

"Thank you for seeing me, my lord," said Chaucer as he stepped inside Calveley's tent.

"Welcome Chaucer, I see that you survived the battle," Calveley replied. He stood behind a table set in the middle of the tent, lit sconces throwing light upon a map laid upon it with stones keeping the curled ends flat. To his left stood Sir Lewis.

"I heard Enrique will be making you Count of Carrion," Chaucer replied.

"Yes," Calveley replied. He added, "He lacked sufficient gold, so I will take the name and land instead."

"You're a Cheshire man, my lord?"

"Yes. Born in Calveley Hall in Bunbury up north. And you're a London man, born in the Vintry, yes?"

"Yes. My da John is a member of the Vintners Company, and I lend a hand when not at court."

"As page to King Edward," Calveley said.

"Yes, my lord."

"But a courier on this journey. You have been lifted high by King Edward."

Calveley adjusted one of several wooden knights on the map before them that were almost surrounding the city of Burgos.

"A map of the battle to come, my lord?" Chaucer asked.

"Yes. We must encircle the city so Pedro cannot escape."

"Does that represent du Guesclin?" Chaucer asked, pointing to the knight next to Burgos. A knight with Calveley's colours stood behind that figure, and Enrique's figure behind him.

Calveley nodded.

Chaucer pointed to a knight inside Burgos. "I hear du Guesclin leads the three armies that have assembled," Chaucer said, searching for a reaction.

He saw only a flick of Calveley's eyes at du Guesclin's name.

I must turn Calveley now, for I am out of time.

"Hmmm" was all that he said.

"Your former enemy, no?" Chaucer added.

"Yes. To be a mercenary is to place loyalty at the foot of gold, land and oneself."

"But can any soldier who has vouchsafed his loyalty to King Edward properly fight for another? And fight for du Guesclin, knowing du Guesclin killed so many good Englishmen?"

"Many English have killed many other English. French, English, Castilian—war is filled with loyal idiots, but a few of the cleverer ones may profit," Calveley said evenly.

Level-headed. Which bodes well for du Guesclin, and poorly for my task.

"And since the Treaty of Bretigny was signed six years ago, we haven't had a proper war, so where is a knight of the realm like me supposed to find gold to feed his family?"

A reasonable question.

"I joined the Free Company for the gold. It's not a proper army but an army of men who kill for gold. The leaders of such men, like du Guesclin and John Hawkwood in Italy, know how to wield a sword and lead men. More importantly, they know how to convince rich burghers to pay gold rather than see their homes burnt and daughters ravaged," he added.

"You admire Hawkwood?" Chaucer asked.

"He is the greatest mercenary alive, a very clever tactician and a fearless soldier, always leading his men into battle, which has earned him the loyalty and respect of all who join his cause."

"And the pope's gold sent Hawkwood to Milan and you and du Guesclin to Logrono?"

"You are too well informed for a courier," Calveley said. "But not as a spy," he added.

Chaucer passed over the comment and asked, "Does an oath to your king not hold?"

"If Edward himself was here, I'd say pay me gold, or I will fight for another who will."

I must try another tack.

"But my good lord, you must consider your reputation. Years, nay decades from now, no one will care about your gold, only the stories left behind that will form your reputation. Stories told by chroniclers like Froissart, Ayala, the Chandos herald and even a poor poet like me."

Calveley, angled toward the door, now turned his body to face Chaucer squarely.

"You ask me to consider my reputation? Why? I buy my reputation with my gold; as a storyteller, you of all people should know that."

Chaucer had no reply, for Calveley was right.

"And you know of Ayala and Chandos."

"Who does not know of them…" Chaucer began.

"And know of the goings on of mercenaries. I say that you know too much for a page," Calveley said over top of him.

"I heard…" Chaucer tried to say.

"And I had heard you were some kind of poet; but *your* reputation must be still in swaddling clothes, for you were not known to me until I began asking about. Your ill-formed attempt to turn me toward your exalted prince and king falls flat, and speaks poorly of your abilities as a storyteller. Do not ever deign to judge me again, for I have beaten, stabbed, bludgeoned, and broken men for far less," Calveley said, his voice rising in volume and tone. "Guards! Lock up this damnable cur and throw him in the stockade with those others, for he is page Monday, poet Tuesday, wine merchant Wednesday. What now shall we call him this day? I say spy," he shouted.

CHAPTER 14
BURGOS CASTLE, MARCH 20, 1366
PEDRO THE JUST

Pedro turned to his knights standing around the large table in the centre of the castle room, his clear blue eyes taking in their worried, scared faces, and he frowned. "So, do none of you have a plan for our salvation?"

Ayala opened his mouth, then thought better of it, and closed it again. Pedro had spurned his ideas once, publicly. He would not be made to feel the same embarrassment a second time.

"Not one of you can see a way out of this?" Pedro asked, and drummed his sword hilt.

Still, no one answered, the eyes of his officers slanting back and forth between Pedro's intense gaze and the hand that sat restlessly—threateningly—on his sword hilt.

"I should have you all hanged," he said in disgust.

"We can successfully fight here at Burgos, my lord," offered one man across the table. "The city walls are thick, there is a good supply of food—"

"And we will run out of water in a week," Pedro interrupted. He walked around the massive table, then stopped behind the man.

Sweat ran down the man's face as he looked behind at his king towering over him.

"Do you have any better suggestions?" Pedro asked.

The man hesitated.

"Surrender?" he replied.

It was difficult to sever a head from its body, but Pedro's very sharp blade was of the finest Milanese steel, sharpened to a fine edge. The man's head fell to the floor and rolled, followed by his body, which toppled forward. Blood sprayed across the table, splashing several of the men. One man vomited.

Ayala had witnessed such violent outbursts from Pedro before, but his stomach still turned at the sight.

"No! I will not surrender to Enrique! I will never surrender to that evil bastard. Anyone else who thinks so should leave now," Pedro said.

Silence thundered through the room as the blood from the headless corpse pooled by the body. The man next to the body shuffled sideways, his boots leaving bloody footprints.

And then another man finally spoke up.

"My lord. We will not surrender to that cur," he said in a confidant, deep-timbered voice devoid of fear. "I propose we instead withdraw first to Seville, and then San Sebastian and Bordeaux to regroup within the realm of your dear cousin Prince Edward. He will surely hear you speak of the danger of a Castile ruled by Enrique, of a crown sullied by a bastard. I say we trust Edward to support your most honoured cause, providing men and gold to finally quash that bastard and place you in your rightful place as the true King of Castile."

"Come forward and show yourself," demanded Pedro.

The man stepped into the light from the narrow window. He was tall, lean and dressed well, his grey-speckled beard and hair covering an oversized head. His eyes, a striking green. It was Cordoba.

Ayala nodded at Cordoba.

"I have seen your face before," Pedro said. "Your name?"

The man bent slightly. "My lord. I am Senor Don Martin Lopez de Córdoba, a knight of little renown, at your service," he said.

"Yours are the first sensible words spoken this day," Pedro replied. "Do I know you?" he asked.

"Don Pero sent me to London in December to put your case before King Edward."

"Yes, now I recall the name, and your good service to my crown."

"I was there when Edward sent an edict to those English mercenaries, including Calveley, to withdraw their support from Enrique and fight for the English, and for you," Córdoba added.

"Yet they have not done so, which tells me Edward holds little sway with Calveley. How do you propose that we protect ourselves from attack as we withdraw? If Enrique and his henchmen Calveley and du Guesclin smell retreat, they will only speed up their advance and catch us. It would be a slaughter," Pedro said emphatically.

"My lord, your insight speaks to your knowledge and experience of such matters. I suggest a quiet withdrawal that might be called something else to all but your loyal lieutenants here. But we could let it be known that we are moving west to make a stand at Leon, and order the first few hundred soldiers, followed by most of our supply carts, to go in that direction. You and the bulk of our army shall follow. Then, under cover of darkness, you shall turn south. By the next morning, you shall be halfway to Seville, where you will be welcomed. If Enrique discovers the ruse, you will be unencumbered by the heavy carts and will be travelling twice as fast as his army, and will reach Seville long before he could catch you," Córdoba replied, all eyes upon Pedro. "From Seville, you might then sail to San Sebastian."

"Córdoba, I find your idea appealing. And you say you are Ayala's man, but how do I know you are not a spy setting a trap?"

"Cordoba can be trusted, my lord," Ayala replied.

"My lord, I will let the merit of my ideas stand in place of my feint reputation," Córdoba added.

"My lord, this will not stand!" said Don Figuera, Pedro's naval captain. "As you say, this man has no standing at this table, and may indeed be a spy."

"And you have a better plan, Figuera? And do you not trust the word of Ayala?"

Don Figuera paused, then said, "I do not, my lord."

"I find the quality of your service, and that of your others," he added, looking around the room, "unsatisfactory. I will ignore your slight to our guest, and instead let his plan stand."

Pedro turned his back on Figuera and faced Córdoba. "We shall do exactly as you say. We shall withdraw—not surrender—and regroup in Seville, then plan for the day when we return with Edward's army at our back and reclaim what is rightfully mine. We shall give up this city for but a few months. When we return, it will be in triumph! Córdoba, I now name you my new grandmaster, for the position has recently been vacated," he said, gesturing at the headless corpse below him. "As I need a man who can keep his head in inclement weather."

"Thank you, my lord, I am honoured."

"We shall depart on the morrow before Enrique has a chance to block our path south. Give the order at once," he said.

"Yes, my lord," he replied.

None of Pedro's knights said a word, for the head on the floor was a mighty suppressant of the words that might yet form.

"The only problem with your plan, I now see, is my treasury. It will take days to load the gold, jewels and plate into wagons; to leave that behind would be to provide Enrique with enough riches to purchase my defeat," Pedro said.

Córdoba looked directly at Pedro and said, "Speed is of the utmost importance, my lord. Take but a portion of your gold; coin and whatever is easily transportable. Bury the rest and return to fight another day. Prince Edward has gold enough for a dozen armies," Córdoba said.

Pedro was nodding his agreement. "Yes, I will bury some, and send some of it on to Seville, and some also to Bordeaux as pledge against a future army. I will travel with some coin, for it may be necessary to buy my way across Castile," Pedro said.

Córdoba bent his head in deference.

Pedro strode from the room, barking a command for his aide-de-camp to accompany him.

Ayala motioned for Córdoba to stay. "You have gained the favour of the king," he said.

"I merely shared an idea to help solve a predicament that adversely affects us all," Córdoba replied.

"That took courage, for if Pedro had not liked your idea, your head would now be rolling next to that one."

They stared at the blood splattered corner of the room where the other head had rolled to a few feet from the body.

"It was worth the risk," he replied.

"It is always like this with Pedro, always walking the cliff's edge. The closer you get to him, the closer to the edge you get. Are you sure you are ready for that?"

"Thank you for your helpful advice, Don Pero. I must ready myself for the coming journey so I can be of service to our king. Good night," Córdoba said, and left.

•   •   •

The next morning, Pedro and a small group of followers, including Córdoba and Ayala, entered the courtyard where squires held the reins of several horses. The western gate, the Arco de Santa Maria, was twenty paces wide, the gate open. They mounted their rounceys and palfreys.

Several servants and merchants who had set up stalls outside the gate and who were in the process of taking them down before the impending invasion entered the courtyard, curious.

"Quickly," Pedro said to Ayala as they settled their mounts.

There were at most fifty travellers accompanying Pedro, including twenty nobles, fifteen valets and esquires, and fifteen knights, along with over a dozen pack horses. Enough men and horses to get the attention of the locals, but not enough to sound an alarm.

Ayala noted a merchant at the gate saying a few words to a boy, who then ran away.

"We must be off," Pedro said to Ayala as he watched two servants struggling to lift a heavy hemp bag onto a cart. They lost their grip, and the bag dropped, the contents spilling onto the cobblestoned courtyard. Gold plate shone in the spring sunlight.

They scrambled to gather up the fallen items.

"Leave it! You're too slow. We must go," Pedro said.

"But the cart has silver and gold plate and paintings and many other valuables," one said.

"Leave it all, I say, do you hear me? Leave it," he shouted.

A crowd of onlookers was forming by the gate.

"My lord. The rest of the treasury is still to be brought down from the tower," Yenez said.

"Leave it. We must depart now," Pedro said, panic in his eyes as he again looked to the courtyard entrance.

Ayala noted the heightening fear on Pedro's face.

"But my lord, Enrique is still…" Córdoba said.

"For God's sake, will you leave it! We must depart!" he screamed.

The crowd at the gate was now blocking the only exit.

"And your crown? Shall we ride first to Los Huelgas to retrieve it?" Ayala asked.

"We must go! Now," he whispered loudly.

"Do you flee your people, Pedro?" cried a woman.

More people began shouting as the crowd flooded into the courtyard, surrounding Pedro.

Ayala noted that several priests and acolytes were now watching from the steps of the Cathedral.

"Why do you dress as a merchant?" asked a merchant.

"Good people of Burgos…" Pedro began, holding his hand out to try to calm the increasingly boisterous crowd. Pedro's horse was spirited, no doubt due to the rumbling crowd, and Pedro kept turning in circles to calm it.

"Why do you forsake us, my lord?" shouted a tall, burly man who stepped forward.

"I must travel swiftly to Seville, for Enrique seeks to take both my family and my treasury," he said smoothly, as if the truth of it had always been on his lips.

A murmur arose from the crowd; some voiced their acceptance but most creased their brows in worry.

"Our enemies are almost upon us, yet you do not choose to face them with your soldiers and defend the city and your people against them. What then would you have us do? How should we defend ourselves if you leave us?" a burly merchant asked.

"I command you do the best that you can do," Pedro said.

Ayala shook his head. Pedro was saying he was abandoning them. They would know this and not forget.

"My lord, if we cannot defend ourselves, will you release us from our oath that we have given to protect this city, an oath we have given three times?" said a courageous merchant.

"Yes, you are released from your oath," Pedro said quickly. "I must depart. Go with God," he added, and whipped his horse forward, forcing his way through them. Ayala, Córdoba and the others followed behind.

The confused men and women stepped aside. Some cried out, "Stay my lord," but their voices were lost in the jangle of harnesses, clomp of hooves and rattle of carts as Pedro galloped through the massive archway.

A priest from the top step of the cathedral shouted, "Coward!" but the noise of the horses and shouts of his men smothered his cry.

Then, in an instant, the royal entourage was gone, and the people were left to make their own decisions. Defend the city, or join Enrique.

Ayala was one of the last to leave and shifted in his saddle to see the crowd descend upon the cart that had been left behind and fight for the plate piled upon it. The last image was of the crowd pushing and shoving to get into the tower.

Ayala kneed his destrier to catch up with the others. His doubts about Pedro had begun with the murder of his friend Jiminez, and had solidified hearing Pedro lie to the people of the city. Ayala knew that if a king could turn his back on his own people in order to save his skin, he would surely turn his back on his soldiers, his friends, and him. Pedro could not be trusted.

Ayala followed Pedro south as they travelled beside the Rio Arionzon. As the others exited the Arco de San Martin on the western wall of the city, no one noticed Ayala steer his horse left and head for the eastern gate at the Arco de San Gil, and toward the advancing army of Enrique.

CHAPTER 15
NORTH OF BURGOS, MARCH 29, 1366
IMPROMPTU PUY

"Hold there," a guard said, trying to make out who was approaching in the dusk twilight.

Ayala held. He had expected to be captured this far north and east, for it was the direction he knew Enrique's army was coming from.

"Who are you?" the soldier demanded.

"Who might I be addressing?" Ayala replied.

"Captain of the Guard. State your business, and be quick about it," the captain snapped.

"I am Don Pedro López de Ayala, Standard Bearer of the Order of the Sash, recently departed from Burgos, with important news for Enrique Trastamara," Ayala said.

"Burgos? Ayala? You are Pedro's lieutenant! Bind this man!" the captain shouted.

Two soldiers approached.

"Hold fast. I *was* Pedro's man, but no more. I have vital news of Pedro that I must share with Enrique," Ayala said.

"How do we know you're not a spy sent by Pedro to murder Enrique?" the captain asked.

"You don't. But you can see I have no weapon. And if you prevent me from having an audience with Enrique and what I have to report comes to fruition, then you will be the one put in chains," Ayala replied.

The captain pondered what Ayala said.

"Bring him," he said to the two soldiers, "But bind him well first, for if he escapes or harms Enrique, it will be the death of you both," he added.

Ayala was led to a huge tent hundreds of yards away, his hands now tied together with hemp rope.

"Halt," shouted a hulking guard standing near the entrance to the tent. He towered over a second guard across the gap.

"A recently arrived noble escaping Burgos. He says he has important news for our lord," the captain said.

"What news? I will determine how important it may be," the guard said, his low voice vibrating with menace.

"I am Don Pero López de Ayala and will speak only to Enrique Trastamara," Ayala said.

The huge guard's eyes lit up. "Ah, you should have said so. Welcome, Don Pero. Your name and reputation are well known in Castile. Enter," he said as he widened the tent opening.

Ayala nodded his thanks to the guard and stepped through the gap into a surprisingly bright space. The tent must have been fifty feet across and forty feet high, with fourscore or more torches blazed in hanging sconces, a fire burning at the centre in a brazier. Smoke wafted up through a gap at the top of the tent, masking a figure standing by the fire.

"So, you are the legendary Don Pedro López de Ayala," Enrique said, stepping forward to greet Ayala.

"My lord," Ayala replied, awkwardly bending one knee in a bow, "I know not that I am legendary, for that would imply my death."

"Up Don Pero. A legendary soldier, poet, chronicler, courtier and nobleman. But tell me—should I now add spy to that list?" he asked.

"I come of my own accord to share news, my lord. Pedro has fled Burgos. He sent hundreds ahead of him west. They think he will follow, but under cover of darkness, he and few retainers plan to veer south to Seville."

"And why would you leave him to tell me this? How am I to verify the truth of this?"

"Send word to the masters of the city. They will tell how the people confronted Pedro in the courtyard of the Archbishop's palace earlier today. He absolved them of their oath to defend the city, told them to defend themselves, then fled. He even left some of his treasure in his haste. I was there. I followed him for a short while then stole away unseen. Your scouts will soon deliver the truth of my words," Ayala said.

"Left his treasure, you say?" Enrique asked, his interest piqued.

"Yes, he took some thirty-six thousand doblas, jewels, gold, and silver jewellery, but left much gold and silver plate and candlesticks. Too heavy to carry. A fortune remains," Ayala replied.

Enrique stared at Ayala. He faced a soldier standing beside him and nodded. The soldier departed.

"Your family is wealthy, and is of very noble blood," Enrique said, as if these facts were accusations. "They have supported Pedro for many years."

"It is true. My family is loyal to his crown, I cannot deny that history. But I also cannot deny the harm he has inflicted upon Castile and my family. He has gone too far, and asked too much of too many, including me," Ayala replied.

"Your family provided gold for his soldiers, who killed my men and my family."

"My lord, Pedro demanded gold, and if we had not paid, we would have been killed, like so many others. When I witnessed him abandon Burgos, leaving the city undefended, I found I could support his cause no more. I could abide by many things he has done, but I can no longer stand by a king who would run from his own people and leave them defenceless," Ayala said.

"A coward in the end," Enrique said.

Ayala nodded at Enrique's words.

"But why join me, Ayala? You could have returned to your family and simply refused to support Pedro," he said.

"Some in my family do not feel as I do. I am my own man, and now seek to see Pedro's reign and power destroyed, once and for all. I want to see a more worthy man on the throne, and that man is you. I know much about Pedro. That knowledge will be helpful to your cause. And then," he added, a smile forming, "once you have claimed the crown, I will chronicle his cowardice and your noble victory and share my words with the world," he added.

Ayala could see that his words had piqued Enrique's interest. Enrique surely knew of Ayala's chronicles and poetry, and he stared at Ayala for a few moments, considering, then replied. "Until my scouts return, you can join the other poets and chroniclers in the stockade."

"Other?" Ayala asked.

"Yes, you poets seem inexorably attracted to this war. The herald of Sir John Chandos, Gawain, was captured just yesterday. Geoffrey Chaucer, page to King Edward, claims to be a poet as well. Do you know of him?"

"Gawain is well known, for he writes well of the many deeds of Sir John. I know nothing of this other man." There was no reason to reveal that he had already met Chaucer.

"You will become fast friends with both. The herald is a clever wordsmith and Chaucer has a clever tongue. Like you," Enrique said, then added in a mutter, "Too clever by half."

•   •   •

The poets were kept in a hastily built stockade of wooden posts, a hemp rope running around each post tying them together. Chaucer noted Ayala's intense black eyes searching his own.

"Falconry, poetry, Boethius, my chronicles, Doña Constanza, my king," Ayala said in his eloquent Castilian.

Chaucer looked about at the men around the fire. Light and shadow danced across the faces of Gawain, Alfonso, and Ayala, who awaited his reply.

"My daughter, my wife to be, poetry, Boethius, and my king," Chaucer replied. His Castilian had improved since he had arrived.

Ayala smiled. "Family first, a noble sentiment. Perchance when I have a child, I will feel the same. Until then, my falcons are like my children, and they will be first," he replied.

Chaucer nodded his understanding.

"But a daughter before a wife? Were you too keen for the first to have the second?"

"In truth, yes, my daughter Elizabeth was born out of wedlock. Then sent to a nunnery. I shall marry my woman once I regain her favour," Chaucer replied.

"And how shall you do that?" Ayala asked.

"Not be in a stockade would be a start," Chaucer replied. Not a complete answer, but one that would suffice.

Ayala opened his mouth to say something, paused as if to consider his words, then said, "Boethius is the next choice for both of us, after poetry. Let us drink to Lady Fortune bringing two souls together who share the same passion for such a philosopher poet." He sat up, reached over and clanked Chaucer's wooden cup with his own cup of wine—provided to them by the guard—then clanked Gawain's to his left and Alfonso's to his right.

"Gawain?" Chaucer asked.

Before Gawain could reply, Ayala asked, "How did you end up here? Are you not the famed herald of the even more famed Chandos?"

"Sir John Chandos sent me to Logrono and Olite to assess the mood of the people of both Castile and Navarre, and to find out if the time was ripe for Enrique to claim the crown. I must have asked too many questions and was taken a week ago outside Olite," he said.

"But that is in land controlled by Carlos, is it not?" Chaucer asked.

"Carlos is loyal to no one but himself. He did not even bother to interrogate me, and sold me quickly to Enrique as a spy," Gawain said.

"You were lucky to have been captured by Carlos, for if Enrique's men had found you first, you might be missing parts of yourself by now," Ayala said.

Gawain broke the sudden quiet, "I would choose a quill, ink and sheets of vellum, and a copy of Herodotus' *Histories* and also Thucydides' *History of the Peloponnesian War*."

"Herodotus and Thucydides? That is all?" Ayala asked.

"That is everything," Gawain said.

Chaucer noted the others nodding, for it said something of Gawain that he knew what was important to him at the age of twenty.

"Family," Alfonso blurted out.

Their heads swivelled to Alfonso, seated on the other side of Chaucer.

"Where is your family, Alfonso?" Ayala asked.

"Everywhere. Navarre, Castile, Aragon. All in this land are family," he said.

"To family," Ayala said, lifting his goblet.

"To family," the three others said in reply, lifting their own goblets.

Quiet settled over the men as they stared into the fire and watched the smoke lifting to the starry heavens above.

"Tell me, Ayala, to which king do you drink now? Pedro or Enrique?" asked Chaucer.

"If you had asked me but a year, month or even a week ago, my answer would be Pedro. But no more," Ayala replied.

Chaucer listened closely.

"He had my cousin flayed alive. The skin peeled from his bones. And do you know why? Because my cousin had the temerity, the courage, to say to Pedro's face he was making a mistake in demanding so much from those who had given so much already. That he was going too far. Pedro said to me, 'I have only just begun to ask for what must be given freely in order to maintain my rightful crown and not let the bastard take it from me'. I will see that dog Pedro killed," Ayala added in a whisper.

He lifted his head and stared directly at Chaucer. "And yet I also have no love for the bastard Enrique, for he upends hundreds of years of tradition and bloodlines by making a play for the crown. And his enmity toward followers of the Jewish faith is distasteful. Yet I will fight with him to see Pedro unseated from his throne, a throne protected by carpet knights and heanlings, their ideals poisoned by ambition," he said. His eyes clouded as he recalled past pains. "That is why I am here now, for I will do all in my power to see Enrique crowned at Burgos," he added.

"Carpet knight? What is?" Alfonso asked.

"A knight who spends more time on the carpet of his lady than on the battlefield," Chaucer replied.

"Carpet of his lady?" Alfonso asked.

"The covering of a lady's room, and also the hair covering her private parts," Gawain replied, pointing to his groin.

The others nodded, except Alfonso, who showed only confusion, but then his face lightened, and he burst out laughing. "Carpet knight. Funny, no?"

They smiled.

"What story will you tell at the puy? One of Pedro's many cruelties?" Chaucer asked Ayala, breaking the silence that had fallen over them like a rain-laden cloud.

"No, for those are well known, and the story must surprise," Ayala replied.

Chaucer smiled, for surprise was indeed key to a good story.

"I may tell a frame tale," Ayala added.

Chaucer's questioning expression led Ayala to continue.

"A tale within a tale. Like *One Thousand and One Arabian Nights*. Do you know of that story?" he asked.

"I have heard of it. I came across a copy of it in Logrono, but I have not read it," Chaucer replied. He didn't mention that Calveley had seized his lovely books.

"Such a story allows one to say what one truly feels and thinks, protected by the fiction of the framing device," Ayala said.

"A most excellent device, and one I would hope to master one day," said Chaucer and tilted his head again.

"Boccaccio also does the same in his *Decameron*. Have you read that book?" Ayala asked.

Chaucer shook his head no. "There are many books I have yet to read. I envy you your library."

"You must read it when this war is won. It is about a group of ten courtiers—seven women and three men who escape the Black Death ravaging Florence and retire to a villa where they each tell ten tales to pass the days; so, one hundred tales in all."

Chaucer and the others listened intently.

"Like the *Arabian Nights*, the frame tale allows Boccaccio to say what he wants through the stories of the courtiers, with wicked men and women, priests and nuns, wealthy and poor held up to the light of the sun, their flaws exposed," he said.

"The book is rare, then? And expensive?" Chaucer asked.

"On the contrary, there are hundreds of copies available now. The pope deemed it unholy and excommunicated Boccaccio and disallowed the book to be sold, even at market," Ayala replied.

"And so, as with most things that the Church tries to repress, it became more popular and can be found through other means, if one knows where to look," Gawain said.

"I would be most desirous in obtaining a copy of such books," Chaucer replied.

"We shall see. The Church is very powerful in Navarre, and one must be careful not to be seen with such books, especially if one is here to…what do you call your task here? Trade in wine? Or is it stories that you trade in?" Ayala said.

Chaucer said nothing.

Ayala took a long draught of his wine and eyed Chaucer directly. "What is it exactly that you are doing here, Chaucer, that would lead you to be locked up with Gawain?"

"I am here for wine, yes, to increase trade for my king. And of course, my trade as a poet is in stories, so I will take any I find and make them my own. It is what I, nay, what we, do, is it not?" Chaucer replied.

"To be here, at this time. with a war afoot? Yes, Chaucer, it is surprising. And dangerous. It is a good story, but I am not convinced it is the full story. You may need more help than you believe, both in the telling and the story told."

Chaucer shivered and did not reply. The days were warmer and the nights colder than in London at this time of the year. He picked up two thicker branches and lay them on the fire, which cackled louder after catching fire, sending sparks and flames upwards.

"Tell me, what rules are we to follow here in the puy?" Chaucer asked.

"Tell the best story and win the gold, as with all puys," Ayala replied.

"I have seen different rules in different puys in my time, each set according to the Puy Society who holds it," Chaucer replied. "And I have seen poets flout such rules and lose," he added.

"'Tis true that there are some rules. Firstly, before beginning, one must bow before the king three times; to bow only twice would mean defeat before even beginning. Secondly, one must never use the king's name, or that of any member of his family, in the telling of the story."

Chaucer inclined his head. "Both rules are easy to follow."

"You forget…rule of happy end," said Alfonso.

"Happy end?" Chaucer asked.

"One must end their story with some happy or uplifting event," Ayala said.

"Happy and uplifting? To end a story such a way would be to twist many stories too far, and thus break them," Chaucer said.

Alfonso shrugged.

"You asked. Those are the rules," Ayala said, also shrugging.

"Who sets such rules?" Chaucer asked.

Alfonso shrugged again.

"They have always been this way," Ayala replied.

Chaucer looked to Gawain, who shrugged.

"But we have no audience to applaud or to choose the champion," Chaucer said.

"We shall each applaud and, as a group, choose the champion," Ayala said.

"But what of the theme?" Chaucer added.

"Ah yes, the theme…" Ayala said.

"To be chosen by the most noble in attendance. We have no lord or prince with us today, but Ayala is of noble blood," Gawain noted.

Chaucer nodded.

"If I must, then I choose loyalty as my theme," Ayala said.

Chaucer pondered the theme. They were amidst a war started because of a betrayal, a broken trust begetting a grievance. The murder of his twin brother, and many others, by Pedro aggrieved Enrique. The enmity within him had been so long in place, the root of it no longer seemed relevant. And mercenaries like Calveley appeared to have no loyalty to his king.

Yes, loyalty was a good theme, a timely theme. For who is loyal? Who is not? Calveley is loyal to gold, yes, but not Edward. Pippa is loyal to the queen, and perchance Gaunt, but is she loyal to me? And how does one prove one's loyalty?

Ayala nodded and began the puy.

"A woman had been married five times. She was tired of men making rules for her and other women that they themselves did not follow, like men who married more than once and were called vigorous, whereas she was called harlot. She complained that the world thought women inferior, when in fact it is they who were more sensible and should rule over men. She then told a tale of a knight, Don Garcia, who assailed a young maiden, a lady named Beatrice, at the court of King Alfonso, and fled the next morning. King Alfonso issued a decree that he must be brought to justice, and when Don Garcia was captured, the king condemned him to death for his dishonourable act. His queen, Maria, pled with her husband to spare his life and allow her to pass judgement upon him. King Alfonso assented. The queen told Don Garcia his life would be spared only if he can learn what it is that women truly desire most, and gave him one year and a day to find the answer. Everywhere Don Garcia roamed he asked women what they most desired, and he never received the same answer—riches, fame, clothes, pleasure in bed. One year to the day later, he journeyed to the court still without the answer. He stopped in a wood outside the castle and spied twenty-four maidens dancing and singing, and as he approached, they suddenly disappeared, leaving an old woman standing in their place. He explained his predicament, and she said she may know the answer, but he must grant her any wish that she desired. The knight agreed, for he had run out of time. At court the next morning he gave his answer to the queen: women desire sovereignty over their husbands, which all the women gathered there agreed to be true, and Don Garcia was freed. The old woman who had accompanied him explained that Don Garcia had promised to marry her, and then asked then and there for his hand in marriage. At first upset, he relented. In bed that night, he was repulsed by the sight of her and she was upset by his reaction. But she then explained that he is fortunate, as no man will desire her and so she will be a virtuous wife. She asked him if he would prefer an old, ugly but loyal wife, or a young, pretty unfaithful one?"

Ayala stopped and took a long drink from his goblet, keeping the others waiting for the ending. It was a storytelling trick that he had learnt long ago, the delay heightening the audience's interest.

He finally continued. "The knight said the choice is hers, not his. Happy to hear that Don Garcia had acceded to her sovereignty, she said he shall then have both beauty and fidelity, for he had truly understood what women desire, and she turned into a beautiful young woman."

Ayala then added, "The woman who was telling the story then ended her tale by saying, 'May Jesus bless all women with meek, young, and submissive husbands.'"

"Bravo!" shouted Gawain. The others clapped.

"Where did you hear that story from?" Chaucer asked.

"My mother passed it down to me," Ayala replied.

Chaucer tilted his head and nodded.

I must remember that story and tell it to Pippa.

"Gawain?" asked Ayala. The fire cast light and shadow across Gawain's face.

Gawain looked up and said, "I will tell a story of King Croesus, leader of the Lydians, and the most famous prediction from the Oracle of Delphi."

Chaucer, Alfonso, and Ayala looked on, curious.

"The most famous king of Lydia was Croesus, known throughout the world for his wealth. Croesus was threatened by the Persian army led by Cyrus the Great. Croesus wondered if he should move against the Persians before they grew stronger.

He first needed to hear what the oracles said, but he wanted to be sure the oracles were accurate in their predictions. He decided to test them and sent messengers to the leading oracles with strict instructions. Exactly one-hundred days after leaving Croesus, the messengers asked each oracle the same question: What was King Croesus of Lydia doing at that moment?

When the messengers returned, Croesus eagerly read the written replies of the oracles. The Pythian priestess of Delphi had written:

'I can tell how many grains of sand lie at the bottom of the sea.

And those who cannot speak can communicate with me.

Now I feel the scent of a dish that is hot,

Lamb and tortoise boil in a big bronze pot.'

Croesus was impressed, for he was at that very time making tortoise and lamb soup in a bronze cauldron. He sent another messenger to Delphi with the following question:

'Should he go to war with the Persians?'

The Delphic Oracle replied:

'If Croesus goes to war, he will destroy a great empire.'

Croesus was pleased, for it surely meant if he went to war against the Persians, the Persian empire would fall. He sent her more gifts and asked one final question:

'Will I reign for many years as king of Lydia?'

Her reply, 'When a mule becomes leader of the Mede, then it is time to flee,' pleased Croesus even more because surely Medes would never choose a mule for their leader, and he would not have to flee. He readied his army to attack the Persians. But the wisest among his advisers warned him against embarking on this war.'"

"Gawain," interrupted Ayala. "How long will your story take? I still need to try to get some sleep this eve."

Chaucer nodded in agreement.

"As long as the story needs to take!" snapped Gawain, and he continued.

"Croesus ignored his advisor's advice. His army met Cyrus at the battle of Pteria, but neither was victorious. Croesus returned to Sardis, and Cyrus followed. Cyrus's most trusted general, a Mede called Harpagus, suggested the camels who had been carrying the bags of the army be put in the front line because horses were afraid of camels. When the Lydian cavalry charged, their horses were terrified, and the Persian army defeated the Lydians in battle."

"Ayala, be so kind as to refill my goblet, for this tale runs far on long legs," Chaucer said.

Gawain shot Chaucer a frown and continued.

"Croesus retreated into Sardis. The city walls were sturdy and high, but a sharp-eyed Persian soldier saw that it was possible to climb up a part of the wall that had not been properly maintained. He clambered up, followed by other Persian soldiers. Soon they were swarming over the battlements of Sardis, who were taken by surprise, heavily outnumbered, and all too easily overcome. Croesus tried to escape by mixing in with the crowd, hoping he would not be recognized. At his side was his one remaining son, who was unable to speak. A Persian soldier ran towards them, and in terror, his son called out, 'Please sir, do not kill my father, Croesus, King of Lydia.' Croesus was immediately captured, and Lydia was defeated. Sardis was in flames. The Pythian priestess of Delphi, on hearing of the loss, said that a great empire had fallen, just as she had predicted, but that empire was not Persia but Lydia.

And as for her advice that Croesus would be safe until a mule became king of Persia, she said, 'A mule is a cross between a horse and a donkey, just as Cyrus was born to a mother who was a Mede and father who was a Persian. And so, a mule was indeed on the throne of Persia.' And that is the story of Croesus and his misreading of the Oracle of Delphi.'"

"No happy ending," Alfonso said.

"I am happy the story has finally ended," said Chaucer. They all laughed and applauded. They were more guidelines than rules, and this was a puy judged by friends, not kings.

When a guard shouted, "Quiet!" they lowered their voices.

"Don Pero, you look concerned," Chaucer said.

"Both Pedro and Enrique are always consulting seers for portents of what the future may hold, especially before battles," Ayala replied. "I fear Enrique, like Croesus, may have misread the signs," Ayala added.

"Which signs?" Gawain asked.

"He thinks defeating Pedro will bring him the crown of Castile, but it will not bring him the love of the people of Castile. Without their love the crown will not be so easily kept," Ayala said.

The men took swigs of their wine. Chaucer poked the fire.

Chaucer looked up. Something in Gawain's story about misreading signs gave Chaucer an idea of how to turn Calveley, with Ayala and Doña Constanza the key.

"I must relieve myself," said Chaucer, rising and leaving the fire.

"As must I," Ayala said.

As the two men pissed onto either side of a tree at the corner of the stockade, Ayala whispered to Chaucer, "And Doña Constanza? Any news?"

Chaucer smiled.

"I last heard Sir Hugh met her and was smitten by her," he said.

Ayala nodded. "I heard the same."

"Perchance through Calveley you two may find a path together," Chaucer said, still sorting out the details of a plan only now beginning to form.

"I don't see that as possible if he asks her for her hand," Ayala said.

They finished up and tucked themselves in, and paused before returning to the others.

"It matters not if they marry. You and she may still find a way to meet," Chaucer said.

Ayala looked at Chaucer, said only "Perchance" and returned to the fire. Chaucer followed.

It was Alfonso's turn to tell the next story, but he was in no hurry. He got up, put a small log on the fire, poked at it with a stick, sat back down, took a drink from his goblet, found it empty and refilled it, and refilled those of the other men, who sat expectant, waiting. He finally began.

"Eleanor de Guzman born in Seville to nobility; her great-grandfather was King Alfonso of León. Eleanor married young, then widowed at eighteen. Met King Alfonso of Castile, León and Galicia when he seventeen. He think she a beauty, but married to Maria of Portugal. So took Eleanor as mistress."

"Alfonso and Maria had two children, Fernando and Pedro—current king. Alfonso ignored wife after children born, and loved Eleanor. She was beautiful, intelligent, well-loved, soon most powerful woman in kingdom. Eleanor and king always together."

"Eleanor and Alfonso had ten children, including Enrique, Fadrique, Sancho and Tello. They were given riches and titles. Eleanor became wealthy landowner. But gained enemies, and in thirteen fifty, King Alfonso died suddenly of pestilence. Pedro became king. His mother Maria ordered Eleanor imprisoned. A year later, Eleanor was executed. Bastard sons Enrique and his brothers went to war against half-brother King Pedro for crown," said Alfonso. "Pedro invited Enrique's twin brother Fadrique to dinner. Crushed head with mace, made blood soup."

Chaucer blanched.

"Angry Enrique joined Pere of Aragon in war against Pedro. Pedro will lose this battle, but will ask Prince Edward to help oust Enrique and win the war."

Chaucer tilted his head.

"Is why you here, yes?" Alfonso asked. "Get Calveley to fight for Pedro, win war."

Ayala and Gawain turned to Chaucer as they learned of his true task.

"Something like that, yes," Chaucer said. Alfonso had a very acute understanding of the politics at play. He would need to stay close to Alfonso.

"Thank you for the story Alfonso, I only knew part of it. Quite illuminating."

"What 'illuminating?'" Alfonso asked.

"Hold a candle in a dark place," Chaucer added.

Alfonso's face changed, revealing an enigmatic smile that could mean joy or sorrow.

"Be careful where shed light. Sometime ugly things appear, yes?" he said.

"But the story does not end happily," said Gawain.

"It does for Enrique, for he has ousted Pedro," Alfonso said.

All heads bobbed up and down.

"Is your name not the same as Sancho Alfonso, one of King Alfonso's ten children with Eleanor?" Ayala asked. "I heard Carlos say it, and he seemed to know of you," Ayala added.

Alfonso was silent for a moment, then the silence stretched and became awkward.

"I am named the same, it is true," he finally replied.

"The Latin for Alfonso means 'noble and ready', said Gawain.

"Are you? Noble? Ready?" asked Chaucer.

"Ready to play game of life and death with those who play game also."

Ayala and Chaucer both looked at Alfonso.

"How very interesting," Gawain said.

"Chaucer, you are next," Gawain said.

Chaucer poked the fire, then stood up. Before he could begin, he was interrupted by shouts and the sound of hooves and armour, followed by several knights arriving in the camp. They dismounted a few yards from the enclosure.

From the shouting and drinking that erupted, they could hear something about Pedro.

"You are free to go," the guard said, swinging open the gate to the enclosure.

"Free?" Chaucer repeated, unsure if he had heard correctly.

"Yes, Pedro has fled Burgos and Enrique is now king and he would have you meet him in Burgos after he is crowned," the guard said, then remounted his horse and headed southwest, towards Burgos.

And just like that, the stories, and the puy, came to an end.

•   •   •

Each was given a mount, and on the journey to Burgos the next day, Ayala recounted to the group his last day with Pedro.

"I chose not to speak of this last night for fear of being called a liar, but I was there when he fled from Burgos with only a few knights and attendants. I watched the people confront him in the palace courtyard. I heard him absolve them of their oath to him and to the city, saying he needed to protect his family and treasure by taking refuge in Seville. I chose then to turn away and made my way to find Enrique," Ayala said.

"Pedro left his people defenceless?" Chaucer asked.

"It is Pedro the Cruel we speak of," Ayala replied.

"Pedro the Just is a phantom," Chaucer replied. "A man's true name follows him around like the stink of shit attached to a boot," he said.

Alfonso nodded.

"Alfonso? What think you of this news?" Chaucer asked.

"Pedro return with Prince Edward's army," he said as he swayed on his palfrey behind Chaucer.

"Maybe yes. He has too much pride and too much hatred for Enrique to let that bastard rule his country for long," Ayala replied.

Alfonso shook his head at the use of "bastard."

"Alfonso? You disagree?"

Alfonso said nothing.

"You rolled your eyes," said Ayala.

"We are all bastards in this land," he said.

Chaucer nodded, but absently, for he was lost in his own thoughts.

I have failed in turning Calveley, and will be surely treated like a bastard upon my return home.

•   •   •

Representatives from Burgos had arrived at the camp, inviting Enrique and his army to enter the city. The next morning, Enrique travelled to the abbey of Santa María la Real de Las Huelgas to be crowned king.

Alfonso, Gawain, Ayala and Chaucer approached Burgos without incident and dismounted, walking their horses as they approached the city. Chaucer was last, for he did not feel like speaking to any of his group. He would join them in watching Enrique crowned, then leave at once for Bordeaux and ask his prince to forgive him for his failure.

The crowds had grown even larger as they had entered Burgos, the streets clogged with people and those from outside the capital who wanted to see a new king wear the crown of Castile.

The bell tower of Las Huelgas soon became visible a mile west of the city. As they neared the abbey, two trumpets announced the beginning of the ceremony.

They passed through the pointed archway entrance into a vast square crowded with onlookers. In the middle was a gorgeously wrought fountain of four intertwined eels, water streaming from the flat ugly head of each eel. To their left was another gated archway that they entered into a smaller rectangular courtyard with a long portico that ran along the west side of the abbey.

They then entered a long corridor, at least fifty feet high, with windows set on either end and filled with people. The trumpets blared again. They pushed their way through the throng halfway down the corridor and turned right into the narthex of the abbey. While not as large as Burgos Cathedral, the abbey was perfectly designed, with two levels of elegant, pointed arches running the length to the eastern end, where the afternoon sun streamed through a tall arched window lighting the altar below. They pushed through the crowd and passed several stone caskets of the kings and queens of Castile and Leon, including Enrique the First, and Eleanor, Queen of Castile, the daughter of Eleanor of Aquitaine. As they approached the middle of the nave, their way was soon blocked by the press of bodies, but they were less than thirty feet away from the altar, where they knew Enrique stood behind the altar screen with the Bishop of Las Huelgas.

Chaucer noted that a few feet before the altar was a tall wooden stand with a massive book laying open upon it. He gave Alfonso a questioning glance and pointed at the book.

"Music. Las Huelgas Codex," Alfonso replied.

Earlier, Chaucer had asked Ayala about the significance of the abbey, and he told him that Castile's kings and queens were baptized, married and buried here. It was the soul and heart of the kingdom. It was where King Pedro had been baptized. He also told him that the nuns of the abbey created the music and played only during a crowning or a funeral. It was music heard nowhere else in any land.

As if on cue, from somewhere above and behind them, voices rang out—the choir. The music had begun.

Just then, the bishop stepped out from behind the chancel screen, followed by Enrique, resplendent in a purple and gold cloak lined with ermine. The golden crown of Castile sat atop a tall table set between the two men. The crown had always been kept here, and Pedro had fled Burgos in such fear that he had left it behind.

The bishop stood facing Enrique, who was rock still, his eyes locked upon the crown. As the song ended, the bishop began to intone about the history of this sacred place, how a new king would be crowned to lead the people of Castile and Leon, and bear the responsibilities that great and honourable power entailed.

The bishop eyed Enrique as he said the word "responsibilities," as if stressing that Enrique should not fail as Pedro had.

A murmur of assent emanated across the abbey, a none too subtle dig at Pedro, who had abandoned his people. They would not soon forget.

"...and I crown you, King of Castile," said the bishop as he motioned for Enrique to lower himself, and then he lifted and placed the bejeweled crown atop Enrique's head. The crowd cheered, and Enrique waved. Then he put up his hand, and the crowd quieted.

Enrique said in a loud, resonant voice, "Thank you, Bishop. I accept this crown and honour the responsibility to protect the people of Burgos, and of Castile."

The crowd cheered. Chaucer knew that Enrique's words were deliberately targeted at Pedro. He would remember that detail for when he chronicled this moment in a poem. The crowd's cheer emboldened him to continue.

"Pedro was a murderer who ruined this great kingdom. Now he has run away to lick his wounds, and will no doubt run like the coward he is into the arms of his protector, Prince Edward. I will never run from my duty to you or to Castile, for I have waited too long and suffered too much to forget the responsibility that this crown brings. I promise to protect you, and in return, I seek your support," he said, his words now almost a shout.

The crowd responded with a louder cheer.

"Now, as King of Castile," he said once the crowd quieted. "I shall carry out my first responsibility. Bertrand du Guesclin, step forward."

Du Guesclin did. Dressed in polished black armour, but without his helmet, he awkwardly kneeled.

"By the power vested in me by this crown, I name you, Bertrand du Guesclin, Count of Trastamara, and Duke of Molina."

Du Guesclin rose and stepped back and faced the crowd, face blank.

The crowd cheered.

"Sir Hugh Calveley, step forward."

Calveley did. He too wore armour, but it was a warrior's armour, dull and dented silver.

"By the power vested in this crown, I formally name you Sir Hugh Calveley, Count of Carrion."

Calveley stepped back.

The crowd cheered again. The choir sang forth.

Enrique took a step forward and began his journey down the altar stairs, then along the middle of the nave, waving at the cheering crowd. His wife and most trusted advisors followed, including du Guesclin and Calveley. The crowd parted, then came together as his entourage passed, following him as he stepped out of the abbey and into the sunlight, to the roar of the crowd in the courtyard, deafening those nearby.

Chaucer knew Enrique would not rest until Pedro had been found and killed. He was a patient man. It had been ten years since his brother Fadrique was murdered, but he would surely have his revenge. With the crown now upon his own head, he would bring its full power to bear upon Pedro. With du Guesclin and Calveley by his side.

But the king had tasked Chaucer with ensuring Calveley was on Pedro's side.

Enrique won this battle yet thinks even now of Pedro's return with Prince Edward and an army. I may yet have another chance to turn Calveley. But how?

And then Chaucer spotted her. A beautiful flower dressed in white. Doña Constanza stood to the side and watched Enrique and then Calveley pass by. She smiled at Calveley, and he smiled back. And Chaucer knew then how he might try to turn Lady Fortune's wheel.

•   •   •

"Where did Pedro escape to?" Chaucer asked Ayala two weeks later. Chaucer was planning his return passage to Bordeaux, for while he had failed to turn Calveley he would still need to report to Sir John Chandos and Prince Edward. And then would consider what to do about Pippa.

"My spies tell me Pedro had dressed as a merchant, and pretended to travel west and then in the dark of night fled south with a smaller band of knights. He must have skirted Madrid, for he had reached the safety of Toledo the next day. There, the people were loyal to Pedro. He then headed toward Seville. At Seville, the Rio Guadalquivir flows into the Gulf of Cadiz, and apparently Pedro told his treasurer Yanez to take his gold, hire a galley and make for Portugal. Pedro left Seville the same day and rode northwest to seek refuge in Galicia, which first required safe conduct through Portugal from Pedro's cousin, the king, but the King of Portugal had refused passage. Pedro finally reached the coast and paid for passage on a cog bound for San Sebastian. From there, I heard he headed north on horseback toward Bordeaux and Prince Edward's safe embrace.

"He could buy an army with his gold," Chaucer replied.

"Well, that's the problem. For as Pedro reached France, he received yet more bad news. Admiral Gil Bocanegra, a recent deserter, had fitted out a flotilla of galleys that had overtaken Yanez's treasure galley before it could leave the Rio Guadalquivir. Most of Pedro's treasure was captured and delivered to Enrique."

"Oh…" Chaucer said.

That would completely change things in Enrique's favour.

"Pedro was accompanied by his one remaining captain, Castro, and eight loyal knights. My spies tell me he only had some silver, jewellery and what remained of the gold he had left Burgos with— only twenty thousand doblas. One tenth of his original treasure, and it would be all that he could offer to Prince Edward for his aid. But he did also now have his three daughters who had joined him, and they were more valuable than jewels, for they carried his royal blood.

"A union of the crowns of England and Castile would be one King Charles of France would despise."

"Exactly. The only problem is the crown now lies atop the wrong head."

CHAPTER 16
BURGOS, MAY 18, 1366
ENRIQUE AND DOÑA CONSTANZA

An overcast sky threatened rain. Chaucer stood outside Burgos Palace in the central courtyard, haggling with a merchant who paused and held up his hand as another merchant whispered in his ear. The first merchant pulled on his beard.

"What happened?" Chaucer asked.

The merchant considered his reply. "Enrique gathered the riches Pedro had inexplicably left behind. His financier told him of the value, and Enrique, in considering the vastness of the empire he now controlled, realized he needed even more riches to fund his throne, and so gathered our five community leaders and merchants and demanded one million maravedis of the five Jewish merchants who stood before him. I was watching their faces that as one expressed shock at the sum Enrique had just shared. One said it was an impossible sum to gather. Enrique said if we don't bring him the gold, their lives, and those of their family, will be forfeit. He then declared a moratorium on Jewish loans to Christians."

"Why does Enrique hate the Jews so?" Chaucer asked.

"You may as well ask, why does the cloud above cover the sun? Who knows?"

Over the next few days, the Jewish merchants didn't receive what they should have when they sold their wealth, for such news travelled quickly, and each buyer drove a hard bargain. However, by the end of the week, the million gold maravedis had been gathered and delivered to Enrique. The community had lived in Burgos for hundreds of years and had never been asked for such a sacrifice. Most of the merchants had long-time relationships throughout the city, relationships built on trust and friendship and mutual benefit. As the rest of the population learned of Enrique's division, enmity against the newly crowned king began to spread. In one short week, Enrique had destroyed any goodwill he had gained the previous weeks in deposing Pedro.

•   •   •

The next day, Chaucer accompanied Doña to the marketplace to purchase some items she needed, and they talked as he accompanied her back to her lodgings.

"Why did you come to Burgos?" Doña asked.

"As you know, I failed in turning Calveley in time, but Pedro will try to return to reclaim his crown. I am sure of it. When he does, if Calveley then sides with him, victory will be his."

"And how will you now achieve what you first failed to do?" she asked.

"I need to first keep Calveley in Castile."

Doña nodded.

"He desires you," Chaucer said.

"Many men do. What of it?"

"Would you turn down gold from Calveley?"

She looked at him, stunned.

"I will seek an audience with Enrique and convince him to give your hand to Calveley in marriage," he added.

She blinked, then let out a chortle.

"Marry that oaf? Never. I love Ayala, and I will not be sold like chattel! I was the lady-in-waiting to Queen Eleanor, not some serving wench!"

"Why have you not yet married Ayala?" Chaucer asked. He had wondered before, after first seeing them together, their desire so keen, and he felt now that the question needed an answer.

"He is from a noble family, but is no longer wealthy since his family disowned him. I seek gold to rebuild my own family that was ruined by Enrique, so I would hope to find a man who can assist me. And it is even harder to consider while he takes gold from Pedro."

"Why?"

"Pedro would soon learn of my time as lady-in-waiting to King Pere's wife, Eleanor. He would not be well-disposed to see his trusted lieutenant marry a trusted servant of his sworn enemy."

"But..." Chaucer began.

"Is a story for later," she said.

But Chaucer would not give up so easily.

"Then marry Calveley. It would be a marriage in name only, providing you gold for your family, an admittedly too small recompense for all that has been taken from you. But if you appealed to Calveley's reasonable nature, you might arrange to still see Ayala. Calveley is not a stupid man and knows where your true feelings lie."

"His feelings lie between his legs, and he would surely kill Ayala if he found me with him," she snapped back.

They passed two men who turned their heads toward her raised voice and unladylike language.

"I think you miss the mark of the man," Chaucer countered.

"Perchance, but you would have me sleep with that man so you yourself can gain success," she said, now in a sharp whisper.

"My success is Ayala's success and your success, for if Calveley joins Pedro and defeats and perchance kills Enrique, you would help avenge your family's death. Ayala would claim his own success and reward, and surely Pedro would look more kindly upon your union. And Edward would recompense you for your effort. In gold. So you would gain the gold you seek, no matter the outcome."

Chaucer was willing to wager gold he did not have, for the stakes were now too high.

And saw her glance up, a sure sign of hesitation.

"Think on it, then give me your answer in the morning. I will see Enrique tomorrow," Chaucer said.

"You put a great amount of trust in me, Chaucer. And what of Enrique? Did he not try to have you killed? Do you not fear he will try to finish the task when he sees you?"

Chaucer had contemplated that very possibility. "With his crown now firmly upon his head, I do not think I pose any threat to Enrique. He now has what he sought."

"I will think upon what you have said, but do not hope too deeply," she said.

Chaucer nodded and strode away. It was all he could ask or hope for now.

•　　　•　　　•

Chaucer requested an audience with Enrique three times but was rebuffed each time by Enrique's advisors and guards. Even Ayala could not help Chaucer gain admittance.

Finally, Alfonso offered to provide Chaucer's message to Enrique.

"How will you succeed where I have failed? Where even Ayala has failed?" Chaucer asked as they drank wine in front of a tavern in the market square.

"I try. Will know soon," he simply said. He emptied his goblet and left.

Chaucer stayed and drank and ate. He sensed optimism in the air, a relief at the war being, if not over, then at least over for the people of the city who did not have to fight Enrique.

Alfonso returned soon with a sealed note in his hand. "Your admittance to the king," he said, and then poured himself more wine and downed it in one long pull.

"Alfonso, you astound me," Chaucer said, then emptied his own goblet.

"Is plain—a compliment, yes?" Alfonso replied.

"Yes," Chaucer said with a smile.

"One thing," Alfonso said as he stood.

Chaucer tilted his head, questioning.

"You speak direct to Enrique, yes?"

Chaucer nodded.

"Your debt to me still remains. You know what that means," Alfonso said.

He wants me to kill Enrique? Surely not.

"You will remain here?" Chaucer asked.

"Close by. I watch you."

Chaucer paid for the wine and they made for the palace. Alfonso's note gained them entrance, and they followed two guards down a long outdoor portico, their footsteps echoing loudly on the polished flagstones. Afternoon sunlight streamed through the top of the portico's arches as they approached the south end of the building where several courtiers, noblemen and merchants streamed out of the Porto de Santa Maria, the main entrance. Most wore smiles, no doubt recipients of Enrique's largesse.

A guard admitted them into an antechamber where they sat, and after a short time, they were told to enter. Chaucer rose and strode toward the hall. He turned to say a word to Alfonso, but he was still seated, a serious expression on his face. He shook his head. He was not coming, and his expression said what his tongue would not: "Take this opportunity and kill Enrique."

Any such thoughts vanished as Chaucer entered the cavernous hall and was bathed in glorious light cast by the stained-glass windows above that splattered multi-coloured hues across the stone walls and floor. Enrique sat in a huge, gilded chair atop a set of stairs at the end of the hall surrounded by guards, advisors, and supplicants. The coloured light twinkled off the jewels encrusted in the golden crown that sat slightly askew atop Enrique's head.

"Geoffrey Chaucer, page to King Edward the Third," shouted a guard.

"Welcome," Enrique said as Chaucer approached. At the bottom of the stairs, Chaucer bent a knee.

"Come closer," Enrique said. "The rest of you, away," he said, waving the gathering to leave.

"My lord, we must…" one advisor said.

"Must what?" he said, his tone sharp.

The advisor nodded and shooed the gathering away.

"Congratulations my lord. To be crowned King of Castile…" Chaucer said.

Enrique cut him off. "What brings you here, Chaucer? You seek employ? You are tired of the heavy chains of King Edward and would now join me, now that I wear this crown?" he asked.

Such an idea had never occurred to Chaucer, and his face showed his thoughts.

Enrique laughed. "I jest. I know you are Edward's man. And surely you have come for something I may give?" he said.

"Yes, my lord. I give thanks for your meeting with me."

Chaucer felt Enrique's eyes judging him.

"There is a delicate matter that impacts both England and Castile and that would benefit your wisdom," Chaucer began.

"I am listening."

"I would ask that you support the bringing together of two souls that would strengthen your hold of the crown of Castile," Chaucer said.

"My crown now sits firmly atop my head," Enrique replied. His crown was, in fact, slightly tilted.

"Of course, my lord. You have rightfully fought for and earned it."

"I am still listening, but my patience wears thin," Enrique said.

"Consider offering the hand of Doña Constanza, the lady-in-waiting to Queen Eleanora of Aragon, whom I believe you know, in marriage to Sir Hugh Calveley to reward him for his efforts in helping you achieve your success," Chaucer said.

"And why would I consider such an arrangement?" Enrique asked. "And why would they consider that arrangement is perchance the better question?"

"I think she may have fallen in love with him, my lord, but is unable to convey such things, for she is a lady," Chaucer replied.

"Ah, I see, you do the work of the lovebird, singing sweet songs to bring these two lovers together, because… why?" Enrique replied.

Chaucer inclined his head slightly.

"To keep Calveley close by, for he would not want to be far from such a woman. Rumour has it that Pedro will be in Bordeaux soon, trying to convince Prince Edward to march south to try to retake the crown that now sits firmly upon your head."

Enrique reacted with an expletive and shake of his head.

His crown tilts further. I must push on.

"Doña Constanza would help keep Calveley here, and that would aid you in fighting the battle-hardened soldiers of Prince Edward, who may threaten from the north."

"I am confounded. Why would you work so against your king?"

"I work for those I care for. And I care for her. Also, you will be in much greater need of leaders, tacticians and knights who can ensure your longevity. Even if du Guesclin leaves, you would still have one proven leader whom the men trust to assist in your next battles."

Enrique gazed at him and then smiled. "You voice my same thoughts Chaucer, for my spies have confirmed Pedro is on his way to Bordeaux, and my mole in Prince Edward's palace has also confirmed that Edward has sent letters across Aquitaine asking his lords, barons and knights to make ready for war. So let us consider your plan as a possibility. How do you see the two lovers coming together?" Enrique asked.

"I would be most honoured to assist, for I have met Doña Constanza and may be helpful in that regard," Chaucer replied.

"And what do you gain from such efforts?" Enrique asked.

"Perchance your good grace would benefit a wine merchant seeking more wine for my king," Chaucer replied smoothly. One of his tasks, after all, was to find more wine for King Edward. And surely what Carlos would have already told Enrique.

Enrique gave Chaucer a smile that could have meant many things. "I will think on what you have said. Good day."

As Chaucer bowed, backed away and stepped from the great hall into the antechamber where he found Alfonso still waiting, he realized that he had not once considered trying to attack Enrique. He was no murderer. Alfonso looked up at the sound of his approaching steps, and his searching eyes sought an answer; Chaucer shook his head no. They made their way out of the palace. His debt to Alfonso still remained. How he would repay it was as yet as cloudy as the skies that now threatened overhead.

•   •   •

"Doña Constanza, welcome," Enrique said.

She had received a note from Chaucer earlier saying he would be seeing Enrique that day, and that she should expect a request to attend him shortly after. After an initial hesitation, she arrived soon after the summons.

"Of course, my lord. It is an honour to meet you," she replied, her voice even, hiding the turmoil of emotions she felt.

She was dressed in a simple white gown that gave Enrique a very clear image of her form beneath. She had ensured her head was demurely covered by what, at first glance, appeared to be a plain white wimple, but a closer look revealed gold thread running through it. She wore white shoes with a gold bow. And her gown was tied by a gold belt. She was a vision of white and gold, purity and wealth. Save her low neckline.

"The honour is all mine, my lady," he said. His voice was controlled, courteous, polite.

But his eyes gave him away, for his eyes gazed at her shape before returning to her face. She had found that men who desired a woman had a particular expression that shone from their eyes, as if their desire somehow lit their eyes from inside.

Yes, his desire was clear enough. It mattered not that they may be distant cousins. Even though he had caused irreparable harm to many in her family and community, he could yet prove useful, and she knew that to be so close to such power would only aid her and Ayala in their goal. And Ayala was worldly enough to know that if she slept with Enrique, or Calveley, or any other man, it was only a means to an end, which was to be closer to Ayala, her true love. And so she smiled and curtsied, revealing a hint of what lay beneath, and Enrique kissed her hand.

"Let me first say congratulations on your victory, my lord. All in the kingdom are pleased to see Pedro gone."

"Truly, he has angered enough nobles to never claim the crown again."

She took a breath and carefully weighed the words she would say next.

"And yet, my lord, I sense hesitation even as you say such words."

"A perceptive woman, as well as beautiful…," he replied.

She smiled at the compliment, holding his gaze.

"Pedro will seek his revenge; of that I am sure." Enrique said.

"Yes, I am told he is already making plans to bend his knee before Prince Edward to seek aid in reclaiming this crown."

"You are well informed," Enrique replied, clearly impressed.

"If Prince Edward accedes to Pedro's plea for help, then you would not be facing only Pedro's rabble, but some of the most successful and best-led soldiers in all of Europe," she said.

Enrique nodded and smiled.

"You are truly something special. And so I must keep both du Guesclin and Calveley in Castile to help face that eventuality."

Doña nodded.

"Tell me about you, and of your lineage. While your present beauty is evident, your past is less so," he said.

Doña had to be careful, for she knew only too well of Enrique's distaste for Jews.

"I am lady-in-waiting to Eleanor of Sicily, the queen of your ally King Pere, my lord. My father was a noble from Castile. My mother was of a noble family from Barcelona. Both are now dead."

"And their parents?"

Constanza hadn't wanted to mention them, but was, at least, prepared to do so. "My parents spoke little of their own parents, for they died young in the Black Death and the grief never left either of them," she replied.

Her answer seemed to satisfy Enrique, for he moved on.

"Tell me. What do you know of Sir Hugh Calveley?"

"I met him only once, in Logrono, but he was chivalrous and I know he is a fearsome and successful knight and leader," she replied. She left out details about his odd teeth and hair and that he looked more like an orange giant, for she knew why Enrique was asking.

"Good. I would that you consider taking the hand in marriage of Sir Hugh Calveley."

"I am flattered, my lord. But why Sir Hugh?" she asked.

"I will not insult your intelligence and say plainly that by marrying him, you would help keep him in Castile in case Pedro attempts to retake my crown."

Exactly what Chaucer said.

"And…is that the only reason, my lord?"

She peered into Enrique's eyes, searching for any sign of his own interest in her.

"I would, of course, be gratified if you visited me twice each year and share with me any news of Calveley. To have you closer to the crown can only cast more light upon it," he said, his careful, courteous words fashioned, like the garment that Doña wore, to flatter the form beneath.

"I would be honoured, my lord, for I believe Sir Hugh to be a very agreeable knight," she said. Her words were not untrue, but calling him 'an agreeable knight,' was hardly a resounding tribute. "He is also renowned as a valiant knight," she added for good measure.

"Your mind is as shapely as your form, my lady, and you craft thoughtful replies. I sense a modest desire for Calveley, and yet no distaste. Perchance, that is enough."

"A woman must be careful when speaking of desire, my lord."

Enrique said nothing.

"Yet desire can grow in time," she added.

Enrique nodded.

Doña smiled and curtsied.

Enrique's eyes shone.

●　　　●　　　●

As Hugh Calveley approached Burgos Palace, he exhaled his pleasure. The sun shone, the birds chirped; spring had arrived. He had received a summons to attend Enrique earlier and had dressed hastily. He was not entirely sure what Enrique wanted to discuss and thought it may have something to do with payment for his efforts. He suspected Enrique had decided to alter their agreement and had prepared a response.

A guard opened one door, and he stepped inside the hall. Within stood dozens of knights, courtiers and ladies, their muted murmurs paused at his arrival. Calveley looked for du Guesclin and was grateful to see that he was not there.

"Sir Hugh, welcome," cried Enrique from the end of the Hall. "Approach!"

As Calveley stepped toward Enrique, the crowd parted. He noted the looks of distaste on many faces, for his hair was unkempt, his surcoat discoloured with blood and dirt. Calveley had not deigned to find a new one, and frankly did not care. For he was a soldier, here to kill the enemy, not show off the latest fashions like the peacocks and carpet knights surrounding him; let the courtiers be damned!

"My lord," he replied as he stopped before the dais and awkwardly bent on the one knee that still functioned properly. The other had taken an arrow five years before and didn't bend as well. Like the rest of his body. And like his will.

"I invited you here this morning to receive that which I am so very pleased to grant to you for your service," Enrique said, beaming.

"My lord," is all Calveley said, knee still bent.

"For your service in gaining me the crown that is rightfully mine to wear, I add to your titles of Count of Carrion a gift of an additional five thousand florins," Enrique stated as a chest carried by two huge Moors was set down in front of Calveley. One of the Moors opened the lid. It was filled to the brim with gold coin.

Calveley smiled.

"You are too kind, my lord."

"Now, I have one last thing to grant to you, but that I will share in private." Enrique stood and motioned for Calveley to follow him.

They entered a smaller anteroom where two chairs, a table, two goblets, and a flask of wine were set before them.

"Join me," he said, sitting down.

Calveley followed, and they both drank.

"The last gift I want to share is of great import, and is not given to you lightly."

Calveley was all ears and long teeth. "My lord," he said.

"I offer you the hand of Doña Constanza Enríquez de Castilla, lady-in-waiting to the Queen of Aragon, as your bride," he said.

Calveley was surprised, as it was well known that the beauty of Burgos was in love with Ayala, the poet soldier and Pedro's confident.

"You know the lady?"

"Not well, my lord, but I had the pleasure of meeting her briefly in Logrono a week ago as we advanced west. We exchanged but a few words, but those were enough for me to see both her beauty and her spirit."

And learn that she is Ayala's lover.

"And?"

"I am grateful for your generous offer, and I have one question," he said.

"Yes?"

"Ayala. What would you have me do with him? It is well known that he is the lady's lover, and he poses a threat as a possible spy for Pedro, despite his fine words."

"I suggest you befriend him, keep him close. If you can allow it, let him continue his dalliances with the lady, discreetly. He may prove valuable. Do you have a wife in England or Aquitaine?"

"No, my lord. The life of a sword for hire is not a life any married woman would enjoy."

"With Pedro defeated, two chests of gold, and a county and castle to call your own, you may now be able to build a home here."

Calveley nodded.

A practical arrangement. But does he seek her to spy on me for him?

"Good. Keep her, and your new lands, and all will be well. I believe Pedro will attempt to reclaim his crown with the help of Prince Edward. I would have you watch and follow Ayala, for even though he said he had left Pedro's service, that may have simply been a ruse allowing him to learn more of our intentions. Should Edward and Pedro join, I would have need of your skills again—but hopefully not too soon. In the meantime, enjoy your newfound wealth and title. Go visit your lands. They are truly beautiful. And go see your bride to be," he said.

"My lord, you are too generous," Calveley said as he stood, bowed, and backed away.

•　　　•　　　•

After Calveley left, Enrique returned to the main hall, sat again upon his throne, and repeated the ceremony, this time with du Guesclin.

"My lord," du Guesclin said brusquely as he bent his knee, as if he had more important things to do.

"Du Guesclin, I welcome you, and honour you for your victory," Enrique said.

"In thanks for your leading the men to this great victory over Pedro, I offer you an additional ten thousand gold florins," Enrique added, as another chest was carried in and set in front of the knight, then opened.

"My lord, I am so very grateful," du Guesclin replied, glancing at the gold before the chest was closed and carried away.

"Was there something else you desired?" Enrique asked.

"My lord, you are perceptive. Yes, there is one more thing I desire," du Guesclin said.

Enrique nodded. "If it is in my power to grant, I will consider it," he replied.

"My lord, I would have Calveley's force disbanded. He may remain in Burgos to carry out your wishes, but I would have his men removed, for they pose a threat to me and my men. Calveley has a strong dislike for me, and I him. At any moment, he could attack me."

Enrique stared at du Guesclin, and then burst into laughter. After a moment, he composed himself enough to reply.

"You two are two of a kind. Too alike by far. No, he will stay, as will his men. I may have need of them soon, for it is rumoured that Pedro bends knee to Prince Edward seeking arms to reclaim my crown," he said.

"You have valued my counsel before, and I would ask that you hear me out now. I ask again, have his men disbanded," du Guesclin said.

"My dear du Guesclin, if he leaves he will return to Westminster or Bordeaux, where he will surely find employ with King Edward, or more likely Prince Edward, and we would soon have to face him on the battlefield, rather than have him lurking in the shadows here. I would prefer the latter to the former. Would you not also?" Enrique asked du Guesclin.

"I have heard enough. I have business in France I must attend to. Good day my lord," du Guesclin said.

He bent his knee, shuffled backwards one step, then gave up the pretense of courtesy, turned his back and strode out of the room.

"I did not say you could withdraw..." Enrique said to du Guesclin's retreating form.

"Ungrateful Gascon! How dare you turn your back to me. I will have you flayed alive!" Enrique shouted to du Guesclin's shrinking back.

But of course, he knew he would not, for he needed du Guesclin in order to exact revenge upon Pedro. And du Guesclin knew it too. But the man's enmity for Calveley did not bode well. The two hated each other almost as much as he hated Pedro. But he still needed both to finally defeat and kill Pedro. He would offer more gold for du Guesclin to return. Later.

PART 3
FOUND

CHAPTER 17
BORDEAUX AND LONDON, AUGUST, 1366
CHAUCER GOES HOME

After Burgos, Chaucer left for Pamplona and then Bordeaux to report to Sir Chandos. The trip over the mountain pass was much easier and faster in summer, but still dangerous. Alfonso had disappeared in Pamplona and so Chaucer had hired two knights to guide and protect him, and he reached Bordeaux safely two weeks after leaving Burgos. The next morning he reported to Sir Chandos, saying that he had failed in his task, for Calveley had helped Enrique claim the Castilian crown. Chandos was not surprised, for he would have known of the outcome well before Chaucer's arrival. But Chaucer was surprised to have Chandos then invite him to dinner with the prince, his wife the countess Joan and several other lords and knights that evening. So Chaucer retired to his room, dressed as best he could, and found himself seated by Chandos at a table below the raised dais where the prince and Joan sat.

She is as beautiful as ever.

To his left was a young squire he did not recognize.

"Joan glows," Chaucer said to Chandos. "A more beautiful lady is surely not to be found," he added.

"Indeed. And this is Thomas Holland, our lady's son," said Chandos between mouthfuls of chicken and bread.

Chaucer pulled his eyes from Joan and smiled at young Holland, his embarrassment at his directness assuaged by Holland's warm smile. Chaucer had heard of the first son born from Joan's first marriage to Thomas Holland, the Earl of Kent.

"Well met Master Holland. I am Geoffrey Chaucer, page to our king. I hope my words of your mother do not offend."

"Chaucer, your words are blunt, more dagger's pommel than steel edge, but please know that many speak so of my mother, for she is indeed beautiful. And my mother speaks highly of you," Holland said.

"Then she is both beautiful and kind," Chaucer replied, his smile widening. "And what brings you to Bordeaux?"

"I am squire to Prince John of Gaunt, Prince Edward's brother, and I arrived yesterday from the Savoy. Do you know my master?"

"Well enough," Chaucer replied, voice now clipped.

"Gaunt will join others gathering south of here near Dax," Chandos added. "To aid Pedro in re-claiming his crown," Chandos said.

"Chaucer, more chicken?" he asked, holding a silver platter before Chaucer.

Chaucer didn't seem to hear him.

"Chaucer?" Chandos asked again.

Chaucer slowly shook his head no and turned and looked at Holland.

"Young Holland, you say you just arrived from London? Do you know of a Pippa Rouet, lady-in-waiting to the queen?" Chaucer asked.

"Pippa Rouet? Yes, I met her but two days hence at the Savoy Palace."

"The Savoy? But she serves our queen at the Palace of Westminster."

"She stays at the Savoy now, for the Duchess Blanche asked her to help prepare my lord's baggage for his journey here."

Chaucer said nothing, his eyes looking to a distant point, a crease upon his brow.

"Not welcome news?" asked Chandos.

"Sir John, I would seek to take my leave and return to London on the morrow."

"An untimely request, but by your visage I see this journey is of some import. I grant you such, but do not tarry too long there, for your service to my prince is now of even greater import."

And I will first see what kind of service Pippa provides to that prince of a man, Gaunt.

Chaucer was on a cog bound for London the next day.

•   •   •

It was low tide when Chaucer walked up the plank and stepped onto Three Cranes wharf and breathed in the fecund air of London, of home.

The grey evening light slowly draped itself upon the shoulders of the once golden day, the Thames now reflecting dull brass. The normal bustle of the wharf had departed with the tide. Chaucer heard only the creak of the stays being fastened to ties on the landing, and a few calls to make way. Most of the men were already in a tavern clutching a goblet to quench their well-earned thirst. But not all.

Chaucer turned at a squeak and watched with a nervous eye as a deckhand onboard the cog he had sailed in attached a hook to the webbed hemp containing several barrels of Bordeaux wine. The hook hung from the end of one of the three massive cranes on the wharf. The deckhand shouted "hook secure", one man on shore cried "hey", and another landed a switch on the hindquarters of a rouncey inside the small hut below the crane arm. The rouncey was harnessed to the crane, and as it moved forward in a circle around the crane timber, a gear turned, tightening the massive rope holding the wine.

"Hold!" the deckhand cried.

"Whoa," the man inside the hut said to the horse.

The deckhand checked that the rope was securely fastened to the hemp. The ten barrels of Bordeaux wine floated in the air, but a few inches off the deck.

Nearby, Chaucer heard a young hand say to another, "Shame if that lot broke, for we'd have to drink up what's left of the broken barrels."

"No need to spend a groat at the Three Cranes Tavern. We can just sip it off the deck," said the other, and both laughed.

"If those barrels break, the owner Master Chaucer would lose several pounds—a year's worth of your miserable wages—and 'e'd have to let you rotten apples go," Chaucer said, reminding the youngsters of how important every barrel was to their common enterprise.

That shut them up, and they quietly watched as the deckhand onboard motioned for the crane man to carry on. The hemp-clad barrels rose, floated sideways and gently lowered to the wharf. The hook was unfastened, the hemp pulled back, and the barrels were rolled one by one into the warehouse.

As the last barrel was safely stored away, the other deck hands picked up their sacks and stepped up the plank to the wharf. Chaucer watched one man step off, kneel, and kiss the stone wharf.

Indeed, how good it was to be on land, and home.

Chaucer turned and stepped into the warehouse to find William, his father's right-hand man, but a worker there said he had gone with the lads to the Three Cranes Tavern. Chaucer needed to speak to William about how he might approach Pippa about Gaunt and the question of marriage. He had entrusted William with many things over their years together, including his feelings about Pippa. He needed his ear now more than ever.

Chaucer entered the tavern, not a hundred paces from the wharf. It was a second (or third) home to Chaucer, as it was for most of the men on the wharf who would retire to imbibe. Where those recently arrived from Calais, or Dublin, or places farther afield, would quench their thirst and hunger and share tales from their travels and feel the connection of like-minded souls who understood the travails and joys of a life at sea.

The tavern was full and the light dim, for the space was lit by only a few lanterns and two small windows that let in the fading light of the bronze dusk that had now settled upon the city.

"Geoffrey Chaucer! Now there's a soul I had not expected to see," said a voice from the bar.

"William," Chaucer said, greeting him with a handshake. "I thought I might find your weathered old face here."

"Snapes. Pour Chaucer a goblet," William said to the server.

Quaffing a goblet or two (or three) after the delivery of a shipment was a long-held custom upheld by Chaucer's father John, to give thanks for the safe passage of the valuable cargo that was so often lost to pirates, storms or theft.

"I thought you was still in Castile at war with that half-brother of Pedro…what's his name?"

"Enrique."

"The bastard, yes. How'd you fare?" William asked.

Snapes delivered the requested goblet, and the two clunked their goblets together.

"Safe passage," William and Geoffrey said, in unison.

Chaucer looked about to see who might be listening.

"Come on Chaucer, it's not like you have secrets to hide from me," said William.

He had known William since he was a boy, for William and his father, John, had built the family business together. He trusted him with his life. But Chaucer had only intimated to William his position as the king's spy and knew he must be careful in the telling of his story, for the memory of Croker's hard words and hand still stung. He looked about and didn't see Croker, but the man may well have followed him home. He was crafty and could be watching and listening that very moment.

"There is much to tell. I sought Rioja wine to expand our business and gain new trade for our good king," he said quietly. "While I was there, the bastard Enrique won a long-running war. His half-brother King Pedro ran away from Burgos and Enrique now wears his crown.

Pedro now bends his knee to his cousin Prince Edward, seeking from him an army to reclaim his crown," Chaucer recounted, sharing only the facts any traveller returning from those lands would tell.

"I know the prince well enough from my time helping your da deliver wine to the palace before you were old enough to do the same. Very keen judge of men. He'll take the measure of Pedro. Sounds like you've been in the thick of it," William said.

Chaucer nodded, saying, "I must return soon though, as my work is unfinished."

"Of course. And did you find any puys in Navarre and Castile?" William asked. He knew of Chaucer's poetic ambitions, and love of, if not success in, the puy.

"Only one, around a campfire in a stockade."

"You were captured again?"

Chaucer nodded. "Held by Enrique with other prisoners, including a talented Castilian poet named Ayala, along with the Sir John Chandos' herald, Gawain, and my guide, Alfonso, but before our puy was concluded, news of Pedro fleeing Burgos reached us, and we were released," Chaucer replied.

"I sense there is more to your story," William said, then leaned over and whispered, "Prefer to talk in private?" and Chaucer hesitated.

"It's just that..." he tried to say, but the words lay stuck in his throat.

"Pippa?" William asked.

Chaucer nodded.

"You asked her to marry you twice before you left," he said.

Chaucer nodded.

"And have returned to ask her yet again, but are afraid she will say no once more," William said.

William was right. He knew him too well.

"Does she love you?" William asked.

"I believe so, yes. But..."

"But?"

"Gaunt..."

"Ah yes. A cuckoo about your nest."

Chaucer nodded silently.

"No sense moaning about jealousy or fear. Go find her and tell her why you returned, and that you love her. You will see in her eyes her true feelings toward you. And don't tarry, for it's almost curfew."

Chaucer hesitated, then nodded, emptied his goblet, put a silver coin on the table, then said, "William, I will see you on the morrow."

Others followed him out the door.

Feeling more hopeful after speaking with William, Chaucer made his way home. After an absence of eight long months, he stepped across the hearth into the great room to see the fire in the central hearth out, a thin trail of smoke the only evidence Pippa had been there.

"Pippa?" he shouted, and dropped his bags.

Silence. No one was home.

He took off his coat, poured himself a goblet of red, cut some cheese and bread, and sat down at the table to eat. Too late to be venturing to the palace, too late to be seeking Pippa on the streets. By the absence of coats, it looked like his parents had already moved to their home at St. Botolph-without-Aldgate that Agnes had inherited, and Pippa was gone. His mind began to create all manner of scenarios. Halfway through his bread and cheese, he found a note from Gaunt lying on the kitchen table.

"The Duke of Lancaster requests that Pippa Rouet, lady-in-waiting to Queen Philippa, attend to his lord to assist him on his journey to Bordeaux on the morrow..." he read aloud, then stopped.

The Duke. Prince John of Gaunt. Third son to our king. Husband to dear, beautiful Blanche. Father of two daughters by Blanche. And father of the bastard child by Marie St. Hillaire, born just before he wed his wife Blanche. He called that daughter Blanche. What kind of man, or prince, would do such a thing? Perchance this prince of a man had fathered Elizabeth also? Even if Pippa would say nought of it, he felt the truth of it in his gut, a truth that would surely out one day. No, I will not let this lie another day. I shall find Pippa. And no doubt Gaunt, and speak my mind.

·   ·   ·

Chaucer carefully made his way to the palace in the near dark. The bells of the nearby St. Mary le Bow Church signalled the beginning of curfew. He had made the journey enough times that he knew how to avoid the beadles keeping curfew. He slid past the looming hulk of St. Paul's where the whores and mendicants congregated in the Church Yard day and night, then made his way down Ludgate Hill. The bells from All Hallows by the Tower to the east joined those of St. Mary le Bow. He waited for the guards to change at Ludgate and slipped through the city's ancient Roman wall to Fleet Street and Fleet Bridge, just as the peal from the bells of St. Bride's ahead and St. Giles Cripplegate to the north joined, and then just as suddenly, stopped.

In the sudden silence he made better time, striding quickly by the dim light of the stars past the fields of Farringdon Without. The black hulk of Newgate prison loomed to the north, and he continued west along the Strand, past the temple at White Friars, the houses of the wealthy nobility lining the banks of the Thames, and finally reached Gaunt's Savoy Palace at the sharpest bend of the river.

Chaucer paused on the Strand, and took in the massive dark palace flecked with specks of light, wondering if Gaunt and Pippa were there together now, warmed by a glowing hearth. He was tired, and getting cold, knew not how he would make it past the guards that would surely be stationed at the entrance, and decided to steal into a nearby hayloft he had frequented before when caught out after curfew and bed down for the night. He made his way in, and but for the rustle of some cows heard nought. He found a corner, covered himself in straw, and sleep arrived quickly.

The next morning, at the crow of the cock, he exited the hayloft, nodding at the surprised stable boy carrying two buckets of water into the barn. He took a piss behind the barn. The sun was just up, the early morning smells of the barn livestock and the river exhilarating, the day full of promise, and he felt more hopeful than before he fell asleep. A handful of barges were just beginning to ply the Thames, and turning his head, he could make out the merchants on The Strand with their apprentices behind them, wheeling carts on their way to the market stalls near the palace. A shepherd guided his goats past costermongers pushing wheelbarrows piled high with fruits and vegetables, and a fishmonger cried out her wares.

Chaucer made his way the short distance to the palace entrance. He was warmly welcomed by the guards and servants who knew him, save for the old valet, who wore a permanent look of disdain upon his face. Chaucer knew from previous encounters that the old goat took umbrage at the inexplicable favour he had found with the royals. But Chaucer was focussed on finding Pippa and had no time to ponder such slights.

He wound his way along the stone corridors and turned a corner and ran into a woman.

"Ah!" she cried.

They collided and both fell.

"Master Chaucer, forgive me. I am in haste to our queen."

"Marie, no, it is I who am at fault, for I dash blindly," Chaucer replied, getting up and holding out his hand.

"Pippa and I did not know of your return," she said, taking his hand and standing up, then adjusting her gown.

Ah yes, comely Marie St. Hillaire, like Pippa, a lady-in-waiting to Queen Philippa. And Gaunt's mistress.

Her attractive form held his gaze for a moment, then he realized he was staring.

"Yes, I came suddenly."

"Sadly for us women, most men do," she said, followed by a snort, then was past him and scampering down the corridor.

He watched her go, then turned and continued on. He approached Gaunt's private quarters, then came to an abrupt stop by Gaunt's voice, followed immediately by Pippa's unmistakable laugh. His brow furrowed hearing Gaunt's deep laugh in response. He took two more steps, then heard their words. Saw light from two sconces, then firelight, then shadows of two figures standing—surely Pippa and Gaunt—cast upon the bookshelves lining one half of Gaunt's study.

They sound like two lovers...just one step further...there. Pippa.

A guard stepped out from behind the doorway.

"Halt!"

Pippa turned.

"Geoffrey," she said, surprise writ across her face.

"Pippa."

The guard relaxed, and Chaucer stepped into the light.

"What are you doing here? I received no letter of your return."

"Pippa...my lord," Chaucer said as Gaunt stepped into view.

Gaunt looked past Pippa to Chaucer.

"Welcome back, Chaucer."

"My prince."

"I heard the war did not go well, and Enrique now sits atop the Castilian throne."

"Yes, my lord," Chaucer replied.

"And Calveley?" Gaunt asked. Chaucer felt certain he well knew the outcome.

Chaucer shook his head 'no,' his mouth tight. "Lady Fortune turned her wheel."

"Lady Fortune does not favour you," Gaunt replied, looking from Chaucer to Pippa. "No matter. Success may follow a second attempt."

Of turning Calveley? Or does he speak of Pippa?

"It looks as though you need to speak to our Pippa, so please do not have her too long, for I still need her, as there is much to do to prepare for my journey to Bordeaux on the morrow. Good day

Chaucer," Gaunt said, then turned his back on them and began looking through some papers. The meeting was over and they were to leave.

Pippa gave a slight curtsy and departed down the corridor. She looked back, nodding for Chaucer to follow, but he hesitated. She turned and carried on. Chaucer looked back at Gaunt, curious to see if he was watching her. No, Gaunt's head was still down as he fussed with his papers.

And then Gaunt ever so slightly lifted his head and gazed at Pippa's receding figure. Gaunt could not see him, for a bookcase stood between them. Gaunt watched Pippa until she turned once more to get Chaucer's attention.

My lord desires her, the woman I love and am to wed. He fathered Marie's bastard. And may have fathered our daughter. My lord, who Pippa serves. I am carked.

Chaucer followed and caught up to Pippa further down the corridor as another page passed them. He reached and caught her arm, and she stopped and turned to face him.

"I looked high and low for you all day upon my return at eventide," he said, trying and failing to veil his accusatory tone. He'd been expecting a warmer reception.

"Lord Gaunt requested my presence to help him prepare for his upcoming journey," she replied, her words matching his, tone for tone.

"And what help did that entail?" he asked.

"You know well enough not to ask such things," she said. Then, after a pause, added, "You sent no letter of your return."

"I came faster than any letter might fly."

"But why? What urgent news brings you home?" she asked, concern writ across her brow.

I must hear her say yes or lose her to Gaunt.

"Us. I came home to talk of us. You and me."

"What about us?"

"Being apart, surrounded by war and death, I thought of you with another, and knew that could not be. I would only have you. I love you, and I will have no other than you."

"What? What are you saying?" she asked.

"You will be my wife," he said.

"Not here," she said, turning and leading them down another long corridor, then along another, until they were alone. They walked silently, side by side.

"Speak your mind."

"I would have you."

"I am not to be had like some whore, but loved like a wife."

"Yes, of course, I meant I love you, and would have you as my wife."

"Loved, not had. And as I told you before, I will marry a valet or knight, not a page."

Chaucer paused then, unsure of how to proceed.

"I had some success in Castile…"

"Yet Enrique now wears the crown of Castile, as our lord just said, does he not?"

"It is true, I was unable to turn Calveley, yet Prince Edward would give me another chance and reward me upon that success," he said.

"But did not yet promote you," she snapped back.

"No, but surely will."

"Your surety is no surety at all, and you already have my answer. I am surprised you would ask. You know that I will not marry until you are made a valet and earn more gold,. We had to borrow from your parents this last year. I will not again, and you cannot afford to keep a wife and grow a family as a page," she replied. "And as a valet or squire, you'd be at court more and in taverns less," she said.

He nodded—all of it was true. She wanted him to change.

"Yes, there is no telling how long it may take to become valet."

"To do well on the king's business would speed Lady Fortune's hand."

Do better, she meant.

"And those puys. You must stop throwing away your meagre earnings playing such games."

Puys? Stop competing in the puys? Had he heard her correctly?

He looked at her closer, as if to make her meaning clearer, but found no ready answer.

He had. She meant exactly that. It was too much. It would not stand.

He turned his back on Pippa and strode the way they'd come.

"Geoffrey? Where are you going?" she called after him.

He stopped and slowly turned and faced the only woman he had ever loved, the mother of his child. He might desire other women— Blanche, Joan and Constanza—but Pippa was always and would always be the only woman he wanted to marry. His heart ached at what he was about to say, but his head had already formed the words.

"You ask too much of me, and you should find another to marry. I will return to Castile on the morrow to do my duty to my king and prince. I may succeed; I may fail, and I may never return, for I shall be amidst a war. If I do return, I will expect nothing of you, save our friendship. I will seek your hand no more," he said, trying to hold back the tears now welling in his eyes and choking his throat. And added, looking towards the direction they had come from, and Gaunt, "Go seek another who will love you as you desire, and fulfill your desires."

Pippa tried to form a reply. Too late, for Chaucer had already turned and walked away.

He made his way from the bowels of the rear entrance up through corridors and passages to Prince John's solar where the afternoon light striped the jumbled open trunks surrounding Gaunt, and his servants scurried about as they busily prepared his belongings for his upcoming journey.

"My lord, a brief word if you might," Chaucer said, more demanding than intended.

Gaunt stopped speaking to his valet and looked up, surprise writ upon his face.

"Chaucer. Again. What an unexpected surprise." By Gaunt's tone, he did not mean a welcome one, but Chaucer did not care.

The two stepped toward each other.

"You depart for Calais, my lord?" Chaucer asked,

"Yes, on the morrow, weather permitting. My brother calls for my immediate assistance, and I will join him in his campaign to return Pedro to his throne. Why do you ask?"

"I would ask to join you on your voyage, my lord," Chaucer said. He would rather join the devil in Hades, but at least he knew this devil.

"Did you not just return from Bordeaux yestereve?"

"Indeed, my lord. But events have transpired such that I would return now, and return to my duty," Chaucer replied. He knew Gaunt could see the pain on Chaucer's face, for he hid his emotions poorly.

"Events have transpired?" Gaunt said. The prince was not stupid. Chaucer would give him that.

"Yes," Chaucer said.

"Are you sure this is what you want to do?"

"Yes my lord."

"Such is the way with women, Chaucer," Gaunt replied. "Yes, join me. But you will have to be quick about gathering what belongings you require for the journey," he said.

"I left most of my belongings in Bordeaux."

Gaunt nodded.

"Thank you, my lord," Chaucer added.

"Yes, yes, of course Chaucer, think nothing of it. It will be pleasing to have your poetic tongue about. I should return to my man, for he vents hot air and would soon burst," Gaunt said. "We leave on the morrow at dawn. Do not partake too much drink that you are late, or you shall have to find your own way to Calais."

Chaucer gave a short bow and backed away under the hot stare of Gaunt's valet.

A short while later, he found his way down to the space under the stairs near the palace's servants' quarters, where he kept some clothes and belongings hidden behind a jumble of chairs and tables that were stored there. It felt then as if his world had shrunken to this small, dimly lit refuge. A place he knew well, where he had spent much time with Pippa, trading barbs, exploring her body, learning what a man and a woman could be like together, and where his lust had burgeoned into love. Where their daughter Elizabeth had been conceived, as best as he could guess. Fathered either by himself, or nearby by Gaunt.

The knowledge that Pippa didn't love him enough to marry him further tarnished these already stained memories, making his heart shrivel. He lived now without desire, without a woman to love. He felt defeated, his hopes for his future dashed by her cold reception.

He needed to abandon this torture, and seek Calveley and his duty and war. Perchance he would die, for he had not the skills of a seasoned soldier. Would Pippa mourn him? It mattered not. His task to turn Calveley still remained. He would do his duty. The final battle brewing between Pedro and Enrique would then be his salvation. Dying on the field doing his duty would be something. Not the nothing that he now felt. No, not nothing. More a cutting wound from Pippa's words thrust deeply into his heart. Next to the old bruise that was Gaunt. And now he was to sail with the man. Perchance that *was* preferred. Simpler. For then he could at least see his enemy clearly in that kind of war, on that field of battle.

CHAPTER 18
OLITE, OCTOBER, 1366
ENRIQUE AND KING CARLOS

"My spies tell me that you have engendered an agreement with Prince Edward for passage through Navarre. I ask that you rescind it. You cannot trust Prince Edward, who will surely seek to take away your lands once his army is safely through the pass. This threat retreats if you make the right choice," said Enrique.

Carlos had been listening, and now poured each of them a goblet of wine. The fall evening had descended, and the fire roared and crackled, partly heating the dining hall. Several courtiers ate at lower tables, with Enrique and Carlos alone at the high table.

"I know nothing of this," Carlos demurred. "Of course, the pass remains closed."

"Come Carlos, we both know the truth of it; this pretense serves neither of us well."

"If what you say is true, such an act would bring great risk, for Prince Edward could easily attack your kingdom as well," Carlos replied.

"His army could just as easily descend upon your land from the west, and of course you are vulnerable to attack from the south," said Enrique.

The threat lay in his tone, not the words.

Carlos was silent and drank from his goblet. After wiping his mouth with the back of his hand, he looked Enrique square in the eyes.

"You forget King Pere of Aragon. He too has been at war with Pedro for ten years and would see him crushed as well. He would not attack me, for we are long-time allies in this war. Blocking the passes against Pedro's ally would also serve him well," Carlos replied.

"Yes, until it doesn't, for if Pere decided to wrest control of the passes, then he would be in position to control the war. Much is at stake."

Carlos turned away from Enrique to hide his reaction.

Of course, Carlos knew only too well what was at stake. There were only two other ways to reach Navarre and Castile, by bypassing the Pyrenees on either the east or west coast, then pushing inland. Both required a much longer journey, larger stores of food and supplies, and a greater risk of attack from travelling mercenaries. The passes were direct, and even in winter, an army could traverse them in only three or four days instead of weeks.

"Your reputation is of a king who is not to be trusted, for you have, on more than one occasion, ripped up an agreement if you felt a better offer was available. Is that not true?" Enrique said.

Carlos turned and faced Enrique with the smile of a predator.

"What is true is that you are the same as me, and would also do whatever you needed to protect your kingdom. Now that you have a crown, you will learn that to rule is to make enemies of friends, and friends of enemies, in order to keep what you have."

"What a curious statement. It leaves trust upon the floor. And without trust, how should we ever truly partner?" Enrique replied.

"Through an understanding that we each must take care of our own interests. When they align, then there is no need for trust. No, let me make this clear to you," he said, holding a hand up to the younger man. "Common interest is a much more powerful force than trust. For trust can be easily broken, but common interest is a bond made forever strong."

Enrique nodded. "You know Carlos. I had always considered you arrogant, like your damnable French cousins. But you have successfully controlled Navarre for nearly twenty years. So perhaps you are not so stupid after all. As for our so-called common interest, it comes at a price, no?"

"Of course. One hundred thousand gold florins. Which I know you have, given that Pedro kindly left his treasure behind," Carlos said.

Enrique smiled. "Perchance. But a kingdom is expensive, and I have only part of his treasure. Fifty thousand."

"Seventy-five."

Enrique smiled again, but there was one more consideration. Calveley might yet seek to return to Bordeaux and du Guesclin to Brittany. Enrique needed to ensure they remained.

"One more thing. That page Chaucer has become a thorn in my side, for I have learned from my spies he seeks to return to Navarre and Castile and help return Calveley to the love of his prince and king, and I would ask your help in returning him to London, or to a grave, I care not which."

"Yes, of course. I will have him dealt with."

Enrique extended his hand, and they shook, saying, "Seventy-five it is."

The next morning a dark-cloaked figure rode through the gates and out of Olite, heading north, in search of Chaucer.

CHAPTER 19
BORDEAUX, JANUARY, 1367
TRUST

Chaucer hovered, waiting in the nave of the Cathédrale St-André. He watched Pedro and Carlos solemnly stand to the left of Prince Edward near the alter where a huge stone basin was placed. Christmas had passed, but a new celebration was before the city, a day after the Epiphany. The archbishop motioned with his hands in the age-old ritual of baptism, then picked up Joan's new babe, named Richard, and lowered him into the waters of the stone basin. A baby's cry rang out, followed by a few final words by the archbishop. Smiles and applause followed from all, including Pedro and Carlos.

Perchance the next king of England.

That both Pedro and Carlos were here together was something of a miracle. Chaucer had helped write an agreement between the two and Prince Edward that was signed four months previously in Libourne. Pedro had given most of northeastern Castile to Edward in exchange of Edward's support against Enrique. Pedro promised to pay the full cost of the campaign, albeit after the war had been won. Edward had asked for more, and Pedro had given over his three daughters as collateral against non-payment. Carlos guaranteed the safe passage through Navarre of Edward's troops in exchange for gold and land paid for by Castile. The agreement also called for Carlos to accompany Edward with four thousand men and join him in the battle against Enrique. Pedro would pay for any damage to Navarre caused by the army's crossing.

Edward gained an ally against the French and extended his control into Castile, but also risked a fortune whether Enrique won or not, for he would be paying for the army. Carlos gained strategic protection. Pedro gained the most and risked nothing, for he had already lost everything, and would finally have an army capable of defeating Enrique. After fifteen years of intermittent battle, Pedro would now be able to see an end to this tiresome war and have his crown returned.

All rested on the word of Carlos, for if Navarre was closed to Edward, the war would end before it began. And Chaucer had found out that Edward's spies had brought news the two weeks before: Carlos had secretly met Enrique to unravel the agreement. So Edward had re-opened negotiations with Carlos, who had asked for more gold, playing both sides to his advantage. The birth of Richard brought them together again, but the signing of a new agreement was the real reason they were here.

Chaucer heard snippets of conversation as he passed outside into the cheering crowd, for it was good luck to be born on the Epiphany before two kings and a prince.

A propitious sign for this prince.

Chaucer gazed at the distant newborn held high by a proud Edward as he stepped on to the steps of the cathedral, and wondered if this was in fact his future king? As son of the eldest son of King Edward, Richard was next in line to the throne after Prince Edward, but many others, including Edward's brothers, also sought the crown of England.

England.

Chaucer thought of London, and Westminster, and the Savoy, and Pippa.

Will we regain the love that lies between us, or remain apart?

Will we ever have another child together?

He recalled before he began his journey thinking that once he helped Pedro claim his throne—a task he would surely achieve—that he would return to Pippa in triumph, and there sit upon the throne of the Vintry, king of his own modest castle.

How empty such a dream seemed now. Standing there, surrounded by thousands of people, he had never felt so alone, never felt so far from Pippa and the love that lay between them. The ambitions of a lowly page seemed of little import with a heart so heavy.

And then a letter from Pippa arrived the very next day. Chaucer ripped it open, heedless of damaging the vellum. He read every word like a starving man offered crumbs. Pippa said she loved him. And was sorry for how they had left things. She begged him to come home safely so they could talk again of the life they might have together. Each word a salve for his wounded heart.

Hope. She sent hope. That was all he needed. And he knew then that he must return to her, and not die on the field of battle.

•   •   •

Later that night, at the dinner Edward hosted in honour of Pedro and Carlos, Chandos gestured for Chaucer to approach him where he sat at the end of the high table.

Chaucer bowed his head as he approached. "My lord, I am at your service."

"Chaucer, our army gathers near Dax. On the first day of the new month, we will march south to Roncesvalles, then cross the pass to Pamplona, if Carlos holds true to his word and keeps the pass open. Then we will march southwest to Logrono, to face the bastard Enrique at Burgos, or somewhere before, and reclaim the crown of Castile for Pedro. But we need the service and loyalty of Calveley and his mercenaries to ensure success. You must now return to Navarre and finally convince Calveley to bear the prince's banner upon the battlefield. You must succeed this time and return with such news, or send a messenger to me. Do so no later than Candlemas. That is one month and one day from this day. To fail again in this is to fail the prince, and to fail England. Do you understand the weight of this task upon your shoulders?"

Chaucer nodded, then said, "Calveley will want gold if he does turn, my lord."

"He will have his gold, and more. But you must first do the turning Chaucer."

Chaucer nodded again, his eyes shifting between Chandos and Prince Edward, who was eating and drinking and laughing, oblivious to the sudden weight of responsibility that he felt. "I value the trust you have placed in me, my lord," Chaucer replied.

"Failure would not look well upon you."

The word failure hung in the air, and he imagined a rope thrust around his neck, then his limp body swaying back and forth.

"Leave at dawn, and make haste," Chandos replied, and then turned back to the courtier to his side. Chaucer was dismissed to his fate.

The next morning, Chaucer departed on a palfrey toward his second crossing of the Pyrenees, a packhorse carrying his belongings. Two of Chandos' personal guards joined to keep him safe as far as Pamplona. He would find and turn Calveley this time, and Edward and Pedro would defeat Enrique. He would gain his promotion and return to London and ask Pippa to marry him and she would accept.

Or he would be found dead, lying face down in some barren, dusty ravine, the crows gorging on his lifeless eyes, and he would see no more of failure and disappointment.

His fate now lay with Lady Fortune. Or in God's hands. He would soon find out.

CHAPTER 20
PAMPLONA, JANUARY 12, 1367
CHAUCER AND CONSTANZA

Chaucer arrived in Pamplona and the next day found Alfonso at the same tavern where they had first met. After a celebratory drink, Alfonso told him that rumour had it that Calveley had cooled towards Enrique, and he was considering a new employer. Chaucer's task seemed more hopeful, but he still did not yet know how he would ensure Calveley would support Pedro. And surety was what was needed.

He also learned from Alfonso that Doña Constanza was currently a guest of King Carlos, who was in the city.

The next morning, he sent word to Doña Constanza asking for an audience. She replied yes, saying to meet her at the base of a little used tower at the south end of the castle walls. He made his way there the next day, where he met one of her guards at the small, wooden door and followed him to the top of the tower. He waited, peering through three narrow openings cut into the stone at the magnificent view of the Pyrenees. He turned when he heard her enter the room.

His heart raced at the sight of her, more beautiful than he recalled. Her black cloak set off the snow white blouse and shapely form beneath, just as her curled black hair set off her almond-shaped eyes framed by long, black lashes. Eyes he could easily drown within.

"Chaucer, I am pleased to see that you have survived to return once again. I have missed your…quick wit and quicker tongue."

"And I your visage, wit and knowledge," he replied.

After they had exchanged further pleasantries, Chaucer got to the matter on his mind.

"You have come to know Calveley these past few months?"

"Yes. I met a knight named Croker who knows Calveley and has been helpful in arranging meetings with Calveley."

Chaucer's eyes widened.

"Do you know Croker?"

"I have met him, yes."

Ah, so that is what he has been doing all this time. Better to keep my relationship with Croker hidden for now.

"Thanks to Croker, I have come to…appreciate Sir Hugh more," she replied, without adding any further detail he hoped to hear.

"And Ayala?" Chaucer asked.

"What of him? I still see him, if that is what you are asking," she replied.

Chaucer pondered her reply before asking what he had come for.

"What would it take for Calveley to turn away from Enrique and return to his king, and join Prince Edward's army?"

Doña Constanza smiled back at Chaucer. "I have been surprised to learn that the man I took to be a heartless mercenary is, in truth, an honourable man, and one who cares deeply about God and beauty. But I also learned that he loves gold and has much of it. The bargain he seeks to make with me is one that would benefit both me and my family, for he would pay me enough gold to ensure my family never has to suffer as we did after Enrique destroyed our livelihood and future. With Calveley, I can recast a new future for all in my family who survived. It is too late for my mother and father. But it is not too late for me."

Chaucer nodded his understanding.

"The trouble is that Calveley follows only gold, as you well know, but your King Edward offers only fealty. And fealty is not enough to satisfy my future husband's desires. So the answer is clear enough. Have you brought gold?" she asked.

"Not that kind of gold, no. But gold awaits, should he turn."

"That would be too late, so I do not have the answer you seek."

Chaucer thought of another path forward.

"Will you truly wed Calveley? And what of Ayala if you do?"

At this Doña Constanza turned away from Chaucer to stare out the slit in the stone window and peer at some distant point beyond the castle where her future lay.

She turned back to Chaucer. "Do I love the man? No. I love Ayala. He is noble, but does not have the gold I need, and the wedding has been arranged, and you well know that love has no place in such an arrangement."

"And yet Prince Edward will very soon return with an army to help Pedro reclaim his crown. If Calveley stays aligned with Enrique, his fortunes will fall, and yours along with them, for not even Calveley and du Guesclin together can withstand the army of Prince Edward. Help me turn Calveley back to his rightful king."

"How could I possibly do that?"

"You have many…attributes and skills," Chaucer said.

She raised one eyebrow. "What are you suggesting?"

"Perhaps there is a way to convince Calveley to leave Enrique, but you must forgo seeing Ayala for a time, for he now supports Enrique."

"I love Ayala."

"And what if Calveley discovered you with Ayala?" Chaucer asked. "What would you do? What would he do?"

"He may kill him, or he may understand that our arrangement is necessary. That is the risk I take for the man whom I love."

Chaucer gave a slight nod, respect writ upon his face.

"And you, Chaucer? You who travel our land and flirt with the local women, are you to wed your betrothed?"

By local women, she meant herself.

"I have asked Pippa to wed me. More than once, in truth. But she will not until I return a success and thus secure our future. My success rests solely on turning Calveley."

"It seems our lives are like grapes that hang side by side upon the vine, to be soon plucked and squeezed underfoot to make something more worthy, no?" she replied.

"Yes."

When she turned back to look out the window, a beam of light illuminated her profile and her black tresses glowed. Her intense beauty left him weak with desire.

"We find ourselves in a difficult…"

"Very difficult…" he replied.

Good God, what an inopportune time to have such a reaction.

Doña moved toward him, putting her hands on his waist, their midsections but a few inches from each other.

She looked down and noticed his physical reaction, then moved closer, her stomach not an inch from his midsection. Her hand crept down and brushed his thigh.

He smelled her then—jasmine and sweat—the combination an intoxicating scent that made him dizzy. His breathing became heavy.

She leaned forward. *Exactly the stance a woman might take before kissing a man.*

Instead, she whispered, "Your desire for me is welcome, and produces in me the same kind of reaction."

They stared at each other, inches apart. "But I cannot follow such desire," she finally said, stepping back a step, her hands lifting away from his waist. "I love Ayala, and you love Pippa. We must honour such love."

He felt bereft; his glazed eyes suddenly focused.

"Perhaps one day we may meet again, and we may each be alone in life, and finally see where our mutual desire leads us. Until then, we must feed the fire of love, not desire."

He was breathing heavily. "You can't leave me like this," he groaned, his voice low.

"But I must, for we cannot be together, at least not now. If Calveley found we had been together, you would be tortured, perchance killed. I would suffer a worse fate. Then I would lose hope of ever being with my true love, Ayala. You know this to be true," she said.

"Yes," he said, his voice barely above a whisper.

She moved to the door, opened it, stopped, then turned. "I will consider what you have said. Calveley may indeed be better off with Pedro and helping to kill Enrique, for to see Enrique dead would be a balm for much pain and loss."

Chaucer breathed out a sigh of relief.

"You can find Calveley encamped with his men in the valley just north of Logrono," she said, before turning and leaving.

Chaucer sighed. He waited a short time, descended the tower, looked left and right along the cobbled street, then also exited and strode toward the barn at the end of the street toward his horse. As he entered the barn, he noted the lantern was lit but the boy who had been tending his horse was gone. He could just make out a tall figure in a dark cloak with a cowl hiding his or her face who stood in shadow in the stall next to that of his horse.

"Who are you, and where is the boy?" Chaucer asked.

"Geoffrey Chaucer, your pass from Carlos has expired," said the figure.

"I was going to ride to Olite to request one this moment," Chaucer replied.

"You must pay a fine for travelling without one."

A man, not a boy.

"Come into the light and we can discuss this," Chaucer said, feeling for his knife.

"Lose this?" asked the man as he stepped toward Chaucer into the lantern's light and held out Chaucer's knife.

Chaucer stepped back toward the barn entrance.

"I can pay for a pass," Chaucer said as he fumbled in his jupon for his leather purse.

"On this day, the price is your life," said the cloaked figure in a low, guttural voice as he took one step forward and raised his sword and Chaucer's knife.

Another dark-cloaked man blocked the door, sword in hand. Chaucer had nowhere to go.

"Gentlemen, surely we can come to an arrangement. I will pay double whatever price you have been paid."

The dark cloaked man took another step forward, his sword point now only a foot from Chaucer.

"There is only one price to pay," he said as he lifted his arm to strike.

Chaucer stepped backward and tripped over a wooden bench used for shoeing horses and fell on his back.

Just then, another cowled figure burst through the barn entrance, slicing the sword arm of the man guarding the door and parrying the downward thrust of the dark cloaked figure.

The two exchanged several blows, turning in a circle until the cloaked figure had the back of the barn behind him, dropped his sword, turned and ran past Chaucer to the other end of the barn and what must have been another exit, and was gone.

"You've saved my life," Chaucer said, gasping for air. He struggled to find his feet and then sought the face of his saviour, who removed his cowl.

"Croker! But how did you find me?"

"I learned a price was put on your head and have followed you since your arrival."

"I am thankful…but who would want me gone?" Chaucer replied.

"Surely Enrique or Carlos, or both, are behind this attack. "

Alfonso arrived, his frown deeply creased by worry. "What happen?"

"I had another unexpected guest," Chaucer replied.

"One seeking to thwart Chaucer's task," Croker added.

Alfonso nodded; he understood too well the stakes involved.

"We ride south for Calveley—will you join us?"

"I am needed elsewhere. You are on your own. Try not to get yourself killed before you find him," Croker said.

"Thank you again," Chaucer said to Croker's back.

Soon after, they rode southwest toward Logrono to seek Calveley, again. The burden of Chaucer's duty was now heavier, even as death's hand was that much closer.

CHAPTER 21
NORTH OF LOGRONO, JANUARY 14, 1367
CHAUCER PLEADS

Alfonso had quietly put out the word and soon heard that Calveley was indeed leading his men east from Burgos toward Navarre, the reason unclear. So Chaucer and Alfonso had ridden southwest through the morning mist along the Camino Santiago to find him. By late that afternoon, the white veil parted and half a day's ride northeast of Logrono they found Calveley's scouts below the ancient Castillo de San Esteban de Deyo o de Monjardínwho. Doña Constanza had been correct. The scouts met and escorted them to Calveley's tent at an outcropping overlooking the valley.

"Chaucer, you are well met this day. How did you find me?" Calveley asked after they clapped each other's shoulders like old friends.

"Alfonso has many eyes and ears across this land. It was not that hard," Chaucer replied.

"If you can find me so easily, then my enemies may also," Calveley replied, consternation flashing across his face.

"And who might your enemies be now?"

"That is a very good question, better asked and answered over a goblet or two of a most excellent and superior wine from the monastery above us. Come, join me. Alfonso also," Calveley said. And they did.

Shortly after, they gathered inside the tent where a couple of dozen pillows lay upon a brightly coloured carpet, after the fashion of the Moors. A huge, dark-skinned servant set a jug of wine and three goblets upon a low table and then lit the brazier next to it. Several torches burned from sconces hanging from the tent poles. A writing table and cot were set on one side of the tent.

"Thank you, Ahmed," said Calveley.

Chaucer noted Ahmed's warm smile as he nodded to Calveley.

"Pedro cut out his tongue for speaking the truth. He is grateful for employment here and is faithful in his duties," Calveley said in answer to Chaucer's unasked question. "His ancestors built the castle that lies above the monastery here. Please sit, make yourselves comfortable."

Chaucer looked about for chairs and saw none.

"On the pillows," Calveley said. "Lighter and easier to pack than chairs, and much more comfortable. The Moors had some excellent customs I happily follow."

Chaucer lowered himself in an ungainly fashion, plopping down on the largest of several pillows set in a semi-circle by the brazier that now cast a warm glow. After Alfonso dropped more fluidly onto a smaller pillow, Ahmed poured the wine.

Calveley finally addressed Chaucer's question about who his enemies were.

"I will surely gain new enemies if I attack towns in Navarre to refill my men's coffers."

"That would not please Enrique. Or Carlos. And might signal you had turned your allegiances to Edward," Chaucer said, shifting on the pillow—he was used to a hard oak chair.

"Yes, it might."

"I see," Chaucer said, shifting again. Alfonso seemed entirely comfortable.

"Do you? Do you see? I am in the middle of a generation-long war, with Carlos changing sides as often as he changes his breeches. An agreement signed even in blood means nothing to him. King Pere of Aragon supports Enrique, and Carlos too, yet both now seem less keen to continue this war than a few weeks ago, even with Pedro gone and Enrique crowned king. I think the threat of Prince Edward is too great and so they prevaricate in case Edward shows his intentions. If he attacks, and they have chosen the wrong side, then they could be destroyed along with Enrique, for Edward will need to pay for his army, and gold from both Barcelona and Olite would fill his coffers."

I must turn this back to the task at hand.

"I see. But what of Doña Constanza?" Chaucer asked.

"I saw her on several occasions last fall and understood that we had come to an understanding. But then received no message from her, so presume she has made her decision."

"I would not presume so much," Chaucer said.

Calveley looked closely at Chaucer. "What do you know of her mind?"

"I would not presume to know a woman's mind, as it can be as inscrutable and unknown as God's plan, but I spoke to her but two days ago in Pamplona," Chaucer said.

Calveley's face was now a cauldron of hope, curiosity and distrust.

"How did you come to be with her? What did she say?" he asked, eyes glinting.

"I met her through an acquaintance. She told me she was to wed you, as Enrique had promised her, in exchange for your support in this war."

Calveley paused before replying, "Enrique promised her, yes. But I know she loves Ayala," Calveley said, hope departing from his face as quickly as it had arrived.

"One can love many people in a lifetime."

This I know to be true.

"Perchance. But one in my position might ask what succour she would find with a man like me, a mercenary?" Calveley asked. "For an unhappy wife is a burden no man should bear."

"Happy? What is it to be happy? To have regular food and wine, a bed, a roof over your head, someone who cares for you? Oh, and servants, land, titles, gold…is that not enough? Happiness is something that can arrive in time like Odysseus."

"I think a woman, nay, a lady like Doña Constanza will want more, will demand more, for she can have any man she desires, and she desires Ayala."

"What you say may be true. But Ayala now supports Enrique. If you supported Edward and Pedro, you might find a way to see both Ayala and Enrique killed or banished, and then all that you desire will be yours," Chaucer said.

"Chaucer, you have a dangerous way with words. Such actions as you describe in the service of desire might be construed as unchivalrous."

Chaucer could see a man turning away from one sure destiny and considering another. He saw his chance.

"Chivalry and desire have always been at war, and yet does not every man take up his sword for desire? The desire to please his king through fealty? The desire to earn riches and gain land through battle or ransom, to gain more in one day than most might gain in a lifetime? The desire to show his lady his courage on the battlefield, and so demonstrate this same chivalry? Is not every true act merely an act of desire?" Chaucer said.

"You are a clever one, Geoffrey Chaucer. I desire all that you say, and of course, desire to be with a woman like Doña Constanza."

And then Chaucer watched Calveley turn and face him as his eyes narrowed, and the light within them dimmed.

"But you are a storyteller, Chaucer. And a storyteller's desire may never truly be known, for one might never know which stories are, in fact, true."

Chaucer's brows knitted in confusion.

Calveley continued. "I see well enough what this is all about. What you are all about. Stories told by Edward's spy," he said.

Chaucer tilted his head.

"I wondered about you when we first met. I asked myself, 'What is the king's lowly page doing in the middle of nowhere, amidst a war, purportedly seeking to trade in wine?' And then you revealed you were on the king's business to try to turn me. Edward sent you on a fool's mission, for he would know I would decline. But I decided to let you and Alfonso join me, in case there were secrets about Pedro you might reveal. After Pedro's defeat, I thought such machinations would end. But I see now that you are using my hatred of du Guesclin and my desire for Doña Constanza as part of your scheme to again turn me against Enrique and toward Edward. Do you deny this?"

Chaucer looked to Calveley's menacing stare, then to Ahmed, still standing like a stone—his very presence a threat.

He turned to Alfonso, who remained silent, and offered no clue to his thoughts, or how Chaucer should respond.

I must be careful of my words or may lose him.

"Yes, all that you say may be true. But you forget the most important thing on that list of accusations."

Calveley's frown did not shift.

"You neglected to accuse me of doing my duty. All that I did was done in duty to my king. Your king. None of my motives in seeking you were hidden. It was only to remind you to do your duty to your king. That is the one thing that *our* king asked that I be sure to convey, above all else. And now I have done so, and done my duty," Chaucer said.

Calveley's face changed yet again, reflecting the emotions that roiled beneath the surface, like a storm that raged and then passed, then raged again.

"Duty, you say? To my king? You think it is only duty I should attend to?" he asked. "After my king paid not a groat to me after I had given years of service and then was left to survive on my own, or return to England, penniless. How in God's name do you think I should reconcile such poor duty from our *king*?" Calveley asked, the word *king* clearly inspiring a strong reaction from Calveley.

Chaucer saw an opening. "What I think of all this is of no import. It is only what you believe in your heart that matters. But think on the oath that you made to King Edward when he granted you knighthood years ago. Then think on the gold and the land and the women and the titles you have gained since. And think now on what remains that is truly valuable. Yes? Have you thought on that, Sir Hugh? What of value remains? Reputation. What of your reputation?" Chaucer asked. "Think on Enrique, who seeks to be a king, but will kill Jews for no reason. Including women like Doña Constanza. There is no chivalry in his heart, only vengeance and some dark hate. He is empty of honour. That is his reputation. That is what the poets will write about him. What will your reputation be?"

Chaucer noted Calveley give a subtle nod of recognition of that truth and carried on.

"For the only things of value that remain are love, reputation and duty. That is all," Chaucer said. "And duty to one's king is a kind of love that can bring reputation, and with that riches," Chaucer added.

Calveley looked away. When he turned back to Chaucer, the storm in his eyes had returned.

"Your words lie too far above your true station, and at such a height sound more lie than truth," Calveley said.

"It is true, good knight, that I am but a mere page, but simple truths are still truths. They know no height, nor rank, but are bred from simple duty," Chaucer shot back. "Duty to one's king. A king and prince, who have won many great battles. And who will win many more, with the help of loyal subjects and trusted knights. Like yourself."

Calveley stared at Chaucer. "Yes, Chaucer, it may be as simple as that."

Chaucer nodded.

"But you neglect to mention one other simple truth," Calveley said.

"And what is that?"

"War. Men like me, we value war. We live to fight battles. To test ourselves. To best others. Some men, and women too, find those battles inside themselves. Methinks you may be one of those. But other men, and yes women, must find a war, wherever it may be, for it gives them a reason to fight, and to live," he said, adding, "The desire for war is one more thing that remains. So add that to your list of what a man may value, and be known for in time. Love, reputation, duty…and war."

Chaucer nodded.

"Some find it within their homes, with their wives and family," Calveley added.

Again Chaucer nodded.

"And some within themselves," Chaucer said quietly.

He had been at war with himself—with lust, with ambition, with jealousy, and more recently, with fear—since leaving London.

It was Calveley's turn to nod.

"I find it here, on the fields of foreign lands, where I might test my skill against others, and against God and Lady Fortune, and find riches that are not just gold," Calveley said.

The words Calveley spoke sparked a memory, and he retrieved a wax-sealed letter from inside his cloak and handed it to him.

"From Prince Edward, to be handed to you in person, on pain of death. Read it, and think on who knighted you on the field of battle, Sir Hugh. I heard rumour Carlos betrayed our good prince and now sides with Enrique. If true, I imagine Edward will be looking to all those he trusts for support in first dealing with Carlos, and then Enrique."

Chaucer's words gave Calveley pause. He took the letter, but instead of opening it, tucked it inside his jupon.

"There is much to consider. Stay the night at my camp and I will give you my reply on the morrow before I return to Burgos to speak to Enrique."

Chaucer noted the frown on Calveley's face when he said Enrique's name, and was, for the first time in a long time, hopeful.

"Thank you, good sir. And I would ask that you think on one more thing. I was attacked in Pamplona by an assassin sent to kill me. Perchance to prevent me from finding you. That means Carlos or

Enrique, or both, now conspire against you. The die has already been cast."

Calveley looked then at Chaucer with his mouth half open, as if about to say something.

He instead turned to Ahmed and said, "Please find Chaucer and Alfonso a place to stay; nothing too comfortable, mind you. Chaucer, sleep safe this night, and I will speak more to you about this in the morning," then turned back to the vellum and scrolls set before him on the small table, the letter from Edward still unopened.

Did I say enough to convince him?

Chaucer followed Ahmed out of the tent to a campfire and a bundle of blankets, Alfonso a step behind him. Dusk was gone; the chill dark of the January night had settled over the campsite. Ahmed handed them each a blanket and motioned to an empty spot around the small fire where no other soldiers lay sleeping. A light dusting of recent snow covered the campsite. He thanked Ahmed, then flopped down exhausted on the cold ground and wrapped the blanket around himself. They sat as close as they could to the dying fire to eke out what warmth remained.

Chaucer stared into the fire until the flames became embers. Would Calveley finally turn? It was possible. He was a man who sought war. He'd made that clear. But what did he need more? Love, reputation, duty or war? Was it always a choice between such things, or could one have them all? When he mentioned Calveley's duty to the king, he noted a reaction in Calveley absent the last meeting. For Calveley to help win another battle like Crecy or Poitiers would be to truly make his reputation. And even Calveley would seek to burnish his reputation with another battle like that.

"You quiet," Alfonso said.

"I have much to think on," Chaucer replied.

"As does Calveley."

Chaucer nodded, then looked up to the stars that sparkled in the clear, frosty January air. Toward the south more lights twinkled from Logrono, where Prince Edward would march once he knew Calveley would join him. But time had nearly run out, for Candlemas, and his deadline, was but a few days away.

He put two branches onto the fire and pulled the blanket closer. Funny how a man might watch a fire die as he himself became colder, too lazy to add more wood to maintain the fire. But the fire must be maintained. As in war. And love.

What do I seek more of, war or love? For it seems my desires are often at war with my ambitions, yet ambition must triumph in order for me to gain the love that forever floats just beyond my reach. Perchance it truly is only duty that matters.

He had done all he could to turn Calveley. He had done his duty. He had no more words in him. Now all he could do was wait. His fate was in the hands of others.

•   •   •

He was awoken by the sound of a horse neighing and muttered voices. He opened his eyes, and it was still the dark of night, but very near his campfire, he saw a cloaked figure dismounting from a horse. The figure said something he couldn't make out to a guard. A woman's voice. A voice that was familiar; also familiar was the way that she moved as she followed the guard—it was Doña Constanza. What was she doing here?

Chaucer scrambled up, pulling his cloak tightly about him as he followed the two figures at a distance. The guard led Doña to Calveley's tent, where a brazier lit the tent entrance.

He paused, keeping to the shadows. He wanted to hear what they would say.

"Try crawl under tent," a voice behind him said. Chaucer jumped at the sound of Alfonso, who must have been hiding in the shadows of the tent.

"What are you doing here?" Chaucer whispered, too loudly.

"Keep you alive," he said.

"How do I get under the tent?" Chaucer whispered back.

"I cut," he said, motioning for Chaucer to follow him.

Darkness engulfed them as they made their way to the back of the tent, Alfonso ensuring Chaucer didn't trip on any of the tent pegs and ropes. Alfonso stopped, crouched, pulled out a thin knife, and silently slit the side of the tent. He then motioned for Chaucer to wriggle through the hole.

Inside, in the dim light cast by the torches, he saw he was in a small space stacked with chests overflowing with silver and gold plate, armour, swords and richly detailed clothing. He was in the back of the same tent he had met Calveley earlier. He could make out Doña Constanza and Calveley sitting on the same pillows they had occupied before. He crawled silently towards them, hiding behind the booty until he could hear their voices. He could also make out the opened letter from Prince Edward lying upon a small table before them.

"...but why? Why would you come by yourself, in the middle of the night?"

"To tell you, I will be with you," Doña Constanza said.

"But what of Ayala? I know it is he that you truly love," he said.

"Yes, it is true, but I would make you a good wife if you would allow me Ayala."

Chaucer knew such words were dangerous for her to say aloud. Calveley could reject her and tell others of what she said, and if the wrong bishop or lord found out, she would be drowned or burned as a harlot by the Church. Or Calveley could simply be angered by her suggestion of keeping Ayala as a lover, and seek to kill him.

But Calveley was silent. After a long pause, he said, "I will think on it. Now return to Pamplona, and I will give you my answer before the next full moon."

"Do not wait too long, for Lady Fortune can change the course of one's life while you wait to change it," she replied.

They stared at each other for a moment, then she strode out of the tent.

Chaucer wriggled his way silently back to where Alfonso was waiting, then slipped out through the cut in the tent. They followed

Doña in the shadows, then watched as she mounted her horse and quietly rode away.

Then, just as he was about to return to his fire and blanket, Chaucer saw Calveley step out of the tent. He took a few steps toward Doña as she rode away. Something only a man smitten by a woman would do. And Chaucer knew at that moment that Calveley wanted Doña Constanza and would fight for her. And for Edward.

He followed Alfonso back to their fire. Doña had come to help him turn Calveley and by all he had heard and seen she had succeeded. And now a battle, and a war, needed to be won. And duty finally done.

CHAPTER 22
BURGOS, FEBRUARY 1, 1367
CALVELEY GIVES ENRIQUE NEWS

"My lord, I depart tomorrow. King Edward asks for my return," said Calveley. After Chaucer's talk, Prince Edward's letter, and Doña's visit, Calveley had returned to Burgos with a clear idea of what he must do next and had requested an audience with Enrique.

"I see. You will return to England, to your king?"

"Eventually, yes, my lord," Calveley replied.

"Or to Bordeaux, to your prince?" Enrique asked.

"I will stop there on my way, yes, to pay my respects."

"But do not tarry too long in Bordeaux."

"And why would you say that?"

"Calveley, we have achieved much together in but a few weeks," Enrique said.

"We have indeed, my lord. I am grateful for the honours, lands, titles and gold that you have bestowed upon me."

"And a lady. And yet…" Enrique added.

"And yet, my lord?" Calveley asked.

"And yet I wonder if in giving my blessing to leave I am tilting at Lady Fortune, for I may very well face you on the battlefield one day."

"Give your blessing? I have not asked for your blessing, my lord, for you and I both know I serve under contract, and that contract has been fulfilled. It is my choice to leave. As to fighting you on the battlefield, one never knows. In the last ten years, I have faced many English knights under hire by the French, or Lombards, or Gascons, who, like me, also fight for gold."

"Yes, yes, of course it is your choice for you to leave," Enrique said, his tone suggesting the opposite. "And yet to have the blessing of a king can be helpful in these dangerous lands. You have a powerful force, but it is small and requires food and lodging. You and your men have a long way to travel between here and Bordeaux."

Calveley's face flushed nearly as red as his hair, and he clenched his fists. "I do not react well to threats, my lord. In fact, I will take my leave now. Good day," Calveley said.

"Please wait. I do not threaten good Calveley. I only inform you of the truth. Now, on a pleasanter note, do you still plan to wed Doña Constanza?" Enrique asked. "Would you depart without her?" he added.

Calveley considered his response.

"My men found her last night. Lost, she said. Thankfully, she is safe now. Her hand, and the rest of her fine self, shall await you, under my care, assuming, of course, you stay allied to my cause, for why would I offer her hand to an enemy?" Enrique said.

Calveley stared at him, his face reddening again.

"I offend you, Calveley?" Enrique asked.

"I am no enemy, as yet. And while Doña Constanza is a fine lady whose hand I would indeed seek in marriage, that will wait, for I must first pay my respects to my lord."

"Do not wait too long, Calveley. A woman like that is sought by many men. You should claim her while you can," Enrique said. "And of course, such a woman must be protected, or Lady Fortune might turn her wheel. It would be a shame if that was the last you had seen of her."

Calveley whirled from him and began striding for the door.

Two guards with spears crossed blocked the exit.

"Move aside or the pointy end of those sticks will end up your arseholes," he rumbled.

They hesitated, looking to Enrique for direction.

Enrique motioned and they moved their spears, allowing Calveley to pass, and watched the soldier stride out of the palace gates. He faced Ayala, who had entered the room silently just after Calveley's hasty departure.

"He now poses a threat," Ayala said. "It would have been better to keep him here longer, and better yet not to have angered him," he said.

"Too costly to keep him, too costly to him let go. A king must make difficult choices."

"But for him to leave feeling disrespected, my lord, is to push him toward Prince Edward," Ayala said.

"He clearly desires Constanza and will not choose against her."

Ayala kept his face toward the empty doorway to hide his reaction. Enrique may have been right about Calveley's desire for Constanza, but Ayala knew enough men like Calveley to know where his greatest desire lay.

•   •   •

Calveley rode hard and later that afternoon arrived at his camp north of Logrono and ordered his eight hundred armoured, battle-hardened warriors to break camp immediately. They left at sunset, travelling northeast toward Pamplona. Enrique must have sent faster riders ahead, for word of the news had already reached other lords who were not welcoming. Calveley and his men were turned away and had to sleep in the cold under the stars that night. The next day they were again rebuffed by nobles when he asked to feed and water his horses and men. The following evening, several riders crept into their camp near the town of Villatuerta and cut the reins of their horses before the alarm could be sounded. In the ensuing melee, they lost four horses and one man-at-arms. Stolen at the behest of Enrique or Carlos—it mattered not now.

Calveley thought of his conversation with Chaucer, who had been right about the rumour, or had known that the letter from Edward spoke of a broken truce, with Carlos again switching allegiances. And trying to have Chaucer killed. The loss of the horses was too much. He had had enough, and he reacted as any mercenary would: he went on the offensive, seizing several towns, including Puente la Reina, about twelve miles south of Pamplona, sacking it, killing the inhabitants and setting fire to the thatched homes and wood buildings. He spared only the pilgrims in the monastery. Calveley would send a message to both Enrique and Carlos that he was sacking towns and villages across southern Navarre. His intentions of which side he would support in the coming battle would now be very clear.

•   •   •

Chaucer and Alfonso had waited in Logrono for news of the outcome of Calveley's meeting with Enrique. When Calveley's forces were spotted north of Logrono heading northeast, they left that morning on horseback and paused midday once the smell of the burning towns reached them. They finally caught up to them a few miles northeast of Punta la Reina. The view of the beautiful valley was marred by smoke from the burning town.

Sir William Beauchamp, who was protecting Calveley's rear from any surprise attacks, galloped toward them with his force of some fifty mounted men to find out if they were scouts, then recognized Chaucer from his earlier visit.

"Chaucer, welcome. You risk much riding without an escort," Sir William said.

"Sir William, I take such a risk to speak with Sir Hugh," Chaucer said as they came within earshot of each other. Alfonso hung back on his swaybacked palfrey.

"He rides several miles ahead," he said, gesturing towards the smoke clouding the sky in the northwest. "The hospitality granted us on our arrival has become less welcoming, so we had to find a way to feed ourselves," answered Sir William. "You would stay for whatever wine and food we have been able to free from the locals?"

"Yes, we would be grateful for the sustenance and company," Chaucer replied.

•   •   •

"Sir Hugh, good day. I see you have given Enrique and Carlos a message," Chaucer said.

Chaucer and Alfonso were now fed and rested, like their horses.

"Yes. I let them both know that I will protect my men against any who threaten me," Calveley said.

"And du Guesclin? Have you heard of his whereabouts?" Chaucer asked.

"I learned just yesterday that du Guesclin has gathered a new force of French and Breton men in France and is returning to rejoin Enrique. And the letter from our lord prince was also as you said, confirming what my own spies have heard. Enrique had increased his offer to Carlos, who accepted it, agreeing to close the pass to Edward, as you had said. Carlos has switched allegiances, and now will pay dearly for that choice," Calveley spat. "And any who choose Enrique now also choose dearly," he added.

The next morning, Chaucer and Alfonso left the city. He needed to convey a message to Prince Edward and had only three days left to deliver it. Alfonso joined him as far as Pamplona.

•   •   •

Carlos soon heard of the pillaging and burning of his lands in the south of Navarre. His future looked less secure with Calveley at his doorstep. When Carlos sent a letter to Prince Edward complaining of such behaviour, Edward wrote of the rumours of the broken truce, and if Carlos wanted Edward to call off his new attack dog Calveley, then Carlos had best ensure the pass stayed open. Calveley had now become the most important knight in their game of chess.

Carlos dispatched the royal standard bearer, Martin Enriquez de la Carra, to mend fences. La Carra was Carlos' puppet when Carlos chose not to risk his own skin. La Carra met Edward in Bayonne and swore that Carlos had no intention of disavowing his pledge, and anything else he had heard was merely a vicious rumour. Edward nodded, said little, and sent La Carra on his way home.

Enrique's spies in Bordeaux had reported that Edward was gathering his army and would surely be sending his soldiers south soon. His spies in Pamplona also sent word that Carlos was turning his favour back to Edward because of Calveley. The winds of war were changing direction, and it was time to act. Enrique made preparations to march his army east of Burgos to Santo Domingo de la Calzada, astride the Camino de Santiago. There, he could face an attack from the north via Vitoria or east via Najera. All that was left was for Prince Edward to march across the Pyrenees in the dead of winter and Carlos to open the pass. Which Enrique could not let happen.

CHAPTER 23
OLITE, FEBRUARY 2, 1367
CARLOS AND DE LA CARRA PLOT

"I signed the agreement and will let Pedro and Prince Edward journey through my pass. I also promised 2,000 knights to join his effort. But I will be in Tudela, and you will welcome them," Carlos said to de la Carra.

The two men were the only occupants of the terrace that spanned the two tallest towers of Olite Castle. They both leaned against the wall that faced Pamplona and the peaks of the Pyrenees that poked above the clouds to the north.

"But why let them come unmolested? You could easily block his army at Roncesvalles," said de la Carra.

"And then earn the everlasting enmity of a powerful prince and his more powerful father, King Edward? With Calveley already burning down my southern border? No, my dear de la Carra, that would not serve our purposes. There are many ways to defeat an army."

De la Carra's face showed his confusion.

"I am appointing you as my viceroy, and you will go to Pamplona and welcome Edward and Pedro in my stead," Carlos said.

De la Carra dropped to one knee. "My lord, I am honoured."

"Up man, for you may soon think differently upon this so-called honour," Carlos said.

"But why would you not greet them?"

"Because I will be behind bars, captured before I can honour my pledge to join Pedro and Edward in battle against Enrique," Carlos replied.

"Ah. I see." Clearly he didn't.

"That is why I chose you, for you understand how these things work," Carlos said. De la Carra just nodded.

"Edward will then seek your advice on how to seek out and engage Enrique."

De la Carra nodded again, more obedient puppy than advisor.

"Tell me, de la Carra, which road would you tell Pedro and Edward to take?"

"Surely the best road for the English would be to travel southwest on the Camino de Santiago to Logrono, cross the Ebro there, and then head west past Najera to Burgos," de la Carra replied.

"Yes, the best for the English, but the worst for us."

"But…," de la Carra began to say.

"Such a large army would eat all the food and drink all the wine between here and Najera, and might also ravish the women and kill the children."

De la Carra nodded a third time.

"No. You will send them north and then west to Vitoria."

"But…but they will starve. The land cannot provide enough sustenance for an army that large," he replied.

"Exactly," said Carlos.

"And then?" de la Carra asked, confusion swirling across his face like the clouds that scudded across the mountains ahead.

"And then Enrique will attack, and both armies might very well destroy each other."

"And then you will be able to dictate terms with whoever survives to claim the crown," de la Carra finally said.

"Yes, you understand exactly. You must above all convince both Edward and Pedro of this route," Carlos said.

"Edward and Sir John Chandos may listen to me, but Pedro will surely know why we would direct them on that path and protest."

"Pedro will want to engage Enrique as soon as he gets through the pass. If he thinks his bastard brother is at Vitoria, he will not care how to find him there," Carlos said.

"But Enrique is at Burgos."

"We know that, but they don't. And if Enrique's spies learn of Pedro's plans to surprise Enrique by attacking from Vitoria, then he will send his army north to Vitoria. I have already planted rumours to that effect. Two of Edward's spies arrived yesterday. You will add to whatever rumours they might spread. Once Edward hears from his own spies of Enrique's movement toward Vitoria, the die will be cast," Carlos said.

"Who are the spies?"

"The brothers Felton. They lead a group of some fifty knights who seek information about Enrique's forces and will inform Edward once he arrives. We will feed them information now and as they travel west." Carlos said.

"We?"

"By 'we' I mean you, in my stead, as I will be behind bars, remember?" Carlos said. "Plead ignorance in all things, if Edward pries. Now go, for I must prepare for my capture."

"One more thing, my lord king," de la Carra said.

"Yes?"

"The spy Chaucer returned to Pamplona hours ago, seeking passage north. What would you have us do with him?"

"He matters not. The die is already cast."

PART 4
WAR, AGAIN

CHAPTER 24
THE PYRENEES, FEBRUARY 13, 1367
CROSSING

As the path narrowed, Chaucer swivelled in his saddle to take in the endless line of soldiers and carts behind them. Snow-covered mountain peaks loomed on either side, and the sky threatened, darkening from the light grey of the overcast morning to the near black storm gathering that afternoon. Chaucer didn't care. After he had turned Calveley, he and Alfonso had ridden as fast as they could to Pamplona where they had bribed a captain of the guards to gain passage and change horses and rode over the pass to Dax to give Edward the news, arriving just before Edward's one month deadline for his return. Edward had gathered his forces, and he and his brother John and the Duke of Armagnac each led an army totalling some 20,000 men. Pedro would have some 4,000 men join once he passed into Castile.

Edward showed his pleasure at the news by inviting Chaucer to ride near the front of the line.

"Chaucer, I cannot quell the ever-present worry that we will reach Roncesvalles and find the pass closed," Edward said.

"Carlos would be a fool to do such a thing, my lord, for he knows Calveley lies to the south, already threatening his border, and we would find another way through and destroy him," Chaucer said, his voice more confident than he felt.

He knew the campaign would be lost before it started, should Carlos change his loyalty yet again. If the weather worsened, and they were trapped and had to turn back, thousands of soldiers would surely perish. They were the second of three armies totalling over twenty thousand soldiers, the largest army ever assembled in memory, crossing mountains in the dead of winter. Edward's brother John of Gaunt was ahead by a day, leading the first army with Sir John Chandos beside him. They were in Lady Fortune's hands now, a lady who played no favourites, and no story, no matter how well told, could change the fate that she had lain in wait for them.

•   •   •

The next day, Edward sat astride his horse and watched his men pass by, struggling against the cold. "Well done, almost there, keep going, and think on the gold and treasure that awaits," he repeated, trying to cheer the soldiers who trudged through the blowing snow.

This was the hardest part, but he was hopeful. Word had reached him earlier that morning that his brother John had found the pass open and had led the first army on toward Pamplona. The weather had turned in the three days since John had left, so Edward had briefly paused. A third similar-sized army was following half a day behind, led by the Count of Armagnac. Both armies were at their most vulnerable part of their journey, for if Edward was blocked, the rest would be as well, and they might all perish. They'd already dealt with a broken cart blocking the narrow path, a horse going over the edge and a small landslide. He prayed no more obstacles would delay them. But now the wind was picking up, and the snow was heavier. He prayed it would not become a true blizzard.

As he sat astride his destrier, calling encouragement to the brave men who passed him, Edward recalled the words of Carlos thrown towards him so effortlessly in Saint-Jean-Pied-de-Port when they were negotiating the final terms of their agreement.

"I carry great risk, for when you pass through my lands, your army may choose to turn on Navarre. What guarantee do I have that will not happen?" Carlos had said, voicing the same words Edward himself had been contemplating. Indeed, why would he not turn on Carlos and claim Navarre as his own? He then would control the pass, and a kingdom. That would provide security to his southern border. But he knew his answer was as true then as now.

"Because to hold such a mountainous land without the support of the people would be to tempt fate. I would need an army five times this size. No, Carlos, I have no desire to lift your crown and wear it, be assured of that. I care only to see Enrique gone, as you do."

The agreement was signed, and a great battle now set in motion.

•　　•　　•

Edward's army made it through the pass and arrived at Pamplona on February 23. Two days later, the army led by Armagnac arrived. At the entrance to the castle overlooking the city of Pamplona, Edward expected to be welcomed by King Carlos, but he was in for a surprise.

"Martin Enriquez de la Carra, viceroy of Navarre, my lord," announced Edward's steward as the new arrival bent low on one knee. "We met once before, last month, in Bayonne."

Edward's scowl voiced silent words. He recalled how he had so effortlessly voiced Carlos' words once before.

Several of Edward's knights and lords surrounded them, nearly filling the hall. A fire crackled behind them, but cast little heat, for it had been lit shortly before. Old, musty wall hangings with smoky hunting scenes covered the cold stone walls.

"Yes, I recall. Up, de la Carra," Prince Edward said, irked at Carlos' messenger kneeling before him instead of Carlos.

The two stood staring at each other for a moment before de la Carra said, "My lord, welcome to Pamplona, and the Kingdom of Navarre."

"Where is Carlos?" Edward asked bluntly, absent his usual flowery words of greeting. He had expected to be met by the king, not his lackey. It was a snub, and Edward had very little patience for Carlos' prevarications.

"King Carlos sends his regrets, my lord. He is in Tudela negotiating safe passage for your army," de la Carra said.

"Tudela?" Edward said.

"Yes. He wants you to know that, should he succeed, you will have safe passage west to Vitoria. Should he not succeed, things may be…more difficult," de la Carra said.

Edward scrutinized the man's face for a hidden meaning, but found none. He asked the obvious question, "And why did Carlos not send you on such a task?" he asked.

De la Carra did not hesitate. "My lord king's cousin is there, and he controls the lands north and west of Pamplona. My king felt his presence in such negotiations would ensure success," he replied.

"I would have preferred to be involved in such discussions," Edward said.

"My lord apologizes, but such discussions arose just two days ago when news of your advance reached us. There were concerns others might not play well, and so my king departed immediately," de la Carra replied.

"I see…" Edward said, not so sure to believe this smooth-talking nobleman's words.

"You and your men must be tired after your crossing. I have rooms ready for you, and your soldiers will be fed as best as we can," he said.

Edward was indeed tired, and still felt bone cold, as did his men and horses, so assented to the invitation. De la Carra had a ready answer for every question and Edward had decided Carlos might indeed be helpful in acquiring safe passage to Vitoria, if that was the route he decided to take. And yet something of the story, and the storyteller, bothered him.

•   •   •

The next night, after the men had found warmth, wine, food and lodging, Edward, Gaunt, Pedro, Calveley, Chandos and several other knights were gathered around a great table in the castle keep. A map was laid before them, candlelight flickering across the small stones laid upon the map to signify towns and cities. De la Carra pointed at the map.

"My lord, from Pamplona, you would be well advised to travel northwest to Irurtzun, and then due west to Vitoria," said de la Carra.

His words were much like those of his king, a silky river streaming effortlessly from his mouth.

"And then, from there southwest, straight to Burgos. Enrique will expect you to take the Santiago de Camino to Logrono. Arriving from the Vitoria route will surprise him," de la Carra said.

"My prince," Sir John Chandos said. "Enrique could simply place his army at the juncture of both roads here at Santo Domingo de la Calzada. He could then await news of whichever approach our army took."

Heads nodded around the table. Save for de la Carra, who shook his. When he finally spoke, his confident, smooth delivery faltered, the pitch of his voice now raised. "My lord, there is another road north of Santo Domingo de la Calzada to Briviesca and then Burgos, so with all due respect to the honourable Sir John, Enrique might still be outflanked by placing his army there. No, I am confident he will expect your approach via Logrono, for that city still remains loyal to King Pedro, and sits astride the Ebro. Control of Logrono would mean control of the valley and the rich land and vineyards surrounding it. And thus it would surely be the more compelling and clear choice in Enrique's mind."

"Yet," said Edward, musing aloud. "If Enrique really did think the Logrono path was clearer, why would he not just go take Logrono and force my hand?"

"A much harder city to defend, my lord," Calveley replied. "If Enrique took Logrono, he could be encircled and attacked from both sides. With the people of Logrono loyal to Pedro, holding the city would be difficult. The entire population would fight, not just the soldiers. Also, you could easily slip around him and head straight west and attack Burgos, his capital. Staying where he is, somewhere west of Najera, assures he is only fighting on one front," Calveley replied.

More nods.

"The Vitoria route carries further risk with less food along the way," Calveley said.

"Our people will provide food, as my king has promised," de la Carra shot back.

Prince Edward trusted neither Carlos nor his lackey. Every word out of the mouth of the viceroy seemed overly chewed. Food was already becoming scarce in Pamplona for an army greater in numbers than the population of the city. The choice of which route to take carried much import; the wrong decision could have disastrous consequences. But he had no more time and needed to decide.

•   •   •

Sixty miles west, Enrique was in doubt that Carlos would honour their agreement, and so marched his forces east from Burgos eleven miles to Santo Domingo de la Calzada, the same location deemed by Chandos as the most strategic location. His scouts would tell him if Edward was advancing from the north or west in time for him to block either path. When he would face Pedro this time and defeat him once and for all, and send Prince Edward back to Bordeaux. The Castilian crown would remain his. No one was going to take it away.

CHAPTER 25
NAJERA, MARCH 30, 1367
CHAUCER AND DOÑA CONSTANZA AGAIN

Edward had decided to proceed north and then west to Vitoria the next day. Chaucer received a missive mid-way along the journey: Doña Constanza wanted to meet Chaucer in Najera, at the west end of the bridge. She had news of great import. So Chaucer told Chandos of their need to travel south, and he had assented without asking too many questions, knowing full well that whatever Chaucer was doing, it was in service to the prince. Late that afternoon Chaucer and Alfonso veered south at Agurain and rode through the mountain passes to Estella and then southwest along the Camino de Santiago, where they camped overnight at a monastery, and the next day reached the bridge over the River Ebro and Logrono.

In Logrono, the people they spoke to were at once anxious and relieved, for news of Edward's army successfully passing into Navarre ten days earlier had set expectations that he would move south to Logrono and then west to Burgos. It was the only sensible route, but it would have meant the town would be taxed with feeding his huge army. With Chaucer and Alfonso's arrival came news that Edward was heading to Vitoria, and a collective sigh of relief arose. But Enrique could still attack Logrono first, given its strategic location. The people of Logrono felt that war would surely return again soon, like spring, as it always had.

•   •   •

Enrique's scouts relayed to Enrique the news of Edward's march toward Vitoria, and a day later Enrique moved his entire army north to the hills just west of Vitoria. Hesitant to attack Edward without du Guesclin, who would be returning from France in a matter of days, he instead had his brother Don Tello send raiding parties to attack and harass Edward's soldiers. They had succeeded beyond expectation. Tello had led hundreds of ginetes down from the hills in a surprise dawn attack that left dozens of Edward's men-at-arms dead and wounded. Edward, short of food and unable to mount an attack on an enemy that could so easily disperse, responded by reversing course and marching his army southeast, following Chaucer across a low mountain pass, and across the Rio Ebro to Logrono two days later. They were running out of time, for his men and horses were hungry and exhausted. He desperately sought one final engagement to end the war. But would Enrique face him?

•   •   •

While Edward was still making his way from Vitoria, Chaucer and Alfonso left Logrono and rode southwest along a valley to the hillside town of Navarette, a third of the way to Najera. If Edward and his army camped in Logrono, any advance toward Najera would come through this valley. Najera could not be seen due to a slight rise to the west before the valley descended.

An army could camp here, some eight or nine miles from Najera, and also remain unseen by Enrique's scouts.

They passed up and over the rise and then descended toward Najera late in the afternoon. As they approached near sunset, dark red cliffs loomed behind Najera, casting a deep shadow over the one bridge that crossed the Rio Najerilla that bisected the town from north to south.

A good defensive position if the army was on the western side of that bridge, and a trap if placed to the east.

Alfonso's network had confirmed that Enrique's army was not far from Najera to the northwest. So Chaucer was keen to quickly conduct his business without discovery, and then rejoin Edward just in case Enrique decided to advance sooner than hoped.

As they approached Najera, Alfonso held back. "I will stay in the shadows and ensure you or she have not been followed. Enrique will have spies here, and we must be careful."

Chaucer walked his horse through Najera and the throngs of people coming and going to the market on the western side of the Rio Najerilla below the monastery that loomed over the town.

Chaucer waited by the bridge, and Doña Constanza arrived soon after. She greeted Chaucer, and she turned and led him into the eastern half of the town and down a labyrinth of alleys and passages. Chaucer soon became disoriented and had no idea where he was. Such care heightened Chaucer's concern. He could not see Alfonso following—which meant Doña Constanza couldn't see him either.

A short time later, Doña stopped in front of a merchant's shop. The merchant immediately began encouraging Chaucer to buy one of his 'beautifully wrought gold chains' in Castilian with an unusual accent, different from the Logrono locals. His clothes were also distinctive. He wore fine silks around his midsection, with a paltok inlaid with what looked like gemstones covering his chest. Gold thread ran through the rich fabrics of his clothing, and he wore a gold chain around his neck and gold earrings. The merchant was wearing more gold than Chaucer had ever seen on a man who wasn't either noble or a prince.

Doña exchanged a few words with the man in a language that Chaucer didn't understand. It may have been Hebrew, as he recalled similar sounding words entering Olite that Alfonso had said were Hebrew.

Doña turned to Chaucer and said, "This is my uncle Ner, and he welcomes you. He was expecting a well-dressed knight on a horse, and took you to be a customer."

Ner smiled warmly, revealing more gaps than teeth. He said a few words to Chaucer in his own language, then nodded at Doña, as if to say, "Translate, please."

"He said, 'My home is your home, and any friend of Doña is a friend of our family.'"

Chaucer smiled warmly at Ner.

Ner widened his smile as he gestured for them to enter his shop, currently without a customer. Every surface displayed beautiful objects of gold and fine jewellery. It felt much warmer than the monastery.

"He has a thriving business," Chaucer said.

"It was not always so," said Doña. "He used to live in Najera, but seven years ago Enrique killed his father, as well as my uncle, my grandmother, and both my mother and father and many other relatives. In fact, he slaughtered all the Jews living in Najera at that time. He said it was one way of getting back at Pedro, the Jew lover, as he called him. It's true Pedro had a Jewish treasurer and protected the Jews, but he also protected the Muslims. He was a pragmatist that way. Enrique, not Pedro, should be called 'the Cruel'".

Ner nodded gravely as she spoke.

"Both your mother and father?" Chaucer asked.

"Yes."

"I'm sorry…" Chaucer said, for once not knowing what else to say.

She stared back at him, her eyes wide with suppressed emotion.

"But why remain at Enrique's court, and also consider marrying Calveley, for both only bring you closer to him?"

"To be close to Enrique is to know where my enemy is, making a sudden strike that much easier."

Ah, now I understand!

"But how was your Uncle Ner not also killed by Enrique along with your family?" Chaucer asked.

"He was in Burgos visiting cousins. One of his cousins had a premonition, or perchance foreknowledge of Enrique's plans, and warned him not to go home to Najera that day. So, he didn't, and he lived. Ner finally returned here after Enrique's threat was gone and has lived here ever since, growing his business. And now watches Enrique's power grow yet again."

Chaucer said nothing, taking in the full weight of the story. A man who had lost so much, and yet had found the fortitude to make so much of his life since, was a man to be listened to.

Doña pulled aside a wall hanging at the back of the shop and entered a back room, beckoning for him to follow. After a moment of hesitation, Chaucer followed her into a modest room that had a low table with two cups and a decanter. The requisite pillows surrounded the table, and lit candles scattered around the small room casting a warm glow in the windowless room.

Once seated on pillows, she poured a deep red liquid into one of cups set before her.

He accepted the cup, curious about the unusual colour.

"What is it?" Chaucer asked, shifting to find a comfortable position.

"It is called pacharan, and is made from endrinas berries, anise and other local ingredients."

He took a whiff—unusual, distinctive—then took a sip. It was cool, sweet and intoxicating. Much stronger than the local Rioja wine.

"It has…a distinctive flavour," Chaucer said.

"It has been known to heal many ills," she said.

Chaucer savoured the pleasant taste, meeting those mesmerizing eyes that seemed to dance in the light of the candles. Was she flirting? Or was it the drink?

"Why have you asked to meet me? Where is Ayala?" Chaucer asked.

She hesitated before answering. "It is for him that I requested to meet you. He is being milked by Enrique for information. I would do anything to relieve him of such a burden. When I offered you a place to stay that first time we met, you would repay me in any way I requested. Now is the time for that debt to be paid, for I need your help."

"Of course, Doña, I am at your service," he said.

"I need you to convince Enrique to let Ayala go free," she replied.

That gave Chaucer pause, for to do so may put himself at risk. He hesitated, then asked, "I would gladly do so, but am unsure how."

"I understand. Only a fool would say yes too quickly to such a request; nay, a challenge. But please understand this truth…Ayala knows much about both Enrique and Pedro that neither would want shared with anyone else. They each have many secrets that they would rather keep secret. Ayala also knows about Enrique's forces, for he is familiar with many of the nobles who serve him. He would be a valuable ally for your Black Prince as he marches to Najera to help Pedro retake his lost crown. And as a court chronicler, what Ayala writes and recites becomes truth once read and heard by others. You are also a poet. You know too well the power that a poet and storyteller can wield," she said.

"How do you know Prince Edward is marching towards Najera?" Chaucer asked, shocked that she would have such knowledge.

"It is no secret. News of Enrique bloodying Edward at Vitoria reached us days ago, followed by news of Edward's sudden departure from that city, and his march south-east through the low mountains. Logrono must surely be his destination. From there, Najera will surely be next. I am certain the war will culminate in a battle within the next few days. I also know Edward's army is suffering from lack of food and supplies; Enrique smells the blood of his hated half-brother, and he does not have much time and the two are fated to meet very soon near here, probably near Najera."

"But you were speaking of Ayala, who chose to leave Pedro and support Enrique freely."

"He did, it is true, and he had good reason. But his anger at Enrique has grown since Enrique promised my hand to Calveley. He says nothing, but I see it in his eyes. One day he may try to kill

Enrique, either a quick death by knife now, or an endless, timeless death by quill and ink for eternity," she said.

"A proud man, with deep roots in Castile, drawn into the intrigues of Pedro through familial ties, and then walking away when he sees only madness and now supporting one only slightly less mad, yet ultimately seeking to be free of both of them," Chaucer said.

"You have not quite captured the full story. Ayala also seeks to be with me, but as you well know Enrique has promised my hand to Calveley, and Calveley now supports Prince Edward, thanks to your intervention, so Enrique's promise of my hand is an empty promise, for Calveley will surely depart soon," she said.

"But if Enrique defeats Pedro, then Calveley may be captured or killed and the marriage won't happen," Chaucer said. "So, either way, you may not have to wed Calveley."

Doña Constanza looked closely at Chaucer. Her eyes narrowed and her mouth twitched.

"Unfortunate accidents occur. An arrow misfired. Calveley slipping on bloody, muddy ground and impaled by a spear. So many things may occur in a battle," Chaucer said.

He surprised himself for saying such a thing, but could see in Doña Constanza's eyes he was right.

"Yes, I have heard of such things occurring in battle," she said evenly, nodding.

She reached out her hand and touched his, seemingly grateful for his understanding.

Her warm touch sent a shock through his body, and his midsection immediately tightened.

Doña's eyes travelled downward.

"You enjoy the touch of a woman," she said, eying his sudden bulge.

Normally he might shift himself to hide his reaction, but he didn't now.

"I do," he said.

"I take it as a compliment, for most woman appreciate such signs of desire. A woman's desire may be less clear to the untrained eye. Yet certain signs are there. Like a flushed face. Hardened nipples. But all such signs may be lost beneath the coverings we must wear to appear as innocent as the Church would have us. So a woman must rely on words and subtleties to convey her desires. A man may do nothing but reveal his desire as it is, direct, not so easily hidden," she said.

He followed her gaze down to his own midsection, then back to her chest, lingering, then up to her eyes.

He shifted.

"You are knowledgeable of such things," he said.

"I was forced to work as a whore for two years when I had nothing after our people were slaughtered and our wealth destroyed by Enrique. Unfortunately, I had to learn what men desire and want, thanks to Enrique. One day I met a wealthy nobleman who took a liking to me, and we became lovers and then were married in Barcelona, and he helped me gain my role as lady-in-waiting to the queen there. He also helped me try to wash my past away. But I failed. Then I met Ayala, and I knew what it was to be in love for the first time. And felt baptized through his love and pure desire. If I were in Aragon, I might be groomed to marry a prince. But here I am not. I am to marry a mercenary. And I prefer to be here," she said matter-of-factly.

"You have seen and felt much in your life," Chaucer said.

She moved her hand toward him, then stopped.

"You engender a certain feeling in me also, Chaucer," she said.

"What kind of feeling is that?" he asked.

She pulled her hand back to her side, got up, and said, "But you must put aside those feelings for now, as I must now return to the palace," she said.

He nodded.

"And will you?" she asked.

"Will I…?" he asked, unsure of her meaning.

"Will you help me with Ayala?" she replied.

"I am still not sure how I can help return Ayala to your side," Chaucer said.

"How can Calveley be led away is the better question. For once he is gone, Ayala will find me, I am sure," she said. "In that, you can help," she said. "And protect Ayala in the battle that will surely come soon."

Chaucer hesitated. "I will do my best."

"Even knowing the danger such a promise brings?" she asked.

Her eyes fluttered, then did his heart.

Chaucer eyed Doña for a few moments. "It would seem I am to give and risk much, yet gain little. And for whom am I taking such risks?" he asked.

"You forget too easily, Chaucer, that you are in my debt."

He thought of all the reasons to say no, the many, many possible explanations he could give to back away gracefully. But he just nodded.

"Chaucer, I appreciate men like you, for your desires are as clear as your loyalty," she said.

She moved her hand to his thigh, an inch from his most pressing discomfort.

Then stood up, her chest inches from his face. "In this we may help each other," she said.

"Of course I will help you," he said, his voice lower.

She turned and left.

He watched her go; his longing as overwhelming as her lingering scent.

CHAPTER 26
LOGRONO & NAVARETTE, APRIL 1-2
OUT OF TIME

"He seems at home here, much happier than in Vitoria," Edward said to Chandos.

The two walked behind Pedro down Calle Portales, Logrono's main street, as it opened up to Plaza del Mercado, the market and heart of the city. Edward felt that the guards surrounding them felt unnecessary, given the warm welcome from the people of this city that remained loyal to Pedro, despite Enrique claiming the city a year earlier. But Sir John Chandos made a compelling argument that Enrique's army was said to be within fifty miles, and spies—or an assassin—could be watching and waiting. So Edward assented and several guards accompanied them.

He felt grateful to be here, his army more or less in one piece. As the exhausted, hungry soldiers crossed the stone bridge into Logrono, they had been welcomed and then fed by the townspeople. They replenished their supplies as best they could, but even that food was now gone, and the battle would need to happen very soon or the army would simply starve to death.

The entourage returned to Logrono Palace, and a scout arrived shortly after. Enrique's army had left Vitoria and was now on the march toward Najera. The battle would begin soon. The next morning Edward ordered the army to march west to the valley below Navarette, retracing Chaucer's steps. The two armies would then be less than ten miles apart.

As they rode toward Navarette, Prince John cantered to his brother. The sun was shining and the sky blue.

"The day looks promising, brother."

"I am glad to have you by my side. We must come to battle and do our father proud."

Gaunt looked over his shoulder at the mass of soldiers marching and riding behind them.

"I wish he were here to see this."

"As do I."

"Tell me, how does this compare to Crecy? Poitiers? You and Chandos fought in both battles," Gaunt asked.

"Our army now is much larger than in either of those battles. But they were both fought on land I knew of. This land is unknown to me, so I must rely on Pedro, who I do not trust, and our scouts. Knowing the land and where to fight is, I have learned, half of what makes a victory."

Prince John said nothing more as they arrived at their camp at Navarette, where tents were springing up across the valley.

Just then, Pedro also cantered toward them. "My lord, my soldiers have joined the fight," he said, pointing southwest, where a stream of men rode toward the camp, a force 4,000 strong.

"Not a moment too soon," is all Edward said.

That evening, the leaders met to discuss their strategy. Prince Edward, Pedro, Prince John of Gaunt, Sir John Chandos, Sir Hugh Calveley and a handful of their most trusted knights stood inside the prince's tent gathered around a rough table made from the sides of a cart. Two months had passed since Edward's three armies left Bordeaux, and they had lost a third of their men to hunger, disease, the ill-conceived march to Vitoria and ensuing attack and desertion. The battle needed to happen in the next day. But how, and where?

"We are completely out of food. We must attack, or our men will starve," said Edward to Pedro.

Pedro, about to answer, was interrupted by Chandos.

"My lord, if Enrique listens to du Guesclin, he will keep his force west of the River Najerilla, and so we would have to fight across the single bridge there, or find a ford to cross the river," Chandos said, pointing at the location on the map spread atop the table. "The river is high with runoff from the mountains. Many will drown. We don't have sufficient time to build a bridge. I suggest we try to draw Enrique out onto the plain and there we may best him."

"You speak wisely, Sir John. But what could possibly cause Enrique and du Guesclin to give up such a strong defensive position?" asked Edward.

A pause hung in the tent.

"Me," said Pedro.

All eyes turned to him.

"The fire of hatred burns as fiercely in his breast as it does in mine," Pedro said quietly.

All heads turned to Pedro.

"But he would be giving up the one thing that might turn the tide of battle," said Edward.

"He has already given up everything and has nothing left to lose except his pride. No, he will come. Trust me," Pedro said.

"But why there? Why choose the plains of Najera?" asked Chandos.

"Because Najera is where I imprisoned him seven years ago when he first tried to defeat me in battle," Pedro said, his voice growing louder. "He had returned from exile in France and had gathered an army with Pere of Aragon, that snake. Our forces met in Najera where I crushed his, and I then imprisoned him in a castle there. His spies freed him. We must bring the battle to him, goad him to come to me. We must advance," Pedro demanded.

Edward noticed Pedro had begun the story addressing both Chandos and himself, but now seemed to be only addressing himself, or the past, or a ghost. His eyes were wild, and a stream of spittle dripped from the corner of his mouth.

"But how and where?" Edward asked. On the table were a number of stones to mark the various flanks of the two armies. A fire in a cast iron brazier cast poor light around the tent, flickering across the faces that stared intently at the map of the land between Logrono and Najera.

"This large rock is Najera. This strip of leather is the Rio Najerilla. These two rocks west of the river are Enrique's forces, with du Guesclin and his mercenaries he brought back from France to the north, and to the south the army led by Enrique," said Chandos. "These other three rocks facing them," he said, gesturing, "are our forces led by Prince John, the second by our Prince Edward, and the third by King Pedro," Chandos said. "This space between them is the plain of Najera, where we seek them to fight them. How do we get them to move across the river to that plain?" he asked.

"Let us advance this very moment; we will be in position by dawn," Edward said.

"And when he sees you coming Enrique will too advance across the river, I am sure of it," Pedro said.

"Agreed, but we also must find a way to bring him to battle on our terms, for his army is much greater in strength than ours," Chandos added. "It is not enough to bring his forces across the river. We must surprise them."

"How?" Edward shot back.

"We must outflank them, my lord."

"Again how, pray tell, do we do that? Their armies stand before us, with mountains to the south, the River Najerilla behind him cutting off any encirclement, and the River Yalde blocking any such flanking move to the north. Assuming we can even entice Enrique to face us on the plain, there is no way to outflank Enrique," Edward said.

Silence. No one had an answer.

"One man may know of a way, my lord," Calveley said.

"Who? Speak up, dammit, who?" the prince said.

"Chaucer, my lord," he replied.

"My father's page. Who helped write out the treaty with Carlos. A poet, page and poor spy. How would he know such a way?"

"He has travelled far and wide in Navarre over the last year with a local guide and knows this land better than anyone here," he said.

"Was he not captured twice by Enrique?" asked Prince Edward. Heads nodded.

"Do you not wonder at both his ability and his loyalty?" he asked.

"My lord, I can attest to his loyalty, for even when I captured him, he made every attempt to return me to your side, which he finally succeeded in doing, as my presence here attests. I see a man who persevered in his loyalty, not one who abandoned it."

Edward was not convinced.

"As for his ability, he has by his side a devoted guide who knows every valley and hillock in this land, and who helped save Chaucer's life," Calveley added.

Prince Edward looked to Chandos, his most trusted advisor.

Chandos nodded. "What Sir Hugh says is true, my lord. Chaucer may lead a listener on a false trail with his stories, but his own journey and duty have been true," he said. "He returned to Logrono before us and awaits his orders."

"Bring him now, for the night is half over," the prince said.

"Find Chaucer and bring him hence!" Calveley shouted to the guards at the door.

•   •   •

Chaucer was just then tilting back his head to drink from a goblet. He sat alone in a small tent in Prince Edward's encampment, sulking.

I should be in the Vintry, Pippa atop me. Instead, I languish in this God-forsaken land.

He felt as gloomy as the shadows cast by the flickering candle that had burned down to a nub. He refilled his empty goblet with more of the Rioja, and was about to take a drink when the opening to his tent opened, startling him, and he spilled wine down his jupon.

"Are you Geoffrey Chaucer?" asked a head peering into his tent.

"For a short time yet, yes. Who asks?"

"Thomas Holland, squire with Sir John Chandos," Holland replied.

Chaucer looked up. "Hang on, we met in Bordeaux—you are the son of Lady Joan," Chaucer asked.

"The same," Holland said, clearly not pleased to be known as such.

"Your mother asked that I look out for you. I am so pleased to see you again," Chaucer said.

"And you also Chaucer, but Prince Edward orders you to attend in his tent at once," he said.

Chaucer spat out a stream of wine, choking. "The prince wants me, does he?"

"I am under orders to bring you without delay," he added. Holland's face showed no sign of jest, and so after a brief clean-up to wipe the wine and detritus of a hasty meal from his hands and face, Chaucer stumbled after him. Holland gestured to a guard who moved aside, and Chaucer stepped inside the prince's massive tent, a low fire from a brazier yellowing the faces of several knights and lords gathered there. He recognized Chandos, who was flanked by the Breton Olivier de Clisson, known as "the Butcher," and on the other side of the brazier, Sir Robert Knowles. Lord Thomas Percy, the Count of Armagnac, the Captal du Bach, Prince John of Gaunt. Men he had come to know since leaving Bordeaux. Including King Pedro.

Sir Christopher Croker stood in the shadows and acknowledged Chaucer with a slight raise of his eyebrows. Chaucer nodded at Croker.

"Chaucer...come forward," Edward said.

Chaucer stopped gawking and approached Prince Edward and bent on one knee.

"My lord, I am your humble servant," Chaucer added, lifting his head.

"Up man. I understand you have travelled across this land and know it well." Prince Edward stated.

Chaucer cast his eye around and landed on Calveley, who nodded encouragement.

"I have come to learn something of the land, yes my lord," Chaucer replied, turning back to his prince, his mind scrambling to make sense of the circumstances.

"Sir Hugh and Sir John both vouchsafe for your loyalty and trustworthiness. I pray that their trust is well placed," the prince said. "Come closer so I may see you better," he added, his tone impatient.

Chaucer stepped into the brazier's light.

"Breadcrumbs and wine stain your clothes," the prince said.

"Excuse me, my lord, a hasty meal," Chaucer replied, self-conscious about his appearance as all the eyes rested upon him.

"A page and courier should take better care with his appearance each day. No matter, for this may be your last. Look here," the prince said, beckoning him to look at the map on the table. "This map shows the position of our enemy by Najera, here, and that of our armies, here. We hope to entice them across this strip of leather, the river, and face them on the plain, here. But we need to somehow surprise Enrique."

Chaucer studied the map where the prince pointed, recognizing the region. "Yes, I see," he said, briefly looking to Chandos once more for help, but the man remained stony faced.

"I understand you have been travelling with a local guide?" the prince added.

"Yes, my lord. A man named Alfonso," Chaucer replied.

"I need to know how our army here," the prince asked, pointing to the figure representing Najerillo on the map, "may outflank Enrique's two armies there, so that we may bring him to battle. Chandos suggests you may know how we might do so," he stated, his eyes piercing in the shadowed light.

Murmurs of dissent floated about the tent.

"Hush!" hissed the prince.

Chaucer flashed to the memory of the gorge, and Alfonso saying the bridge there was the only crossing for twenty miles.

"My men all tell me we cannot outflank Enrique. Shall we prove them wrong, Chaucer?" asked Edward.

Chaucer looked from lord to lord, and saw only cold, unfriendly eyes staring back, save for those of Chandos and Calveley. He looked down at the map, his mind rapidly considering the options. When he looked up at the prince, he hesitated, knowing the audacity of what he was about to suggest. The crossing near Huercanos was but a narrow bridge where an army would be forced to cross single file. It was the perfect place for an ambush, where only a handful of well-placed archers could destroy an army. Their army. It was also the only path forward to outflank Enrique.

"Come man, do you know of another passage?" said Edward, shedding impatience like a dog shakes off water after a swim.

Chaucer took a deep breath. "My lord," he said, adopting the tone and expression he used for the puy. "I have learned something about this land this past year, of families, cities and a country divided by blood, gold and loyalties," he said.

"None of that concerns me, Chaucer. What I need to know is how we can get behind Enrique to surprise and defeat him before the sun rises on the morrow," Edward said, his words clipped, his tone impatient.

Chaucer looked to the circle of lords one more time before facing Edward. He said, "Yes, I know of a way, my lord," and proceeded to tell them. As he spoke, he could see the expression on the face of Prince Edward change from gloom to hope.

Pride swelled in his chest but for a moment, for he realized that the success of the entire campaign now rested upon his shoulders.

CHAPTER 27
NEAR HUÉRCANOS, APRIL 2, 1367
THE BRIDGE

As Doña Constanza got out of the bed to take a drink of water from the goblet on the table across the bedroom, Ayala eyed her naked form as she gracefully moved across the moonlit room. Every time he was with her, he fell deeper in love. Every time he left her, he wept. He knew such feelings would be the death of him.

He had snuck away from Enrique's camp north of Najera and ridden hard to this ancient tower on the east side of the River Yalde where they'd agreed to meet. The tower was the last remaining structure of a crumbling castle built to guard against any trying to cross the bridge below to attack the town of Huercanos, two miles east. Or Najera, four miles southwest. Ayala had paid his cousin, who owned the lands upon which the castle sat, for the exclusive use of it. Until Enrique's soldiers had taken it over the year before. Now the soldiers were gone, and it had become the lovers' secret refuge.

He saw her smile at him from across the room, and his heart filled to overflowing.

"You will survive, my love, if you can avoid the arrows," she said, as if reading his thoughts. "But I believe Pedro will win this battle," she said.

"And why is that?"

"The English longbows, superior armour, and more experienced soldiers will crush Enrique's ginetes," she said in a matter-of-fact voice.

"You can see the future?" he teased.

She didn't smile this time. "My uncle is knowledgeable about warfare. He says Prince Edward and Sir John Chandos were responsible for the victories at Crecy and Poitiers and Auray, victories tied to their strategy in using the longbow. As standard bearer for Enrique, you will be in the centre of battle, with many English arrows aimed your way. I worry about you," she replied.

"Have no fear, my love," he said, holding out his hand to her. "I will come back to you."

She returned to the bed and kissed him and urged him on again.

•　　•　　•

The armies of Prince Edward and Pedro the Cruel left Navarrete as soon as dark masked their movement to any spying eyes. They marched northeast, around a low mountain set between Navarette and Najera. The noise from the men's footsteps, armour, horse harnesses and clang of metal against metal and leather brought the nearby villagers outside, holding torches and gawking at the horde of soldiers as they passed.

Chandos rode next to Edward, with Chaucer and Alfonso, acting as guide, right behind them. Once the decision had been made to trust Chaucer, Alfonso had been brought by Edward's side to provide directions.

Edward turned in his saddle. "Alfonso, do you know where we are? Should we ask the villagers to douse their torches?"

"My lord, this is Cenicero. Low mountain to left hide us. No light reaches Enrique. After this village, at hill ahead, light seen."

"Sir John, order the men, on pain of death, to douse all torches as soon as we have passed this village," Edward replied.

They travelled slowly in the dark, but Alfonso guided them well. It was still dark when Alfonso finally said, "We are here, my lord prince."

"Here? Where is here? I cannot see anything," Prince Edward replied.

Just then, a knight rode out of the dark and stopped before Edward. "My lord, the scouts say we have arrived at the lip of a gorge."

"It is bridge over Rio Yalde, near Huercanos," Alfonso said, adding, "must get across now before dawn, and before Enrique's scouts see us."

•   •   •

As they began to make love for a third time, Doña stopped Ayala and sat up, listening keenly.

"Do you hear that?" she asked.

"It's nothing…," he said, reaching for her, his senses attuned only to her body.

But she moved his hand away and leapt out of bed, moving to the narrow window on the southeast side of the tower. A light smudge ran across the eastern sky.

"There, again. The sound of cartwheels creaking and the jangling of horses," she said.

He got out of bed and stood beside her, and heard it now too.

Horses. Carts. Soldiers.

And then he could see their shapes less than a mile to the northeast, moving as silently as such a mass of men could move.

"It is the Prince and Pedro. His army arrives. And his archers."

Ayala needed to cross the bridge before the prince's army did. He needed to warn du Guesclin or Enrique's army would be destroyed, and he might never see his Doña again.

"I must warn Enrique!" Ayala said as he reached for his clothes.

"No. Give yourself up to Edward. Our future is there, with him."

"I cannot. I must honour my men and my duty. I may not respect Enrique, but I respect the banner that I shall hold in battle."

"But what about us?"

"We will be together again soon."

After the battle, which would begin. Very soon.

•   •   •

Soldiers led by Sir John Chandos arrived near the lip of the gorge above the River Yalde as the first stripes of dawn coloured the black sky. They would now be only four miles from Najera. If they could cross the Rio Yalde and if Enrique crossed the Rio Najerilla, then the battle could begin. Unless enemy scouts found them first.

Chaucer and Alfonso rode behind Chandos. Chaucer had learned much about the famed knight since their first meeting the previous year, and was impressed as much by his knowledge of men and women as his knowledge of military tactics. He willingly put his own life before his men by leading, rather than ordering, his soldiers into battle, which engendered their everlasting respect, loyalty, and admiration. And which gave Chaucer some confidence in the outcome ahead.

A soldier atop a small palfrey approached them. He was not a large man, and the unstrung longbow he wore diagonally on his back looked much longer than he was tall.

"My lord?" the man asked as he came alongside.

"Sir Giles. This is Geoffrey Chaucer, King Edward's page and courier, and the man responsible for finding this bridge," Chandos said.

"Alfonso gets the credit for—," Chaucer said, but Sir Giles interrupted.

"Good day Chaucer. My lord, my archers should dismount and ring this side of the gorge in case of any attack while the rest of the army crosses," Sir Giles said.

"Yes, good idea. We must hold this bridge until our army can pass over," Chandos replied.

Sir Giles nodded to Chaucer and galloped away.

"My lord, with dawn near breaking, we may be seen along the lip of the gorge by any scouts or soldiers looking up. I suggest Alfonso and I dismount and crawl to the edge to see who and what lies below." Chaucer said, then sneezed suddenly.

Chandos nodded. "Don't even think of going down there yourself," he warned.

Chaucer soon found himself looking down, and needing to pee, which reminded him of their first visit to the bridge the previous year. But this time they were on the eastern side of the gorge. In the valley below, he could see flickering firelight and several men milling on the bridge. They were too late. The bridge was already guarded. He sneezed again.

"Not soldiers," Alfonso said.

"How can you tell?" Chaucer asked.

"No horses."

"We need to go down and make sure," Chaucer said.

"Giles won't like," Alfonso said.

They both looked toward Sir Giles, but he was talking to his archers.

Chaucer nodded to Alfonso, and the two made their way down the goat path, trying to beat the dawn's light that was already brightening the sky. The gorge remained in deep shadow.

"No sneeze," Alfonso said quietly.

As they descended, they saw there were about a dozen men guarding the bridge, and they were clearly soldiers, with swords at their waists. Alfonso, for once, was wrong. Several soldiers also stood near a fire at the eastern end of the bridge, their view blocked partially by a tall bush. Spears leaned against the end of the stone bridge.

The two made their way to the bottom of the path and snuck toward a small building, providing shelter for the guards about thirty feet away. The roof had collapsed, but the walls provided cover for men now clustered around their campfire.

The large bush they passed lay between the building and the bridge and looking back and up, Chaucer could not see Sir Giles or any of his archers, which was fortunate, for that meant that Enrique's soldiers couldn't either.

Chaucer could hear the murmur of their muted conversation, and was about to ask Alfonso if he could make out what they were saying when he sneezed.

Alfonso looked at him in alarm, then looked at Enrique's soldiers, who turned their heads as one towards the unexpected but unmistakable sound.

In no time Chaucer's hands were bound, a leather horse's rein tied around his neck, the extra length of it curled on the ground below him. Alfonso had melted away unseen.

"Lift him up," said an older soldier to the two men who held Chaucer.

Chaucer resisted as the men forced him onto the four-foot-high pony wall that ran along each side of the narrow bridge. The wall was only a foot wide, so Chaucer immediately stopped struggling. With his hands bound in front of him, he had to take care to gain his balance and not tip and fall into the gorge that lay at least fifty feet below him.

"Tell us where the prince's army is," the older soldier said as he held the end of the leather rein that was tied around Chaucer's neck.

Chaucer shook his head, and kept his gaze on the lip of the gorge, seeking some sign of Sir Giles or Sir John. Or Alfonso. He could see no movement.

The leader motioned, and two soldiers jumped onto the wall on either side of Chaucer to hold him. They tilted him forward and his body hung at a steep angle above the gorge, the leader standing in the middle of the bridge holding the end of the rein. Chaucer's feet remained on the pony wall, the leather strap around his neck the only thing keeping him from falling to his death on the river rocks below. The sight below him was dizzying, but that was the least of his problems as he began to cough and choke as the rein began to tighten around his neck, strangling him.

The leader let out a bit more of the rein and Chaucer tilted further forward, facing the broiling river and rocks below. A sure death either way.

"Last chance—speak now or go meet your creator, or the devil—I care not which," the leader said.

"Hold!" rang out a voice.

Chaucer turned as best he could towards the voice at the east side of the bridge. He saw a knight astride a destrier trotting toward them.

Chaucer was close to passing out from lack of air, but recognized Ayala, looking splendidly authoritative in his knight's attire. Another rider, more diminutive, sat behind holding onto his waist, wearing a black cloak with a cowl hiding the face. Ayala approached the group and reined his horse, giving no hint he recognized Chaucer.

"State your name," demanded the guard holding the rein.

"I am Don Pero López de Ayala, second lieutenant of King Enrique Trastamara, of the Order of the Sash," Ayala replied.

Chaucer then saw Doña's face peering at him from behind Ayala.

"Show me your signet ring," the nearest guard demanded.

Ayala held out his hand.

When the guard leaned forward to peer at the crest on the signet ring, Ayala kicked the man in the face. He screamed, falling to the ground but somehow keeping hold of the rein.

Four other soldiers on the west end of the bridge ran toward Ayala.

"Chaucer, I will buy you time for Edward's archers to find these soldiers, for first light is upon us," Ayala shouted in English.

Chaucer watched Ayala's destrier rear up and kick out as it turned, and the guards blocking him stepped out of reach of the hoofs. But one was too slow, and was struck in the head by a hoof and flew over the pony wall to his death below. Three soldiers still stood between Ayala and his escape. Again Ayala's horse reared up, and Chaucer, head twisted, recognized Doña, holding him tight.

"May God be with you! I will see you on the battlefield, God willing," he shouted as he spurred his destrier forward. He swung his sword arm, slicing one soldier's shoulder, used his horse to knock another off the bridge, and the last stepped back and let him gallop past and then up the steep goat path.

•　　•　　•

Ayala reached the western lip and shifted in his saddle.

"Can we not help Chaucer?" Doña asked as another group of Enrique's soldiers ran onto the bridge behind them.

"Edward's archers will soon do that work. We must be away," he said.

They both looked up and watched as a row of archers, outlined above the gorge, pulled back the strings of their bows and let fly their arrows.

Was he too late? Had he given Chaucer enough time?

The distance the arrows flew was considerable, yet each found a target. His heart rose and then sank at the sight. Chaucer would survive with such archers at his back. The army of Enrique would probably not, as Doña had said.

He watched for a moment longer as the archers, followed by a swarm of Edward's soldiers, flowed down and across the bridge, a seemingly unstoppable stream of men intent on their victory.

He turned and gave spurs to his destrier, galloping toward what he felt in his heart would be the beginning of the battle, and defeat. But he would do his duty and hold the standard of the Order.

•   •   •

The soldiers on Chaucer's left and right both flew off the side of the bridge and into the gorge below, arrows protruding from their falling bodies.

The leader had since risen and as he stepped toward Chaucer, an arrow smacked into his shoulder, the force of the blow twirling him forward and over the ledge. He grabbed Chaucer's leg as he fell forward.

The length of leather rein that lay upon the bridge began to uncurl as the leader plunged over the edge.

Alfonso, who had been hiding in the tall bush, ran past to the bridge and grabbed the end of the rein as the last curl straightened and he jumped off the other side of the bridge as a human counterweight.

The nearest guard reached for him but an arrow took him in the back and sent flying over the edge. The leader held onto Chaucer by his boot. The leather strap was taut, running from Chaucer's neck up and over the pony wall across the bridge to the other wall and down to Alfonso, who hung off the other side holding the end of the rein, his legs dangling below him. Chaucer clawed at the leather around his neck that was strangling him, and he coughed and struggled. His face was bright red.

"Hold on," Alfonso cried out.

Chaucer kicked at the leader below him one more time, but the leader held his ankle in a tight grip.

Alfonso was being pulled up by the weight of both men and braced his feet against the bottom of the bridge to stop himself from being pulled up and over, which would send all three down to the river below.

Several soldiers had run toward the bridge when they saw their leader take an arrow. But within a few seconds, the soldiers were all dead or wounded by the English bowmen.

Chaucer could not breathe. He kicked at the leader's hand and missed, and the leader tried to grab Chaucer's boot and climb up his body. Chaucer tried again and finally connected with the leader's hand, forcing it to open and the leader fell, landing with a thud on the rocks beside the river below, and did not move. But Chaucer was still tied to Alfonso, and could not breathe and began coughing. Alfonso tried to get a handhold on the ledge to climb back on the bridge, but couldn't quite reach it. Each kept the other alive, but Chaucer was losing consciousness.

And then hands were pulling him up and over the wall of the bridge. Alfonso was pulled up next. Chaucer's hands were unbound, and he coughed and gagged as he struggled to remove the leather strap around his neck and breathe.

Sir Calveley laughed at Chaucer, handing him a skin of water. "Your face is as red as a beetroot," he said.

Chaucer struggled to speak, his voice only managing a croaking whisper. "I…have never been so relieved…to see you, Calveley. How did you know…we were in trouble?" he added.

"Sir Giles spotted the disturbance. They saw you being lifted over the edge."

"Each arrow must have travelled…well over a furlong…and nearer to three hundred yards," Chaucer said, still hoarse.

Sir Calveley nodded to Sir Giles as the archer approached, his bow across his back.

"It looked not good for you, with things hanging in the balance, so to speak," Sir Giles said to Chaucer, flashing a smile.

"Thanks to you and that damn fine bow of yours, I am alive. I am forever indebted to you, Sir Giles. That was surely the finest show of archery I have ever witnessed," Chaucer said.

"Not at all. Bit lucky really," he said.

Alfonso just said, "Is plain."

With that, Sir Giles turned and made his way toward his companions, who were now streaming down the goat path, leaving both Chaucer and Alfonso with a deep respect for the skill of the English bowmen.

Chaucer thanked Alfonso again.

"What did you mean by 'plain'"?

"No luck. Is plain that Enrique no win against such power and skill," Alfonso said.

CHAPTER 28
NAJERA, APRIL 2-3, 1367
DU GUESCLIN AND TELLO

Du Guesclin had argued with Enrique about tactics. He said they should stay on the west side of the river, but Enrique would not hide behind the river in the town he had been captured and held in by Pedro. Enrique would meet Pedro and Edward on the plans of Najera. Pedro had been right.

And so after crossing the Rio Najerilla at dawn the day before, Enrique's army had made camp facing the long valley to the east from which Enrique knew Prince Edward and his army would attack. A low mountain rose at the northeast end of the valley, blocking their view of what lay beyond its peak, but Enrique's spies reported that the prince's army was camped south of that mountain in the valley below Navarrete, some eight miles east. The spies had also reported that Edward's men were tired, starving and out of options, and the army would need to march toward him and begin battle with his own army, twice the size. They would surely advance that very morning.

Du Guesclin placed his fifteen hundred mercenaries in the centre of the formation, with Enrique and his guards behind him. Ayala and his thousand knights and esquires of the Order of the Sash would be to his immediate left on the northern flank; Enrique's brother, Don Tello, would lead his ginetes furthest north. Tello had proved successful in harassing Edward's forces the week before in a series of raids. But this was different, and he was unsure of Tello's courage facing a well-disciplined army. On his right, the southern flank would be his strongest division, led by Don Alfonso, the Count of Denia, who shared leadership with Pedro Monez de Godoy.

Don Tello and du Guesclin were on a slight rise of land, sitting astride their destriers and looking east toward the faintest of glow that hinted at dawn's approach.

"My lord, Prince Edward's army was last sighted past Navarrete over that ridge and to the right of that low mountain in the east," du Guesclin said, pointing. "We know Edward must attack straight down this valley today, here, so I suggest that we move farther to the northeast to outflank and surprise him. And surprise counts for much on the battlefield."

Don Tello showed no signs of listening to du Guesclin. Instead, he was leaning forward, head next to his horse's neck, murmuring to his horse.

"Did you hear me, my lord?" du Guesclin asked through clenched teeth.

"Prince Edward is to the east, yes, I know," Don Tello curtly replied, giving his horse a last pat before sitting tall and gazing to the east.

"We must move north to outflank him," du Guesclin repeated.

Still, Tello ignored him.

At the sound of hooves approaching, they turned to a soldier approaching.

"Any sign of Ayala?" du Guesclin asked him as he reined in beside them.

"He has not yet returned, my lord," the soldier replied.

Damnable idiot running off to bed that whore just before battle.

"Tell the men that we will move into position farther north, there, and by the sun's full rise will surprise Edward as he comes down that valley," said du Guesclin to the soldier, ignoring Don Tello.

"It is not wise to give up our position with the Rio Yalde protecting our back," Don Tello finally said.

Du Guesclin tried to hide his hatred for Tello, but he couldn't prevent his mouth from curling and his fists from tightening into balls. He would like to hit the man, but he kept his voice calm as he explained basic tactical warfare to the idiot before him.

"Don Tello, surprise accounts for more than half of the success of any battle. It creates chaos in the enemy, and with chaos comes opportunity. If we reposition now, the soldiers of Prince Edward will advance to find us not facing them, but on their flank, and they will be forced to wheel about in disorganized panic to face us. It is then that you will drive your soldiers forward into their heart. We will smash them between our two crab pincers. Do you understand?" du Guesclin added, as if explaining a simple lesson to a child.

This child, it seemed, had no interest in learning.

"To march before the light of day is dangerous, for we could end up lost, in the wrong place," Don Tello replied, his voice wavering.

The sound that escaped from du Guesclin was a cross between a sigh and an unintelligible oath. "Don Tello, in war, one must risk to win. I have learned this through some twenty battles. And the sun will be up soon. Tell me, where have you learned your tactics? What battles have you fought in to gain such wisdom?" he asked.

Don Tello, used to the flowery pleasantries of court, was taken aback by du Guesclin's pointed question. "I fought a resounding victory near Vitoria," he said in a wavering voice.

"You make my point, for in Vitoria, you surprised Chandos and caused such chaos that you were able to kill several before they reorganized themselves."

"Du Guesclin, moving our army now is not a prudent path—" he tried to say.

All pretence of civility vanished in du Guesclin's reply. "Prudence be damned. We will march now. We will surprise and then strike, and we will be victorious. Go tell your men to prepare," he snarled.

Don Tello did not move forward. He sat and watched his men respond to du Guesclin's orders, barking at them like the Breton dog that he was. The soldiers, mounted and on foot, obeyed him and began to move northeast.

He still sat astride his horse, unmoving. Soon he was alone, dust clouding his view. He bent down and again murmured to his horse as dawn spread gentle pink fingers across the plain of Najera.

CHAPTER 29
NORTH-EAST OF NAJERA, APRIL 3, 1367
CHAUCER AND CALVELEY

Chaucer was behind Calveley and Croker, saying nothing as he rode along the stony path they followed in the dimmest of light. Thousands more rode and marched quietly, at any moment expecting a crossbolt or arrow, followed by a shout from the enemy. The men were tired, starving and thirsty and ready for battle. But they would prefer to fight an enemy they could see.

Calveley had not spoken to him since they had crossed the Rio Yalde. Many had heard him chastise Chaucer for disobeying his orders and almost getting himself killed, and more importantly, losing the element of surprise. Not to mention that Enrique's soldiers could have escaped to sound the alert. Chaucer took the tongue lashing in unaccustomed silence, for the crossing had ultimately been a success, Edward was pleased, and they were marching toward battle, which would come soon.

Calveley finally turned in his saddle. "Chaucer, your silence shouts at me. Speak your mind," he said.

"I worry for the upcoming battle, my lord."

"You worry about what you cannot control. Such worry is a waste."

"Perchance, but I worry nonetheless," Chaucer replied.

"What is the worse that may happen?" Calveley asked.

Chaucer paused then, for he hadn't actually voiced such thoughts.

"The death of those I have come to care for. Including my own self."

"An honest reply. But war inevitably means death. One does not occur without the other. As soon as you agreed to serve King Edward on this journey, you knew war would come. And so you agreed to the greater likelihood of seeing death. Chaucer, the deaths that you worry about are inevitable. A war just quickens that outcome. For in the end, we must all die," Calveley said.

"I worry that I may not return to London to see my wife to be," Chaucer said.

"Chaucer, I tell you this now only because I may not live to see the stars this eve, and I would have you remember me as more than just a sword for hire. I do not fear death; what I fear most is the loss of a love I have not yet had," Calveley said.

A scout arrived just then to interrupt their maudlin thoughts. "My lord, the enemy has been sighted some two miles ahead," he said.

•　　　•　　　•

"What think you?" Chaucer asked. He and Alfonso sat astride their horses on the high ground a few yards to the side of Prince Edward and his entourage. Before them, the entire army was moving toward the huge smudge that was Enrique's much larger force, a smudge breaking in two with part of it moving to face them.

"English will win battle," Alfonso said.

"Tell me, who paid you to serve as my guide and find Calveley?"

Alfonso turned his head to face Chaucer. "Córdoba. That day you wait for him Pamplona. I know him from court. He pay me to meet you instead," Alfonso said, then added. "But I have own reason. To get revenge, finally," he added, a smile upon his face.

Chaucer realized it was only the second time he'd seen Alfonso smile.

"Revenge?"

"Today Enrique will finally be defeated and killed," Alfonso said.

Chaucer looked more closely at Alfonso.

"My mother kitchen maid. Name Eleanora. She work castle Valladolid. Love stable boy who love her back. But taken first by the fair-haired King Alfonso, also fifteen."

Chaucer nodded.

"She sent to nunnery. I was born. Nun told me truth and cared for me until I was young boy. My mother could not afford to raise me, so I was given to a noble woman who had lost her own baby. Lady raised me as her own, and I learned to speak Latin, and Castilian, and courtly ways, but not the Basque of my own mother. But at fifteen, at same age of mother when she birthed me, I felt deep longing to find her. So I left castle one night and travelled to castle in Madrid where King Alfonso lived, and asked servants about mother. It took time to find answers as I was unknown and had little gold to pay. But I was clever and made friends and learned of her fate."

"Enrique also learned of me, his other bastard brother, and found my mother and tortured her to try to reveal my name and location. She refused and was thrown in river, hands and legs tied. Enrique sought to find me for years, as I have claim to throne. He send spies, but no find, for I call myself another name. Until now."

Chaucer's nodded. He knew most of the story, but Alfonso had added more detail.

"Enrique dies this day. You help me, your debt paid."

A horn blast stayed Chaucer's reply.

The battle was set to begin.

PART 5
BATTLE

CHAPTER 30
PLAINS OF NAJERA, APRIL 3, 1367
THE ARMIES CLOSE

Du Guesclin gazed north where over one thousand dismounted Knights of the Order of the Sash stood waiting, the second line of soldiers who would face Prince Edward. Over their armour, they proudly wore their white surcoats with the red field and golden two-headed dragon running diagonally across the sash. Enrique's brother Sancho rode at the head, and he would lead the Order into battle.

Twisting in his saddle, du Guesclin could just make out the third line of soldiers that lay two hundred yards behind them, consisting of some fifteen thousand Spanish infantry ranging from well-armed professionals to reluctant conscripts. Behind them, to the west, the cliffs of Najera were still a dark mass.

Du Guesclin then shifted his attention to the thirty-five hundred heavy cavalry arrayed in the two wings protecting King Enrique. They were ready.

He could make out the shape of two flanking forces of Spanish light cavalry, the ginetes, where Don Tello led the left northern flank, and the Count of Denia led the southern flank. Closer behind du Guesclin was the centre of the line, led by Enrique with the cream of his heavy cavalry, fifteen hundred strong. Immediately behind him stood fifteen hundred hand-picked men-at-arms and five hundred crossbowmen, the first line of soldiers facing Prince Edward.

In total, some thirty-five thousand soldiers stood battle ready behind du Guesclin awaiting the army of Prince Edward.

But the left flank was a scene of confusion, not order. Du Guesclin's efforts to outflank Edward had only begun, and in the pale light before dawn, he could see only chaos. Some soldiers had obeyed du Guesclin's orders and shifted, others were awaiting orders from Don Tello and refused to move, while yet others had decided to move backwards, pushing into the forces behind them. Confusion was beginning to spread.

A rider galloped toward du Guesclin and pulled up in a cloud of dust. It was Ayala.

"My lord," Ayala said, gasping for breath. "The army of Prince Edward…is approaching from the northeast," he said between gulps of air, as if he himself had run the distance.

"*Northeast?*" du Guesclin shouted, craning his head in that direction, unable to see an army; "I see only a smudge of dark dust there."

He was expecting the attack to come directly from the east, where the expansive plain ahead of his army sloped gently down from the high point between Najera and Navarrete. How was it possible that Prince Edward's army could appear like magic to the northeast, outflanking him, just as he was trying to do the same?

He turned to Ayala, scowling. "That is not possible!"

"Before dawn, the English passed near Huercanos."

A tremor ran through du Guesclin. "But how? There is no way through," he demanded.

Du Guesclin looked northeast again. The sun was just now rising, and his eye caught a glint of reflected light and movement, and a moment later he heard the distant sounds of the approaching army.

A murmur amongst his troops grew into shouting as the soldiers around him pointed in the same direction.

"They crossed a bridge at Yalde," he said. "When I arrived at the bridge, I found the guards all dead, full of English arrows, stuck like hedgehogs." Ayala had altered the timing of events, but the results were the same.

"Clever bastard."

"My lord?" Ayala asked.

"How many?" barked du Guesclin.

"At least twenty thousand, my lord," Ayala said. "Possibly more."

"Sound the call to arms. Now!" du Guesclin shouted.

Drums rang out, beating time, and several thousand soldiers and horses and hundreds of wagons began to change direction to face Edward's army.

The smudge of dust was now a cloud lit golden by the sun just now cresting the Pyrenees.

Behind them, the cliffs of Najera were suddenly shot red with light. Day was upon them.

Don Tello cantered to du Guesclin's side and pulled up the reins, the silver breastplate of his horse matching his own shining silver armour.

"Du Guesclin—what force is that?" Tello asked, dressed more for a joust than a battle.

Du Guesclin shook his head slightly in disdain and shouted, "Don Tello. Get your ginetes ready to move. Prince Edward advances from the northeast. We must stop his advance," he said.

"Northeast? How is that possible? How many?" Don Tello asked.

"At least twenty thousand. His entire army. Against our thirty-five thousand. The odds are in still our favour, but we must move or remain outflanked," du Guesclin replied.

"My ginetes will draw them to the plain where there is room to attack," Tello suggested.

"The English bowmen will pick them off before your ginetes would be able to reach their infantry," du Guesclin replied.

"Nonsense. My cavalry is too fast to be hampered by archers," Don Tello replied.

Du Guesclin paused in his reply, for he could not believe Don Tello was so ignorant of the power of the English longbow. Every man, woman and child in Europe knew the stories of how the French were so badly defeated at Crecy at Poitiers thanks to the English longbow.

Just then Enrique arrived on his destrier.

"My lord, Prince Edward arrives there," du Guesclin said, pointing northeast.

Enrique nodded. "Unfortunate. We should attack."

"Your brother would send his ginetes to the plain there," du Guesclin said, pointing ahead to the right of the dust cloud. "But forming up on the plain would mean the River Najerilla would be at our backs, with the small bridge there hampering any retreat we may need to make."

"Retreat? There will be no retreat," said Enrique.

"My good brother, your famed commander has lost confidence," said Tello.

Du Guesclin opened his mouth, but Enrique cut him off. "No retreat."

"We outnumber them. We have cavalry. Our troops are fresh and eager, and have yet to lose a battle since we began this campaign. They are tired and starving. No! We will form up on the plain, and by God we will stain the ground red with English blood," Don Tello shouted.

"Your brother underestimates the power of the English bowmen," du Guesclin tried once more, scowling. "Your light cavalry will not be able to evade English archers and successfully outflank them. The archers are accurate at a distance of three hundred yards, the hardened steel-tipped arrows able to punch through even heavy armour. But the knights in your light cavalry are wearing only hardened leather jerkins and little armour. Your riders might be experienced swordsmen, and courageous, but they are no match for thousands of steel-tipped arrows. I have seen what those arrows can do."

"Nonsense. You shout fears like an old woman. We will dispatch them as we did in Vitoria. Our cavalry will easily outflank the archers.

Once they split their forces, our infantry can push forward. We have double their number and we shall crush them!" Don Tello said.

Du Guesclin fumed.

"You command your men, du Guesclin. I command the army," Enrique said.

Du Guesclin, his gaze on the approaching army, could waste no more time arguing.

"My lords, as you say," du Guesclin snapped.

Still fuming, he wheeled his horse and galloped towards his men. He also had doubts about their superior numbers. The White Company mercenaries would best any force alive, that he knew; yet there were only fifteen hundred truly exceptional warriors among the army. The several thousand additional conscripts had more confidence than experience, gained after a few wins against untested soldiers defending the towns they had taken since leaving Zaragoza. But the time for reflection was over as a horn announced the arrival of the English.

•   •   •

The men under Prince Edward were exhausted, sleep-deprived, starving and thirsty; yet to a man, they knew they held the advantage. They had indeed surprised the army of Enrique the Bastard, for his troops could clearly be seen now scrambling in disorder.

Chaucer crested the hill and saw Prince Edward astride his huge destrier, both prince and horse covered in polished black armour. The prince had drawn his horse to a stop atop a small promontory ahead of him, with Chandos at his side, and Sir Gawain several yards behind and to the side of him. Pedro, a hundred yards to the south, was cantering towards the group.

"Gawain, have you seen Alfonso? He was just behind us," Chaucer asked Gawain as he approached him.

"I last saw him as we crossed the bridge," Gawain replied.

The two surveyed the scene before them, the two armies approaching each other, the one clearly much larger than the other.

"Enrique's army looks twice the size of our own," Chaucer said to Gawain.

"Size, as the ladies say, does not always matter," Gawain said, producing a chuckle and a nod from Chaucer.

Gawain continued. "Sir John has told me time and again that the quantity of the soldiers does not account for as much as their quality. Most of our men have fought several battles, and they wear the best armour available. Based on the wounded soldiers we captured at Vitoria, and those at the Rio Yalde, most of Enrique's soldiers wear only toughened leather, light armour, or older, thinner armour. And many of Enrique's soldiers have fought in only this campaign. No, I think the odds are more equal, which means it will come down to the character and courage of the soldiers, and the skill of the leaders in how they are deployed," he said.

The plan, Chaucer had been told, was for Prince John of Gaunt, with his three thousand well armoured infantry and three thousand archers, to engage du Guesclin's force. Prince Edward, together with Pedro's four thousand soldiers—half of them archers, the rest infantry—would engage Enrique's heavy cavalry. Flanking the Prince were two similar forces under Captal de Buch and Sir Thomas Percy. Edward's third line, the rearguard, was led by the King Jaume of Majorca and the Count of Armagnac with three thousand foot soldiers and another three thousand archers. And Calveley. At the core of the army were over ten thousand battle-hardened Anglo-Gascon men-at-arms wearing high-quality armour. They were supported by thousands of mercenaries and soldiers from Aragon and Navarre. Four thousand English longbowman were in the advance guard.

"In all, I would wager some fifty-five thousand soldiers are arrayed on the plain before us," said Gawain.

"As a herald, you appear to know much about military tactics," Chaucer replied.

"Sir John has shared his knowledge freely with me," Gawain replied.

"He knows your busy quill will capture his exploits for eternity," Chaucer said. Chandos was a chivalrous knight, but one not unaware of the power of reputation."

Gawain nodded.

The first rays of the morning April sun now swept the barren plain; only a few small trees and bushes dotted the landscape.

"How close to the battle do you expect to get?" Chaucer asked.

"As close as I need to in order to recount the day's exploits," Gawain replied, kicking his horse forward, to be closer behind Chandos. Chaucer followed.

"Ah, Gawain. Welcome. And Chaucer too," Chandos said. "You intend to chronicle the battle? I suggest that you retire to our baggage, where you will be safe."

"I must be close enough to recount your exploits, my lord," Gawain said.

"As you wish, but be careful, it would not do to have the exploits of this battle left to those with fantastical imagination and poor memories," Chandos said, and then rode forward to where Prince Edward, Prince John of Gaunt and King Pedro now stood in a final war council. Chandos dismounted and joined them.

Chaucer and Gawain rode forward, stopping beside a squire who stood next to the royals holding a furled banner.

Prince Edward ordered the vanguard to dismount and squires led the horses to the rear. He could see that Du Guesclin had done the same with the force directly facing him. Edward smiled at Chandos. "See how du Guesclin and his men scramble? We have surprised them. We should attack immediately."

"We have instilled chaos, to be sure my lord, and Tello knows not his ass from his mouth," Chandos said.

"Is it not time to unfurl the banner?" asked Edward of his most trusted knight.

"My lord, I have served you these many years. Everything God has given me comes from you, and you know full well that I am wholly yours and will be always. It is truly a fitting time and place to raise your banner," Chandos said.

The prince nodded, took the furled banner from the squire, and unfurled it then and handed the shaft to Chandos.

The banner was well known across Europe, quartered with three golden lions on a scarlet background in each of two diagonal quarters, and several golden fleur-de-lis on a blue background on the two other diagonal quarters. The symbols of both the English and French monarchies, united, reflecting the ambition of both son and father to hold both crowns.

"Sir John, I ask that you show prowess and gain honour for us in the battle to come," the prince said.

"My lord, I am honoured, and I will do the best of my God-given ability to lead your men to victory," Chandos replied. He then re-mounted his horse and galloped back to his men, the standard bearer with the unfurled pennant flying in the wind, galloping beside him. A great cheer arose from the men.

Chaucer could hear the man's booming voice echoing back from across the field.

"My lord Prince Edward exhorts each and every man here to fight for honour on this day," Chandos shouted as he rode along the line of waiting soldiers..

Another great cheer arose.

Chaucer felt a prickle along his arms and neck. *This truly will be a day to remember, whatever the outcome; if it pleases Lady Fortune, I will live to recount it.*

Prince Edward now mounted his magnificent warhorse and trotted in front of his advance guard of men, shouting, "We are hungry. We are thirsty. We face an enemy laden with food and wine who have slept on soft beds with softer women, and with the River Najera at their backs, are puffed up by false confidence."

Only the creak of metal and a few coughs broke the silence between the prince's words.

"Let us pierce their thin skins with sharp arrows and blows of lance and sword and dine this eve on their food and wine at Najera. Let us dine on victory this day, and never be hungry again, for we will be immortalized as victors," he shouted, raising his fist in the air.

A cheer arose from the men in reply.

Edward then turned to his brother Gaunt and said, "Let us believe that we were not born to be considered unworthy. Let us be overcome and ruled by an ardent spirit, having given our oath to stand and fight, for if we flee for fear of the bastard, we shall be the laughingstock of the Scots, Franks, Danes and Goths. Therefore, remember whose offspring you are and that you act with righteous authority. Be mindful of your undefeated ancestors…and trust in God, I beg you. Now let us kiss one another, and afterwards advance on foot," he said, finishing with a flourish of his arm.

Another great cheer arose.

Gaunt bowed and replied, "My lord, my brother, I am your servant, and we shall prevail."

Edward smiled at his younger brother and then said to a knight beside him, "So help me Jesus, today you shall see me a good knight, if death causes me no hindrance."

Gaunt nodded to Chandos, who then knighted several squires, including Thomas Holland.

Gaunt then said to William Beauchamp the same words the prince had said to him. He then said a prayer to himself, then gave the order to advance his banner.

He turned to Pedro and said, "My cousin, on this day you will have your crown once more. Have firm faith in God. Would you like to say anything to the good and loyal soldiers arrayed before us?"

Pedro shook his head no.

He turned back to his men and shouted, "Now forward, forward banner! Let us take the Lord God for our protector and let each one acquit himself honourably."

Horns blared, and the army marched at double time toward the enemy.

CHAPTER 31
PLAINS OF NAJERA, APRIL 3, 1367
BATTLE

Chaucer sat atop his palfrey on a small hillock behind the main force and watched as the two armies approached one another. It was a sight he knew few if any had seen before: fifty-five thousand soldiers about to begin the largest battle fought in their lifetime.

Gawain, astride a small rouncey a few yards to his left, kneed his horse beside Chaucer and pulled out a small book from a leather satchel.

"Master Chaucer, I have greatly enjoyed our time together. I do not know how this battle will end, but I would that you accept this small token of my appreciation of our friendship," Gawain said as he handed the book to Chaucer.

"A kindness, thank you Gawain. The writing is faded. What is the title?"

"*On the Consolation of Philosophy* by Boethius. You know of him?"

"I know only that he wrote it in a dungeon before he was executed. What is it about?" Chaucer asked.

"Many things. The transitory nature of wealth, fame, and power, and the ultimate superiority of things of the mind. That happiness comes from within, and that virtue is all that one truly has because it is not imperilled by the vicissitudes of Lady Fortune. He was the writer who named Lady Fortune."

"Ah. I see. And what does Boethius say of war?"

"Only that those who understand and accept the capricious nature of fortune will not be unduly affected by the outcomes of war. Instead, they will focus on cultivating inner strength and wisdom," Gawain replied.

"Hard not to be unduly affected by the vicissitudes of a yard of ash through one's chest," Chaucer replied, turning toward the battle beginning before him.

"In that, I can agree. Look there. Du Guesclin still tries to reposition his soldiers to face us. I see chaos in their lines," Gawain stated.

Du Guesclin was at least half a mile away, but he was unmistakable astride his massive destrier, galloping forward toward the northern flank of his forces.

"Perchance our lord Chandos will reach them in time to take advantage of such chaos," Chaucer replied.

·   ·   ·

Du Guesclin was screaming at the ginetes to form up, but they looked back and forth between du Guesclin and Tello, unsure of whom to obey. Tello sat still on his horse and just stared back at du Guesclin.

"Du Guesclin, stop that barking and hold that ill-formed Breton tongue and watch as my men attack," Don Tello snapped, his right arm raised.

Before du Guesclin could reply, Tello lowered his arm and all eight hundred ginetes in three formations galloped toward the infantry of the Captal du Buch.

Ironhoof shivered, as if expecting to follow, but Du Guesclin pulled back the reins to quell his horse. He shook his head in disgust, swore, and then sniffed the air. "I smell fear, sweat and dust. And soon I will smell Castilian blood," he said.

·   ·   ·

Chaucer and Gawain rode forward to get a better look at the advancing enemy, and the English awaiting them. He could just hear the Captal du Buch, some fifty yards ahead, shouting to his captain of archery, "They ride swiftly, I'll give them that. Let's see how these famed ginetes ride stuck full of hardwood. Give them your best, men."

"Archers…knock…pull…release!" shouted the captain.

Chaucer watched the first flight of ash, goose-fletching and steel fly in a whoosh and twang, arising like a swirling flock of long-nosed sparrows flying skyward and, a few seconds later, down. On their tail followed another flight of arrows. Then a third. Five thousand arrows from twelve hundred English longbows landed in quick succession, their sharpened steel tips tearing through leather padding and slicing through flesh and bone. In seconds, hundreds of men and horses were down or falling, the screams of agony resounding across the plain.

"Signal the infantry to advance!" shouted the Captal du Buch.

The Castilian ginetes still alive wheeled in retreat leaving hundreds of dead and wounded behind. Chaos ensued as horses and men alike screamed from the sharp steel that sliced apart muscle to embed in bone, or cut through legs and arms. One rider, an arrow stuck in his eye, screamed his last words as he rode toward the archers until a second arrow took him in the neck and he fell, his wild-eyed horse veering off, an arrow in its hindquarters.

Chaucer could now clearly see du Guesclin astride his massive horse, shaking his head, and beside him Tello sat immobile, as they watched the slaughter unfold.

Du Guesclin then nodded to his captain and hundreds of slingers stepped forward and flung their battle stones toward the enemy and Chaucer, who instinctively turned his palfrey to retreat but the distance was still great and only a few stones found their mark in the first line of the English archers.

•   •   •

On the south flank, the Count of Denia looked north and watched Don Tello's ginetes launch their attack. He ordered his own riders forward. The English and Gascon enemy lay atop a hillock and had a stronger defensive position, but the Count had the advantage in numbers.

"We shall ride and we shall defeat these ill-gotten whoresons. For King Enrique!" he shouted and a great roar rose from his one thousand riders as they galloped toward the enemy as if shot from a catapult.

A whirring sound was followed by a dark mass filling the sky, and then thousands of steel-tipped arrows hit home. Hundreds of men and horses fell with screams of agony. It seemed a repeat of the northern flank, and yet Denia and those unharmed advanced. His men wore heavier armour and some of his first riders reached the Count of Armagnac's troops but were soon repulsed by a second volley of arrows before they could engage. Some of Edward's men were struck as well. Denia ordered the remaining cavalry to retreat.

•   •   •

"My lord?" asked Saladan, who rode behind du Guesclin.

"Send the crossbows, for the ginetes are being destroyed but we can still down some of their archers," du Guesclin replied.

Saladan shouted an order and several hundred of du Guesclin's crossbowmen trotted toward the Captal du Buch on the northern flank.

Enrique galloped to du Guesclin, pulling on the reins as he brought his mount to a halt. "Why doesn't my brother engage further? He must advance with the rest of his force or will be wiped out by the English longbows. Did you order my brother to disengage?" Enrique shouted in anger.

Du Guesclin shook his head no. "Of course not. But he does not listen to me, my lord," du Guesclin replied.

And neither do you, he wanted to add.

"I will deal with my damnable coward of a brother!" Enrique snarled, wheeling his horse and galloping toward Don Tello, who still sat frozen upon his mount, well behind his decimated troops. Du Guesclin could hear Enrique shout, "Tello! Order your soldiers to dismount and advance on foot with shields held above their heads!"

Du Guesclin knew that Don Tello had never faced a real army before. Two weeks earlier, Tello had led the raid near Vitoria that had surprised Edward's scouts, killing several, and claiming a great victory. But that was nothing like what he faced now, an organized force of thousands led by successful soldiers backed by the English longbow who never faltered. Du Guesclin saw the abject fear in Tello's face and eyes.

"I wwww…will not…ask my ginetes to dismount," Tello stuttered. "It would be humiliating for them."

Enrique kneed his destrier closer to Tello so he could lower his voice.

"You must find courage, brother. If not, then your men will all die. They *must* engage with the English archers at close quarters in order to win the advantage. We have the numbers."

His brother looked white, shaken.

"We must alter our tactics. I order you to dismount and follow me!" Enrique shouted.

Still Tello did not move.

"Are you now coward? After all, we have been through together to bring Pedro to justice for the murders he has committed against our family. You will let me, and them, down? You would let Pedro win by failing to fight?" Enrique exclaimed.

When Tello didn't respond, Enrique spat, and said loudly, so all could hear, "You shame me. You shame our family name. You shame yourself. You are my brother no more!"

"My lord," said a nearby knight.

Enrique turned to see the English mounted knights and infantry on foot press forward and the two armies now only one hundred yards apart.

The Castilian crossbowmen let loose more iron bolts. While they did not have the range of the longbows, they succeeded in instantly felling dozens of English infantry.

"Knock, pull…release!" shouted the English archery captain in response.

The arrows fell among the Castilian crossbowmen, with many impaled. As were dozens of ginetes still awaiting orders from Don Tello.

The English continued to close and were now only fifty yards away. Knights and squires wielding long swords, men at arms bearing swords, poleaxes, maces, war hammers and flails advanced. Most wore well-made armour, and they knew their business.

Du Guesclin ordered his crossbows to loose a third volley, and they dropped several archers and a few unlucky mounted knights whose heavy armour failed to protect them. He then tilted his head to his captain, and the slingers sent more stones toward the English. This time they were in range and dozens of bowmen, men at arms, and a few knights were struck. The battle stones, weighing over a pound, had sufficient force at that range to crumple steel armour. A few English had their heads caved in, arms broken, and legs shattered.

But the bowmen were faster and again the whirring flight of death rose from the English archers and then fell upon the melee of riders and infantry, dropping far more. After the crossbows and archers traded one more volley, they stopped, for fear of taking down their own.

Enrique rode past du Guesclin and shouted, "Du Guesclin, do something before we lose this flank. I must tend to this damnable Prince Edward," and galloped past toward Count Denia on the south flank. Denia was bloodied but still mounted, an arrow sticking out of his armour by his shoulder between his left rerebrace and pauldron.

"Denia, how do you fare?" Enrique demanded.

"My lord king, the English archers know their craft. But soon they will have no arrows left. Then we will close on their mercenaries," Denia said between clenched teeth.

"Then let us charge."

•   •   •

Du Guesclin ordered Tello's captain to reform the remaining ginetes, and a confused mess ensued as some heeded his call while others trotted toward Don Tello.

"My lord, what are my orders?" asked his second captain.

"Order the French and Castilian mounted men-at-arms to charge and drive a wedge into the centre of Sir John's men. If we gain the centre, we may yet turn their flank!" du Guesclin shouted, and the captain galloped away.

Several hundred heavily armoured knights soon galloped toward the English. The charge surprised the centre of the English army. The infantry commanded by John of Gaunt and Sir John Chandos were not yet formed up and as they were struck by this wave of lance and armoured horse and sword, they were pushed back. A third, smaller group of ginetes heeding du Guesclin's orders to dismount and abandon their horses charged at the north flank, reaching the English and Gascons on foot and hurling their lances and spears. The English archers, now empty of arrows, wavered as some were hit, but they recovered and joined the fight with their swords and daggers.

In the centre of the melee, men at arms and knights from both sides were fighting and falling, wounded or dead. Chandos slashed and stabbed with his long sword. A mounted Castilian knight struck his chest with a sword, but his Milanese armour deflected the strike. The fighting was close, and he parried several more strikes, and those he could not were turned away by his armour.

Then a massive blow to his helm stunned him, and when he shook his head, he saw through his visor a huge man, larger than himself, getting ready to strike him a second time. He recognized the Castilian knight Martin Fernandez, who swung his sword in a large arc, finding purchase where his shoulder guard and breast plate met. Chandos, briefly stunned by the blow, recovered and struck Fernandez on the mail protecting his otherwise exposed neck. Fernandez stumbled backward, shook his head, and the two traded more blows back and forth, like great beasts battling for dominance, and then Fernandez got inside Chandos' reach and grabbed him and threw him to the ground. In the struggle, Fernandez dropped his sword. Chandos reached for his own sword, but Fernandez found his dagger first and thrust it through Chandos' visor. Fernandez then grasped his sword with his bloodied gauntlet, rose on one knee and pushed himself up to standing and then lifted his sword above his head in triumph.

The ground ran red under Chandos' helm. He did not move.

The English soldiers looked upon the prone body of their champion, still unmoving, a dagger hilt sticking out of his visor. He was surely dead, and a great sigh of despair arose from the English soldiers.

Fernandez turned to his own men, raised his helm and shouted, "I have vanquished the great Knight Sir John Chandos, the flower of English chivalry, the greatest warrior of our age," and a cheer erupted. Enrique's forces were emboldened and attacked with even more vigour, surging at the English, swords raised, voices screaming victory.

The English looked upon their fallen hero and quaked, for if Chandos had been felled, they would surely be next. A quiver of hesitancy and fear swept across the English line just as Enrique's men attacked them. Several knights died as they paused, swords striking between the gaps in their armour deep into flesh. A battle was no place to hesitate.

The English line continued to falter, and the Castilians pushed their advantage, breaking through the English line in places.

"Keep attacking!" shouted Du Guesclin.

·   ·   ·

Don Tello had not seen the English centre collapse, for moments before he had suddenly wheeled his horse, dug his spurs into its flanks and galloped west, fleeing the battlefield and riding past his brother Sancho toward Najera.

Sancho called after him, "You are a coward to turn your back on your brothers. Enrique should have never trusted you again. You are a traitor to our family!" Sancho spat out each word, but Tello did not turn or falter.

Some of Tello's gitanes followed him, and seeing their cavalry turn, some of the foot soldiers under Tello also retreated. These men had not stuck a single blow, and their departure bred panic. No sooner had the men turned than they were killed, for the Captal de Buch and the Lord of Clisson and their men fell upon them mercilessly. Du Guesclin, watching the men flee, paused his own attack and sent two hundred soldiers north to quell the retreat before it turned into a rout.

•　　•　　•

Chandos moved his leg.

"Look! Chandos lives!" shouted a Gascon knight.

Fernandez turned, but too late, for Chandos had pulled a dagger from his belt, rose onto one knee, and thrust it between the armoured plates above Fernandez' gut by his heart, sinking the dagger up to its hilt. As Fernandez fell, Chandos saw the surprise in his eyes even as the claws of death dragged him to the reddened earth, his own blood mingling with that of Chandos.

Three English knights encircled Chandos, protecting him as he struggled to stand. He grasped his sword with both hands and pulled himself to his feet and flung off his visor. Blood poured from his ear where the dagger had pierced it, missing his neck by an inch.

"The English are not so easily vanquished. Death to Enrique!" cried Chandos, his words filled with a steely joy as he strode toward the nearest Castilian soldier and sliced the man almost in half, then continued to pour death onto every man he faced.

A great cheer arose from the English, and each man faced the enemy with renewed vigour. The English line surged forward, and this time, it was the Castilian line that quailed.

Du Guesclin's attack was stayed and a great din and reek arose as the hand-to-hand fighting reached a crescendo.

•   •   •

Chaucer searched the battlefield for the order of the sash that Ayala would surely be holding. The battle was now a chaotic affair of soldiers and mounted knights slashing their way through globs of infantry. Then, looking to the south of the centre, he found it. The sash. And Ayala. Ayala held the banner with one hand while fighting for his life. Then he spied a group of Castilian horsemen on the north flank dismount at the English line and surrender their swords, kneeling in defeat. Don Tello's men. Then watched Du Guesclin's wave of reinforcements move toward the gap left by Don Tello.

Chaucer turned back to Ayala and watched him fight valiantly, parrying sword and mace, even as more infantry to the north lay down their arms and knelt in surrender. In the centre, the English were now surging forward. He sensed the tide was turning and Ayala would not survive alone. He needed help. But to ride into battle, this battle, would be suicide. He was no soldier. He had already tried soldiering once, and was captured without lifting a sword, his group surprised during a morning scout outside Reims. Either Gaunt or King Edward had paid his ransom—to this day, he was unsure. All he knew was that riding into this battle would not end well for him. He had to think of Pippa and Elizabeth.

"Afraid you'll be captured again, or worse?" said a familiar voice.

Chaucer turned—Gaunt approached on horse, his retinue at least a hundred yards behind.

"My lord, I learned at Reims that I progress more with quill than sword," Chaucer replied.

"Indeed, this is no place for a soft hand," Gaunt replied, then turned to view the battle raging before them.

Does he mock me?

"Still, the battle is yet to be won, and every extra sword would help turn the tide."

Gaunt turned to Gawain, and added, "Or two."

Gawain bowed his head. "My lord prince, who then would be left to recount the exploits of the great knights and princes if the storytellers die on this field?" he replied.

"Better to die with honour, than live without, I say," Gaunt said.

"I do not understand, my lord," Chaucer said.

"You understand the term carpet knight?"

He does not mock, he goads.

Chaucer nodded. He knew enough such men who were showered with honours, sword sheathed, even as they unsheathed other weapons upon the carpet of the ladies of the court.

"You will be rewarded by my brother Edward for finding that bridge and surprising Enrique. Mayhap promoted in your station. But would you want to be known only as a carpet knight, a scribe who stood idly by while his brothers in arms died in front of you?"

He calls me a carpet knight? This prince of a man? I will not stand for it.

Something inside Chaucer changed in that moment. Perchance it was the doubts about Elizabeth that he'd carried for three years. Or it could be that Gaunt's words were true, that Chaucer had no honour. It mattered not in that moment, for Chaucer was gripped by a sudden hot anger, and unsheathing his diminutive sword, he shouted, "Gawain, follow me!" and spurred his mount forward.

"I must remain by my lord Chandos…"

"Do you value Ayala and the poetry he has yet to write?" Chaucer shouted over his shoulder.

Gawain nodded.

"Then unsheathe your sword, follow me and try not to get killed," Chaucer shouted.

Chaucer held his own small sword high in his right hand, his left hand holding the reins as he tried to guide his palfrey forward, kneeing his mount to some kind of gallop, bouncing about as if to fall at any moment as he rode toward the battle.

Leaving Gaunt sitting atop his horse, a smile upon his face. His retinue arrived, and they cantered after Chaucer and Gawain toward the enemy.

"My lord?" asked the officer, who arrived first.

"Now we will truly see how a deft hand with his quill fares with a sword," Gaunt replied.

•   •   •

On the south flank, Enrique led his knights in a second attack on Armagnac, and this time, with the bowmen having exhausted their supply of arrows, he was more successful, pushing the Gascon forces back and up the hillock.

The entire battlefield had shifted like a massive wheel turning from north to south, with the Captal du Buch pushing northwest into space left by Tello's defection, and Enrique pushing southeast against Armagnac. The centre held as both sides fought for every inch.

The battalion under Prince Edward and Don Pedro attacked what had been Enrique's central position he left when he rode south. The men of Castile parried the attack, slinging stones with such force they could split a helmet in half, bringing down scores of English and Gascon soldiers.

The English archers with any arrows left retaliated with devastating effect. The battle cry of "Castile for King Enrique" was answered by an equally loud "St. George for Guyenne." Yet the French and Aragonese under du Guesclin defended the English attack.

Calveley sat astride his horse in the rear guard behind Gaunt's line and watched the first attack by Denia's ginetes push forward, then be repelled, and now saw the second attack find some success. Now was the time to still the momentum and push Denia back down the hillock.

"On me!" Calveley shouted as he spurred his horse forward, even as the banner of both Denia and Enrique moved toward them up the hillock. His eight hundred mounted knights extricated themselves from the battles they were fighting and galloped after Calveley. His forces met Denia's light cavalry on the downslope of the hillock and a bitter battle ensued.

•   •   •

Chaucer had ridden with Gawain to where he thought Ayala was, but could no longer see him. A man at arms swung a sword at him and he leaned back to avoid the blow and almost fell off his mount, then recovered and kneed his horse forward past the faceless assailant. He was ill-trained to use his sword. No matter. He would aid his friend, who had saved him.

There, ahead. The Order. Ayala.

And just then a pike was thrust toward him, and he parried the head aside and rode past.

Chaucer turned and could see English standards flying toward du Guesclin in the centre. If they could connect with Percy and Clisson, du Guesclin would be encircled and the battle would be over. And Ayala would surely perish. He had to keep going. All now hinged on the centre.

To the south, Calveley fought his way through the forces of Denia and Enrique. Through a heroic effort, he and his knights were able to push them back and down the hillock. Calveley then spotted the Order of the Sash standard to the north, in the centre of the battle, and while he couldn't see him, he knew Ayala would be protecting the standard, for it was his sworn duty. Calveley cut his way north. He would end Ayala now and take all that had been promised to him.

Chaos ensued as the English cheered and pushed forward, even as du Guesclin's heavily armoured and well-trained mercenaries pushed back. Some of Enrique's men began to retreat, but Ayala and Enrique's personal guard were able to turn most of them around and restore a semblance of order.

Ayala turned at a shouted warning from one of his comrades and saw Calveley's banner heading straight toward him, but two hundred yards away.

•   •   •

Alfonso had completed his task of helping Chaucer turn Calveley. Now it was time to complete his own task—of finding and killing Enrique. After slipping away from Chaucer, he had carefully led his horse to the edge of the battlefield unseen behind and to the south of Chaucer and Gawain. There he had put on the chain mail he had hidden there the day before, for he had correctly guessed where the battle would begin. He then watched Enrique from behind a bush, waiting patiently for his chance to finally exact revenge. Calveley had broken through, and Enrique had retreated to the centre. Alfonso saw his chance and kneed his horse and galloped toward him, sword unsheathed.

Enrique did not see him coming, for Alfonso was riding slightly behind him at an angle to intercept him. Alfonso was only ten yards away, sword raised and about to strike, when his own horse was knocked off stride by the horse of another knight. Alfonso was then hit by a blow to his shoulder that stunned him and knocked him off his horse. Alfonso crumpled to the earth and lay still.

Enrique, unaware of the threat, rode on, fighting his way toward the standard that Ayala still held, now joined also by du Guesclin in the centre.

"Edward is winning the battle," Enrique shouted to Ayala, ten yards away. "We must turn the tide. Bring up the reserves!"

"All of them, my lord?" Ayala asked. To commit all the reserves was to roll dice. Ayala looked south and could see Calveley, but a hundred yards away.

"All of them, now, or the battle will be lost," he shouted back. The din was so loud he could barely hear his own words.

Ayala leaned to the man behind him, and passed the order, and he blew his horn. A dozen of Enrique's men at arms surged forward, blocking Calveley's advance. Many more followed to the centre.

He could see Edward's archers being resupplied with arrows by squires. They then waited patiently until the mass was within bowshot, and they loosed more arrows.

With the soldiers massed so tightly together, every arrow found a mark. Ayala watched as the wave crumpled upon itself. The arrows kept flying; Enrique's men kept dying. Some of Edward's men also fell. But too late, for Enrique's soldiers faltered, broke, and fled.

At the sight of their enemy fleeing, Ayala heard a great roar from the English. Those of Enrique's soldiers in pitched battles turned to the sound and saw their own men fleeing, then fled as well.

Ayala looked about him and saw the fleeing men and then the English and Gascon forces closing in from both sides. They would shortly flank the Castilian army. Du Guesclin was still fighting in the centre. The Captal du Buch was approaching from the north. They were almost encircled. Then he spotted Calveley, not fifty yards away, staring and pointing his sword toward him.

"My lord, your orders?" Ayala shouted at Enrique, who had just fought off a Gascon man at arms with a poleaxe, cleaving his head with his sword.

Enrique looked to Ayala, and to the battle raging around him, and was about to answer when a sword followed by the arm of a metal clad knight struck toward Enrique. Ayala leaned across his horse and sliced the arm off at the elbow. The knight's scream was drowned out by the screams of many others. Too many.

Ayala drew alongside Enrique and lowered his voice. "My lord, our position is soon lost. We have been outflanked and will soon be encircled. We must retreat before this battle becomes a rout," he said as evenly as he could.

"Rout? We can claim victory still…" Enrique said, but his tone did not match his words.

An arrow sliced past his visor.

"It pains me to say the words, my lord, but we must sound the retreat now, before it is too late," Ayala said.

"I will not retreat and give Pedro that satisfaction," Enrique snapped.

"Then our men will be slaughtered," Ayala said. "As will your nobles…as will you, my lord," he added as he parried a blow from a man at arms.

"Nonsense. We will be ransomed," Enrique countered, also parrying a blow and killing the soldier.

For a moment, they were alone.

"Pedro will seek vengeance, and that vengeance will begin with you."

The mention of Pedro caused something to shift in Enrique. He had fought alongside his men valiantly, but knew Pedro would indeed seek vengeance first upon him. He would die.

The two men stared at each other a moment longer, and then Enrique nodded once at Ayala, snapped his reins, and put spurs to his horse's flank. He galloped west toward Najera and his escape, his guards following. When the foot soldiers spotted Enrique's banner flying west, they too turned and fled. The English and Gascons saw what was happening. The rout had begun.

• • •

Chaucer kept riding. He could hardly believe he was still alive. To his left he could see Calveley, fighting his way toward the Order of the Sash standard and Ayala. Ahead, he could make out the banners of Percy and de Buch coming together behind du Guesclin; his flanks had been turned. Now only the centre remained where Ayala held the banner upright. He watched Ayala deflect a blow from one of the three English knights now surrounding him. Another knight attacked him, and he furiously fended off the blows, holding the standard in his left hand as he swung his sword with his right. How could he possibly survive such odds? While holding the pennant? And then Chaucer saw them. Two pennants approaching Ayala. One he knew too well, two lions either side of and holding a shield, and on that shield, in quarters, two lions and two castles, each castle with three turrets. Leon and Castile. Pedro. The other pennant, two black calves atop a red band, and one calf below, against a white field. Calveley. Both were angling from different directions toward Ayala, but thirty yards away.

There was no way Ayala would survive an attack from both of them. And just then Chaucer saw Enrique's banner suddenly move west. Was he fleeing?

And now too Edward's banner appeared, approaching from the centre. All were coming to Ayala.

I must save Ayala, and so save myself.

Chaucer and Gawain weaved their swift mounts around and past what soldiers were left fighting in hand-to-hand combat. Avoiding fallen soldiers and mounts was the greater challenge. Chaos reigned, for some of Enrique's men had followed him west, and some, like Ayala, had stayed to fight.

Suddenly, Chaucer saw Sir Christopher Croker not ten steps ahead of him, shield broken, sword on the ground, defenceless, facing a huge Castilian knight lifting his sword to strike. As Chaucer rode past, he pulled his reins hard left and his horse bumped the knight. Turning his head, he saw the knight slipping and Croker plunging his own sword into the knight. Croker looked up, nodded his thanks. Chaucer nodded back and turned to face the battle ahead.

One debt repaid, finally.

They were but thirty yards from Ayala when Gawain was knocked off his horse as an injured and riderless horse crashed into him. From astride his horse, Chaucer held the reins as Gawain tried to re-mount, but before he could he himself was caught by a glancing blow of a poleaxe that sent him tumbling off his own mount. The soldier holding the poleaxe pulled back to finish Chaucer, but another sword sliced into the soldier under his arm. Thomas Holland wielded the sword and finished off the interloper with a series of quick thrusts.

"I am in your debt, Thomas," Chaucer shouted.

"You may not have to wait long, Chaucer, for Lady Fortune's wheel will surely turn," Holland replied, and then was off to strike another.

Chaucer picked up the discarded poleaxe and this time it was Gawain who held his rouncey steady as Chaucer re-mounted.

Ayala was now only twenty strides away.

Chaucer's eyes widened when he saw Calveley over Gawain's shoulder only a few yards behind him, hacking his way toward Ayala.

But Calveley had now been stopped in his tracks by two soldiers on foot wielding poleaxes.

Gawain was still on foot in front of Chaucer with only one knight between him and Ayala. Two of Ayala's men at arms lay still, felled by arrows. A knight entered Chaucer's vision and swung a huge mace that bludgeoned Ayala's shield, splintering it into three pieces. A second blow would surely end him.

Chaucer shifted forward and swung the long poleaxe, aiming the barb of the weapon at the knight's visor. His aim was lucky, for it caught the knight's helm, and Chaucer yanked backwards, forcing the knight to pull away from Ayala to regain his balance on his horse.

As Chaucer turned to recover his balance, the knight raised his bloody mace to attack Gawain, now standing between him and Ayala, but Ayala buried his sword deep into the knight's underarm. As Ayala withdrew his sword, the knight fell off his mount, falling dead at Gawain's feet.

"Ayala, Calveley is close by and seeks to end you. Yield to Gawain," Chaucer shouted.

Ayala, bloodied and bruised, nodded his understanding and had already raised his sword to surrender but then shifted to impale a Gascon who suddenly appeared on foot at Gawain's left.

Another Gascon on foot lifted a poleaxe to strike at Ayala. Gawain knocked him sideways with a blow from his sword.

"Yield to Gawain!" Chaucer shouted again.

They all turned then at a deep guttural sound; Calveley's roar of rage from upon his destrier, not ten feet away, sword raised. He was willing his way through the crush of horse and men and weapons and looked unstoppable.

Gawain took hold of the reins of Ayala's mount and loudly said, "Sir Ayala, I capture you in the name of Sir John Chandos."

Ayala still clutched the standard and his sword, and shouted back, "I yield to you Gawain."

Calveley leapt off his horse, sword raised and shouted at Gawain, "Leave him, he is mine."

Chaucer shifted his mount to come between them. "Calveley, he has been rightfully captured by Gawain. You must give way," Chaucer said.

"Try to stop me Chaucer, and you will die," Calveley shouted back as he lifted his sword to strike Chaucer.

"Hold fast, Sir Hugh."

Calveley held, for he looked up at Prince Edward, who now sat stride his horse, his armour covered in mud and blood, his visor open, a small stream of blood dripping from a cut to his dirty cheek.

•   •   •

Du Guesclin spotted a familiar hulking form in front of him. Roland. His former servant. Who had fought to save him once before, and who now stood before him, his chain mail a reddish brown from blood and mud, holding a massive mace by the handle, the pointed iron head lying on the ground beside him next to the curled end of the iron linked chain.

"It's been too long, my friend. I see you have found a new home," du Guesclin said.

"Chandos treats me well," Roland said.

"You have come for one final battle?" du Guesclin asked.

Roland just nodded.

Du Guesclin dismounted and held his sword before him. The trail of dead men that lay behind Roland spoke of his strength even though he was old and injured.

Roland lifted the mace head off the ground as if it was a toy and shifted the weight, preparing to swing it.

Just then, a great cry arose along the battle line. A cry of confidence as the English and Gascon troops pushed the Castilians backwards. Some Castilian soldiers fled, realizing the battle was lost. The English, tasting victory, surged forward with renewed vigour. In no time, the entire Castilian centre had folded. Roland had no need to swing his mace.

Du Guesclin looked left and right; his force was surrounded. One quarter of his men were dead, many more were captured and most were injured.

Sir John Chandos, still bleeding from his ear, dismounted from his destrier, raised his visor and stepped forward. "You have fought valiantly, old friend, but your cause is lost. Surrender," he said.

Du Guesclin also raised his visor, but not before first striking down an English man-at-arms who had the discourtesy to approach while he was being addressed by Chandos.

Roland nodded at Chandos and stepped backwards.

Chandos again asked for his surrender.

"It appears you have won this day, Sir John," du Guesclin replied. "I believe we remain even at three battles apiece," he added.

"You are correct," Chandos said, a grim smile spreading across his blood-smeared face.

"Until our next meeting then, when we shall decide once and for all," he said, and finally plunged his sword into the blood red dirt and gestured to Chandos, who stepped forward.

"Roland, in thanks for your loyalty, I would that you step forward and accept du Guesclin's surrender. He will be yours to ransom," Chandos said. So turning the soldier servant into a wealthy man.

CHAPTER 32
PLAINS OF NAJERA, APRIL 3
RETRIBUTION

Chaucer spied Pedro approaching behind Edward. He needed to block his advance, or Pedro would surely slit Ayala's throat for treason. And Chaucer still owed Doña Constanza a debt.

Chaucer turned toward Ayala. "Ayala…."

"There is much to say…" Ayala replied.

"Let us speak another time, for Pedro arrives anon," Chaucer said.

"I must ask one more favour," Ayala said. Pedro's banner was but ten yards away, Pedro now visible. Although there were pockets of men here and there still engaged in hand to hand fighting, the battle was over, with nothing to impede Pedro.

Chaucer did not wait to hear Ayala's words and kneed his horse toward Pedro, and shouted to Edward, "My lord, look who has yielded to Gawain!"

"Out of my way, Chaucer! I will have that traitorous bastard, Ayala," cried Pedro.

Chaucer turned his palfrey sideways, blocking Pedro's advance.

Gawain let go the reins of Ayala's horse and Ayala trotted his horse toward Edward.

"My lord," Chaucer called toward Pedro.

"Out of the way, fool," Pedro shouted.

Edward had dismounted, his arms resting on his massive broadsword. His face was smeared in dirt and his cheek still dripped blood.

"My lord, Prince," Ayala shouted.

"Do I know you, good knight?" Edward asked, as Ayala dismounted and bent one knee before him.

"I am Don Pero López Ayala, once a loyal supporter of Pedro, but now fighting for Enrique. I find myself on the wrong side of this battle, and I have already surrendered to Chandos' man Gawain, my lord," Ayala said.

"No, he is mine!" cried Pedro, who just then arrived on his white destrier, his doublet splattered with blood. "I demand that this traitor surrender to me," Pedro shouted.

"You are too late, cousin, for he has already been claimed," Edward said.

"I am a king on this field, and will not have some peasant claim my prize, And you shall obey me in this and show fealty to me!" Pedro exclaimed.

Edward stood taller.

"I control this army, and it is I who have won you back your crown. And I choose to show mercy to Don Pero, as is just and right according to the laws of chivalry. If you do not respect my wishes, then this battle may yet need to continue," he said in a low threatening voice that only carried as far as the tight circle surrounding them.

"Your man Chaucer blocked my passage," Pedro spat.

"Well then, Chaucer knows where his true loyalty lies," Edward replied.

Chaucer dismounted and walked his mount past Pedro, stopping by Edward's side.

"My lord, would you care for a mount to continue this battle?" he asked, ignoring Pedro.

"Thank you, my dear Chaucer, but that poor beast would not carry my weight," he said. Another knight brought forward his destrier and Edward took the reins, mounted and looked back directly at Pedro to see if he had any fight left in him.

Pedro's eyes blazed, but he said and did nothing.

Edward looked past Pedro to the west.

"I see Enrique followed his brother Tello and chose to flee with his men," Edward said, and all eyes turned to the mass of men and horses fleeing towards Najera.

"Ayala, you shall come with me. Calveley, Gawain and Chaucer too. Cousin, I suggest that you tend to your own men," and with that Prince Edward rode away, leaving Pedro alone.

"Ayala, I will find you and kill you, you traitor. And Chaucer, you shall also pay," Pedro called after him.

Chaucer mounted, then said in reply to Pedro, "I congratulate you on your victory, my lord. I respectfully remind you of what may be written about you on this day by the many chroniclers gathered here. For it is your actions, and your words also that will be the story told of this war, and of a reputation passed on for generations to come."

Pedro bored his eyes into Chaucer, but Chaucer held his gaze for a moment, then turned and rode toward his prince as Pedro mouthed a reply he did not hear.

"Well done, Chaucer," said Edward. "Pedro would have flayed Ayala alive were it not for your timely interruption. I cannot abide by Pedro's lust for vengeance. Chivalry is lost upon that man."

Ayala caught up to them.

"My lord, I am in your hands, and in your debt," he said.

"You are in Chaucer's debt, and he will hold that debt in my stead," Edward replied, and then spurred his horse forward, leaving them alone.

"I thank you doubly, my good Chaucer. You saved me from ransom and death by that knight Calveley, and then a sure death at the hands of Pedro," Ayala said.

"I was merely doing my duty and repaying my own debt, good Ayala," Chaucer replied.

Chaucer and Ayala just nodded at one another and smiled, and rode side by side, two storytellers bonded by fortune, fate and courage.

Suddenly, the sound of hoofs and the jangle of armour and sword caused Chaucer to turn his head in time to see two riders galloping toward Ayala from behind, not a spear's throw away. One was Calveley. The other looked vaguely familiar.

"Calveley," is all he had time to say to Ayala, who at once pulled out his sword, ducked and turned, parrying Calveley's sword stroke just in time. The clang of the two swords continued and their horses danced a circle.

Chaucer had taken his eyes off the other rider and now, looking back, saw, too late, the sword slicing at him, and the hood of the cloaked rider shadowing his face. Chaucer sensed a memory of the figure before the sword found purchase, cutting through his hauberk.

Chaucer sent an awkward thrust toward the man's neck, and the man pulled sharply back, his hood falling, revealing one blue eye and one black eye that blazed from the grim pale face. Chaucer knew him. The assassin. Who smiled then, revealing yellowed wooden teeth.

But before the assassin or Calveley could land killing blows, four of Edward's mounted knights shouted their approach. Seeing the advantage lost, Calveley sent one final sword thrust toward Ayala with all his might, breaking Ayala's sword and slicing into his leather. Then he galloped away, shouting, "I will finish you one day, Ayala." The assassin also broke and galloped after Calveley.

The four knights reached them just after their assailants had ridden off.

"Ayala—you are injured," Chaucer said.

"It is nothing. A glancing blow. He is a skilled swordsman, but I, too, know how to protect myself. Thank you for the warning. But you—you have been cut. Are you injured?"

Chaucer ran his hand along his chest where his hauberk had been sliced open and pulled a small book out. His Boethius had the top third cut nearly severed. The book had saved him.

"Only my pride. And I can now say that the quill truly is mightier than the sword."

The two soldier poets smiled at the moment and then turned west and kneed their mounts forward. They soon approached the banner of Sir John Chandos and found him surrounded by his men. His helm was off, and blood was streaming down the side of his face, but he was laughing as he gulped wine he happily squirted down his throat from a bota they had taken from a dead soldier.

"We are victorious this fine day," shouted Chandos. "The bastard Enrique has fled with his rabble."

"They escaped?" asked Chaucer.

"He and his cavalry were able to scatter north and south, but the infantry could only escape west toward the narrow bridge at Najera to escape those bent on vengeance. Many of Enrique's men died by a sword to the back, and many more reached the Rio Najerilla and finding the bridge clogged with men trying to cross, threw themselves into the boiling waters where they drowned, pulled down by their armour or inability to swim."

·   ·   ·

Soon after victory, Edward sent four knights and four heralds to search the field of battle and report on the number of nobles dead and wounded, and to find out if Enrique was among them.

Chaucer joined them and searched the ruined field for Córdoba, Alfonso and Thomas Holland, whom he had not seen since earlier in the battle, and he had made a vow to Joan to watch over him. He covered his face with a cloth, for the stench of blood and shit was overpowering. He gagged, then saw Córdoba's pennant lying in the dirt. He looked more closely and as the crows began to descend, he found a body. He couldn't be sure, for the man's skull had been smashed in, but the armour looked like Córdoba's. A spear was still stuck in his body, and one hand almost completely severed from his wrist. If Córdoba, then it was a sad ending for a man much like himself who had raised himself up to become advisor to a king. Such was life, for Lady Fortune cared not.

Chaucer carried on stepping over bodies. He found neither Alfonso nor Thomas and sighed. He had had enough of death and loss on this day, and remounted and rode slowly toward Najera with a tiredness he felt deep in his bones. He had somehow survived. And then spied a knight riding ahead of him and recognized his form. He spurred his tired horse forward.

"Croker?"

The knight turned. It was indeed a now smiling Sir Christopher Croker who turned to face Chaucer.

"I am glad to see you survived the battle," Chaucer said as he caught up to Croker and rode beside him.

"Chaucer. I survived, thanks to you. You, or your horse, saved me from that knight who I was able to dispatch."

"A debt doubly owed."

Neither said anything as they rode past dozens of bodies. The stench of death was strong. Some were being stripped of anything sellable by locals. Some were missing limbs, or their entrails were flowing into the blood red dirt.

Both men had seen enough death that day.

"I am parched and would kill for a drink. Shall we find some Rioja?" asked Croker.

•   •   •

Late that afternoon, Prince Edward entered Najera and took possession of the town and the many buildings where Enrique had been lodging, and found an abundance of food and wine and passed the evening in great revelry. After feasting, the knights and heralds returned from the bloody field of battle and reported to the prince and Chandos, who stood by his side, wearing a cloth patch over his ear to stem the flow of bleeding.

"The bastard, is he dead or taken?" asked Prince Edward.

The knight paused, then shook his head. "We did not find his body, my lord."

"We counted five hundred and sixty knights and men-at-arms and some seven thousand five hundred common soldiers slain, my lord. And many more drowned trying to cross the river."

"And our losses."

"Only one hundred and forty knights, ninety-four archers, and some two hundred and forty men at arms slain, my lord. We also have a great number of prisoners, French knights and squires under Bertrand du Guesclin, with a large number of Castilian nobles and knights, including de Ayala, my lord."

"Ayala is no prisoner. He is a knight, a poet and an honourable man and shall not be ransomed. Did you know that Enrique was held prisoner here by Pedro seven years ago? Methinks Enrique was always seeking the final battle to be held here to gain his vengeance. Now there is some beautiful justice," Edward said.

As captors were brought before him, Edward showed compassion and chivalry to each.

Pedro gained an audience with Prince Edward that evening and demanded that he be given all the knights that had been taken prisoner.

"After all, we are fighting the same war and are of the same noble blood," Pedro said.

"No, I will not grant you such rights, for you would put them all to death," Edward replied, then added, "and noble blood is the only thing we have in common."

"How dare you…" Pedro shot back.

"How dare I? How dare you consider such actions! What kind of leader are you? You hire Moors to fight your battles while I was fighting to save Jerusalem against those same Moors. I paid for pilgrims to journey on the pilgrimage to Santiago de Compostela to receive a blessing from the Bishop of Santiago there. You murdered him. I seek, through words and actions, to be a devout Christian and Catholic. You, through your words and actions, have been excommunicated by the pope. And you have no sense of chivalry or honour, slaying captors who have been disloyal to you. Unless you want me to order my army to place you in irons and have the crown of Castile and Leon placed now upon my own head, I suggest you close your damnable mouth and thank our God above for what has been given to you on this day. Now get out of my sight."

Pedro stared at Edward without saying anything, burying the fury writ upon his face. What Edward had said was true. Edward controlled the army, and he could, if he chose to, easily wrest control of the crown Pedro had fought so hard for these last ten years.

"I must be to Burgos, to be crowned King of Castile, my *prince*. It would be courteous of you to attend," is what Pedro said instead once had had composed himself.

Only a mere prince is how it sounded to all gathered there.

"Until then," is all Edward said in reply.

Pedro turned his back on Edward and left.

CHAPTER 33
BURGOS, APRIL 4, 1367
PEDRO'S RETURN

Prince Edward departed the next day. Pedro and his entourage had ridden for Burgos at dawn and Edward had waited, for he had no desire to ride with Pedro. By late afternoon Edward had approached the city walls which he skirted, riding along the south side of the River Arlanzónv and quartering at the monastery of Las Huelgas, across the river and a mile west of Burgos.

Edward had asked Chaucer to serve as his eyes and ears and remain close to Pedro, and so he had ridden ahead by a southern route and had quietly joined the end of Pedro's entourage as it approached the city. Chaucer also had no desire to be seen by Pedro, who had vowed vengeance to his face on the battlefield but one day before.

Pedro's group stopped before the eastern Gate of Saint Martin, built in the style of the Mudejar when the Moors controlled the city. Countless armies, both Muslim and Christian, had passed through it since. The gate was also used by pilgrims as they departed on their route to Santiago de Compostela, and it was held in reverence by those who lived nearby.

Pedro dismounted and carried out the age-old tradition of swearing respect to the local codes of the city before entering. Chaucer noted how quiet the people were, with no welcoming cheers. In fact, some of the locals scowled as they peeked out from behind doorways and windows. Silence rather than shouts of welcome greeted Pedro as he re-mounted and entered the city and descended toward Burgos Cathedral.

Chaucer turned to the cowled knight to his right and asked, "Why are the people so quiet?" he asked.

A familiar voice replied, "Is plain."

"Alfonso? You are alive?"

The knight pulled back his cowl to reveal the grizzled face of Alfonso.

"You survived! How?"

"I try kill Enrique and took blow to head and lay on the field until night. Then caught up to you."

"I am very glad to see you alive."

Alfonso gave the slightest hint of a smile.

"Is plain the people do not forget how Pedro left their city undefended, fleeing like a scared child," Alfonso said. "He lost their respect that day. Any cheers you may hear today are for duty, not respect."

"It is indeed a dull imitation," Chaucer replied.

Seeing Alfonso alive raised Chaucer's spirits. He thought he had lost him. A man who had guided him to Calveley, to the bridge, and guided Edward and Pedro to victory. Who had become a friend. It felt wrong that he would be slain.

The next day, Pedro formally took possession of the city, and the following day, retributions began across Castile for those who sided with Enrique. Pedro's knights seized Jean de Cardalhac, Archbishop of Brago, and imprisoned him in the castle of Alcala de Guadayra. However, he did not forget those who supported him. Pedro confirmed the grant given to Calveley by Enrique as a reward for his support in the victory over Enrique.

Pedro then received a letter from Edward, who had remained two miles away at the abbey of Santa María la Real de Las Huelgas where Enrique had been crowned, asking for his debt to be paid: two hundred thousand gold florins. A fortune Pedro did not have, for whatever buried treasure had been found was quickly spent paying those nobles still loyal to him.

Instead, Pedro replied to Edward, stating he would need more time to gather the gold.

Edward said his army would remain in Castile until he received the gold he was due. Edward then asked Calveley to journey to Aragon as an emissary with a letter to seek King Pere's support in finding Enrique. It would not do to have come all this way, spent all that gold, and to have let the bastard live.

•   •   •

Two days after Pedro had re-claimed his crown, Doña Constanza and Ayala sat in a corner of a tavern in Najera.

Lit by a small candle on the rough table, Doña sat with a hood over her head, her hair covered. The tavern was full and noisy. A few men looked at her askance, for women were not known in taverns, but she had paid the owner enough to be left alone at a table at the back. Once Ayala joined her, no one paid them attention, and they returned to their tales of the riches that had been stripped off the dead soldiers and the many stories of the battle won that day.

"I cannot stay long," she said.

"I heard Edward has sent Calveley to Barcelona to offer Pere terms to capture Enrique," Ayala said.

"I have heard such, yes," she replied.

"Also involving your hand in marriage to Calveley, ensuring Aragon does not come to harm from a mercenary like him," Ayala said.

"Yes, I journey to Barcelona on the morrow," she said.

A pause hung in the air like the smoke from the fire that glowed in the hearth at the other side of the tavern.

"You must be careful of Pedro's vengeance. Where will you go?" Doña asked.

"France."

"It is goodbye then," Doña said.

"Yes. But I will come to Barcelona in time and find you."

"I will be married in but a few months."

"It matters not. We shall be together again soon enough," he said.

His confidence drew tears to her eyes.

"But you must make a life for yourself and not wait for me," he said.

She nodded.

Ayala got up, bent down and kissed her deeply, then walked to the tavern door, looked back once and left.

Doña wiped at her tears and stared into her goblet.

"It will be all right," said a familiar voice.

She turned and saw the speaker at the bar a few feet away, and watched him get up and make his way to her.

"Father!" Doña said, mouth open. "You are alive? How?"

Alfonso took a step forward and stopped.

"I thought you were murdered with mother three years ago. Where have you been? Why have you not sought me out before?" Doña asked.

He took another step forward. "I went into hiding, knowing that if I tried to see you, I would be found out, and your life put at risk, so I plotted my revenge. I'm so sorry to have left you alone, for I know you have suffered."

"I suffered, yes, and then became stronger for it. But you look so different. Your hair. Now white, not black. You look as old as your father."

"Part of the ruse."

Alfonso took one more step toward Doña. She stood.

"And Enrique? I saw him flee the battlefield, and a bounty is now upon his head," she asked.

"I tried and failed to kill Enrique during the battle and was knocked off my horse and fell, unconscious. When I regained my senses, the battle was over, and Enrique was long gone. I laid low for a brief time, then I was finally able to look for you."

This time, Doña closed the gap between them and hugged him.

"I have missed you so much," she said between sobs as she cried tears of both sadness and joy, and he hugged her hard in return.

"And I you. When Chaucer told me that he had met you, I was hard pressed not to tell him the truth. But to do so would have been to put your life—and his—at risk."

She wiped tears from her eyes and smiled her understanding.

"You are lucky," he said.

"How is that? The man I love has just walked out that door."

"Yes, but you have a man that you love. And that loves you just as deeply. Many never find such love. You will see him again before too long, for love in time of war is stronger."

She nodded at the truth of her father's words, and said, "I have your love," and hugged him again.

"Will you continue to look for Enrique to avenge my mother's death?" she asked.

He looked toward the door of the tavern and beyond, to where his future lay.

"Until my final breath," he replied.

CHAPTER 34
LONDON, MAY 1367
CHAUCER RETURNS

Chaucer stepped off the cog onto the Three Cranes wharf. He bent down and kissed the hemp and dirt-covered stone beneath his feet. He stood, smiled and said hello to the hands he knew, and was welcomed in return as one of their own.

"Bordeaux this time?" asked a young apprentice, pointing to the barrels of wine hanging in a hemp bag from the end of the crane.

"Yes, the finest in the land, and also some Rioja. A gift from Prince Edward," Chaucer replied.

"Prince Edward, is it? Not the king himself?" the lad replied.

"Stop your nattering and get on with it," snapped the master wharfman.

The young lad quickly led the horse he held forward by its bridle, making the crane turn toward the wharf and the hemp bag descend—too fast.

"Easy, lad, or you'll break the barrels," the man shouted, and the young hand slowed the horse. The hemp bag gently came to rest on the wharf.

Just then, William arrived and cuffed the lad across his head. "You ass, this is Geoffrey Chaucer, newly returned from the glorious victory at the Battle of Najera with his reward from our good Prince Edward for helping win said battle. Now get back to work, you whoreson, before I throw you and your teenful mouth into the Thames where it belongs," he said.

Chaucer saw the lad open said mouth as if to protest, but then noted the ire of William's glare, closed it and unhooked the hemp bag from the crane.

"You made good time," William said, turning to Chaucer with a welcoming grin.

"Favourable winds," Chaucer replied.

"Lady Fortune also favouring you of late."

"We both know how fickle she can be," Chaucer said. "I must go see my own lady and so tempt fortune again. I will seek you out soon enough and share my many tales over a goblet, or two, I promise," he said, and then stepped toward his home.

•　　•　　•

"So, you returned whole and finally did your duty to your prince and king," Pippa said.

Chaucer stood in the doorway to his parent's house on Thames Street and smiled. He could always count on Pippa to at once welcome and cajole him. Her saucy half-smile made her chide more endearing.

"I failed to keep away. It seems Lady Fortune had my balls in a sling," he replied.

"Better if I have your balls in my sling," she said, sliding his cloak off his shoulders, taking his hand, and leading him up the stairs.

"Where be my parents?"

"I sent them out," she said, pausing on the stairs.

"When will they be back?" he asked.

"At the right time," she replied, pulling him up.

He pulled back.

"Are you well?" he asked.

"I will be better soon if you shut your trap and drop your breeches, for a woman can only wait so long for her pleasure," she said.

•   •   •

Later, lying in bed, he asked, "Any letters for me?"

"These came yesterday," Pippa replied, reaching to the bedside table and handing him two letters, one with the king's seal on it.

He opened the first letter without the seal.

"What news?" she asked.

"A letter from Ayala. Calveley has married Doña Constanza, the princess of Aragon, in Zaragoza."

"A beautiful lady who gave you pause, I would expect," Pippa said.

He said nothing as all three of the ladies who had given him pause, Blanche and Joan and Constanza, flashed across his mind.

"Open the second," she said.

He did and after reading it, he handed it to her, saying, "I am called to the palace to see Edward on the morrow."

"Good. Then return after you see the king and we will continue our play. We have much coming and going to catch up on," she said, at once flirtatious and challenging.

How I love you.

CHAPTER 35
PALACE OF WESTMINSTER, JUNE, 1367
THANKS

"Welcome Chaucer. Good tidings precede your arrival, for I have heard of your success in finally turning Calveley and his men back to the warm embrace of England, and of my son's resounding victory at Najera. A truly momentous battle," said King Edward.

Chaucer smiled first at his king, then at Croker standing beside Edward. A year and a half before he had been set on by the king and had slunk away in disgrace. Now he stood in the king's good graces. He knew it was only through good fortune and the help of his new friends—Croker, Alfonso, Ayala, Calveley, Gawain, and Doña Constanza—that he could claim such success. And of course Pippa, for she had inspired his journey, and his ambition, with her love.

And he must credit King Edward for trusting in him as a reluctant spy.

"My lord, you do me too much honour. I was mere witness to history," Chaucer replied. His voice sounded strange to his ears in the echoes of this vast room. He felt small amidst the dozens of courtiers standing behind him, the Great Hall larger than he remembered.

"More than a witness Chaucer. Nay, from what my sons and Sir John Chandos say, you helped shape a great battle, a story that will now be shared for generations to come."

Chaucer bowed his head.

More likely my name expunged, with only noble names remaining. No matter.

"Step up, man." Edward said.

Chaucer took two tentative steps up toward the dais.

"Closer. I do not bite, unless famished for news," he said.

Chaucer climbed three more steps, and was now but a few feet from Edward.

"Now tell me. How is that you, mere page and poet, changed the outcome of the Battle of Najera? And how did you turn Calveley?"

Chaucer hesitated, for he did not want to appear boastful.

"Come now, we must hear the full story, for I have heard only part of it," Edward added. "My son in his letter spoke of your helping him outflank Enrique's army. How so?"

"My lord, it is not thanks to me, but to a local guide Alfonso, who led me to a bridge that allowed Prince Edward to cross a river and surprise Enrique," he said.

"Yes, so I heard. And was that guide not named Trastamara, of the same name as the bastard Enrique?"

Again, Chaucer paused. Murmurs spread out across the room like ripples on a lake.

"Yes, my lord. Alfonso is Enrique's half-brother," Chaucer replied.

Louder murmurs rose across the room.

"But were you not fighting Enrique?" Edward asked.

"Enrique had murdered Alfonso's wife and many in his family. Alfonso fought to avenge their death. And so helped me find Calveley, and the bridge to outflank and defeat Enrique."

"But he was your man, and because of your efforts, we claimed a resounding victory. For this, I award you twenty marks a year, for life," Edward said, handing Chaucer a parchment bearing the royal seal.

"Open it," Edward said.

Chaucer did, and read. *I have also been named valet. I must tell Pippa!*

"My lord, I am eternally grateful for such largesse," Chaucer replied, bowing.

Just then, Alice Perrers, the Queen's lady-in-waiting, approached the king and whispered something in his ear. He bobbed his head at her words and his gaze lingered on her form as she returned to her place in the line of other courtiers and servants who surrounded them. Then faced Chaucer again.

"And Calveley? How did you turn him?" Edward asked.

Chaucer hesitated. "My lord king that story requires much time to tell in full, but suffice it to say that Calveley is a man who finally learned the importance of both duty and reputation."

"And you yourself have learned much these past months, it would seem," King Edward replied.

Then Edward leaned forward so only Chaucer could hear. "I had my doubts about sending you on this journey, Chaucer. One word of advice. Your passion for wine and poetry is noted. Be thoughtful of your goblet, and of which poems you compose, and for whom. Words are as powerful as swords. Nay, more so."

Chaucer nodded.

"And a poem about my son's victory at Najera would not go unnoticed," he added.

He seeks to buy my quill? A quill already bought when I began this journey, it seems.

Edward leaned back and said, "I may call on your services again soon. Do you know the Milanese courtier Benzo?" he asked.

"I know of him, yes."

The weasel who short-changed Sir Lewis Clifford.

"Your expression says more," Edward said.

"I do not trust him, my lord," Chaucer replied.

"Good man. Neither do I. Yet we seek to deepen ties with the Visconti in Milan. I may need to call upon your services again to journey there in aid of the crown. Until then, I suggest you take the hand of our good lady Pippa and listen to her advice."

Chaucer nodded, said "Yes my lord," followed by, "I am forever grateful," and backed away.

CHAPTER 36
LONDON, AUGUST, 1367
QUEEN OF THE VINTRY

"Watch your head, little sparrow," said William in the doorway to the kitchen. Elizabeth sat astride his shoulders like a princess.

Or a queen. Chaucer smiled at the sight of William and his daughter.

William lowered his bulk and carefully made his way into the kitchen.

"I am Queen Boadicea atop my chariot. You must bow down to your queen. What say you?" Elizabeth shouted.

"I say you make a fine queen," Pippa intervened, "ready to slay the Romans. I also say it is time for your chores, my flower."

William slung Elizabeth down from her perch and gently set her on the oak-planked bench next to her father. William leaned over to present himself to Queen Boadicea.

Elizabeth kissed William on the forehead, then shifted sideways and snuggled in Chaucer's arms. "Papa, may I play at the palace with Philippa and Elizabeth, and then do my chores?" she asked.

Chaucer looked at his daughter and smiled. She had grown so much in the eighteen months since he had begun his journey. Now six months shy of turning four summers old, she was polite and courteous, yet still had a fierce imagination and a wildness of spirit. The nuns at St. Helen's Bishopsgate had done well to cultivate the first while not snuffing out the latter. But with pride came also a sense of loss for that time not spent with his own daughter.

"Your duty first, then yes, of course, if your momma allows it," he added, looking to Pippa, who smiled as she watched them with moist eyes.

"Put away your clothes first, then William will, I'm sure, gladly walk you to the palace."

William and Elizabeth had formed a special bond of late, the hulking manager of Chaucer & Co. holding a very soft place in his heart for the sweet girl. Chaucer knew Elizabeth reminded William of his own girl lost to pestilence while Chaucer had been in Castile.

Soon, Chaucer and Pippa were alone again, the house quiet.

"Valet? It's now in writing?" Pippa asked, not believing what she had just heard.

"Yes," Chaucer replied.

Pippa now stood by the large table in the kitchen chopping vegetables where Chaucer's mother Agnes had stood before his journey had begun. She paused her chopping and poured wine into a goblet that she set before Chaucer and seated herself at the table and poured another goblet for herself. He nodded his thanks and took a sip from the goblet.

"Why?" Pippa asked after taking a sip.

"For my service in Navarre and Castile."

"What in the name of God did you really do there?"

"I helped Prince Edward and King Pedro defeat Trastamara at the Battle of Najera," he said, as if he did such things every day.

"But how?" she asked, still incredulous about his turn of fortune.

He told her, leaving out the boring bits.

"That is quite a story," she replied, shaking her head.

"There is more," Chaucer said.

Pippa tilted her head.

He pulled from his leather purse a rolled note of vellum and handed it to her.

She unrolled it, and, as she read, her eyes grew wide.

"What? Is this true?"

"Yes."

"Twenty marks for you, for life?" she said, not believing it.

"Yes. You'll have to marry me now."

She turned, her face half lit by the cool light of the fading day, and half by the golden glow of the fire in the kitchen hearth.

"Perchance. You seem to have done the impossible and returned to me whole. More than whole by the look of you," she said.

Chaucer's smile widened. He was stout, yes, and he knew she loved him for it.

"But do you not still long for your dark Castilian ladies?" she asked.

He hesitated for a moment as thoughts of Doña Constanza coursed through his body.

"Ah, I see I touched upon a fond memory or two," she said.

"The one Castilian lady I met, Doña Constanza, was in love with a very fine soldier, poet and nobleman," he replied.

"But there are three more ladies I cannot stop thinking about," he added.

Pippa tuned to him, brow furrowed.

Chaucer reached into the leather travelling bag he had placed on an empty chair and pulled out the three books he had purchased in Logrono. He set them on the kitchen table.

Pippa's curled mouth transformed into a wide smile of delight.

"They are indeed beautiful ladies," she said, inspecting them.

"When can we be married?" he asked.

"I heard a rumour yesterday at the palace, of a storyteller who may be asked to travel to Milan," she replied, deflecting his question.

Chaucer hadn't told her of Edward's mention of Benzo. "Yes, Edward said that I may be needed with some business brewing with the Visconti."

"And so face deadly black-haired Lombard beauties?" she teased.

He smiled at her. "We should wed soon," he said.

"Two things first need to be answered," she replied. "The first, and of greatest import, is this: Have you learned in your travels what women most desire?"

Chaucer's smile expanded to a laugh that he failed to stifle.

"Why do you cackle so?" she asked.

"I laugh at myself for being such a dullard and dotard. When I left for Castile, I thought that you most wanted me to succeed in order to advance and gain more gold, and I would sit atop the throne of the Vintry upon my return, and you would have me then."

"Yes, I recall," she said.

"In Logrono, Doña Constanza had tried to tell me a different truth, but I had not understood."

Like Croesus, I had misread the portents, and like Don Garcia, only learned the truth through experience.

"But now I know that what you most desired then, and now, is for you, not me, to sit atop the throne of our home in the Vintry. I bow to you now, my queen," he said, bowing his head.

Pippa's smile widened, and she stepped around the table and stood before him, her hands cupping his face as she looked down at him.

"You said there was one more thing I need to answer?" he asked.

She reached down and claimed his hand, holding it in hers.

"I was going to ask, shall we make another babe? But it is a question no more."

She pushed him onto the bed.

The next novel in The Storyteller series, **The Storyteller's Reputation,** *finds Chaucer battling his nemesis Jean Froissart for the coveted court poet position. Both are then sent to Milan to face the ruthless Galeazzo Visconti and try to return home with a rich wedding dowry—and their lives. See more at* <u>www.jccorry.com</u>

HISTORICAL NOTES

Names. The Spanish version of names is used where possible (so 'King Carlos' is used instead of the Anglicized 'King Charles').

Politics. The Iberian peninsula, what we now call Spain, was a collection of separate kingdoms in 1365 with deep ties to both England and France.

The Treaty of Bretigny had been signed between King Edward the Third of England and King John the Second of France in 1360, pausing the formal war that had been raging between the two countries for several decades (what we now call the Hundred Year's War). But a proxy war was still being waged to the south.

The Kingdom of Castile was ruled at that time by Pedro the Cruel. His half-brother Enrique Trastamara was allied with King Charles of France (who succeeded his father King John), and had been trying to take his crown for a decade. Pedro was allied with King Edward.

To the north, Aquitaine and Gascony were ruled from Bordeaux by King Edward's eldest son, Prince Edward (known in later centuries by the sobriquet 'Black Prince').

King Pere ruled Aragon to the southeast from his capital in Barcelona. Pere also had a long-standing feud with Pedro, and so was naturally allied with Enrique. King Carlos ruled Navarre and controlled the passes over the Pyrenees mountains between Aquitaine, Navarre and Castile.

The Battle of Najera. Considered one of the largest battles, by number of combatants, to have been fought during the Hundred Year's War. The best account of this battle is from the exhaustively researched and highly readable *To Win and Lose a Medieval Battle* by L.J. Andrew Villalon and Donald J. Kagay. In it they compare the accounts of the main chroniclers of the day—Jean Froissart, Pedro Lopez de Ayala, the Chandos Herald, John of Reading and the anonymous Canterbury Chronicle. From these they posit the size and make-up of each army, as well as the location of the battle. I have used their research extensively in both the lead up to the battle (Edward did in fact outflank Pedro and surprise him), the size and formation of the armies involved, and the battle itself.

Was Chaucer at the Battle of Najera? We know from *Chaucer Life Records* (Crow, Olsen, 1966) that Geoffrey Chaucer, then a page at the court of King Edward, was in Olite, Navarre where he received safe passage on February, 22, 1366 to journey across Navarre. This was just two weeks before Enrique, du Guesclin and Calveley attacked cities held by Pedro, reigniting the decade-long war. The implication that Chaucer, son of a wine merchant, was acting as a courier or spy (or all three) is posited by Marion Turner in her excellent biography of Chaucer, *Chaucer: A European Life,* and this suggestion formed the genesis of the story. Given that Chaucer's father John was a wine merchant, and Geoffrey would have been well-versed in the wine trade, and would have spoken English, Anglo-French, Latin, and possibly some Castilian learned on the docks, it seems reasonable to position him also as wine merchant seeking wine for trade, as he sought Sir Hugh Calveley to try to turn him to aid King Edward's ambition in defeating Enrique. And so the story took shape, and I continued the thread to the logical conclusion of Chaucer as a spy, a reluctant one, helping to shape the outcome of the battle.

Was Chaucer cuckolded by Prince John of Gaunt? The jury is out, but there is evidence to support both cases. Sexuality was encouraged during King Edward's reign. Gaunt was the anonymous donor who paid for Elizabeth Chaucer to lodge at the convent St. Helen's Bishopsgate. Pippa received a lifetime annuity from Gaunt for her service to the crown. Chaucer's son Thomas (born in 1368 soon after the events in this novel) was eventually granted a coat of arms that did not bear any symbols of the Chaucer family coat of arms. Each fact interesting, but insufficient on its own to make the case.

But patterns and behaviours speak to one's character, and Gaunt had a track record as an adulterer. That he slept with Kathryn Swynford outside of his marriage to Constanza, and Kathryn went on to became his wife after his Constanza died, is well known. Kathryn was Philippa (Pippa) Chaucer's sister. Pippa served Queen Philippa as a lady-in-waiting before being asked to move to Gaunt's household. Some historians argue that Gaunt sleeping with both sisters would be a breach of protocol, unchivalrous, and even considered incest requiring additional papal dispensation in order for him to eventually marry Katheryn. Which may be true, but it doesn't hide the fact that before Gaunt's affair with Kathryn began, Gaunt had an affair with Marie de St. Hillaire, a lady-in-waiting to Gaunt's mother, Queen Philippa. He was at the time betrothed to Blanche, the Duchess of Lancaster. In fact, Marie gave birth to a baby girl just before he married Blanche. The name of the daughter? Blanche. Leaving off for the moment how hurtful that would have been for the Duchess, this fact clearly shows that Gaunt had absolutely no moral qualms about sleeping with other women, providing a clear picture of Gaunt's character.

Time and Dates. Given that clocks had only recently been introduced across Europe, time was not yet spoken of in terms of an hour as a specific and unchanging period representing 1/24 of a day. The term 'hour' at Chaucer's time had a more flexible definition, and could vary in length.

Christian scholars divided the day and night into twelve equal segments or hours. But that meant where you lived (latitude) and the time of year determined how long an hour was. On the spring equinox (March 21 or so) in London, England, one twelfth of the daylight hours equal one twelfth of the nighttime hours, or about 60 minutes. By contrast, around Christmas, a daylight hour in London contains about 40 minutes, while a nighttime hour contains 80 minutes. These figures are reversed in midsummer. For this reason I try to avoid the use of "hour" and "minutes" in this story.

Speaking of Christmas, the beginning of the year, the "New Year", changed. From 1087 to 1155 the English year began on January 1, and from 1155 to 1751 it began on March 25. In 1752 it was moved back to January 1. So festivities to celebrate the New Year in 1366 would not be in January, but in March, and a researcher coming across a mention of a "New Year's celebration", but no date, would need to understand that fact.

Dates are also tricky. In 1366 Europe used the Julian calendar, which was based on three years of 365 days and a fourth leap year of 366 days. This was replaced by our current Gregorian calendar, by almost all European countries, beginning in the late 16th century. For a researcher, the question is, does one use the date of a record when written, or does one transpose that date to the current calendar? For example, the record locating Chaucer in Olite is dated February 22, 1366 in *Chaucer Life Records*, and the editors state that "All dates of any importance are converted into modern equivalents." Which means Chaucer was in Olite on February 14, 1365 according to the Julian calendar of his day, but a year later according to our Gregorian calendar (see https://stevemorse.org/jcal/julian.html for a handy calendar conversion tool).

Clear as the colour of the Rio Najerillo on April 3, 1367, which either flowed red with the blood of thousands of soldiers, or brown from the spring runoff a week earlier on March 26, 1367.

While this research is important, it hopefully stays hidden, beyond the reader's mind, allowing the story to stand on its own, but informing the events.

GLOSSARY

I have tried to only use words that were known to be in use within Chaucer's lifetime (~1342-1400), with a couple of words that may have come into use slightly after Chaucer's death. Abridged definitions of the following medieval-period words are from the Oxford English Dictionary.

Spouse-break: Adulterer.

Bibber: Likes to drink.

Blab: One who has not sufficient control over his or her tongue; a revealer of secrets or of what ought to be kept private; a babbler, tattler, or telltale.

Blonk: Large, powerful horse.

Carked: To be anxious, full of anxious thought, fret oneself; to labour anxiously, to toil and moil.

Carpet knight: A knight who accomplished more on the carpet of the lady's boudoir than in battle; term of contempt.

Clatterer: One who clatters (also chatterer, babbler and tattler).

Costermonger: An apple seller who sells his or her fruit in the open street.

Destrier: Large warhorse able to carry a fully armoured knight into battle.

Fealty: The obligation of fidelity by a feudal tenant or vassal to his or her lord.

Garderobe: Toilet.

Grutch: To murmur and complain.

Heanling: Humble or base person.

Jangle: To talk excessively or noisily.

Jupon: A close-fitting tunic or doublet worn by knights under the hauberk, sometimes of thick stuff and padded; later, a sleeveless surcoat worn outside the armour, of rich materials and emblazoned with arms.

Palfrey: A horse for ordinary riding (as distinct from a warhorse).

Poleaxe: A weapon for close combat, having a head comprising an axe blade or hammer-head, balanced at the rear by a pointed fluke.

Paltock: A man's short coat or jacket; a sleeved doublet, worn beneath armour.

Queynte: Vagina.

Rouncey: Horse used to carry heavy loads.

Sell-sword: A mercenary who only works for money.

Surcoat: An outer coat or garment, commonly of rich material, worn by people of rank of both sexes; often worn by armed men over their armour.

Tattler: One who spreads gossip.

Tittler: A person who spreads rumours or gossip; a tattler, a telltale.

Tale-teller: A teller of tales or stories; a narrator.

ABOUT THE AUTHOR

J.C. Corry's first childhood memory was peering through rose-tinted stained glass in a Battersea church in London, England, colouring a passion for historical fiction emboldened by his father's hole-ridden Normandy helmet that sits above his writing desk. An army brat, he lived in ten homes by the age of ten in Canada, England and Australia, studied literature (where his love for Chaucer began) and film, produced television documentaries about artists, and now leads a thriving corporate communications career in Vancouver, BC, where his two grown sons literally look down upon him. He loves travel, good wine, singing, dancing, live music, theatre and film, forest walks, and scrabble. Visit his website www.jccorry.com to learn more.

NOTE FROM J.C. CORRY

Word-of-mouth is crucial for any author to succeed. If you enjoyed *The Storyteller's War*, please leave a review online—anywhere you are able. Even if it's just a sentence or two. It would make all the difference and would be very much appreciated.

Thanks!
J.C. Corry

We hope you enjoyed reading this title from:

www.blackrosewriting.com

Subscribe to our mailing list – *The Rosevine* – and receive **FREE** books, daily
deals, and stay current with news about upcoming
releases and our hottest authors.
Scan the QR code below to sign up.

Already a subscriber? Please accept a sincere thank you for being a fan of
Black Rose Writing authors.

View other Black Rose Writing titles at
www.blackrosewriting.com/books and use promo code
PRINT to receive a **20% discount** when purchasing.